M000305519

A THOUSAND STRANDS OF BLACK HAIR

A THOUSAND STRANDS OF BLACK HAIR

By Seiko Tanabe
Translated by Meredith McKinney

THAMES RIVER PRESS

A Thousand Strands of Black Hair

THAMES RIVER PRESS
An imprint of Wimbledon Publishing Company Limited (WPC)
Another imprint of WPC is Anthem Press (www.anthempress.com)

First published in the United Kingdom in 2012 by
THAMES RIVER PRESS
75-76 Blackfriars Road
London SE1 8HA

www.thamesriverpress.com

Original Title: Chisuji no kurokami
Copyright © Seiko Tanabe 1974
Originally published in Japan by Bungeishunju, Tokyo
English translation copyright © Meredith McKinney 2012

A CIP record for this book is available from the British Library.

ISBN 978-0-85728-246-0

Cover design by Laura Carless.

This title is also available as an eBook.

This book has been selected by the Japanese Literature Publishing Project
(JLPP), an initiative of the Agency for Cultural Affairs of Japan.

A single strand of
black night hair
entwines your fingers as they fall
heedlessly straying
over it

FOREWORD

Every country has its romantic literary figures, writers whose life stories grip the imagination and are known to many more people than ever read their work. In Japan, there has been a long tradition of romantic woman writers. Among the greatest of them is the early modern poet Yosano Akiko, the subject of this book.

Akiko, as she is familiarly known, shot to fame in 1901 at the age of twenty-three when she published *Tangled Hair* (*Midaregami*), a collection of poems that was as shocking as it was impressive. The poetry was passionate, often daringly sexually explicit, and gave powerful new voice to the young women of her age, scandalising the older generation. But Akiko's poetry was not only new and shocking in tone and content – she was also in the vanguard of a poetic revolution then taking place, and what's more she clearly had immense poetic powers. The poems in *Tangled Hair* were as beautiful as they were new and audacious, and they immediately established her as one of the finest poets of her time.

That era, the late Meiji Period (the period from 1868 to 1912), was one of ongoing innovation and upheaval in Japan. By Akiko's time, the first chaotic rush to modernize and "Westernise" had passed. Now the changes were no longer largely imitative. They had begun to bite deeper, destabilising traditional society and culture. They were also bringing upheavals to the literary norms. Poetry, which had until now been written in the short traditional *tanka*, or the even shorter *haiku*, forms, was now increasingly liberated to find its way in Western-style free verse. *Tanka* and *haiku* were not simply abandoned, however. They continued to be at the forefront of poetry, while succumbing to pressures of change that increasingly liberated them from the old rules and styles. At their most daring, the traditional forms became outrageously avant-garde expressions of emotion and experience. Akiko's poetry represented this bold extreme.

She was far from alone, however. This book tells the story not only of Akiko but of the circle of poets around her, who were swept along on the same exciting tide of poetic reform. Unlike today, poetry then was widely read and played an important role in cultural life. Readers followed these young writers almost as avidly as pop stars are followed today. And then, as now, the scandals of their private lives were the source of eager gossip.

The poems of *Tangled Hair* would certainly have invited gossip, with their blatantly erotic overtones. Akiko's poetry in fact soon evolved to become more subtle and mature, but it is the passionate excesses of her first poems that are still read and loved today – and the story behind them that still fascinates readers and non-readers alike.

This book vividly retells the story of Akiko's early years, spent in a deeply traditional household that did not allow her the liberty even to leave the house alone, and traces the astonishing transformation of that shy young girl into a passionate and liberated woman far ahead of her time. The key to the transformation was the man who became her husband, Yosano Tekkan. When he first met Akiko, Tekkan (he was known by this pen name, as was commonly the case with writers of the time) was himself at the forefront of the revolution in poetry, a kind of romantic young god of poetry with whom she quickly fell in love. He was a Byronic figure, whose unruly relations with women form a sub-plot in this book. Together, these two passionate young lovers created a poetic movement that was embodied in the journal *Myojo*. This book tells the story of that journey, and of the tempestuous love that lay at its centre. The story is presented as a seamless blend of fact and fictional recreation. Details of individual scenes are not necessarily presented as they happened, but the author has based the story closely on the known facts. Translations of poems are my own.

CONTENTS

PART I. THE SONG OF THE SEA

1

I first came across the poems of Yosano Akiko when I was a student at a girls' secondary school in the pre-war school system.

The poems of hers that were included in our textbook were vividly drawn, highly descriptive landscape poetry, utterly elegant and ornate. (This being austere wartime, naturally her early love poetry with its overt eroticism was banished not only from school textbooks but from all her published work.)

> Crossing through Gion
> on my way to Kiyomizu
> everyone I meet
> so beautiful
> on this moonlit cherry-blossom night
> • • •
> Pouring thunderously
> across Bandai Mountain
> the white sideways-blown
> torrent of rain
> enters the lake
> • • •
> Summer's wind
> comes blowing from the mountains
> and across the fields
> shaking the ears
> of three hundred young colts

Sho, as Akiko was called, loved the great Edo period haiku poet and painter Yosa Buson (1716–1783), and it is clear that his techniques influenced her work but, quite apart from this style of natural description, the beauty of the sheer rush of words here is peerless.

In girls' schools, the Japanese literature textbooks began with examples of traditional *tanka* poetry from the conservative Keien school, whose techniques harked back to those of the great classic anthology *Kokin wakashu* (early tenth century), which usually were followed by the poetry of Sho and her husband Tekkan. The impression of freshness and vigour given by these latter poems gave was thus greatly enhanced by comparison to the stolid *tanka* that came before. I was deeply interested by and attracted to Sho's poetry. As further examples of poems likely to appeal to a girl, or rather, specifically to a schoolgirl of my generation, I could add the following well-known *tanka*, poems beautiful both to the eye and to the ear:

> Kamakura
> a midsummer grove –
> Buddha though he was
> Shakyamuni
> was a handsome man
> • • •
> Summer's low cuckoo call
> at the temple
> where at thirty the mother
> of the fated child emperor
> chants her sad sutras
> • • •
> I long for the sea
> for my parents' house
> where I grew from girlhood
> counting the sounds
> of the waves' distant pulse

Through such poems, I sought to know Sho more deeply.

And so I searched for and obtained a volume of her poetry, though I don't think it was in the school library room that I found it. I seem to recall that at the time the library room doubled as an extra-curricular emergency drill room or some such; this was where we wartime girls learned how to tie bandages, staunch bleeding, perform artificial respiration, make splints and so forth. Later, the whole student body would be put through its paces in practical training, running about carrying stretchers out in the school yard under the scorching sun. Thus, as I remember, desks and chairs had been removed from the library room, and there was no sign even of books. I think I must have bought Sho's volume at a second-hand bookshop near my house. Casually opening its pages, I was taken aback by poetry extraordinarily different from what I had encountered in our textbook.

Essentially, Sho's first and most famous volume of poems, *Midaregami* (*Tangled Hair*), is far from easy. I should think that, at my age, there were many that I read without really understanding them, and no doubt I skipped quite a few. And yet, I was instantly entranced by the spirit of youthfulness, romantic love and shamelessly bold sensuality, which drew me deep into the world of her poetry.

There I found tones and evocations of astonishing clarity. The colours, too, were sumptuous − crimsons and purples, demonic colours to arouse the heart. All plants were poisonous here, the bells rang out arrogantly, blood dripped in love's breath, and the air was vibrant with the mad peals of a woman's laughter.

What an opulent, terrifying, expansive world this was! Avalanches of words. Words that were in themselves unexceptional would, when they fell from Sho's pen, burst into mad flame, transform into weeping sorrow that crouches kneading its flesh, writhe in jealous agonies, leap suddenly from the depths of torment to a boundless delight − what exquisite phantasmagoria!

> You who preach the Way
> who never reaches
> to touch the hot throb of blood
> beneath soft skin −
> are you not lonely?
> • • •

> Hands pressed to my breasts
> softly I kicked open
> the doors to mystery's realm –
> how richly scarlet
> this flower.
>
> • • •
>
> Spring is transient
> Why speak of immortality?
> said I, and let
> his hands grope for my vigorous breasts.

As I read, each word on the page reached me swathed in an emotion that rose like a shadowed form, shifting the very air. The opening poem, renowned for its difficulty:

> There amid the stars
> once I lay cloaked in curtaining night
> whispering all my heart –
> now in the human world below my hair and heart so tangled.

or this:

> My blood burns.
> Oh let me give you this dwelling place
> for one night of dreams.
> Gods, do not despise
> us who travel life's throbbing springtime.

These struck me as radiant and stunning by very reason of their difficulty. The more arduous to read, the more a poem was for me filled with dazzling beauty. I could not really claim to be awestruck by grasping the meaning of this poetry. Rather, I was drunk on the language, astonished by the vaulting spirit that could so boldly and freely choose those words.

For me, or rather, for the age we lived in then, such exhilarating release of the spirit was unthinkable. That is not to say that we young people thought of ourselves as so languid and sunken – war had been a constant distant roar in our lives from the day we were born, like the ceaseless sound of waves.

Adults would say knowingly, Don't do this, You mustn't do that. Because of the war – when the war ends – will it ever end? – No, there'll be a still bigger war.

One war (the war with China) was not over before another war began on top of it. We schoolgirls thought this was the way of the world. But looking about we realised that between one moment and the next ribbons and chocolate, long-sleeved kimonos of printed silk, pressed flower bookmarks, letter paper bearing the drawings of Nakahara Jun'ichi – all had disappeared, and now look, there was nothing to be seen but the stark and brutal khaki of soldiers everywhere. It was a world without music or colour or scent. All one saw was drained and exhausted figures dragging their limbs wearily along.

Tangled Hair appeared in 1901. If one were to ask which of the two – that earlier period or the later wartime Japan of 1942–43 – was the darker, the more cramped and restricted, conservative and hardline, I would answer that it was the latter age. That decade around the turn of the century saw a fresh new literary movement; it was the height of the era in which Meiji romanticism bloomed. On the other hand, in Japan before its defeat, people's hearts gave birth to not a single thing. All that existed was a cheerless and menacing despair that pressed down upon our heads. The abscess that was Japan at that time was still swollen and crimson with its unburst pus.

Turn hither and yon as we might, there was no answering echo. In the midst of this, Sho's poems spoke to us of a sky that lay beyond the grimness.

In her later years, Sho rejected her early poetry. She was ashamed and saddened that people spoke only of those first poems, which she herself felt were so unsatisfactory, and that they barely paused to consider her later poetry.

Her writing life spanned forty years, with over fifty thousand poems; she spoke of this early period as "the age of lies," and called her mature, later self "the truth that emerged from the lies." Of her late poetry she said, "I have a confidence and pride." Indeed, her assertion was that her literary beginnings were modelled on the work of Shimazaki Toson (1872–1943), a poet and novelist whose innovative "new style poems" paved the way for the revolution in poetry which Sho and other younger poets espoused, and the essayist and poet Susukida Kyukin (1877–1945). Sho's earliest works amounted to no more than this, or so she later declared.

And yet, although there are poems that are undeniably no more than imitations as she claims, how could one label as "lies" the dense, heavy, sweet sense of reality that other poems in the collection evoke? And if one labels those as mere lies, fictions and replications, what then should one call the poetry of her middle period that took these early poems as its springboard and grew out of them, those verses that have the convincing weight of stubborn truth? I must confess that today it is this work of Sho's middle years that I most love.

My twenties passed in the hectic postwar bustle. On all sides lay scorched earth, with not a bookshop to be found. In those days, I was a student at a women's college, specialising in Japanese literature, and I was constantly borrowing books from the college library room. Luckily, this college had escaped the wartime bombing. Although I was enrolled to study my own country's literature, in fact I spent my time reading translations of foreign classics. Our house had burned down in an air raid two months before the war ended, and my father had died in the following December. My mother, younger brother and sister and I lived a life of privation that is unimaginable today, never sure how or whether the next meal would come into our bellies. I suspect that it was for this very reason that swallowing down those ridiculously huge and verbose foreign novels was such a diversion for me. It was at this stage in my life that I consumed Tolstoy and Dostoevsky. I barely touched poetry at all. For me, poetry was something that could be properly tasted only when body and soul were relaxed and at ease.

After the war, in fact, Sho's poetry became widely known by the general public and, riding the expansive spirit of liberation abroad in the world at large at that time, most people became familiar with poems such as "Preacher of the Way" and "Spring is transient." The oppression of the war years had unleashed an instantaneous and indiscriminate flood of erotic publications and culture that inundated the streets, and Sho's poetry was picked up and whirled away by this, sullied and misused.

Today, I don't imagine anyone who reads "Preacher of the Way" simply as a poem would be bowled over or shocked by it. This is, after all, an age in which sex itself is glaringly exposed in all its nakedness. In this age, then, it is only if one takes the trouble to read such a poem in the light of the time when it was written, in other words to read it in a spirit of scholarly inquiry, that it will surprise us.

For this reason, there are those who consider Sho merely in terms of the differences between her day and our own, as a pioneer in her time. This strikes me as a very superficial point of view. For me, this poem should not be considered simply in the dimension of historical comparison, as something that lives only in relation to the age which produced it – it is an eternally living truth. We can understand this when we look at the poems she wrote throughout her life. This early poem echoes and speaks to poems that she wrote in her thirties and forties.

When I turned thirty, I chanced to take up the work of writing. I went on to meet and part with many and various people and, after surviving many minor twists of fate, to make an extraordinary marriage. I grew from a schoolgirl in her sailor's uniform into a woman nearing forty.

Sho's early poetry had lost none of its colour, and remained for me as bewitching as ever. But what to make of these eerie moans of rancour and bitterness that came after those first victorious cries affirming love?

> In a list of "Dispiriting Things"
> should also be placed
> the man newly awake
> from love, the woman
> newly awake from love
> • • •

To be loved by you
who with your powerful heart
raise that stone hammer
and come again and again
to beat upon my breast…
• • •
I must have aged.
How boundlessly
nostalgic now seems
all that everyday life
of last year and the year before.
• • •
That time of love
when my young heart
felt tortured as to death
now at last
is over.

These are poems from Sho's thirties. Just as the love poems seduced me as a schoolgirl into a world of mad and hidden passions, so in my thirties my heart was fed by these poems.

The little autumn cricket
a song heard from deep within
the pile of empty letters
between a man
and a woman

Poems like this are just the sort of thing for a mature woman. While youth may have passed in a flash, she is yet aware that another life is in the process of emerging – a life that glows, that sparkles with an energy unlike that of mere physical youthfulness. Women reach a point in life when they know this.

This new brilliance does not emerge in any straightforward way in a woman – rather, it lies heavy and sunken within her, a murmuring, subliminal presence.

In these poems, the breath of this presence in Sho has grown until it escapes in a long gasp. Here she sings of her life during those years of heavy brilliance. They are poems of nearing forty.

> More and more certain
> who it is that I admire
> now that I have passed
> my thirties – I comb
> my long black hair.
> • • •
> I feel myself
> a rose
> so weighted, so ripe
> that I might hardly
> have a human form

In short, it seemed to me, Sho's poems were not simply a kind of way station that a reader passed through in youth, but rather poems with which one could spend a lifetime. At sixty I may well find magnificent consolation and delight in those elegantly simple late lyrics such as "I have a confidence and pride."

When I was young, I believed that the woman who wrote such beautiful poetry must herself be beautiful. Now, however, my research has brought to light a number of photographs, which show her as far from what is normally considered a beauty.

That manly face, with its sturdy, strong-willed jaw.

Those thick and vigorous eyebrows.

Such heavy, imposing shoulders. Her breasts are high and generous, and the kimono is somewhat loosened around the collar (a style peculiar to the Kansai region where she grew up, in which this looser look goes with an obi tied low around the hips). Most photographs show her excessively thick lacquer-black hair tousled as in the title of her first book of poems. One imagines this hard, strong, thick, long hair resisting all attempts to control it, like her own passion.

It seems to me, however, that her face is in fact suffused by a particular kind of beauty.

The large, brightly shining eyes contain deep wisdom. A firm-bridged nose like a man's. The mouth, with its somewhat protuberant lower lip, is turned down at the sides, hinting at her formidable determination. She maintained this extraordinary expression over the course of her long life. It is an expression that speaks of confidence in her own talents, passion of a depth beyond her own control, a woman living life profoundly.

Kobayashi Masaharu's third daughter, who married Sho's son and became Yosano Michiko, recalled seeing Sho, then in her forties, when she was a child.

"Her eyes shone like obsidian beneath the ledge of her brows, with the clarity of pools brimming with thought and feeling; child that I was, when those eyes gazed at me I felt transported, and trembled in heart and body."

This same look is evident in the photographs of her at twenty-two or -three. The rounded girlish cheeks are pretty, but in the bewitched eyes flashes the hint of a ferocious sensibility. The following poem, from the collection *Dancing Girl*, seems to describe her at this time:

Fortune teller,
speak to this lovely girl
whose face is wasted
with love and desire,
say welcome words.

It is at this point, in her early twenties, that Sho met the man who would be the love of her life, Tekkan.

2

"That young dearie Sho, she never fussed much about her appearance, I must say. Hair done up in a simple twist, and all over the place just like the book says – too busy with the shop to bother with it, I suppose."

This description comes from Maeda Chozaburo, schoolmate of Sho's younger sister (Shichi Sato) at the Shukuin Secondary School in Sakai. Until very recently there were elderly people still alive who remembered Sho as a girl sitting behind the counter of the family's long-established confectionery shop, Surugaya, in Sakai.

The old women recalled, "There was a girl there in the shop, yes, not sure if it was one of the elder young dearies or the younger." And these unassuming old women, who have grown old without ever leaving Sakai, shake their heads in amazement at why everyone now makes such a fuss about Surugaya and the "young dearie" there – for Yosano Akiko had been, as it were, stoned out of town in her youth. Back in the Meiji period, this older generation had not forgiven the girl who seemed so honest and upright, but who had strewn poetry everywhere and then fled her parents' house to join a married man. They told the tale contemptuously, as a story of local shame, and Emura Mineyo, a Sakai poet and member of the Akiko Study Association, says, "I'm guessing it would have discreetly stolen its way right through the entire community."

These days, of course, no one misunderstands Sho in this way, yet Emura was only able to carry on her research because she was born in Osaka rather than Sakai, and thus managed to avoid this invisible yet entrenched wall of resistance. In the middle ages, Sakai was the site of Japan's first system of self-government, and boasted the expansive atmosphere of a prosperous free city – only to wither at last to this pitiful state. By mid-Meiji, Sakai had declined into a backward little out-of-the-way place, ridiculously constrained by outmoded tradition and plagued by deep-seated conventions and rules.

From the age of twelve, with her simple twist of hair, Sho sat in the little office behind the counter of the family shop, keeping the business accounts.

Surugaya was a traditional confectionery shop with a reputation not only locally but as far afield as Osaka and Kyoto. It was located in the district of Kai, on the Kishu Highway that linked Osaka to the Wakayama area. Sho's grandfather was a resourceful man, who invented the black sweet *yokan* (bean jelly) studded with whole beans, which he marketed under the elegant name "Night Plum Blossom." It became famous, along with the octagonal shop sign in the shape of a large clock that decorated the plaster walls.

A dark blue shop curtain hung from the eave beneath the gaslight, with the words "Yokan Surugaya, Main Shop" written with a thick brush on the indigo-dyed background. In the inner gloom beyond sat Sho, ensconced in the little lattice-fronted office, hair unoiled and in a yellow *hachijo* silk kimono, calculating sales or organising entries in the old-fashioned account book.

She was apt, however, whenever there was a pause in her work, to turn over the book lying there face-down and begin to read, and once she began she could not stop.

"Sho. I say, Sho…"

"Eh? What is it?" Sho looked up, startled. Sadashichi, the shop clerk, stood smiling beside her. He was a small young man, with pale, pinched features.

"You really are deep in that book… Bet you didn't even notice that customer who was just in."

"I see." Sho lowered her eyes to her book again, as if shielding her blushing cheeks from Sadashichi's gaze.

"You're a smart young dearie, you are. That's a pretty hard-looking book you're reading."

"Mmm…"

Sho did not look up again.

"What's the name of it?"

"It wouldn't mean a thing to you if I told you, Sadashichi."

"Yeah, I guess that's true."

Unperturbed, Sadashichi craned over to peer at the book in her hand. "*Shigarami-zoshi*. Is that a novel?"

"Yep," Sho replied briefly. *Shigarami-zoshi* was a literary journal first produced in 1889 by Mori Ogai and others, who sought to establish a new direction in Japanese literature. (Sho's future lover Tekkan was among its contributors.)

Sadashichi was a gentle, foolishly honest, earnest lad of seventeen or eighteen, a few years older than Sho, who admired her for her love of reading and writing and looked on her with special affection, which Sho took as her natural due.

"Really does look hard… Wow, Sho, you're really something," he said, attempting to run his eye over the page again. Sho quickly shielded the book with her arm.

"We've got different kinds of brains, you and the rest of us," said Sadashichi.

"True enough. I'm not like you lot." Sho spoke with unquestioning assurance. Sadashichi nodded deeply. "That's for sure," he agreed with conviction, and set about carrying the freshly-made bean jam buns out to the shelves.

Looking out from the dimly-lit lattice behind where she sat, Sho could see the main street, lit with brilliant sunshine.

This highway ran north-south through Sakai. Fields of yellow mustard flowers were scattered among the houses that lined it, while across the way she had a view of another shop belonging to Surugaya, this one specialising in imported liquor. Far in the distance beyond its roof stretched the hazy mountain range of Katsuragi.

The dark blue curtain at the shop's entrance flapped in the breeze, which brought with it the scent of the sea.

Sakai sat on a harbour facing the sea. Depending on the direction of the wind, you could sometimes hear the waves, and from the second floor balcony where the laundry was hung out to dry, you could count the sails of passing boats. Sho was born in this house.

When she was an innocent little girl, Sho would get the shop's apprentice to recite for her the names of Sakai's districts: "Kai, Ichi, Yuya, Ebisu, Kushiya, Kuruma, Zaimoku, Shukuya, Shinmei, Kuken, Yanagi, Sakura, Nishiki, Aya, Hatago, Hancho…" The list moved north from Kai, the district where they lived, and it was spoken to a soft little tune, just like a song.

The names have an old-fashioned elegance and beauty, as befits an old town.

Hide-bound and conventional as the town was, it was also the place that had earlier produced Sen no Rikyu, originator of the tea ceremony, and Ryutatsu, who founded a style of song popular around the seventeenth century. Even in the Meiji period of Sho's day, Sakai was known both for scholarship and artistic pastimes.

Sho had loved books since she was a primary school student, when she read the literary magazines of her time such as *Mezamashi-gusa* and *Bungakkai*, but her onfectio works were found in her father Soshichi's library. From reading *Kogetsusho*, the seventeenth-century commentary on *The Tale of Genji*, she had come to read *The Tale of Genji* itself, which had given her a taste for the difficult court tales and poetry collections of the Heian period (794–1185). Soshichi was by temperament more scholar than confectionery-shop owner, a dilettante who loved the arts and owned a vast collection of books.

Most owners of such traditional establishments, large or small, in Sakai at that time probably shared his elegant tastes.

"The young Surugaya dearie is a real bookworm," the townspeople said of Sho as she sat behind the lattice.

The old women who later recalled her spoke of "the elder dearies" and "the younger dearie," using an affectionate local dialect word to speak of Sho and her two elder half-sisters by a different mother.

Sho was her father Ho Soshichi's third daughter.

In the time of Soshichi's grandfather, the Ho family had moved to Sakai, taking with them a branch of the old Surugaya shop. Soshichi had an elder brother who, in the normal course of things, should have inherited the business, but he was a scholar who did not take to shopkeeping, just like his grandfather's eldest son, Soshichi's uncle.

Soshichi's strong-willed mother disliked his first wife, and once she had borne him two daughters she was sent packing.

After the divorce, Soshichi's mother chose another wife for her son. This was Tsune, Sho's mother. Tsune seems to have been a clever, hard-working woman, with a rational turn of mind. Perhaps Sho and her siblings inherited their clearheaded intellect from their mother, and their love of the arts from their father.

After the first son, Hidetaro, came a second, Tamajiro, who died early. Soshichi had it in mind that the Surugaya business should follow tradition and be handed down through the second son, and his heart was fixed on the birth of another boy. However, near the end of 1878, on December 7th, Tsune gave birth to a girl. She was not especially beautiful.

Soshichi was filled with disappointment. He took long walks, driven to distraction by the peevish child's endless crying.

Soshichi named the girl Sho. The combination with their unusual family name, which was written with a single character ("phoenix"), produced the slightly ludicrous reading "Ho Sho," creating a strangely foreign, Chinese impression. One explanation of the origin of the name Ho was that the family had originated in a village about two miles south of Sakai whose name literally meant "large bird" or "phoenix" and the character for "Ho" was an alternative reading of the village's name. In fact, however, in the beginning of the Meiji period when commoners were first allowed to take a family name,

Soshichi, who was erudite in the field of Chinese classics, arbitrarily chose this elaborate character to register for himself. (The affectation of choosing a Chinese pronunciation of a Japanese name was not uncommon among confectioners of the time.)

Not only was Soshichi the sort of well-to-do gentleman-merchant who took an interest in elegant pastimes such as tea ceremony and Noh singing, he was apparently also something of a libertine, squandering his fortune in the gay quarters of Ohama and going off on long trips accompanied by several rickshaws full of geisha.

Those walks he took after Sho was born were also made possible by the fact that he could leave matters in the hands of his mother Shizu, who was firmly in power in the household. For this reason, as daughter-in-law poor Tsune was put under constant strain. She now also blamed herself for her husband's disappointment, and she was slow to recover after the birth of her daughter. What's more, she couldn't produce milk. She sent the baby to the home of her married sister over in Yanagi district to be looked after. They were a wholesale fishmonger, and every evening after the shop closed and everyone had gone to bed, Tsune would arrive at the back door with her lantern, having walked the mile from home to Yanagi to see her baby. Sho may have been Soshichi's third daughter, but she was Tsune's first.

"Boys and girls are both equally delightful, after all. Poor creature, to be rejected and shunned just because she was born a girl…" As Tsune held the howling baby in her arms, she considered her own fate as the daughter-in-law in this contradictory, difficult merchant family.

"Yes little Sho, isn't that right, it's no good being a girl…"

Two years later when Sho's little brother Chusaburo was born, she was finally brought back home. But Sho's aunt's household had in fact made a fuss over the little girl; they also had a gourmet approach to eating fish, only natural given their line of business (though the same held true for Sho's own home). In this they followed the ways of old and historically important towns, especially this Inland Sea port with its wealth of available seafood. (In later years, when she married Tekkan, she was astonished at his poor and simple taste in food. Accustomed as she was to eating well, she said this was the hardest thing for her to get used to.)

Sho was considered an odd, taciturn child. By this time she also had a little sister, Sato, and Soshichi seemed at last to have settled down and begun to treat Sho with affection. He seemed to feel she had a certain promise.

"The girl's bright," he said, and at the age of five he tried sending her off to primary school, but she was still too little and came running home in tears. He then waited until she had reached school age, and sent her to Shukuin Primary School. This was 1884. Soganoya Goro, later a famous actor and playwright, was in the same class.

When she was nine, she was sent to the local school of Chinese learning called "Chishinjuku," run by a Chinese scholar named Higuchi Shuyo, where she began with rote readings of the classics as a first step towards understanding them.

Also gradually introduced in her education were the traditional arts of flower arrangement, tea ceremony and traditional dance in the Fujima school – Sakai, being an old-fashioned town, was home to a great many geisha and thus very strong in these feminine arts, so Surugaya's "young dearie" would have needed to hold her own in this sphere.

In time, Sho graduated from Shukuin Primary School, completed upper level studies, and entered the newly-established Sakai Girls' School. Ever since primary school, she had been particularly good at maths. Considering that her elder brother Hidetaro went through Tokyo Imperial University's electrical engineering faculty to become a scholar in the field, and Sho's daughter Yosano Uchiko also became a mathematician, there can be no doubt that her family was blessed with keen bright minds.

Still, all things considered, the reason that all the children, girls included, had so many years of schooling was probably because Soshichi, despite being a merchant, was a dilettante lover of literature who dabbled in *haiku* and ink painting, bought the latest books and magazines of the major literary scene, and was in short a man of understanding and sensibility.

The custom of those days dictated that merchant families should bring up their children accordingly – the boys going into business and devoting themselves to the abacus, girls spending their days practicing the traditional feminine arts of flower arranging and so forth, together with sewing and cooking. It was rare indeed for a confectionery shop's sons and daughters to go on through to higher education, and it was surely thanks to Soshichi's love of learning that his children did so.

Nevertheless, the education at Sakai Girls' School, as with all girls' schools of this period, emphasized needlework and household management, with the aim of producing "good wives and wise mothers," as the well-known Meiji-era saying expressed it. The school had in fact developed from a needlework school that had been set up as a practical school for girls. It was a three-year course of study, giving classes in ethics, arithmetic, geography, history, reading, writing and housekeeping, but the greater part of the time was given over to homemaking, mainly needlework.

Sho was good at needlework. In later life, she would sew a dress or kimono for one of her children in a single evening. She was clever at whatever she laid her hand to. There were competitions at school to see who could sew the fastest, in which the girls would set to work at the order "Start!" to sew a cotton kimono or the like. A hush would fall over everyone as they sat there silently in the classroom, pincushions crammed with threaded needles beside them, gazing intently at their work while their hands flew. Less than an hour later, the first girl to finish left. Sho was fast. She was never beyond second or third place. At first glance a gentle, ordinary girl, she burned with a fiercely competitive spirit.

Whatever she did, she did better than others. She felt she deserved better than this girls' school with its poor standards of study, but higher education was not open to women, and so she withdrew into herself and fretted, unable to give vent to her dissatisfaction.

Behind this feeling lay a constant envy of her elder brother Hidetaro, who had proceeded from secondary school to the prestigious Imperial University in Tokyo.

"Mum, why do you think it is that boys get to study and girls don't?" she asked Tsune.

"Well, they're boys, aren't they? Boys are different from girls."

"How come?"

"Boys have to make their way in the world, so they need to study. Girls don't. Study's useless for girls. Girls marry into a household."

"That's stupid. I think girls are just the same as boys…"

"So what will a girl do with her learning, eh?"

"Hidetaro's got it lucky. He gets to go to Tokyo and study all he wants…"

"Just listen to you! You were born a girl, so you mustn't overdo the studying…"

"I'd just love to go to Tokyo and study like Hidetaro."

"So who's going to do the sewing and kitchen work if girls go studying? You going to make the men do it?"

Tsune chuckled at her own joke. She had seen her mother-in-law laid to rest, and had settled down as mistress of the household by now; she was quite content, and no longer had any doubts about a woman's place in life.

"…"

Whenever Sho had an argument with her mother, she ended by falling silent. Tsune took this as a sign of her obedient nature, and was pleased, but in her heart Sho was not convinced – she was simply not prepared to speak her defiance aloud. She grew increasingly taciturn.

As a young girl, Sho loved her mother's warmth and tenderness, yet on another level she was coldly critical of her ignorance, narrow-mindedness and naïveté about the world. Privately, Sho could not but be constantly aware of this seed of criticism that grew so strong and sturdy within her breast. For this unnaturally mature girl with her overdeveloped mind, made so worldly and wise by the books she read, it was impossible not to react against the things she saw in everyday life.

Nor did she have any real friends she could talk to. There were, of course, good-natured girls among her school companions to whom she was drawn, but from Sho's point of view they were unbearably infantile, all very well for girlish friendship but not anyone to open her heart to.

As for the teachers at her school, they were all bigoted and rigidly old-fashioned.

"Miss Ho, if you read novels you will fail."

This is what her teacher told her when she handed in an essay on the newly-published novel by the contemporary novelist Ozaki

Koyo for her reading class. Sho was silent. Silence was her only option, in fact. Her teacher, she thought, had no idea who Koyo was, and had likely never tasted the soul's boundless delight at reading a work of literature.

In his ethics class, this teacher talked of nothing but loyal and virtuous heroines, and recommended old-fashioned books that told their stories – *The Zen Nun Matsushita*, *Princess Kesa*, *The Wife of Hosokawa Tadaoki* and so forth. Privately, Sho rebelled fiercely against these clichéd, prejudice-ridden morality tales. She felt proudly confident that she was very probably many times more skilled and prolific at reading than her teacher, and had a finer sensibility. She nursed this hidden pride like an animal will its wound, licking and caring for it, so that gradually it grew sturdier and stronger within her. Yet she said nothing, simply watching with her dark eyes. Then she would lower her gaze, bow and withdraw. Her heart, twisted with these unspoken feelings, grew pliant and strong, crouching like a wild beast awaiting its chance to hurtle out at last with terrific force. Would a time come when this creature would at last break its chains and leap out free into the wide world?

Sho walked home from school alone through the willows that lined Okoji Street, dressed in *hakama* trousers that were the school uniform at the time and holding to her breast a cloth bundle containing her sewing materials. To look at this ordinary girl, who would know that inside lurked an unseen beast, that this was in fact her true self?

Once home, she sat at the office desk, where she passed the time writing up accounts. Shop gossip bored her, and she took no interest in the chatter of the wet-nurse Outa or her mother's maid.

Sho took down book after book from her father's shelves, reading at random. Not altogether comprehending them, she delved into classic historical tales such as *Okagami* and *Eiga monogatari*, the old poetry collections of *Kokinshu* and *Shinkokinshu*, and various works of early court literature.

It was at this time that *The Tale of Genji* first seized her imagination.

Teru and Hana, her two older half-sisters by their father's first wife, had recently moved in. Teru spent only a brief period as the girl behind the lattice doing the accounts before she went off as a bride to the home of a doctor named Takemura. Her younger sister Hana then took over, but soon handed the job over to Sho because she herself was busy preparing for marriage.

She was a gentle girl, however, and would sometimes take time out to help Sho. "Why don't I take over for a bit, little dearie?" she would say, and settle down at the desk in Sho's place. Living amidst her stepmother and half-siblings, Hana was always diffident and solicitous of others, an unobtrusive presence.

Hearing this, Sho would jump up delightedly and go straight to the library. Here, under the feeble light, she could immerse herself in reading any book she liked without worrying about what anyone might say. With the aid of a seventeenth-century commentary, the *Kogetsusho*, she tried to grope her way through *The Tale of Genji*. Back and forth she went, reading the beautiful, difficult sentences over and over, stumbling along from one word to the next. At first she barely understood a thing, but after three or four years of reading and re-reading, the brilliant and voluptuous thousand-year-old world of this ancient love story gradually began to reveal itself before her eyes, as if some gossamer veil had been finally torn away. At last, though still only dimly, Sho could glimpse the world of *The Tale of Genji* – the Shining Prince, Hikaru Genji, who loved a forbidden woman, and the anguish of the dark and beautiful illicit love into which he strayed.

Swirling petals of unhappy love! His fierce remorse at the transitory love affair with the beautiful Fujitsubo, who bore his child despite being his stepmother, Fujitsubo's decision to become a nun out of self-reproach for her unforgivable sin, and the appearance of the delightful little girl Murasaki, like a light set aflame in the midst of the dark sufferings of Genji's troubled heart.

And then the dramatic death of the pretty Yugao, and the madness of Lady Rokujo, Genji's older lover. The breathless fascination of those multifarious people and the complications of relationships made and broken. Genji's official wife, Aoi, chilly and reserved; Lady Rokujo, a woman of unsurpassed wit and beauty who yet could not withstand her oppressive demons. Not one of these women embodies the ultimate, but the various aspects of feminine nature are laid before us in dazzling array.

Lady Murasaki, who could be called the ideal of womanhood, she whom Genji had fixed upon as his true love when she was still a child, and whom he himself had raised precisely as he wished, was unable to bear a child. How enviable was this author's insight and empathy for people!

And at the last, Genji's own crime comes back to haunt him in the form of the secret affair between his own wife Sannomiya and the young man Kashiwagi. He is repaid by the rigorous hand of fate.

Call it the karmic cycle, or karmic retribution – this picture scroll tale that opens so brilliantly draws to its close reverberating with strong, dark, fearful overtones.

In this world, one who usurps love from another must have his own love taken in turn – by a vast, unknowable power, a kind of grave and magisterial universal will.

In any case, this emotional young girl's heart was deeply affected by the world of Genji.

All her life, for over fifty years, Sho continued to love *The Tale of Genji*. Her translation of it into modern Japanese takes a different approach from that of the novelist Tanizaki Jun'ichiro, who aimed at faithfulness to the original's atmosphere. Sho's translation penetrates more directly and deeply into the heart of the tale, cutting to the quick and instilling a fresh flourish and an uninhibited freedom. It is a *Genji* that borrows her voice and speaks in her own tones. I love it. In the process of her intimate reading of *The Tale of Genji*, she almost physically digested it. The volumes of *Genji* and the same period's famous historical tale *Eiga monogatari* deeply imbued her with a taste for the world of early court literature – she was forever enchanted by the beautiful, the noble, the elegant.

3

When Sho was fourteen, her stepsister Hana married a landowner from nearby Otori.

Hana was a shy, lonely girl who had been uprooted from one household to another and who found it difficult to warm to her younger siblings.

Sho was unaware of the fact that Hana and an elder cousin were in love, but her father would not allow a marriage between cousins; instead, he arranged marriage for her with a different man.

Sho noticed, however, that as the wedding day approached Hana was increasingly depressed and silent.

"Is becoming a bride really such a miserable thing?" she wondered to herself.

If that was the case, where was the joy in a woman's life? Staying at home meant having to do the housework there, and getting married meant helping out with that family's business. It was one gloomy thing after another – poor downcast Hana, going off to be sacrificed in her bridal veil. "What's so great about being a bride, then?" Sho could only think, defiantly.

Misfortune dogged poor Hana – she bore a child, and not long after she fell ill and died. She was just past thirty.

After Hana married, Sho could no longer leave her post at the desk. She kept the accounts and assisted in the shop, helping to wrap the *yokan* in their bamboo-bark wrappers in her spare moments, and at night she worked further, helping with the making of the *keshimochi* (poppyseed bean jam cakes).

Then, when the work was done and everyone was sound asleep, she secretly read her books.

"Sho! You're still up?!" thundered her father's frightening voice from down the corridor.

"Ye– yes… I'm just going to bed," was her confused reply. Then she read stealthily on, careful not to make a sound as she turned the pages. Before long she became so absorbed she forgot the time. Then suddenly the electric light went out. It was midnight.

Surreptitiously she lit a lamp, shielding its glow behind her kimono hanging on its rack, and went on stealing through the pages. This was when Sho most envied her elder brother.

Her brother Hidetaro had graduated from the science faculty of Tokyo's Imperial University, gone on to postgraduate studies, and was commencing his career as a scholar. He was an up-and-coming young researcher of whom much was hoped for the future, with plans to study abroad in Europe in a few years' time.

"Please give my little brother Chusaburo the business," he told his father. "I want to devote myself to scholarship." When he heard this, Soshichi and his wife resigned themselves to the fact that the inevitable moment had arrived.

Soshichi was proud of Hidetaro, so he agreed without hesitation. There was, in fact, an odd custom already established whereby the eldest son did not inherit the Surugaya business, so no doubt he was privately prepared for this eventuality.

Sho's little sister Sato also left Sakai Girls' School and went on to the research area of the Kyoto Prefectural Secondary School.

"Why should she go all the way off to Kyoto?" her parents grumbled reluctantly, but Sho backed her.

"These days you'll fall behind in the world if you don't learn English. Surely even girls should get all the education they can?"

She pitied Sato's potential fate of being buried behind the lattice like herself. Bookworm that she was, she could preserve her own private world, but Sho was apprehensive at the thought of the pure and innocent Sato sinking into the grime of the mundane world.

And besides, in the last few years everything in Japan had surged ahead. The ferocity of the rate of change was astonishing. When Sho had entered the girls' school, there was still no secondary school such as girls like Sato could now attend, and few families even bothered to send their daughters to school anyway.

But after the Sino-Japanese War of 1894–95, in which Japan was the victor, everything changed completely. Factories sprang up in great numbers, there was an increase in both male and female factory workers, and many more people had cash. The Nankai train line was extended throughout the area where Sho lived, all the way to the coast at Hamadera and Takasago, providing easy access to Osaka.

Telephones were installed, and people wearing Western dress became less of a rarity. With each passing day, the winds of this new civilization penetrated more deeply. It was now an age when sending a girl to the high school in Kyoto was no longer anything particularly unusual.

The nation had been stunned by Japan's easy victory over China, another major nation, and then by the fact that negotiations by Russia, France and Germany had, nevertheless, forced Japan against its will to return the Liaotung Peninsula, which they had taken in the war. This rallied the people's urge to see Japan's strength as a nation grow. The Japanese government, determined that Japan be included among the great imperialist powers, fanned the flames of this sentiment.

"Polish the sword for a decade" was a popular phrase of the time.

Another expression clamoured about was the Chinese phrase, "To lie on firewood and lick bitterness," expressing the need to submit to mortification as a penance.

Japan, in other words, must never forget the humiliation of its subjugation at the hands of the three Western powers. It was an age when the whole nation was in a state of heady exhilaration. Trains ran everywhere now, mills and factories were spreading – people's lives were changing, and with them their hearts. Such changes in how people lived and thought about the world naturally meant that the idea of letting your child become a scholar was becoming nothing out of the ordinary. One must incorporate new concepts and work hard to help build the country's power and wealth. This passion throughout the land encouraged social development, and lit the fuse that would lead, at length, to the Second World War. A long fuse indeed.

The next flashpoint was the Russo-Japanese War, ten years later.

During those ten years, Sho's fate would undergo a dramatic change.

But who would have guessed it then?

"Well, if Sato goes on to high school, you'll be stuck doing the account books forever, you know," said her mother, astonished at Sho's support for her sister. "All things being equal, you'd be passing on the accounts work to Sato about now, and getting yourself ready for marriage."

"I've no mind to do that yet," Sho responded with a laugh. "Spare me from being a bride! I'll keep on doing the accounts until Chusaburo gets himself a wife."

Chusaburo, two years younger, had stepped in instead of his elder brother the scholar and left Sakai Middle School to enter the family business. He was now busy learning the trade as Surugaya's "junior boss."

"Come now girl, you'll be an old maid if you go on like this – you'll get a bad reputation with our relatives and neighbours, you know." Tsune knitted her brows.

"Old maid," that derogatory name for a woman past marriageable age. In Japanese, the term literally translates as "the widow who doesn't leave home," and had about it a humorous edge associated with the Osaka dialect spoken in the Ho household. The term would have a deeply humiliating ring to a parent's ears.

Sho was, in fact, getting a number of marriage offers, but she merely shrugged them off, paying no attention to any of them.

Rather, her heart was devoted to the kind of princely men who reigned in her imagination, lovers far more real to her than such unappealingly practical fellows like the son of another cake shop or the second son of a kimono silk merchant (although no doubt among them were some fine young men).

At Mr. Higuchi's school of Chinese learning, which Sho had been attending after school since she was very young and where she still sometimes went, by special request she had studied Bo Juyi's long verse romance, *The Enduring Remorse*. Reading *The Tale of Genji*, she had discovered that the depiction of the tragic love between the Kiritsubo emperor and his court lady alluded to a section of this famous Chinese classic, and now she felt compelled to read it through.

The Chinese emperor Hsuan Tsung's obsessive and fateful love for the great beauty Yang Guifei was the model for the Kiritsubo emperor's love for his lady in waiting, though Yang Guifei's end was even more gruesome.

"Oh, alas, for this maiden of but fifteen years, who had determined to die by the sword as had Yang Guifei."

Sho was herself just seventeen when she read *The Enduring Remorse*. She could manage to get away with the excuse that she was "still young… I'm not twenty yet!" when she turned down offers of marriage.

Her soul was captivated by the delights of straying in the world of fantastical romance; mere reality was as insubstantial as drifting smoke.

In *The Enduring Remorse* she read:

> In the Yang household there was a daughter who was just
>   growing to maidenhood,
> raised with care and profoundly beautiful, as yet unknown to
>   others...

How could one fail to discover such heaven-ordained beauty?
And when one morning she is chosen to take her place beside her
monarch...

> She had but to roll her eyes and give a single smile,
> and she was overwhelmingly seductive,
> No need for the adornments of the palace's concubines...
> Three thousand gorgeous ladies lived in the Inner Palace
> yet all the emperor's love that was due those three thousand,
>   was focused on her alone.

The beautiful girl and the emperor, in love, must leave the capital
because the An Lushan Rebellion has broken out; some hundred
leagues west of the city gates, hostility toward the emperor and his
lover overtakes the loyal army.

"It is Guifei who is the real danger threatening the nation. We
must have her head!" clamour the soldiers. Despite his attempts to
pacify them, the army refuses to obey his orders. The emperor is
forced against his will to hand his beloved Guifei over to the soldiers.
She dies before his eyes, her flower-like visage soaked in blood.

"The sovereign covers his face, unable to save her." He and his
loyal followers gaze at each other and soak their robes with tears.

Ripped apart by cruel fate, never to so much as glimpse each
other again in this world, these two lovers have vowed:

> "If we are born in heaven, may we be as inseparable as
>   lovebirds;
> If we are born on earth, may we cling together as two entwined
>   branches."

The poem ends with the emperor, distraught and weeping, as he
moans, "Infinite is my longing, knowing no end."

Sho decided that, since she was doomed to live as a woman, she must follow in the footsteps of Yang Guifei – she would live fiercely with all her might and with a woman's full strength, a life splendidly squandered in the full bloom of youth. She yearned to commit herself, body and soul, to loving and being fiercely loved, to love without regret.

In the gloomy recess behind the lattice, Sho's maiden heart smouldered with boundless and irrepressible dreams.

Where at this moment was the man whom she would love?

Would he some day come for her? Or was the prime of her youth fated to wither and fade while she sat on in this shop?

Secretly in the bath, Sho would regard her own chaste body. She would gaze at herself in the mirror as she wound up her long, stiff hair.

She murmured the description of Yang Guifei bathing in the pool:

> "The waters of the spring slid smooth over her lustrous skin
> When the servant helped her from the bath, she drooped alluringly."

Seen through the water of the bath, her own pale skin looked particularly beautiful.

Some time before, oil paintings of nudes had been displayed at an exhibition in Tokyo, causing a great stir: "Exhibition or no, what can they be thinking of," stormed a newspaper editorial, "to bring in such deviant objects?" There was a general uproar of criticism and attack. Sho had not seen the exhibition, of course, but it seemed to her that there was nothing more beautiful than the skin of a woman at the height of her youthful beauty. Surely it was only natural for an artist to want to capture this in a painting? Kept hidden from sight, a woman's glory only deepened in intensity and grew richer in its bouquet. Sho did not think herself a conventional beauty, but when her thoughts soared upward as if astride some angelic steed, she could not but be drunk with self-adoration, imagining herself a pure and fascinating beauty.

I let my hair,
this long black hair, hang down
against my fine skin
as if to say
Suffer, sinful man!
• • •
Though I have reached the age
of ripeness,
no glorious Prince Genji
has come to call
upon me yet.

People still alive today who knew Sho's dilettante father say that he had not a few examples of erotic *ukiyo-e* woodblock prints in his collection. In that case, it may well have been that Sho, rummaging around in Soshichi's library, happened one day to chance upon them. Perhaps, seeing those gorgeously-hued amorous fantasies may well have deepened further the rich voluptuousness hidden within her.

When Sho was nineteen, her mother suffered a slight brain hemorrhage.

Sho devoted herself to nursing her mother, making it clear to both parents how useful it was to have an able-bodied young woman around the house.

"Thank you, Sho... I had the idea that because you're such an odd one, always with your head in some difficult book, you wouldn't be the type to rise to the challenge like this, but you've changed my mind. I'm deeply grateful to you." Tsune gazed happily up at her suddenly adult daughter. Sho was a thoroughly considerate, alert and efficient girl, but somewhat quiet, subdued and unapproachable in appearance. It took an emergency such as this to bring out her true colours.

Sho loved her mother, so it was a shock when she fell ill.

"Recover as quick as you can and get back to normal again, Mum... I don't like worrying about you like this."

"Yes, indeed. This is the most important moment, with none of my own children married yet, so I've no intention of up and dying," replied her mother with a laugh. "My plan is to stick around, come what may, till you've found yourself a husband, and Sato's married, and Chusaburo has a wife and I've seen the face of my grandchild."

"That's right, Mum, it'll all happen." As she said these words, Sho clung to her mother like a little child. In reality, she was still an unsophisticated girl who couldn't get by without her mother's protection.

And yet, despite all this, her heart tugged with the contradictory urge for a life of freedom.

Thanks to Sho's care, her mother gradually improved, and at length she could somehow limp about, dragging one leg. After her illness, she seemed to rely more on her daughter, for she left the detailed running of the house to Sho.

Sho was aware that ever since her father had become a member of the Sakai City Council, he had been spending a considerable amount of his own money, making it hard for her mother to make ends meet. Soshichi liked to play the rich man and spread money around, and he had an easygoing approach to business. His method was old-fashioned and, since the war, prices had risen and competition had increased. Theirs was a large household and besides, Soshichi's work as a city council member not only consumed time and energy but even began to eat into the family fortune, so that the Surugaya enterprise was almost imperceptibly beginning to wane. This being business, though, Sho's mother had to keep the problem to herself, so she agonized alone in the kitchen over how to manage the household.

"You know the saying, 'It's when help arrives that the burden feels heaviest'?" Tsune remarked with a laugh. "The moment I realized what a fine dependable lass Sho is, something in me relaxed and went limp…"

Now that her mother had come to rely on her, one after another Sho found herself taking over the jobs of the lady of the house – maintaining relations with the relatives, keeping watch over the workers and clerks in the shop, dictating instructions to the maids and so forth. The weight of the household began to lie more and more heavily on her shoulders. When her mother had been ill, she clung to her forlornly, but once her mother's health had improved again, Sho found herself bitterly cursing the fate that kept her cooped up in this house.

Sho was at last beginning to weary of the long summer of her maidenhood.

Soshichi was by nature something of a wastrel and man-about-town – dabbler in the arts though he was, their influence in no way extended to his personal philosophy and moral code. Like all parents of the Meiji era, he never thought of his daughters' education in terms other than as the making of good wives and mothers. He was happy to send his son all the way to Tokyo for his studies, but he wasn't prepared to allow his daughters even to step out alone, let alone go for an idle excursion somewhere. From time to time he would take his daughters with him to Kyoto or Nara, but this was Sho's sole form of amusement, and the long monotonous days weighed heavy on her. She was sick and tired by now of the pagoda at Myokokuji Temple, the ginkgo trees on Honganji's temple grounds, the Katsuragi and Takama mountain ranges, and the scent of the nearby sea. She had no close friendships and, naturally, being the strictly-raised daughter of a good family, had never had any relations with the opposite sex. Wherever she went, even to her lessons on the wifely arts of tea ceremony and the like, she was always accompanied by a maid, while going out after dark was absolutely forbidden.

Sakai was full of geisha, and hence its moral atmosphere was rather lax; there were apparently occasions when Soshichi feared for his daughters to such an extent that he locked them in their rooms.

In later years, looking back on her girlhood, she wrote, "My father was a drunkard, my mother was ignorant, many of the employees were ill-mannered, while my relatives were either stingy or avaricious, and the area was full of people who were wily, vulgar and lewd."

One can imagine that for Sho, a girl drawn to literature, who was aware in her Kansai backwater town of the exciting new literary stirrings in distant Tokyo, at some point her surroundings came to feel crude and irksome.

Surely, however, this long period Sho spent fretful and miserable turned out to be a blessing for the seed of her own unique literary life that would soon burst into being. Fine wine must lie long in the barrel to gain the full richness of its flavour. During this period, little by little, Sho's extraordinary nature began to glow stronger and stronger; the wine of her soul was fermenting its particular vintage.

Sho had early begun to read the magazines from Tokyo; in Sakai at this time, there were only two young people who were buying and reading the literary journals *Bunko* and *Bungakukai*: Sho and the poet Kawai Suimei.

Sho was much moved by the groundbreaking anthology of free verse, *Seedlings*, by Shimazaki Toson. This was a world completely new and different from that of her beloved *Tale of Genji* and *Enduring Remorse*.

> When I saw you under the apple boughs
> your girlish fringe brushed back for the first time
> you seemed to me a blossom
> with your flowery comb upon your head.

Entranced by this fresh lyricism, Sho's imagination was filled with thoughts of Tokyo, where lively young literary people were gathering like clouds in the sky to create new modes of thought that would revolutionize Japanese literature.

Sho was particularly stimulated by the woman writer Higuchi Ichiyo's fiction, *Takekurabe* (*Growing Up*) and *Nigorie* (*Troubled Waters*), published respectively in *Bungakukai* and *Bungei Kurabu*. Confident as she was of her own abilities, Sho could not help but feel a surge of rivalry as she read them, although in fact Ichiyo's novels were in another league altogether from Sho, whose literary seed had yet to forth shoots.

In 1896, when she was nineteen, Sho became a member of the Sakai Shikishima Tanka Society. The poems she produced then constitute her first printed work.

> Deer on the Mountain Peak

> Oh autumn night's soft rain
> please do not fall so thick
> for the stag who seeks his mate
> there upon the mountain ridge
> will grow more drenched with dew.

Bell at Evening

Would that they could hear,
those people of the city,
the evening's temple bell that tolls
in this mountain village as
the autumn rains sift down.

These mediocre, pseudo-classical poems that hark back to the pre-Meiji period in tone and style speak of the way in which Sho's addiction to the classics was an unfortunate fetter on her talents. Ever agile, however, Sho soon shook off this bond and entered new territory.

Toson's *Seedlings* had stirred the hearts of young people throughout Japan to a wild enthusiasm, and the same thing was about to happen in the realm of traditional *tanka* poetry. As with that new free verse style, so too the flames of a *tanka* revolution were beginning to flicker.

Sho could not forget a strange poem she had seen in the *Yomiuri Newspaper*. Knowing her love of literature, her brother Hidetaro, studying in Tokyo, had kindly sent her a note saying, "Ozaki Koyo's novel *Konjikiyasha (Demon Gold)* is causing a stir here, with everyone saying how interesting it is, so you should read it," and enclosed the edition of the *Yomiuri* that carried the serialization. Its culture page featured some poetry, among which was the following:

Spring still young along the path
over Dokan Mountain
where at a lone tea-house
a student sits eating rice cakes,
wearing *hakama*.

The poet's name was Yosano Tekkan.
Tekkan…
Sho had immediately taken notice of the impressive-sounding, masculine pen name of this poet.
Tekkan, written with characters that suggest a steely action, brought to her mind an image of a chaste plum blossom flowering

in fierce cold. His rough, intense poetry echoed his name. He was a belligerently argumentative young poet who, in 1897, at the youthful age of twenty-four, made his debut in the literary world with the collection *Tozai Namboku* (*The Four Directions*), followed the next year by *Tenchi Genko* (*Black Sky Yellow Earth*), which were greeted with a storm of enthusiasm by young readers everywhere.

When *Tozai Namboku* came out, Sho read it immediately. The poems were not to her taste – all were swashbuckling, rough, and fiercely passionate.

But this new poem, "Spring still young," bewildered her. It was of an utterly different sensibility from his poems that she had read before.

At first glance it seemed a straightforward and unexceptional poem, but it had a fresh new realism not to be found in previous traditional poems with their obsession with technique.

There were none of the usual clichés here – no cherry blossoms, no waves or moon or insect song. In fact, despite dragging in the everyday ordinariness of rice cakes, Dokan Mountain, a student and *hakama*, it was essentially a sure and convincing sketch of reality.

The next poem read:

> A lad dozing at noon
> and from the pocket
> of his school uniform
> violets tumble –
> they say he's eight years old.

This too struck Sho as refreshingly original.

In her poetic treatise *Yabukoji* (*Wild Citrus*), she relates how she thought at the time, "If this is the new poetry, I think I can write it too."

4

A fresh new vigour was evident in the literary movement around Osaka at that time – this particular moment in postwar social development had produced the same effect not only there, indeed, but throughout the nation. Though it didn't yet amount to a clearly defined "Kansai literary scene," about twenty young literature lovers came together to form the Naniwa Young Men's Literary Society and produced a magazine, *Yoshiashi-gusa*.

Among them was Nakamura Kichizo, who later published novels under the pen name Shun'u (Spring Rain), as well as Takasu Yoshijiro and Kobayashi Masaharu. These young men, like all Meiji-era literati, were enthusiastic in submitting work to literary magazines. The supreme honour was to have a piece accepted by *Bunko* or *Shonen Sekai*.

Literary journals in those days, typified by the somewhat later *Myojo* and *Shinsei*, were a combination of trade publication and literary coterie magazine, which also accepted submissions from non-members among the general public. Unknown young writers could make their debut in the literary world within these pages. They couldn't really be classified simply as the coterie members' publication, since high-ranking writers also frequently submitted work to these journals, and besides, they were eagerly snatched up by readers as soon as they hit the bookshops, while young people in provincial literary associations also awaited their publication with impatience.

Both Nakamura and Takasu spent their days earning a monthly wage of ten yen at the Hakkenya Postal Bureau in Osaka, and their nights at evening classes where they devoted themselves to literary study.

Kobayashi Masaharu, who looked after the group's finances, was the son of a blanket wholesaler with branches on Osaka's Azuchimachi and Shinsaibashi Streets. He provided their material support.

Their spiritual support was provided by a young man named Kawai Matahei, a Sakai kimono shop owner, a poet who went by the pen name Kawai Suimei. He was both leader and pioneer of the Kansai modern literature movement, a man deeply respected and trusted by the young writers' group.

A youthful photograph of Suimei reveals a firm, placid, gentle face.

Born in 1874, he was the oldest member of the group, and since he was at this time the editor of the poetry column for the national magazine *Bunko*, the other members must have gathered around him to imbibe a whiff of the literary new age. Suimei had taken over his family's long-established kimono shop called Kawamata, located in

Sakai's Kitahatago district. Misfortune had dogged his family; both parents had died within a short time of each other, leaving him alone with his grandmother. He had married his cousin, and inherited the family business. But Suimei was a deeply literary young man, who at the age of eighteen had already been published in the collection of new-style *tanka*, *Seinen Shoka-shu* (*Songs of Youth*), and he had no desire to toil away in obscurity in this provincial kimono shop. He defied the opposition of his relatives and went to Tokyo, but then gave in to their pleading and entreaties and returned home again. Meanwhile, his poetry grew and developed; his fresh, lucid poems were becoming increasingly admired, sought out and well-known. This was the same period during which the Kansai literary group was flourishing.

Suimei agreed to act as poetry editor for the group's magazine, *Yoshiashi-gusa*.

"What do you think?" he asked Kono Tetsunan. "Could we form a branch of the group in Sakai?"

Tetsunan was the pen name of Kono Tsugai. He too was a lover of literature who, like Suimei, came from Kuken in Sakai. His father was the priest at Kakuoji, a branch of the Nishihonganji Temple of the New Pure Land sect.

"Yes," he mused, "I can think of seven or eight people who'd join the group, including myself, Taku Gangetsu and Kawai."

"Great. And if we change our name to the Kansai Young Men's Literary Society, that will make us even bigger… It's essential to get more members and increase our numbers if we want to become a breeding ground for new literature," agreed Kobayashi Masaharu, the young blanket wholesaler. They sat together long into the night, unaware of the passing time as they filled the air with literary talk and dreamed of the future of their group. Now was the time in the contemporary literary scene when the old guard was becoming moribund but the new wave was still gestating, or had only just emerged, and not yet gathered real strength, they told each other.

Within the older generation of writers, Ozaki Koyo was ill, and couldn't even muster the energy to continue writing the serialization of his *Konjikiyasha*, the novel that had garnered such praise. Koda Rohan was prone to silences, and the novels he did occasionally publish were increasingly dogmatic and difficult, far from the sort of writing that young readers felt any interest in supporting. The great novelist Mori Ogai had left Tokyo for Kyushu. Now, in the third decade of the Meiji period, all the writers who had more or less formed the core of the literary scene were on the point of handing their place over to a new generation.

"It's true," said Taku Gangetsu, son of a Sakai wine wholesaler called Yamahisa, his eyes shining. "Sukida Kyukin's poetry collection, *Boteki-shu* (*Flute at Nightfall*), is marvellous, no doubt about it, and even those stubborn old fogeys in the so-called Imperial University School can't deny it, I'd say."

Kyukin was a young poet who had made a dashing debut with a style redolent with original language and profundity. He had neither education nor money, however, nor any contacts in the literary world, so his talent was ignored and unrecognized. The novelist Goto Chugai, who loved his work, had excited the young writers by doing battle with what he termed the "imperial literature" clique, criticising the cronyism of the literary scene, which was distorted by academic old-boy factionalism.

"Yes indeed," agreed Suimei, calm as befitted his greater years. "There's a special feel and expressiveness to Kyukin that you won't find in Toson or Bansui, or even in Tekkan." Suimei had a literary sense that could sniff out the real thing, and he had a genuine passion for it as well.

"New talent gets recognized by the new youth. As with Toson, as with Tekkan."

"Now Tekkan's one who supports and values Kyukin highly. He's a real representative of the younger poets."

"Speaking of Tekkan," said Kono Tetsunan on a sudden thought, "How about the idea of asking him to be the *tanka* editor for *Yoshiashi-gusa*? I'd say he'll agree."

"Good idea," they all agreed. Everyone knew that the two were old friends, and in fact Tetsunan had borrowed the first character of Tekkan's pen name to create his own. Tetsunan, however, had a mild and gentle character, quite the opposite of the swashbuckling Tekkan.

"What do you say to joining the *Yoshiashi-gusa* group, sis?" said Sho's younger brother Chusaburo, coming upstairs after finishing his work in the shop. "Yamahisa was here just now and he suggested it…"

"Yamahisa? Oh, you mean Taku."

"Yes, Taku Gangetsu. He says if you join you can submit free verse and stories and *tanka* to the magazine."

"Yes, that magazine – who's behind it?"

"Well, Osaka seems to be the headquarters, but Kawai Suimei's apparently at the centre of the Sakai branch. You know, the kimono shop Kawamata…"

"All right, I'll do it if you will, Chu." As she spoke, Sho peered over at the copy of *Yoshiashi-gusa* that her brother was thumbing.

She and her brother were close.

Chusaburo, having taken over the family business in place of his elder brother, was a gentle-hearted, literary young man, who loved his sister. He seemed to take his own pride in her bookishness and poetic scribblings, and often read her work at the Shikishima Tanka Society meetings.

"I may just be saying this because we're family, but it seems like surely they'd take something of yours if you submitted it."

"Well, I don't know about that…" Sho rejected the suggestion, blushing. "But won't Mother and Father object if you and I both join up with this Kansai Young Men's Literary Society?"

"Don't you worry, leave it to me," Chusaburo replied cheerfully. "It's not as if we'd be going to a bad part of town, and I bet they'd let you go to meetings as long as I was there with you. Submitting pieces wouldn't be a problem, either – you could do it from home, in your spare time."

"That's true… All right then, let's join."

"Yeah, let's."

And so, with a friendly exchange of smiles, the two of them decided to join the group.

The theme for the call for poetry submissions was "Spring Moon." For all her talk, Sho's heart surged with desire to go into battle. As she turned the pages of the journal Chusaburo had left with her, a fierce conviction that she would win out swelled within her.

In contrast to her gentle and pliant exterior, within Sho dwelt a hidden steel. As her eye fell on each poem, her first response was one of self-confidence – "I could write something as good as this stuff."

She spread a sheet of paper on the desk before her, and dipped her brush in the ink.

Phrases floated through her head like passing clouds, one after another, but none would cohere into a poem.

"You and I… fine wine… pale crimson cheeks… a heartless smile…" Fragments of poems read who-knows-where slipped through her fingers as she grasped at them. Sho sighed, laid down her brush, then picked it up once more.

All she could do was seethe with a vague simmering energy.

What she tasted was a mixture of the soaring delight of creativity, and the pain of frustrating groping. Her heart was now lit, now darkened by confidence and despair in turn.

Far in the distance through the midnight hush, the song of the sea thundered.

PART II. YOU WHO PREACH THE WAY

1

You and I, long parted,
tonight in this sweet inexhaustible wine
tasting the joy of meeting
and there, upon your cheek
tinted with softest crimson
your hair plays softly
swayed by the spring breeze.
How joyous this evening,
spring in the thin night clouds
must know our love
Beneath the soft-scented moon glow
Shall I offer my young life
to your artless smile?

Sho's first free verse poem was published in number eleven of *Yoshiashi-gusa*, which came out in February 1899.

"Hey, sis! It got in!" Chusaburo brandished the magazine, opened to the page, and showed it to her. Sho was on the shop floor, sorting beans for the *yokan*. The soft and steamy air thickened around her, filled with the scent of beans boiling to make sweet bean jam buns.

The poem had been selected under the theme "Spring Moon." Sho flushed at her brother's announcement.

"Really...?" she murmured. Her eyes dropped to the page. The delight at seeing a poem of her own, printed in a national magazine for the first time in her life, made her heart pound like waves upon the beach.

She couldn't bring herself to read it.

"What's all the fuss about?" Soshichi demanded of Chusaburo, grumbling as he emerged from the inner room. Hearing the news, he hastily donned his spectacles to look at the magazine.

"Who's this 'Ho Shoshu'?"

"Er, that's my pen name." Sho's shoulders cringed into a shrug as she replied.

"Well, well, just fancy, Sho turning out something like this…" Soshichi read the poem aloud to himself again.

He turned sternly to look at her. "So who's it about? Surely you haven't been getting up to mischief behind my back have you, Sho?"

"It's a poem, Daddy… It's just made up, not about anything real."

"That's all very well, but it's about love, see… and it's you who wrote it, see… it's disgraceful. What will people say? A young girl like you writing this sort of thing and showing it about in public…"

"Dad, poetry is…" began Chusaburo with a laugh. "It's a beautiful… embellishment of reality within the world of the imagination. That's the power of art, what's called the soul of poetry. It doesn't in any way mean that she's had a real lover like that, does it, sis?"

"But poetry has always been about elegance, ever since the old days," objected their father. "It's tasteful and refined, you know, about praising the moon, or the snow."

"Dad, these days it's popular for young people to write their own kind of poems, that express their feelings directly. There are good things about the old style of poetry, but Western-style poetry has arrived now, and…there's a new way of writing poems. This one of Sho's is a new-style poem. You have to write about new things if you're going to write in a new style. Isn't that so, sis?" Sho smiled meekly and remained silent. She didn't want to defy her father, and she had no inclination to set about earnestly explaining things like her brother.

She felt Chusaburo was more good-natured than she. He was someone who didn't rub people the wrong way, a person with truly fine qualities. Compared to him, she wasn't such a good person perhaps. There was no real point in explaining to her old-fashioned father the differences between traditional poetry and free verse – he wouldn't understand. She smiled, and stayed proudly silent.

For all that a new whirlwind was spinning in the literary world, on the face of reality, not a thing had changed. Her father's level of comprehension was in fact at the higher end of the scale. There were many in the real world who felt that poets and literati were not to be counted among fully-fledged adults like themselves, that they were well down the social scale from real workers such as public officials, merchants, company men or tradesmen, indeed were both powerless and poor, mere imposters and hooligans intent on corrupting the public morals.

But here was Soshichi, apparently thrilled by the sight of his daughter's work displayed for all the world to see in a magazine. He even called his wife Tsune to have a look.

"My, my, you mean they've been kind enough to publish a poem of Sho's? So this is a good poem…? Well, that's wonderful, we should be grateful for such an honour." Tsune spoke almost as if the editor was some kind of god.

"Who's this now, could it be the lad from the Kawamata shop?"

"That's right."

"You must pay a visit and thank him."

Thank him…?"

"Yes indeed, he's not far away after all. You go along and pay your respects."

Yes, Sho thought suddenly, why not seize this opportunity to meet Suimei in person, to introduce herself as a new member and thank him for selecting the poem? Her heart leapt at the thought.

2

There were sixteen members in the Sakai branch of the Kansai Young Men's Literary Society, a far more impressive number than expected, and Suimei, their sponsor was delighted.

His interest was piqued by this girl who went by the name of "Ho Shoshu" and had written the "Spring Moon" poem he selected for the magazine.

"That lass from the *yokan* shop has had a few traditional *tanka* published in the Shikishima Society newsletter, but judging from this free verse, it seems she reads modern stuff too. Impressive, don't you think?"

"She's certainly a diligent one," remarked Gangetsu. "It takes real enthusiasm to order magazines all the way from Tokyo and read them in this backwater."

"Quite unusual in a girl. She's a real find… It's just a shame that girls' talent withers away once they marry. I wonder if she's still single?"

"I wonder. She's always sitting there in the shop. Her brother Chu and I have been friends since we were kids, so I sometimes poke my head in, and I always see her there."

"Is she a beauty, this talented girl?" asked Kobayashi Masaharu on behalf of the other members who still hadn't met her, and everyone laughed.

"Hmm, well…" Gangetsu searched for words. "Well, she's a young girl, so…"

He was trying to say that her youth gave her whatever beauty she had. She wasn't what the world would normally call beautiful.

A later poem of Sho's reads:

> My mother felt it as a curse,
> my lack of beauty,
> and raised me
> the more lovingly
> to shield me from harm.

Her two married half-sisters were both beauties, but Akiko had a very plain face. Gangetsu had noticed, however, that though not lovely she was a girl who embodied the ripeness of youth.

But the other members of the group were fascinated by the thought of this sole new female literary talent that had appeared among them with the lovely name of Ho Shoshu (which literally read as "Phoenix Little Boat").

Sho came calling, dressed in her finery, with her nurse Outa carrying a gift of the special "Night Plum Blossom" *yokan* her family had created.

She removed her sky blue crepe hood to reveal, beneath the rich black hair done up in her own unique style, an anxious look. In the full bloom of youth, Sho was tall, and while her prominent masculine eyebrows lent her face a forbidding expression, her demeanour was soft.

One might even say that she was timid, out of place as she felt.

She wore a kimono of golden-brown figured silk with a bold pattern, and it did not take the professional eye of the kimono shop owner Kawai to see that it was not particularly stylish. Indeed it was gaudy, with a loud design of Chinese lads pulling flower carts, with blossoms scattered as far as the hems and sleeves and even over the chest.

"How do you do. My name is Ho Sho." She sank to the floor and bowed to Kawai, hands politely on the floor before her forehead.

Kawai set about praising her poem and chatting about literature in an effort to ease her tension. He was a straightforward and kindly man.

After a time, lured by his words, Sho at last relaxed and began to answer him easily.

Shy as she was, it was immeasurably discomforting for Sho to sit talking like this face to face with an unknown man.

"I've read a little in *The Tale of Genji*, the *Kokinshu* and *Manyoshu* collections and that sort of thing... As for modern works, I find Toson's *Seedlings* very impressive." Her speech was politely formal, but the conversation had sparked her interest, and she blushed to realize how enthusiastically she was talking. What a new joy it was to find someone, aside from her brother Chusaburo, with whom she could speak like this about the modern poetry she so loved.

"Now that you mention it, your 'Spring Moon' does bear the influence of Toson's *Seedlings*. But your phrasing has something unique about it too, you know. I'd say very soon we'll be seeing free verse poems and *tanka* that could only have been written by you." Frank and honest poet that he was, Kawai praised her with equivalent candour. He had intuited that hidden within this seemingly ordinary local girl there lay a formidable strength.

"We've never had the opportunity to properly meet before, have we, despite both living in Sakai."

"It's true." *Though actually, I've wished for this chance for a long time* – the reticent girl didn't let these words slip out, but her eyes shone softly with happiness.

Kawai sensed the unspoken reply. "Well, now that we know each other, please continue to submit work to *Yoshiashi-gusa*. All the members are very much looking forward to seeing more," he added in kindly encouragement.

"Thank you very much. For my part, I would deeply appreciate your guidance and instruction. I don't know much of anything about all this, you see…" With this gentle, polite response, typical of a merchant's daughter, Sho lowered her blushing face and left.

Kawai had been left with a good impression of this girl in the bloom of youth, from her bewildered innocence of the world to the clothes she wore – evidently her mother's choice – and her looks as well. She had at first been reserved and mumbling, giving an impression of indecisiveness, which reinforced her choice of the pen name "Little Boat," so suggestive of a gracefully elegant lady poet; and yet, he thought, recalling the strength that emanated from her strong brow, inside she seemed rather vital and unyielding.

Nevertheless, that vitality and genius were at present dammed up within her, hesitant and tentative. Kawai's poetic intuition sensed in Sho's bearing something oppressively inert that, once the floodgates were open, would hurtle forth.

But for now, judging only from her "Spring Moon," Sho's genius remained an unknown quantity. There was no way to tell from this Toson-style poem just what she was made of, but Kawai was inclined to believe that once she was tossed in among the *Yoshiashi-gusa* members, if she was concealing a jewel it would surely begin to sparkle.

This conventional merchants' town of theirs had produced a rare thing, a girl who cared about literature, and Kawai was touched by and felt generous towards her. It also occurred to him that perhaps he was seeing in her a double of his earlier self, someone struggling in the darkness of youth, the urge towards poetry suffocated by the worldly bonds of family and dependents.

The next poem that Sho submitted to *Yoshiashi-gusa* was a *tanka*. It appeared that year, in issue number eight.

Burial Mound
Who is the lord
who rests so quietly
there in his burial mound
hearing endlessly the pure
melody of the village stream?

But this was still poetry that sprang from old-fashioned conceptions, the kind of ordinary poem typical of the official poetry academies of yore.

Before long, however, Sho found her place, and published a rapid succession of poems in the magazine. The style was still old-fashioned, but little by little the tone was becoming uniquely her own. Some examples:

Occasional Poem
My beloved lass
unties her cape
and as she does she hums
softly, whisperingly,
"Can this be a dream?"
• • •
I will not weep
I will not mourn the world
or those in it, I said.
Yet why is this silken sleeve's
crimson lining soaked with tears?

Although these poems still lacked a conspicuous originality, they could not help but draw attention to themselves, their flowing and elegant diction the mark of a woman's work standing out like a single drop of scarlet amongst the many male poems surrounding them. In Osaka at this time there was a young woman writer named Masuda Miyako – a true beauty – who Sho and the others were aware was submitting work to the national magazine *Bunko*, but within the *Yoshiashi-gusa* group Sho stood out, a fact that did not escape the notice of Yosano Tekkan in Tokyo. At this stage, however, Sho was still not even acquainted with many of her own group's members, and of course had no way of knowing Tekkan.

Despite the sensation caused in the Sakai branch of the Kansai Young Men's Literary Society by the appearance of this poetess by the name of Ho Shoshu, Sho was not in a position to come and go freely among its members discussing literature.

Her brother Chusaburo, on the other hand, attended meetings from time to time, but he was busy with the family business, and before long he was begging off going to meetings, though he was delighted that his sister's poems were being published.

The first time Sho met the *Yoshiashi-gusa* members – Kobayashi Masaharu, Kono Tetsunan and the others – was on 3rd January 1900.

3

The town of Sakai faces Osaka Bay. The area is shaped like a large basin, and the surrounding sea was once called by the name of "Chinu." In the old days, the shoreline was famous for its scenic beauty, and people from Kyoto were fond of taking excursions to see it.

The area now known as Hamadera was once known as Takashi Beach, a place famous in classical poetry and No plays. It had once been an elegant *utamakura*, a place name evocative of specific poetic associations; among the famous poems composed about it is one by Lady Kii:

> These sleeves so damp –
> is it those famous waves
> fickle and wanton on Takashi's beach
> (so like your heart)
> that has wet them thus?

At Sho's time, during the Meiji period, it was still a beautiful beach, with famous restaurants and summerhouse-style open tea stalls.

One day Sho and her brother received a notice informing them of a New Year's banquet to be held by the Kansai Young Men's Literary Society on the third of January at a Hamadera inn named Tsurunoya.

Sho was desperate to go, yet she quailed at the thought of being the only woman among that great crowd of men… Chusaburo told her he had another gathering to go to that day, so he couldn't attend. Courageous and determined though Sho was, on the other hand she had a fearful side to her. A later poem of hers goes:

> This heart of mine
> so feeble, so delicate,
> I see it as the wound inherited
> from my upbringing
> in old Naniwa.

But her "Naniwa" upbringing (Naniwa was the old name for the Osaka area) was not really to blame. In fact, Sho's earnest and rather ponderous nature was never able to deal lightly with things, which was perhaps complicated by her strong sensitivity and an almost distorted degree of empathy for others. This is not to say, of course, that she lacked a sense of humour. She understood it in others, and could herself be witty. What was missing was the ability to be jocular.

However there was no repressing her surge of desire to meet the members of the group.

"Could I go?" she asked her mother.

"Well, now…" Always indulgent of her children, Tsune herself felt no hesitation, but she gave a noncommittal reply, carefully monitoring Soshichi's expression.

"Forget it. Going off alone like that to a banquet where there'll be nothing but men…" Soshichi looked disgusted.

He had been a man about town himself in his younger days, taking a certain pleasure in book learning, cultivating the elegant arts, patronizing the geisha tea houses, but when it came to his own daughter he was an incorrigible old fogey. He was happy enough to let her indulge in a little dabbling in the fine old arts of writing *tanka* and *haiku*, but it seemed that as a father he couldn't permit his daughter to have anything to do with the kind of literature that dealt in dubious words like "love" and "ardour."

Sho wilted, and miserably lowered her gaze. In the New Year she would be twenty-three by the old reckoning, in which a child at birth is a year old and a year is added to one's age at the beginning of every year. She was a full-fledged adult by now, but it was the sorry lot of women to be forever treated as children.

Tsune pitied her disappointed daughter. Recently, she had been reading the poems Sho wrote and asking about the group, so she knew the ins and outs of the situation and couldn't agree with Soshichi's sweeping condemnation of the idea. She trusted Sho, and took good note of the things she said. And so, with a mother's combination of cajoling sweetness and boldness, she said,

"It should be fine, surely. The maid will go along with her, after all. She just has to be sure and come back early before it gets dark. Do let her go, Papa."

Sho was delighted, but when the day came she grew hesitant again. Nevertheless, there wasn't likely to be another occasion when her father would give his tacit consent like this, so she screwed up her courage and set off with Outa.

The early days of the new year were still chilly, but the weather was beautiful. Sho sat far back under the rickshaw awning, out of the cold sea breeze, a shawl around her shoulders. From where she lived in Sakai's Kai district it was not far to Hamadera, and they soon arrived at Tsurunoya. The lovely pine forest by the shore soughed in the breeze off the bay, the fresh clear sound blending perfectly with the festive atmosphere of New Year.

Tsurunoya was a large old inn that also had a restaurant.

In keeping with the festive time of year, Sho cut a strikingly feminine figure in an elegant purple woven satin kimono with a deep red kimono coat, and on this day there was not a hair out of place in her careful coiffure. She gave her name to the maid at the entrance and stood waiting, heart pounding, for one of the party to come out to meet her.

Just as she entered, she had heard high-spirited male chatter and laughter from a window beyond the wall, and guessed it to be the group she was there to meet. Sure enough, there was a heavy tread approaching along the corridor from that direction, and two young men appeared before her and looked with surprise at Sho and the maid Outa, who stood behind her. One of them was Gangetsu, the man whom she saw at the shop from time to time; the other she did not know. He was a handsome young man of around twenty-seven, with a pale complexion and a gentle face.

"Ah, it's Miss Ho!" cried Gangetsu delightedly. "Well, well... welcome! So glad you were able to make it. Here you are, come on in," he urged, almost seizing her by the hand as he gestured for her to step up from the entrance hall.

"Um, I've just come to pay my respects to everyone quickly and then I must be off again right away," mumbled Sho, face lowered. She was self-conscious to be the only woman joining a sizeable group of unknown men.

"Come now, no need for that... Hey, everyone, Miss Ho Akiko has just arrived."

Taku Gangetsu strode ahead into the room to announce her. She had recently given up the pen name Shoshu in favor of the name Akiko, an alternative reading of the character for her given name, "Sho," with the addition of the feminine "ko."

Left standing there, the other young man unfolded his arms and dropped his hands to his sides, giving a slight bow. "Welcome, Miss Ho," he said, smiling faintly. "I'm Kono Tetsunan, from Kakuoji Temple in Kuken."

Ah, thought Akiko. She recalled seeing a poem of his in the last *Yoshiashi-gusa*, on the Burial Mound theme, a very male sort of poem.

> Everyone lives
> on a great mounded tomb
> where corpses lie in millions –
> and this they proudly call
> "the capital."

This young priest at Kakuoji was a far more modest and agreeable youth than Akiko had been led to imagine from this poem, as well as from his name. His gentle face also made him extremely handsome. Tetsunan showed the blushing Akiko into the room.

She hung back again at the doorway – passing her shawl to Outa, she knelt in a formal bow in the corridor beyond the sliding paper panel, her fingers to the floor before her knees.

"Please come in."

"Do join us."

Male voices rose from within. Akiko still hung there, timorous. The deep red of her coat stood out like a flame in the doorway.

There were around twenty young men in the room – the budding physician Nakayama Kyoan, present editor of *Yoshiashi-gusa*, Kobayashi Masaharu (Tenmin), Ishiwari Biyo and others were gathered, conversing happily, with Kawai Suimei at the head of the table.

Takasu Hojiro (who went by the pen name of Baikei or "Plum Valley") and Nakamura Kichizo ("Spring Rain"), who had earlier been involved in *Yoshiashi-gusa*, had gone up to Tokyo two years earlier. Takasu now worked at the publishing company Shinseisha in Nishiki-cho in the Kanda area, helping with the editing of their magazine *Shinsei* while he studied at the school that later became Waseda University; Nakamura was working his way through the same school, as well as being an apprentice under the novelist Hirotsu Ryuro. Everyone was afire with the desire to make their name in the literary world. These two had despaired of waiting for their chance in the provincial Kansai area, and had made off to the capital.

Kawai, too, was hatching a secret plan to do the same thing in the coming year.

"Hello there, Miss Ho. So glad you could make it." Kawai welcomed her with much the same words as had Taku Gangetsu. When he sent the invitation, he had been resigned to the fact that there was little likelihood a girl from a strict old merchant household would be allowed to join a group of men.

Noisy talk and laughter suddenly filled the room, and the maid Outa, sitting out in the corridor, was invited in to sit beside Akiko at the near end of the table.

On behalf of the Sakai branch, Kawai gave his New Year felicitations. He then went on, "As you all know, in November last year Yosano Tekkan founded the Tokyo New Poetry Society (Shinshisha). He's said that he plans to put out a newsletter from these parts. He'll be soliciting members from the Sakai branch as well, he said, so I would urge you all to join. Kono and I intend to."

"The Tokyo New Poetry Society, eh? That's a strong move, typical Tekkan. What will the magazine be called?" someone asked.

"*Myojo*, so I hear."

Akiko didn't know who had replied. She had been introduced to them all one by one, but she hadn't raised her gaze, so she had no idea who was whom.

Dazed, she registered the powerful beauty of the name *Myojo* ("Venus"), while an image of the two vivid characters that comprised its name reverberated through her mind.

Celebratory sake cups were exchanged among the group, the sake bottle went round, male voices rose louder and louder, and a lofty discussion ensued.

"Yes, weren't those old fogies at the Imperial Literature School praising Kyukin and his *Twilight flute*?"

"True enough, they've actually recognized its worth. I quote, 'Aside from Bansui and Toson, one is bound to count Kyukin first among the poets.' They've lost! They've had to admit defeat before a new talent, authorities though they are…"

Kyukin was twenty-four. His new, youthful talent would continue its splendid evolution and be welcomed by the world.

"The age of poetry has arrived!" someone cried. "The year 1900 will be a new era of poetry!" There was a general commotion.

Akiko was in the midst of the crowd, half drunk despite having imbibed not a drop.

The only two in the gathering she knew were Gangetsu and Kawai, but she had seen the names of all present in print, so there was already a certain sense of familiarity with them.

These men treated her as an equal, had high hopes for her talent, and they respected her.

This "woman," restricted until now by the conventional upbringing of a merchant household, could here transcend gender and, on the strength of her own gifts, engage in free and open literary discussion face to face with men.

She was experiencing a broadening of the spirit, a liberation of the heart, as fresh and carefree as the sea breeze of Hamadera.

Tetsunan, seated next to her, passed her the little brazier. He was obviously a thoughtful and considerate youth.

"What about you, Miss Ho. Will you join *Myojo*?"

"Oh no, I'm far too immature a poet, I'd only get in the way," responded Akiko falteringly, overcome with shyness.

"No, no, that's not true at all. We've already told Tekkan that the Sakai branch has this talented jewel among us by the name of Ho Akiko, and he's written back urging you to submit your work."

"Gracious!" Akiko's eyes were wide. "Have you, um, been acquainted with Mr. Yosano for very long?"

"Oh, we've been friends since we were kids." Tetsunan seemed an unsophisticated youth. He spoke with head lowered, not meeting her eye, glancing from time to time at his companions. "When he was young, Hiroshi – that's Tekkan's real name, you know – was adopted to be the future heir by the priest of a temple called Anyoji in Oriono. My dad used to take me there from time to time, and he and I often played together. He was two or three years older than me, probably around eleven then. He was going to a private Chinese learning academy in Sakai, and he was far and away the best there. Young Ando Hiroshi was known as a child prodigy back then. A bit later he developed ambitions to make his name in literature, and he up and left his adopted family – that's how he came to take back his old name Yosano again… Anyway, he wandered about in Yamaguchi, then in Tokyo, and before long he came to be known for his traditional verse. He was born up in Kyoto, in the Okazaki area, so he knows Sakai well… Well, since he went to school in Sakai he probably feels even more at home here than in Kyoto."

"I see. In that case, I wonder if he might have occasionally passed our shop…"

"Yes, I should think he did."

"You never know where a connection will spring up, do you? Well, well, so Mr. Tekkan may have…"

The two exchanged glances and smiled.

"Hey there, what are you two up to? Tetsunan's monopolizing our talented jewel, everyone. Shame on you!"

The room erupted with affectionate teasing.

The banquet festivities were by now in full swing.

4

But what did Akiko make of these young men who made up the Kansai Young Men's Literary Society? She had guessed at their personalities from reading their work, and one can imagine that a glimpse or two of the real people would have increased her goodwill and affection for them all. One can also guess that she would indeed have used her creativity to augment her sketchy impressions, so that her portrait of these young men was revised into something even more agreeable.

Akiko had few actual opportunities to see men in her life; her only way to know them was through the window of literature. This window, however, could sometimes intoxicate, confuse the standards of judgment, or aesthetically distort. Akiko recreated each of these men in a way to suit herself, which had nothing to do with the men themselves.

She was in thrall to her own rich imagination, dragged hither and yon by its powers, and unable to observe the world clearly and objectively. Nor would she have been in an environment where she could learn to do so.

One can suppose that for Akiko, this year when she met the group's members constituted the happiest, most incomprehensibly thrilling time of her life to date. With her understanding of human nature nurtured as it was on old romantic tales and poetry, she set about embellishing and glamorizing the real men before her.

Among all these young men, there was one on whom she fixed her sights. This was Tetsunan.

It seems that Akiko, herself naïve, would naturally choose a man who was similarly innocent.

She had left the New Year banquet somewhat earlier than the others, and once home she retired to her room.

Downstairs, her father had gathered a group of like-minded friends, and they were chanting Noh librettos together. There was a generally festive New Year's atmosphere in the house, with braziers scattered through the rooms, lights blazing, and even the maids laughing and chatting boisterously together.

Akiko could not forget the young man she had just met, Tetsunan. Quiet and composed, warm, and with a deeply thoughtful expression, his gentle goodwill towards her had been unexpected. From his poems, she had imagined a man with a philosopher's rational sense of mind, and strong feelings.

Unable properly to express herself face to face, Akiko wrote Tetsunan a letter.

In flowery classical language, it began: "I count it an immense delight, and one ne'er to be forgot, to have had the honour of finding myself in the presence of your tender and most solicitous voice, and treated without the reserve that my gender might normally provoke – you, whose name alone was known to me until this day, and before whose poems I had long trembled, sensing therefrom how great must be your manly powers."

Having taken up the brush, she found it rushing on with a life of its own, one which far exceeded the words she herself would have spoken.

The words poured on and on in a white heat of effusiveness. What she wrote inflamed her feelings further, and this in turn urged her language to greater heights. As she wrote, from one moment to the next Akiko's heart was fanned by her own rhetoric into an intoxication with Tetsunan. This was a trap of her own devising, but her fall gathered unstoppable momentum as she tumbled.

Surely this was the man she had been waiting for. Surely Tetsunan was the very one who would take charge of her fate and set fire to her life.

In her secret girlish vanity, Akiko had taken the kindness that Tetsunan happened to show her to be an expression of affection for her, and her heart raced at the thought.

"When the time is appropriate, I will request a letter from you, so I beg you to await my message..." she wrote in conclusion.

There was little else she could do, this beautiful girl held captive and fearful under the stern eyes of her parents.

Not long after this, Tetsunan came to the shop. He placed an order for bean jam buns for a memorial service – and, more importantly, happened to exchange a few words with Akiko before departing.

He hovered there in the shop, apparently finding it difficult to tear himself away.

"At our regular gathering the other day, Yosano Tekkan's poem 'If I choose a bride' generated quite a response," he said. He had kindly intended to tell her this news.

"Ah, that must be from *Poem of Yearning*... I think it's wonderful too," Akiko replied, eyes shining.

"Yes," Tetsunan went on eagerly, "it's an excellent poem, isn't it? It's a bit slapdash, but I don't think it's a poem anyone else could write. I really like it too." His pale cheeks had suddenly flushed, and, averting his eyes, he recited softly:

> If I choose a bride
> she will be gifted,
> lovely of feature,
> tender of heart...

It had appeared in the February issue of *Yoshiashi-gusa*, and Akiko too loved to recite this musical poem with its tense rhythms that expressed so directly the pride of a youthful heart.

> If I choose a friend
> he will be a reader,
> six parts chivalry,
> four parts fire...

Akiko recited with Tetsunan, her heart beating wildly.

Tsune walked in from the back room.

"Mother, this is the gentleman from Kakuoji—", began Akiko, but before she could introduce Tetsunan her mother broke in,

"Well, well, how do you do, thank you for all you've done for my daughter. Please, do come in." Though he was Akiko's friend, Tsune spoke with the courtesy due to a respectable son of a temple, young though he was.

"No, no, I'm afraid I mustn't... Goodbye." Tetsunan took his hasty leave as though intent on fleeing.

"Dear me, do stay!" Tsune cried after his departing figure.

Tucking her disordered hair back into place, Akiko said to her, "He's gone already."

"What a shy young man," Tsune smiled. "So does he write poetry too?"

"He does."

"He's all right at it, then?"

"Oh, far better than I am of course."

Arrogantly assured, albeit inwardly, of her own talent, Akiko was quite prepared to stand aside in favour of the man she fancied.

A few days later, on her way back from her tea ceremony lesson, an issue of *Imperial Literature* that she'd finished reading tucked under her arm, Akiko took a roundabout route home via the Kuken district and dropped in at Kakuoji.

On this occasion she wasn't accompanied by Outa, her usual maid, but by another named Oume.

"What business might you have at a temple, miss?" Oume asked inquisitively. Outa would simply have come along without question, and it annoyed her to have to explain everything to Oume.

"I'm returning a book I borrowed," Akiko replied, but of course this was just an excuse. She had suddenly been so overwhelmed with a desire to see Tetsunan that she had been unable to prevent her feet from taking her in the direction of the temple.

Kuken's streets were lined with old temples, among them this Pure Land Buddhist branch temple. The fleeting winter sun was already deepening the shadows in the temple courtyard when they arrived.

Kakuoji was a small and plain temple but ancient and historic, said to have been founded by Kono Michimoto, the son of the famous Michiari.

Just as she was about to set off toward the priest's living quarters, Akiko stopped in her tracks.

She wanted to see him, but she couldn't think of what she could say once they met.

For his part, Tetsunan wasn't the kind of garrulous person who could easily be induced to talk, either. The two of them would lapse into silence together.

Akiko was painfully bashful, and her inability to speak in front of someone she liked irritated even herself. This fact can be gleaned from her correspondence. Though her letters were loquacious and persuasive, with a rich store of vocabulary, in reality she was taciturn and shy.

When she pictured how Tetsunan might now be sitting by a window, his pale face lowered over a book, Akiko's heart raced.

"No, I won't bother…" She found herself turning on her heels.

"Miss… Miss, you said you had something to do here, didn't you?" cried Oume loudly, pursuing her.

"For heavens sake, lower your voice, Oume! They'll hear you."

"But you've come all this way…"

"I've changed my mind." And with these words Akiko went hurrying down the street.

But just at that moment a young man who was coming from the other direction along the temple's long earthen wall suddenly halted in his tracks.

"Well, good heavens!" he exclaimed. It was Tetsunan. He was dressed in traditional everyday clothes, with a matching dark blue splash-patterned coat and *hakama* trousers. "Where are you…?"

"Um, I just dropped by your place…" Akiko could not raise her eyes.

"I do apologize. Won't you come in? I'm so glad I ran into you."

"No, I'm afraid I can't…"

"But we can't talk here, it's too cold…"

"Sorry, there's really no reason for my visit, I must be going."

"Oh, I see." Tetsunan chose not to press her further, and fell silent. Akiko too was silent for a moment, then she opened the cloth-wrapped parcel she held to her chest and almost thrust the magazine towards him, saying, "Please take it…", and hurried off. Both were so awkward and ill at ease that Oume watched in puzzlement, unable to comprehend what was going on.

Now face to face, there was not the slightest mention of the letter Akiko had sent. No doubt she would have died of shame had Tetsunan happened to refer to it.

Yet this repressed feeling was, in fact, the very thing that had driven Akiko to write her fiercely love-maddened letter. Though she had called him "brother," her language breathed with all the passion of a love letter: "I long indeed to speak all my heart in your presence."

Truth be told, it was not Tetsunan alone who received letters from her – Akiko also wrote to Taku Gangetsu and Ishiwari Biyo. To Gangetsu she sent the following poem:

"Wind in the pines
pierces me through,"
Waiting, I write to him,
while my tears
quietly drench me.

This letter consisted simply of pretty but empty phrases, though Akiko was bothered by the fear that Tetsunan might hear of it from Gangetsu and get the wrong idea. Akiko was deeply attracted to Tetsunan's gentle, earnest character. He was the one her heart had settled on – and yet she couldn't deny herself the enjoyment of dashing off idle epistles to these other young men behind her parents' back.

One suspects, in fact, that Akiko would have long been littering her desk with quite a number of such poems and phrases – only now she had somewhere to send them.

In effect, what she sent to Gangetsu and Biyo and Kyoan were nothing more than jottings from her notebook; she had simply designated their names as recipients. The young men were not to know this, however.

"Though I truly suffer, if you alas no longer feel as once you did, yet think with pity of this suffering girl if only in her role as 'poet of the gods', and send me some message soon I beg you. If I wait two or three days and yet no missive arrives, I will surely die."

Kono Tetsunan was astonished and confounded when he read this.

Priest though he was, he was still quite innocent, a sensitive literary young man.

This rarity in Sakai – a talented poetess who could speak of literature and write her own poems – interested and pleased him, but what he felt for her was not romantic love.

Akiko's letter, however, had a whirlwind power that threatened to sweep him into a romantic entanglement. But Tetsunan was quite perceptive, and he saw through her letter to the truth that lay behind it: Akiko heaved with sweet and passionate adoration for him, but it was not true love.

Hers was a phantom love – she was in love with love itself. Wise beyond his years, the prudent Tetsunan wrote a carefully noncommittal reply.

Akiko's next letter spoke of her reverence for the great ninth-century poetess Ono no Komachi, who was renowned for her beauty and romances. What she yearned for, Akiko declared, was Komachi's fate – to make her way in life having love affairs with various men and, in the end, to die a wanderer upon the wayside. Komachi's skull is famously described as sprouting pampas grass through its eye sockets, which soughed in the autumn wind as if crying "alas my eyes, my eyes."

Akiko wrote: "I should think it would be a wonderful thing for the chill autumn wind to blow over my bones, the skull bewailing as in the old description of her death."

Tetsunan, however, did not reply to this bizarre and eccentric letter.

> White violet?
> Cherry blossom petals?
> Or the red plum? –
> which shall I enclose
> with this letter I send you?

Akiko chose to send this poem with cherry blossoms. The effusively sentimental literary gesture provoked an understanding smile from Tetsunan – What a little girl she still was!

Yet it was as if a sudden bright flush of colour had pervaded his forlorn and changeless, poverty-stricken life, and he could not repress a gentle sentimental glow, like a lamp in the dark.

He was aware that Akiko had also sent a beautifully expressive letter enclosing a cherry blossom to Taku Gangetsu, for he had shown it to him. It contained this poem:

> Hid beneath fluttering petals
> of blush-red plum,
> youthful, I weep
> this evening
> over my youthful love.

Suimei had also received a letter, enclosing a palm frond, the kind that was once used to write on.

When Tetsunan learned this, he felt troubled – *There, you see, it's just the silly romanticism of a bookish girl. She's only dreaming, sending off faux love letters to all and sundry. She doesn't care who the other person is. She's simply swept along on a literary impulse in search of an object.*

This is what he told himself. Habitually discreet, he now became still more prudent and careful in his dealings with her.

But Akiko's heart was filled only with fervent thoughts of her "Lord Tetsunan."

Looking back on her poetry, we realize that there are many poems that are deeply concerned with priests.

> At the sound of the flute
> the hand that copies
> the Lotus Sutra
> halts, and he knits his brows,
> still so young and innocent.
> • • •
> Spring waved her pretty sleeve
> at the window, awakening
> the innocent young priest,
> and his pile of sutras
> tumbled in disarray.
> • • •
> Late to row home
> at evening in your boat,
> young priest, are they so many,
> those red lotuses
> those white lotuses?

Akiko's favourite stories from the fanciful picture scrolls were those in which an austere and pristine young priest is matched with a beguiling and passionate young beauty. She became the heroine in her own fantasy, adding further fuel to her feverish love for Tetsunan. From her point of view, Tetsunan's restrained response was infuriating.

He must surely know how she felt!

She was deeply frustrated by this man who would not rise to her own heights of passion, who would not seize her and sweep her away.

Of course, the two of them had never met except under the eyes of others. Nor could they hope to. Still, this man was too concerned with what people would see and think.

He was also too afraid that Akiko's passion would knock him off his feet and leave his life in disarray. Akiko sensed this, and it filled her with dissatisfaction.

For his part, Tetsunan attempted to keep their relationship on the level of literature. Being more grown up and familiar with the ways of the world thanks to his dealings with his parishioners, he was very concerned not to become the laughing stock of those who were always watching for signs of young romance. Actually, the fact was that he was not interested in Akiko as a woman. It may well be that she was simply not his type.

Anyhow, he said to himself, *the world is full of gossipers. It would be too bad if Akiko became the butt of rumors.* Tetsunan was in the thrall of his own conscience.

5

In April, Tekkan's new magazine *Myojo* finally appeared. Akiko first laid eyes on it when Tetsunan showed it to her.

It was in tabloid format, with sixteen pages, and the paper was rough and cheap. "Published by Tokyo Shinshisha," it said. The price was six *sen*, and the publisher and editor was listed as Hayashi Takino.

Akiko had no idea who Hayashi Takino was, but the editor in chief was Yosano Tekkan.

The overall impression of the magazine was somewhat crude – a ragbag of critical essays, creative works, traditional poetry – and yet, the pages overflowed with youthful passion. The "official manifesto" read as follows:

1. Professional poets aside, this Society is a group for the study of traditional *waka* poetry and modern free verse.
2. Yosano Tekkan has been nominated editor in chief.
3. Members shall submit poems each month or in alternate months for consideration by the Editor in Chief.

4. Besides their own works, members shall pay a sum of thirty *sen* for expenses per issue, and three *sen* for return of manuscripts submitted…

Tetsunan encouraged Akiko to submit her poems to *Myojo*.

"Look," he said to her, showing her a piece of paper, "Tekkan's sent a poem."

She read it:

> Though I have yet to see you,
> Lady Akiko,
> your name
> means much to me –
> do send your poems.

"Good heavens! Fancy Yosano-Sensei saying such things!"

Akiko thought it was bound to be thanks to the recommendation of Tetsunan and Kawai. While on the one hand she was delighted that such a famous writer should deign to look at her poems, she was also afraid that her own poor work would earn his ridicule and bring shame on Kawai and the others.

Nevertheless, *Myojo* was of an impressive standard, even if the editing was slipshod.

Its particular glory lay in the incredibly fine piece titled "Traveller's Lament" that Shimazaki Toson, presently a teacher in Komoro in Shinshu province, had contributed to grace the inaugural issue.

> By the old castle of Komoro
> among white clouds the wanderer sorrows.
> No sprouts upon the green chickweed
> nor does the new grass spread its sward.
> Upon the silver-cloaked hills
> rivulets of pale sun-melted snow…

The poem's fluid beauty would never be forgotten once the lips had spoken it.

Akiko was enchanted both by "Traveler's Lament" and by *Myojo* itself.

Still torn between a sense of inferiority and a reflexive confidence, Akiko summoned her courage and decided to join the group and submit her poems. She was no longer the shy girl who had sought her brother's advice before timorously joining *Yoshiashi-gusa*.

"How embarrassing it is to be sending these to someplace as exalted as *Myojo*! I can only imagine doing it if you cover for me, brother," she wrote to Tetsunan in the letter accompanying the poems she had chosen to submit.

The second issue of *Myojo* included six rather girlish poems by Ho Akiko. One, titled "Hanagatami" ran as follows:

> Cringing embarrassed
> at the letter I send
> informing you
> that I have let my sleeves out
> and am now an adult.

Akiko officially joined the group in May, the same month the issue appeared.

Myojo also contained a single poem by one Yamakawa Tomiko (though admittedly it appeared in the column of fillers).

Akiko could only gaze at her own poems printed within. She felt almost as if she had suddenly been transported to the centre of Tokyo and thrust into the limelight, and the sensation was not so much enjoyable as unnerving. But her mettle was up. There was no retreating now, and the thought fired her to produce further *tanka*.

The third issue contained the following:

> When I waited for you
> amidst the low grasses
> blooming with lilies
> there at the field's edge suddenly
> a rainbow glistening.

> • • •

Perhaps it was the dew
from the young leaves in the grove's darkness
that soaked them through
drops fallen
on the pair's clasped hands.

The poetry she was writing now had an exquisite delicacy that foreshadowed her later work.

Nevertheless, like her letters from this time, her verses still lacked the impact of genuinely moving sentiment.

The rhetorical language may be rich and the tone beautiful, but it went no further than the pretty-picture idle amusement of a literary girl, and showed no more talent than any other woman writer in the Meiji era.

This was because, although romantic love gave her poems their force, Akiko had not yet encountered true love.

The same issue included four poems in its "New Poetry: Drafts" column by the member Yamakawa Tomiko. She had previously been submitting work to both *Shinsei* and *Bunko*.

The fourth edition appeared. Already, Tomiko's talent was being recognized. She had nine poems in this issue, presented in a special column of their own, on a par with Akiko's seven.

They were beginning to be referred to together as "The two new poetesses, Akiko and Tomiko" and "The twin jewels of fine poetry."

Akiko had quickly become aware of Tomiko's talent. At first (in the second issue) her poems had had a pseudo-classical tone:

Hanging the birdcage
on a low, still branch
I count the day's
slow length
in the peach's blossoms.

But once she had joined *Myojo* her undeniable poetic genius began to shine, and she outdid Akiko in her power to astonish. The romanticism of her poetry was both sophisticated and compelling, and readers could not resist its attraction. The young audience of the period went crazy over her poems.

> Born as I am
> a maiden with long hair
> face lowered
> to the white lily
> oh it is you I dream of.
> • • •
> Do not compare this breath of mine
> to the breeze in the cotton rose,
> for with a single puff
> it snaps
> the lute's thirteen strings.

Looking now at the photographs of Tomiko that remain, one sees someone reminiscent of a gallant young man – pale, with keen, bright eyes, a handsome mouth, and beautiful hair.

I visited Yamakawa Tomiko's birthplace, the town of Obama in Fukui Prefecture, one summer in late July. Silk trees bloomed along the way, and the monument inscribed with Tomiko's poem was half obscured by their soft pink flowers.

The monument consists of a blue inkstone-shape set into a pillar of natural stone. The effect is a little harsh for such a fragile poet. The poem reads:

> The deep–fathomed waves
> smile at the clouds
> that cross this sail –
> I have been called
> one from the northern lands.

No doubt it is a reasonable choice for a monument that stands in her birthplace, but one feels it would have been more suitable to have chosen something with the flavour of romantic beauty that so enthralled her young Meiji readers.

Obama is a lovely and traditional old castle town on the Japan Sea coast with an important early history, and so many temples that it is sometimes called "Nara on the Sea." Tomiko was the daughter of a local samurai family, and in her beautiful face we can discern a steely dignity that the merchant-class Akiko lacks.

Though Tomiko was a pristine Japanese beauty, with a sweetness precisely reminiscent of the flowers of the silk tree, she lacked that inner spirit driven by fierce determination.

She was born in July 1879, the fourth daughter of the Sakai clan samurai Yamakawa Teizo. She was a year younger than Akiko.

The Yamakawa family traditionally provided the superintendent officers and for Wakasa province's feudal lords, the Sakais. Among his eight children, Teizo had a particular affection for his beautiful and talented daughter Tomiko. He was a strict disciplinarian, as befitted a man of an old samurai family, but he was also a cultured man, rumoured to have held monthly poetry competitions. Tomiko respected and loved her father.

In 1895, she became a student at Baika Women's School in Osaka. This provided the highest level of education a woman could obtain at that time. One can only admire the wisdom of a man who would send his daughter from deep within the provinces to study in the city in this way. Baika was a mission school, so it had an atmosphere of freedom and Western modernity. She graduated in three years. Displeased with the thought of returning home and being forced into a marriage not to her liking, she chose to stay on in Osaka helping in the school office, while boarding at the home of Kawahisa Uemon, the household into which her elder sister had married.

The two women, aware of each other's existence and respectful, if privately rather hostile toward each other's talent, had yet to meet.

The first time they met was in fact on the same momentous day on which they both met Tekkan for the first time.

It was the summer of 1900 – the festival of the first of August at Sumiyoshi Shrine was behind them. Feet had been clad in traditional wooden *geta* with thongs of scarlet velvet; blue cords were strung in front of all the houses, from which hung curtains bearing the household crest, and young girls were wearing light summer kimonos of plain white with red damask obi sashes. And then there was the festival food – the special *gomoku* sushi, chilled noodles, octopus tentacles and eel. Akiko's twenty-second summer was threatening to pass uneventfully, like every other summer.

But that year, a special destiny was in store for her.

On one of those hot mid-summer days, when the cooling water that people sprinkled about seemed to evaporate as soon as it hit the ground, she was treated with the rare sight of Kono Tetsunan and Taku Gangetsu together parting the shop curtain at the entrance of Surugaya.

"Ah, welcome." She rose from behind the lattice with a smile to greet them. In response, Gangetsu burst out,

"Tekkan's coming to Osaka! He's giving a lecture. Imagine – Tekkan!"

It was indeed an epoch-making event for Osaka's young literati.

PART III. TEKKAN THE TIGER

1

No modern *tanka* poet was more praised nor more censured than Yosano Tekkan.

Some deprecated his work as crude and lacking in literary sensibility, while others hailed him as a pioneer, the most radical among the poets of the current *tanka* revolution.

The great novelist Mori Ogai extolled Akiko's talents, alongside those of critic and translator Ueda Bin, while also being sympathetic to Tekkan. Mori had even lauded him in his preface to Tekkan's volume of poetry *Love Lyrics*.

"Who is the man who has both engendered and nurtured what is known as the 'new wave' of poetry? Only one person can answer 'It is I' – that man is none other than Yosano Tekkan."

In photographs, at least those taken in his prime, we see a rather swashbuckling intellectual type – glistening black hair with a lacquered sheen, a clean-cut oval face with pale complexion, a fine bridge to the nose, a strong, tense, irritable-looking mouth, and a firm and manly chin that draws the whole effect together.

The description "statesman" might be more fitting for this man than "poet," but one feels that, as with Akiko, he was someone whose handsomeness became evident once one saw him in person and heard him speak.

Opinions are completely divided on his character and behaviour – some have called him a superbly cunning philanderer, while others praised him as a candid artist. He must have been the kind of multi-faceted and mutable person who is difficult to grasp when seen from a single angle. Perhaps the only one to truly comprehend his inner nature was his wife Akiko. Even his own children seem to differ in their assessment of him. He was the type of dubious character who defies definition, even in photographs, and one can well imagine that he was the sort of complex man to be of great interest to women.

Yosano Hiroshi (his birth name) was born in the Okazaki area of Kyoto in 1873, the fourth child of Yosano Reigon, the priest of a Nishihonganji New Pure Land sect temple called Ganjoji. Reigon was the son of Hosomi Giyuemon, the village headman of Atsue in Yosa county in the Tango area.

Reigon appears to have been a clever man. He tried his hand at a number of endeavours that were radical and progressive for his day – excavating for hot springs, producing medicine and pure drinking water, founding a hospital and so forth – but, as so typically happens with pioneers, in every case his only reward was debt. Both the temple and its land were relinquished to repay what he owed, and the family moved to a branch temple in Kagoshima on distant Kyushu.

Reigon was a priest with loyalist tendencies, and he was well-versed in the nation's poetic heritage, which led him to a friendship with the great poet and nun Otagaki Rengetsu. It is said that Rengetsu gave Hiroshi his name.

His mother Hatsue was the daughter of a Kyoto rice dealer. Hiroshi later spoke of his mother as "the preeminent daughter of a Kyoto clan family," but she tasted hardship and poverty in following her wandering husband. Among Reigon's poems is the following:

> In this world
> where so many live
> parent and child together
> we live
> apart and distant.

He and his wife had five sons and a daughter, but both the eldest and the second son were adopted into another family, Hiroshi being adopted at the age of eleven by the priest of Anyoji Temple in an isolated village north of Sakai called Ono. A son is generally adopted by a family to inherit the succession, so the term has an impressive ring, but in Hiroshi's circumstances it was most probably a case of shedding children to reduce the number of mouths to feed.

Loud-voiced, when together
we quarrelled –
now I live apart
from Mother and Father,
they maintain a silence.
• • •
I hang the pan above the fire
and as the steam rises
from the potato gruel
I cup my chapped hands
over it for warmth.
• • •
Even in this house
where the rice bill goes unpaid
for three months
spring sunlight shines in –
we need not eat.

Thus wrote Hiroshi, recalling the poverty of his childhood. His
wanderings began early in life. But he was no ordinary boy. "He
displayed a glittering talent from an early age," states his biography,
"and was known far and wide as a prodigy with an encyclopaedic
memory."

All his siblings were gentle and sincere by nature, and it seems that
Hiroshi alone was wilful and hot-tempered.

"I grew up with a reputation for oddness from the age of five or six
– when I was five I moved to Osaka, where, oppressed by relentless
scolding from my agonized adopted mother, my heart was full of
complaints that I could never speak. My only comfort was to throw
myself into reading – I spent every day and all night sleepless before
my desk, sipping occasional bowls of watery tea-rice, and thanks to
this my poor hot-blooded young body developed a weak stomach
which ultimately affected my brain and drove me to madness."

This is a sketch of his own unhappy youthful years. However,
his adopted father Ando Hidenori was delighted to have a child
in the family with a reputation as a prodigy, and sent him to study
the classics with a Chinese scholar in Sakai by the name of Takagi

Hidemizu. Hiroshi walked the several miles to Sakai and back for his studies. One of his schoolmates there was Kono Tetsunan.

It seems likely that Tetsunan's mild and wholesome personality would have been effective in calming Hiroshi's fierce and fiery temper on numerous occasions. Hiroshi loved him, and this early friendship endured throughout their lives. It was at this time that Hiroshi, who loved plum trees, took the pen name Tekkan from the line of a poem: "the ancient plum tree's trunk has put out fresh bud" ("Tekkan" or "iron trunk" is a poetic term for the trunk of an old plum tree).

Before then he had used other pen names, including Tetsurai ("iron thunder"). His friends, including Tetsunan, copied him by also taking pen-names including the character "tetsu." As he grew older, the name of this beautiful and talented young man became known in his hometown of Kyoto.

> Ah, those days
> when people in the capital
> spoke of me, awed,
> as a genius
> and a handsome youth.

Along with Chinese prose and poetry, Tekkan also studied Buddhist scriptures and English. Eventually, thanks to his teacher Takagi Hidemizu's recommendation, he was invited to join both the painting and calligraphy gatherings and Chinese poetry competitions held in various parts of Osaka, where he composed Chinese poems and painted in the Chinese style alongside adults. The prodigy's name spread further and further afield.

But Tekkan was now fourteen. He felt he couldn't bear to live out his life in this little backwater – he wouldn't be content with local fame. What's more, though he had followed his father's orders and been ordained as a priest, he was determined not to rot here in this remote country temple as its incumbent.

In the spring of 1886, at the age of fourteen, he fled his adoptive family and threw himself on the mercy of his elder brother, Wada Daien, down in Okayama. When he set off, Tetsunan went with him.

One cannot guess Tetsunan's feelings as he followed Tekkan. No doubt it was a gesture of youthful rashness, a vague urge to leave home behind and go wandering, spurred on by Tekkan's extravagant and fanciful enthusiasm.

However, Tetsunan's family came searching for him. The two were discovered at Osaka's Kawaguchi pier as they were boarding a boat, and Tetsunan was taken home.

It was indeed a strong childhood friendship, it seems.

Tekkan joked in a poem:

It must be a whim
of the gods
that made Tetsunan a man
for he is a lover in the old style
like the dashing courtiers of ages past.

His adoptive family was enraged at his desertion, and there were considerable complications over annulling the adoption arrangements. His distressed father Reigon came to see him in Okayama, but it wasn't until several years later that Tekkan reverted to the family name Yosano.

His elder brother, Wada Daien, was the incumbent priest of Anjuin Temple in Okayama. Under his kindly brother's protection, Tekkan for the first time felt "heart and self expand and breathe, and I found the universe I longed for," but his tempestuous nature did not abate. One day, he took out a farm horse and rode it in devil-may-care fashion through rice fields and vegetable patches, breaking its leg, for which his brother had to bear the costs. He also smashed close to a hundred eggs along with their container, threw an unworn piece of clothing on the bathhouse boiler fire, and then declared it had made him feel grand. Such actions could only invite a reputation as a reckless hooligan or at the least an eccentric.

"There's a lass who's good at singing *shinnai* with the *shamisen*. Why don't you have a listen? It might cheer you up a bit."

At the urgings of a local man, Tekkan called the girl along and listened to her sing "Akegarasu" ("The Crow at Dawn"). Her name was Oyasu. She wasn't particularly beautiful, but she was a very gentle, good-natured country girl. When Tekkan in a fit tore off tile after tile from the wall of the temple compound and smashed them, she did her best to calm him down, rubbing his chest with the top of a wooden smoking box and clinging to him, weeping and begging him to restrain himself and be patient – "Oh, sir, calm yourself! Calm yourself!" She cringed as if she were herself to blame for his crazy fit. Perhaps it was the dark and tumultuous passage from boy to young man that was sending the highly-strung Tekkan into such bouts of confusion and derangement.

Once he even lifted a bundle of books and made as if to hurl them into the fire of the kitchen stove. Oyasu rushed to him, stumbling and with hair flying. She clung to his arm, and when he threw her off and she fell to the floor, she scrambled up and clung to him again, shrieking with all her might.

"Oh, sir, what are you doing? Surely books are the soul of a man, are they not? If you're in a rage, better to smash this *shamisen* and throw it in. How could you live, to lose your soul? Sir! Oh, sir!"

Tekkan staggered, and his raised arm fell to his side. Oyasu was weeping at his feet. He was surrounded by gentle people in life – Tetsunan, Oyasu. Throughout his harsh early years, he was blessed to have about him these tender souls, who protected and nurtured his fragile, sensitive, emotional self. He was at heart a gentle person himself, straightforward and prone to tears.

Now under his brother's roof, he attempted to enter the Okayama Normal Secondary School (later Okayama Ichi Secondary School), but failed, because his mathematics was not up to the required standard.

He had never had any formal schooling, and no matter how deep his knowledge of the Chinese classics, this could only be seen as a partial education in the modern age.

His failure to gain admission completely floored the self-confident Tekkan, who was used to being regarded as a child prodigy.

In despair, he went back to the home of his real parents in Kyoto. But though his parents had returned from Kagoshima to the temple in Kyoto, his father was as poor as ever, and furthermore, he wanted Tekkan to become a priest. Tekkan had, of course, been groomed for this profession all along, but he hated the idea. He was seventeen now, more quick-witted and alert than ever. He could not bear the thought of wasting his life away looking after a temple.

He fled Kyoto, this time running to the home of his second brother Akamatsu Shodo, in Tokuyama in Yamaguchi prefecture. Fate awaited him there. It was 1889.

2

Akamatsu Shodo was the incumbent priest of Tokuoji temple in Tokuyama, the adopted son of Akamatsu Renjo and married to his daughter Yasuko. Yasuko was renowned for her wifely wisdom, and together with Shodo was devoted to the encouragement of women's education in the area.

They were a virtuous and upright couple, devoted religious believers as well as educators, still praised today by the local townspeople. Tekkan's brothers all seem to have been distinguished and well-regarded. To judge from the remarkable diversity of opinions about Tekkan, he appears to have been the sole exception.

Tokuyama is an old castle town in southeast Yamaguchi prefecture. Behind it looms the Suo Range, in front lies a fine natural harbour, and both mountains and sea are serene and beautiful.

In the feudal period before the Meiji era, the town had flourished as a large centre for trade and transport ruled by the Mori clan, and it was still a prosperous place. Tekkan's spirits were soothed by this unexpectedly beautiful and cosy country town, and he felt inclined to settle down there.

As his brother Daien had done, Shodo too welcomed his wayward and unruly younger brother with kindness. He was running the private Hakuren Girls' School in Tokuyama, located in the grounds of Tokuoji Temple, which in 1890 changed its name to Tokuyama Women's Private School.

Thanks to his brother's helping hand, Tekkan was given a job teaching Japanese and Chinese literature at the school.

He was an enthusiastic young teacher. One of his pupils, who was still alive and well until WWII, had this to say of Ando Sensei (at this stage he still went by his adoptive name):

"He always used to say, 'People must have five spirits – the spirit of bravery, the spirit of determination, the spirit of chivalry, the spirit of hard work, and the spirit of intelligence.'"

During the summer and winter holidays, he held special courses on the famous anthology of one hundred poets, *Hyakuninisshu*. He was the kind of person to throw himself into whatever he did.

Besides teaching, he also performed various other tasks at the school, as well as editing the self-improvement magazine that his brother published for the Yamaguchi Prefecture *Sekizen* Society.

It is interesting that Tekkan should preach the virtue of "the spirit of hard work." At this time, he wrote the following about women's education:

"Women must have the educational grounding and determination to achieve independence. To this end, there should be no scorning the power of hard work. They must labour alike in the trivial matters of everyday life."

This was the period that saw the appearance of the female activists Nakajima Shoen and Kageyama Eigo. Shoen, well-known as a speaker for the Liberal Party, was also an author, writing critical commentary and novels. Tekkan was no doubt impressed by the activities of these women's rights activists, and enthusiastically attempted to instil in his pupils the principle of developing a free and independent individuality rather than conforming to the womanly ideal of "good wife and wise mother" prevalent at the time.

One of his pupils was Asada Sadako. She was the eldest daughter of Asada Giichiro, a powerful man in the town. Giichiro was one of the town elders, head of an old landed family. With the onset of the Meiji period, he had turned his hand to the businesses of books, kimono and textiles, Western and traditional clothing, and general merchandise, growing wealthier in the process. He had also founded the Inland Sea Shipping Company, but irresponsible management had led to the company's bankruptcy, and it was said that this had squandered the family fortune.

He was, however, of fine old stock, and renowned in the town, a highly educated man with a high reputation for his dedication to the industrial prosperity of the region. And despite the decline in his fortunes, he was still a man of impressive wealth in the area, the owner of large tracts of farm and forest land.

Sadako was a sickly girl, and had entered school rather late, so she didn't graduate until the age of twenty-two. She was three years Tekkan's senior, but she was still an innocent, brought up a virtuous maiden hidden away deep in the house, and much younger than her years.

She loved poetry and fiction. Who knows which of them was the instigator, but Sadako took to borrowing books from Tekkan and discussing her impressions with him.

Prior experience had not inoculated her fragile heart, and very soon she fell for this charismatic, talented young man who emanated such refreshing youthfulness. Perhaps it was Tekkan, all too eager to accept her feelings, who made the first move. The news soon spread through the gossipy town.

When they learned of the young girl's romance, the family decided that she ought to marry Tekkan − not on account of his personal qualities, but because he was the younger brother of the virtuous and highly respected Akamatsu Shodo. Sadako's father, however, looked into the matter and forbade her to marry him with the simple statement, "That Yosano fellow has no educational qualifications."

("Educational qualifications"? What could that mean?)

Tekkan's self-respect was deeply wounded. His self-confidence, grown fat since childhood on his reputation as a prodigy, was in fact precariously sustained above a deep insecurity about his lack of formal education.

He later wrote:

> Fallen to earth,
> no university education,
> doesn't read the Bible,
> and thanks to the world and love
> reduced to a shabby down-at-heel.

One may imagine that all his life he yearned for a university education. In those days, universities had an incomparably higher status. He was all the more interested and enamoured with them for his lack of connection with such institutions. This complex about his lack of education dogged him all his life, and made him belligerent in his career.

Though of good birth, and with a highly educated father, Tekkan had been born into a poverty-stricken temple family and had grown to manhood in straitened circumstances, with a strict adoptive family; hardly a favourable environment for gaining a formal education. Asada's ruthless criticism had driven the point home. On the verge of twenty, Tekkan was still an ingenuous and inexperienced youth. His view of the world was naively optimistic. He had assumed he would be allowed to marry Sadako – after all, he had a good reputation at the girls' school where he taught, and his father and brothers were well-liked. But this indulgent expectation had been shattered by reality.

"Sadako, my brother is telling me I should leave Tokuyama. But I don't want to go without you. Would you consider coming with me?"

In their secret rendezvous on a mountain path, Sadako wept in his arms.

Sadako's complexion was pale, and her voice was beautiful. She was a reserved girl, considered to be calm and prudent, yet at some point, unbeknownst to everyone, she had slipped into a relationship with Tekkan. A typically modest and respectable young Meiji girl, the eldest daughter of a wealthy old rural family, had pulled off the daring feat of conducting the kind of audacious love affair at which even modern girls would balk.

Sadako had first grown close to Tekkan through their shared literary taste in novels and poetry and the pleasure of their conversation, but from one moment to the next Tekkan's passionate nature had swept her off her feet. Once in love, this taciturn and well-behaved girl was transformed in a way that astonished Tekkan.

"Sensei. Yosano-Sensei," she would call softly below his window. (He had by now reverted to his former family name.)

When he hastily opened the window and looked out, she was standing there in the darkness, nothing on her feet but white *tabi* socks.

"Sadako. What are you doing?"

"I wanted to see you…I just stepped straight out of our living room into the garden and left the house…" she faltered, blushing.

Though she mumbled the words and couldn't raise her face to look at him, when he offered her his hand she clambered in through the window. Putting out the lamp, she flung herself at him, sighing "Yosano-Sensei!" Dazzled and confused by her ardour, Tekkan told himself that such passion must be love.

And thinking it was love, Tekkan also believed that Sadako would therefore follow him anywhere. In the face of this triumphant love, he was convinced that as a matter of course it would lead her to abandon her home and family for him.

Yet now Sadako did not answer, she only trembled. In his arms, wrapped tight in a young man's indigo kimono sleeves, she wept, her cheek pressed to his breast. Meek as she was, she could not face leaving behind everything to flee with this man she knew not where.

Tekkan was her first love, her first man. If she let him go now, she felt she would be relinquishing forever this precious moment of youth, of love, which would never again come her way. Yet she could not bring herself to raise her head, to nod, to acquiesce. Her passion was a secret thing, a thing confined to the night, which ran to him unshod through the dark; it could not find the daring to withstand the glare of daylight, to boldly expose itself to the eyes of the world.

For Sadako, conventions and morals were insurmountably powerful forces. If her parents forbade it, she did not have the courage to go against their wishes. There was nothing in her life that would have given her the wherewithal to do so. In this, she was no more than a common country girl. In his arms, she simply wept.

"Yosano-Sensei, are you really leaving?"

The students at Tokuyama Girls' School were fond of serious young Tekkan, and they were sad to see him go.

As for Tekkan, he felt no regret at the end of his two years as a teacher. Though he was leaving, as it were, under a hailstorm of humiliation, and entering a rootless existence, this only served to stir his fighting spirit. Yet among his present students, there was one who was close to his heart.

She was the eldest daughter of a wealthy man from Izumo Village in Sado. Her name was Hayashi Takino.

She had just entered school, and was still a child, but already her beauty was turning people's heads. Since she came from quite a distance away, she was a boarder, but she missed her mother so much that she and her little cousin once ran away from school together. Her father would visit with sweets to cheer her up.

"What school will you be going to, Sensei?" she asked Tekkan innocently.

"Oh, I'm not going to be a teacher any more."

"Really? What are you going to do now?" Takino opened her beautiful eyes wide in wonder.

"Well, I don't actually know myself. But if I make a name for myself somehow, I'll let you know right away."

Tekkan was nursing his sensitive pride, and dreaming of the day he would show the world what fine gifts he possessed.

"You caused me a few problems, didn't you, Takino? When you first arrived all you did was whisper about how you were going to get back home again."

"I missed home…"

"Still, your marks have generally become the best in the class, haven't they?"

"That's because you were always kind enough to give me top marks, Sensei. I remember I once had to tell you that you'd marked my answer right when it was wrong," Takino ingenuously replied.

Tekkan burst out laughing. "Did you indeed? I don't remember that." He was hastily covering his confusion, for he was drawn to this clever, beautiful girl, and it was true that she had always been his favourite.

"You're an honest girl, and you don't approve when things aren't right, do you? It's a fine quality." He managed to bluff his way through the conversation, but in his heart he was loath to part from this beautiful young girl.

Wounded by the parting with his first love, Sadako, he felt that the only person who might bid him an innocent farewell was Takino. His memories of Tokuyama had become focused on her. He left behind nothing but scandalous tales of his dealings with women.

"Sensei, write us something as a farewell present," cried his students as they gathered around him. He took a narrow strip of paper and jotted down a clichéd little poem for one of them.

Though I live in a world
crooked as the bent bamboo
and as thick with sorrows
I will never alter
the straightness of my purity.

"One for me too please Sensei!" Takino begged for a copy of this old-fashioned poem that smacked of worthy girls' school anthems.

But no sooner had he given it to her than she managed to lose it. Young as she was, she had only a vague impression of him, and she later remembered him as a young teacher who for some reason had treated her as a favourite student.

Little did she know – this beautiful, fresh young girl in her maroon schoolgirl *hakama*, with a white ribbon in her braided hair – that she would later become his wife in a relationship full of pain, that she would suffer, and cause suffering to him, as well as to his second wife Akiko.

A later poem written by Hayashi Takino reads:

You knew me early
as a youthful maiden
scented
with the odor
of Yamaguchi's orange blossom.

3

In 1892, at the age of twenty, Tekkan left for Tokyo, with the five *yen* he had borrowed for the journey in his pocket. He set out for the capital knowing nothing of what might await him, with a daringly triumphant heart, prepared to battle his way out of his current predicament.

Tekkan had two or three times sent prose pieces to the women's magazine *Fujo* in Tokyo, which had published them. This was his only lead within the city. He didn't have the confidence to imagine he could eke out an existence through selling his writing, but his youthful high spirits gave him the nonchalant faith that it would all work out somehow.

Yet though he had come to Tokyo full of resolution, nowhere would take him in. No school would open its doors to him unless he could pay the fees, nor could he find employment, as he had no guarantor. In dire straits, he went knocking at the gate of Ochiai Naobumi.

Naobumi was a *tanka* poet who wrote under the name "Haginoya." He had formed a society called Asakasha that was devoted to reforming *tanka*.

His poems attempted to infuse a new sensibility into the techniques of the old school. There was a newness about the plain style in which he wrote that intrigued the young poets who were tired of the conventional old Imperial poetry school.

> From the box
> in which the maiden placed
> those silkworms
> two lovely butterflies
> have now emerged.
> • • •
> Rustling softly
> at the white jaw
> of the little sea bass
> I caught –
> the autumn wind.

These were calm, temperate poems, quite lacking in any ferocity, but there was a coolly refreshing touch to them.

While Naobumi had a talent for encouraging and training his disciples, and a solid grounding in the literary classics, he knew almost nothing about the Western literature that was so important in the modern age; this, coupled with the nature of his talent, made him no more than a half-hearted and transitional reformer. Among his followers were the *littérateurs* and *tanka* poets Omachi Keigetsu, Onoue Shibafune and Tekkaneko Kun'en, who carried forward Naobumi's reforms and each made names for themselves in the literary world. It was thanks to their teacher Naobumi's magnanimity that these men all came to display their own unique talents.

Naobumi had a high opinion of Tekkan, for he likewise generously supported Tekkan throughout his career. But in the months before he came to stay at Naobumi's house, Tekkan seems to have literally not known where his next meal would come from. He had found his way into a dormitory for indigent students in Kichijoji, where he cooked the students' meals in exchange for the fifteen-*sen* boarding fee. He made what living he could by producing the tinted stone rubbings that were popular at the time, making do with nothing but water for the day if he had no money, or devouring a roasted yam if an odd coin fell into his hands. On the wall of his room in the Kichijoji dormitory, he wrote the following Chinese poem:

> Homelessly wandering about the earth, what sufferings have I
> known these past ten years?
> Oh do not sneer at the stains on my sleeves, half are the trace
> of tears and half of dust.

Even in the midst of grinding poverty, Tekkan's precocious and tempestuous talents remained keen. He was a man whose fighting spirit only rose the more fiercely the more straitened his circumstances became.

Under Naobumi's guidance, his followers dedicated themselves to the reform of *tanka*, but Tekkan gradually grew dissatisfied with the party line, and set off at full tilt on his own trajectory. There were some who later scorned him with the accusation that he was "no more than a talented man," and indeed his free-ranging genius with words was really more akin to journalism than to poetry.

The following poem expresses his pride and confidence:

> I'll smile as I press
> the earth
> in one small hand –
> this world I live in
> works with a sneering wit, alas.

His mentor Naobumi sang Tekkan's praises to the publisher of the newspaper *Niroku Shinpo* and in 1894, while working there, Tekkan published a fiercely-worded treatise on *waka* – traditional thirty-one syllable verse poetry – titled "Sounds of Ruin to the Nation." It was subtitled "In Scorn of Today's Sickly *Waka*," and was a scathing attack on poets of the hidebound Imperial poetry and Keien schools, men such as Takasaki Masakaze and Hachida Tomonori. It was Tekkan's belief that *waka* must not be restricted by the old conventions, such as the elegant beauty of nature, puns, conventional poetic place associations and so forth, that belonged to the old style of poetry and were perfected a thousand years earlier in the classical Kokinshu era. What he had in mind was a completely new style of *waka*, one in which the kind of poetic images seen in his mentor Naobumi's ground-breaking free verse poem "Song of the Faithful Daughter Shiragiku" could be crossed with *waka* to produce *shintaishi* – something new that was at the same time in the style of free-verse poetry.

Tekkan was, as he said of himself, "irascible," a rough-edged, passionate man with a short fuse. This plus a wealth of talent meant that when he took up his pen or spoke, the flames were inevitably searing for others.

"My own poems will be more vehement things… readers will feel they are brushing flame… my poetry will sway hearts more wildly, shock, soar far up, beyond nation and society, out of the common world to the heights of beauty… they will be poems of modern language and sensibility, yet reaching back to the muscular style of old… poems full of ardour and passionate intensity, like the voice of a man raised in song…"

Thus dreamed Yosano Tekkan.

But he still held the conviction that love was not a subject befitting of a hero such as he saw himself to be. He had not yet gained a clear sense of how to proceed. Having rejected the conventional *waka* style and chosen to part ways with the elegant tastes of the old-style literati, he was left with the "manly hero" style of verse. Tekkan realized that, by chance, his own beliefs and his nation's fate intersected.

It may help to mention that this was just after the end of the Sino-Japanese War, in which the newly modern nation of Japan had astonished the world by defeating China. Korea, which had become Japanese territory in the subsequent treaty, was introducing a Japanese educational system, and was teaching Japanese in a newly established public school funded by subscription, called Itsubi Academy.

Naobumi's younger brother Ayukai Kaien had been invited to be the head of this school. He and Tekkan were close, and Kaien suggested he come along and teach there.

Though he had found a job at *Niroku Shinpo* and was somehow managing to make ends meet, the mention of a position at Itsubi Academy must have struck him as welcome news, with its promise of a career. Elated, Tekkan decided to go. In those days, Korea was a choice prize for the burgeoning Japanese nation to have obtained, and since China had lost its battle for supremacy there, Japan had been given free run of the country, so to speak. It was a new and undiscovered world that stirred the ambition and ardour of politically disaffected youth and those willing to try their luck. With wanderlust in his blood, Tekkan was particularly attracted by this opportunity.

Kono Tetsunan, hearing the news of Tekkan's decision to go to Korea, arranged to meet up with him at Yuteiji Temple in Osaka, and wished him well for his ambitious undertaking. Tetsunan read the poem Tekkan showed him, written on a strip of scroll paper:

> Those Korean people
> who plant upon their mountains
> the cherry tree –
> I'll teach them
> to sing Japanese songs.

'Parting From Friends' was the title of Tetsunan's following poem.

> Though you venture
> to the far wilds of Korea
> where lurk tigers fierce,
> Surely you'll not forget
> the truth of friendship.
> • • •
> Heroic I feel you,
> you who leave today
> to sing
> the songs of manhood
> in distant Korea.

In response, Tekkan wrote:

> Even should I die
> in the tiger-lurking wilds
> my friend, how could I forget
> the truth
> of friendship?

The exchange is replete with the exuberance of youth. Yet these emotions were not Tekkan's alone, but also the destiny of the nation itself. Since its overwhelming military victory in the Sino-Japanese War, Japan had gained a powerful voice with regard to Korea. Men, and in particular young men, held forth heatedly on matters of state, and gloried in striking patriotic poses.

Huge numbers of Japanese were flooding into Korea. The politically disaffected, revolutionaries and down-and-outs, nay, even shadowy types who may have been Japanese government spies and the like, were all floating about there, and the capital was a hotbed of unrest and ferment. Aswim in their midst, Tekkan encountered high-level Korean bureaucrats, associated with political thugs, fell in love with prostitutes in the gay quarters, and generally threw himself into the life of a youthful vagabond.

Tekkan would later travel to Korea several more times, but it is unclear to what extent reports of his political activity there are exaggerated.

The headnote to the following poem reads: "Composed with Kaien in autumn, on the day we left the capital. At this time the tyranny of Queen Min was growing daily, and the political power of the Japan Party had suddenly plunged."

> The autumn wind
> will be rising in
> those Korean hills
> I stroke my sword
> thinking somehow of myself.

This referred to an event called the "Eulmi Incident."

The imperial Yi family of Korea were divided into warring pro-Japan and pro-Russia factions, and Queen Min, who was of the pro-Russia faction, was scheming to impel the emperor to rid Korea of Japanese power. Learning of this, the Japanese in Korea – the politically disaffected and self-styled patriots – performed a *coup d'état* and assassinated her.[1] This led to an explosion of anti-Japanese feeling in Korea.

The Japanese government gave careful thought to the incident's repercussions for its foreign policy, and arrested and jailed the ringleader and others involved. Tekkan was hospitalised at the time, having contracted typhoid fever, and one might say he thus had a lucky escape from being implicated.

This event occurred on 8th October 1895. The young diplomatic attaché Horiguchi Kumaichi (father of the poet Horiguchi Daigaku), who was in the capital at the time, was involved in the incident. He and Tekkan were good friends, and it may well be that Tekkan would have fallen in with him had it not been for his hospitalisation. He was in fact suspected of involvement and taken back to Hiroshima for questioning, but later released.

His mentor Naobumi again came to his rescue. Itsubi Academy had by now closed down, so the following year, with the aid of the editor in chief at Meiji Shoin Publishers, he was recommended for the post of literature teacher at Atomi Women's School.

He did go back to Korea again, but it is uncertain how much political activity he could have been involved in. His subsequent writings and actions, however, give the impression that he single-handedly bore Japan's fate upon his shoulders, and played an active part in the affairs of the nation.

Tekkan seems to have allowed this impression to develop among his literary admirers and those around him after his return to Japan. No doubt he intentionally failed to correct the well-meaning misunderstandings of others, and acted the patriot for them.

[1] Translator's Note: Historians now agree that Queen Min was murdered by Japanese assassins hired by the Japanese Minister to Korea, Miura Goro. The incident led to political chaos, but did not result in a *coup d'état*.

Here are two other poems from this time:

On hearing a tiger roar thrice in the snow as I travelled along the Kankyo Road:

> Come, tiger,
> confront me if you will.
> I'll skin you inside out
> and use your hide
> for this sword's scabbard cover.
>
> • • •
>
> How fiercely the tiger
> roars on Mount Onoe –
> this evening
> the wind
> must be rising.

He became known as "Tekkan the Tiger," and his poetic style – the blustering, restless heroics – gained the name of "the Tiger and Sword Style."

According to Ayukai Kaien, who was often together with Tekkan in Korea, he had in fact never travelled to the sort of place where a tiger's roar might be heard. Those who call Tekkan a fraud point scornfully to facts such as these.

For Tekkan, however, it was imperative for the tiger to appear in his poems about Korea. His tiger is a creature which leapt brilliantly into being within a dream of snowy mountains, hovering nimbly on the border between reality and fiction. Once Tekkan had caught it in his poems, this phantom tiger became real. Those who are more down-to-earth have no comprehension of such artistic secrets.

The inheritance of his father's blood was also part of Tekkan's disposition. Reigon had been a loyal supporter of the emperor during the upheavals of the Meiji Restoration, and he too had thrown himself into the affairs of the nation.

Perhaps in Tekkan's veins too there ran the Oriental posturings of the loyalist. He was hot-blooded, a man of strong emotions. One can imagine how he would easily have been imbued with the bravado of the politically disaffected people he associated with.

While in Korea he fell in love with a courtesan by the name of Hisui.

> Let me go with you
> begged my Korean geisha Hisui –
> with what reluctance I stood
> and came here
> alone.
> • • •
> How splendid those special clothes
> in Korean style
> she wore at New Year
> my little Hisui, just eighteen
> and I was twenty six.

He was drunk on the soft flesh of this graceful and beautiful foreign seductress, who spoke no Japanese.

Declaiming soberly on national and world affairs by day, by night drunk in the lap of the beauty he was bedding, Tekkan's self-absorption far outstripped reality.

Tekkan's loyalist pose, and his loyalist love, surpassed the man himself in their exaggerations.

Yet perhaps it is in exaggeration, embellishment and distortion that the truth in fact lies.

The Four Directions, Tekkan's volume of poetry from this period, was published in July 1896, not long after his return from Korea. Its rough, forceful poems and *tanka* took the young men of the day by storm, and Yosano Tekkan quickly became their idol.

This work, indeed, is replete with a truth that could be called "the intoxication of youth"; its poems give full voice to a particular aspect of Meiji youth. This happened to coincide with Japan's great victory in the Sino-Japanese war and the return of the Liaotung Peninsula, which had briefly become Japanese territory, through the Tripartite Intervention, an incident that stirred the indignation of the Japanese people and sparked a surge in nationalist sentiment. This swelling of patriotism infused everyone with a kind of warrior spirit.

In barbershops and public baths, voices were raised in rage against the three nations of France, Germany and Russia that had forced Japan to relinquish its hard-won territory. It was at this point that Tekkan's fiercely masculine poems appeared. Natural momentum lifted Tekkan, or Yosano Hiroshi, to the role of the nation's darling.

Tekkan's poetic inspiration had perfectly captured public sentiment.

There may be some who assert that this was simply the result of Tekkan's journalistic instincts, but this is not the whole story. If it were so, Tekkan would not have missed the bus in the shift from the decline of the so-called Myojo School to the next wave of writing in which Naturalism was in the ascendant. But Tekkan's fate and Meisei's were one.

When its role was at an end, and *Myojo* had flashed for a brilliant moment and then perished, Tekkan's poetry too lost its vigor.

Tekkan's talent coincided precisely with the flourishing of Meiji's youth.

He was above all a symbol of them. His strong, new poetry captured the emotions that the young people of the era felt in their bones. But he had to wait for Akiko before he was able to take the next step, and challenge the old familiar world and conventional social morals as he planned. The Tekkan who embraced the "soft flesh" of his courtesan could not yet write the daring mockery to be found in his later poems.

PART IV. WHITE LOTUS

1

Now a successful poet, Tekkan nevertheless did not for a moment forget the humiliation he had been dealt at the hands of the family of his first love, Asada Sadako.

One by one, he sent each book that was published with his name on it to Sadako. No doubt it was primarily not so much to impress Sadako, in fact, as from a spirit of revenge against the Asada family.

At the same time, he did not forget his promise to Hayashi Takino to send his books. He was an amalgamation of vindictiveness and pure-hearted innocence.

His second volume, *Heaven and Earth*, was published the following year, in 1897, and he returned to Korea a second time. It is not clear what he did there. One can guess that in this unsettled foreign clime, seething with anti-Japanese sentiment, he engaged in vaguely political activity of some sort, and took a certain indefinable pleasure in being caught up in it all. The fact was that at this time politics were a tastier dish to him than literature.

Tekkan returned to Tokyo at the beginning of 1898. In summer that year, his father fell ill while he happened to be staying with his second son Shodo. Tekkan went to Tokuyama to help look after him, but his father died, and the funeral was held at Shodo's house.

Tekkan had thought he'd never return to Tokuyama, but he could not repress his nostalgic response to the landscape. Once his father's funeral was safely over, a desire to see Sadako grew strong in him, and he asked for someone's help in getting in touch with her.

The conservative and gossip-ridden country ways of the area meant that since the rumours of Sadako's love affair had surfaced she had had no decent offers of marriage, and was still humiliatingly single. She was in a position to yield to Tekkan, who was now a man of fame in the capital.

When Tekkan called around to visit her, her father probably felt less antagonistic than before, but was still not prepared to allow a marriage or resumption of relations. Being a businessman, her father Giichiro had no patience for the risky undertaking of the *littérateur* or poet. He knew that Tekkan was penniless, and for that reason he apparently had his suspicions that Tekkan might try to entice his daughter away. It was not only Giichiro who thought this, in fact, but the world at large.

It is difficult to say. It seems to me that there must have been some element of calculation concerning her family's wealth in Tekkan's intimacy with Sadako. One could even wonder whether he would have felt the love he did if she had come from a poor family.

Did Tekkan not perhaps feel a strong attraction and adoration for this maiden who had grown to womanhood in a rich household, under the prudent watchfulness of her parents? His love and his dreams found their germinating soil in such romantic imaginings. Tekkan's taste in women and perception of them could only be conceived of in terms of a world all too different from his own. It was not so much the woman herself as the protective and financial power of the parents behind her that must have been a powerful attraction for the destitute Tekkan, and one can only imagine how his psyche would have been enticed by it.

For this and the following year constituted a particularly eventful and difficult period for Tekkan. Strength and willpower he had, but not the money to allow them fruition. It was just the moment for a longed-for patron to appear.

Early in the spring of that year in the *Nihon Newspaper*, the *tanka* poet Masaoka Shiki had published a critical essay, titled "Letter to a *Tanka* Poet." Shiki's aim was both to break new ground in the classical *haiku* form, and to do away with the conventional *tanka* to create a form replete with a fresh, free spirit. He was hostile to poets such as Hatta Tomonori of the Keien School and Takasaki Masakaze of the Imperial poetry school, who followed the ancient *Kokinshu* style to the letter. Of course Ochiai Naobumi had also created a *tanka* revolution and established his own school of poetry on the same grounds of opposition to these conservative poets, but in Shiki's view he too was old-fashioned.

What was necessary, he maintained, was the creation of a new way of seeing things, an approach that accurately "sketched" from nature, and a fresh, vivid rhythm imbued with the living voice of the present new age. Shiki was already ill and semi-bedridden with tuberculosis when this essay was written, although at the age of thirty-one, his view was high-spirited and full of abundant energy. He stood in opposition not only to the Keien School but to Naobumi's Asakasha, and was dissatisfied with the plain style of such poets as Sasaki Nobutsuna of the Chikuhakuen School. He was also put off by the fierce roughness of the poems written by Naobumi's disciple Yosano Tekkan. When it came down to it, he was opposed to every contemporary school of *tanka*.

In "Letter to a *Tanka* Poet" he made the following firm statement:

"Ki no Tsurayuki (c. 872–945) was a poor poet and, oh, how boring the *Kokinshu* is!"

The thousand-year-old authority of the *Kokinshu*, that single path by which so many generations of poets had learnt their trade, he crushed with a single blow.

"I cannot fathom those worldly types who hold that art consists solely in imitating this poetry. It astonishes me to witness the disgraceful way they can milk the dregs of these ancient poems – bad enough if it were for ten or twenty years, but no, for two or even three hundred years.

"What nonchalant fools parading as poets! To hear them, they are forever boasting that poetry is the greatest good, but this is the sheer self-flattery of men who in fact know nothing but poetry."

Among the many who cried for the reform of *tanka*, none had ever produced such a powerful bombshell as this. Shiki was an intelligent and clear-headed man highly skilled in his art and blessed with the double gift of being both a fine poet and a critic; and while on the one hand he was busy destroying the old style, on the other hand he was producing modern works.

Meanwhile, there was a poet named Doi Bansui, whose fame rivalled that of Susukida Kyukin. His poems were indignant deplorations in the solemn, manly style of the noble Oriental idealist. His poem on the ancient Chinese hero Shokatsu Komei had a particularly devoted following among young students.

> Sad autumn winds blow fierce on Mount Ki
> and on Gojo Plain the serried clouds ride dark.
> Thick lies the patterned dew.
> The horses fatten on the hay
> but from the banners of the Szechuan armies the light has gone
> and the sounds of drumming now are stilled.

> General Josho's illness wracks him.

It is easy to imagine how this sad Chinese-inflected lament captured the hearts of the youth of Meiji. It broke new ground, to the extent that later student poems and dormitory songs always included reference to it. Bansui was twenty-eight at the time he wrote it, a secondary school teacher in Tokyo. The previous year, the twenty-six-year-old Shimazaki Toson had published his free verse volume *Seedlings*. Its flowing, elegant lyrics were likewise loved by young readers. Thus around 1897, a number of talents were vying with each other in the same field.

It was indeed as if all the flowers of spring were bursting open together.

Tekkan, who had made his debut with *The Four Directions* and *Heaven and Earth*, must have felt he could not sit idly by. It must also have excited him to witness Shiki founding not only the *haiku* journal *Hototogisu* but also the Negishi Tanka Society and the Association for Tanka Reform.

However, it is cruel and unfair to say that he therefore turned to this rich country family in his search for the funds to fulfil his ambitions. He was not so unscrupulous. Granted, over and over again he may have acted in such a way as to suggest that he was, yet most assuredly, this was not what was in his heart.

It does seem that this is a matter in which Tekkan is easily misunderstood. And yet, as I have already indicated, it cannot be maintained that his approach to Sadako was not tinged with self-interest. At the least it can be said that the fact that this merchant family's daughter, unlike Tekkan, was brought up with all the money she wanted was an added attraction that paved the way for his rush to love.

I do not believe that, as some will firmly maintain, Tekkan was a crafty schemer and a smooth-talking tactician. If he had a fault it was to be too passionate, too honest, too hot-blooded. He was not one of those people who are clever in the true sense, who comport themselves discreetly and keep a constant eye on others. He was recklessly and ridiculously honest. Even if he chanced to hatch his version of a plot, it was a poor and innocent thing, and others soon saw through it and uncovered his secret. It seems to me that, pure though his heart was, half a lifetime of such bitter experiences served to make him considerably wiser to the ways of the world. Though he had experienced all the hardships the world had to offer, and knew the taste of what it is to live, he was unaware of a deeper existence beneath this. He battled on in his own way, a mixture of purity and worldly wisdom. But his underbelly was still vulnerable. I believe that the criticisms of Tekkan are really in essence expressions of how unsullied he was by the evils of the world.

If Tekkan were the wily fox that people make him out to be, he would certainly not have acted in a way that allowed himself to be caught. No, he would have been bathed in praise and admiration.

This goes both for the affair with Sadako, and his relationship with his future wife Hayashi Takino. I have expounded here at length on Tekkan's character because he was later criticized for his relations with women.

When Tekkan met Sadako again, she was twenty-nine.

2

Sadako was still single. She was more beautiful than before – in fact, the depression that had afflicted her through the flower of her youth had now added to her affecting charm. She had suffered the scorn of those around her in silence, inwardly bewailing the fate that left her to rot in this backwoods place through the bloom of her maidenhood.

What must she have felt when this high-spirited and radical young poet who was taking the literary world by storm returned to see her, his old love unforgotten? Though every time he sent her his latest published work she had been reaffirmed in her faith that their bonds were unsevered, how could she project any future for their romance? But now, here he was again before her eyes. She was no longer the rustic, innocent girl who had wept on the mountain path. She was now a fully mature woman.

And Tekkan too was a very different person. He had become a man who was accustomed to dealing with women. Gone was that callow youth who had once written "Although my age/has reached one score and six/I yet know naught of love" – Tekkan now had under his belt his experiences in Korea, those constant rounds of wine, women and politics. He brought to Sadako's arms a shamelessly indifferent, macho masculinity. One wonders who seduced whom.

> Like the pure melody
> of an old song that
> flows in the air anew
> I meet my love
> once more.

This time when they met, the two found themselves giving their bodies to each other.

> Now into my hands
> Oh joy, seven long years later
> a jewel finer than coral
> a flower that exceeds the lotus
> ah, into my hands – you.

This poem of Tekkan's was written in October 1898, so there is no question that the "you" is Asada Sadako.

Sadako found herself pregnant. Her parents howled with rage, and cursed Tekkan. This time he was not merely stoned out of town, he was driven away with fire and brimstone.

But now, Sadako went quietly with him.

"I will come with you." Those who knew her still say of her today that hers was a mild, self-possessed and cautious nature. Yet this was a girl who dared – just once in her life, and what is more, in the conventional world of the Meiji period – to disobey her parents and follow love.

I find Meiji women fascinating.

A rain of criticism inevitably swirled about not only Sadako who had followed him to Tokyo, but Tekkan himself. "My brothers all abuse me and call me stupid. And it is difficult to attempt to justify myself," he wrote, and indeed it was so.

There is no record of their life together, so we can only guess at it. According to what Tekkan later told his friend Kobayashi Tenmin, however, when he was married to Akiko she drove him mad not just with her jealousy of Takino but also of his first wife Sadako. One may imagine that Sadako, who had followed her man for a love that her home forbade, burned with a far fiercer passion than would a girl who merely gave herself to the husband her parents had endorsed.

The problem was, did she have the strength of character to maintain such passion? The world's censure was such that even Akiko, who likewise later turned her back on home and parents to become "disowned by family" for Tekkan, found herself praying, "Oh grant my heart be brave." Even a woman as strong and courageous as Akiko endured so much in being with Tekkan that many times she considered suicide.

Sadako's joy in love was short, and her suffering long.

For their part, although angry at Sadako, the Asadas cherished their pregnant daughter, and sent her quite a lot of money. This all went to pay the rent or repay debts, however, and the young couple were constantly hounded by privation. Her heart torn by poverty and by the enticement of her parents' repeated pleas in letters – *Leave him, leave him and come home!* – in the midsummer heat of August Sadako gave birth to a girl. In a card postmarked 10th August 1899, Tekkan wrote the following to his friend Tetsunan in Sakai:

"My wife bore a girl on the night of the sixth. It feels most peculiar to find myself become what is known as a 'parent.'"

This was Tekkan's first child. No doubt after his own fashion he was pleased. The little girl was given the name Fukiko.

> I do not pray that you
> might be a fairytale princess
> or Murasaki Shikibu
> but may you have at least
> everlasting skills in poetry.

Fukiko was born to parents who were not officially wed, and registered as illegitimate. This was partly owing to the family register laws that applied in Meiji Japan, under which the eldest daughter Sadako, whose parents refused to allow her to remove her name from the Asada register, was unable to be registered elsewhere as married, as was also the case later with Takino.

But Fukiko died forty days later of meningitis. This was registered as follows: "Died at twelve noon on the seventeenth day of September 1899, in Sakuragi-cho, Ueno, Shimoya Ward, Tokyo."

> You have died
> with a smile on your lips.
> Alas, and here in this world
> your father
> longs to live though he starves.

Sadako wept day and night in an abstraction of sorrow. Until the birth of her child, she had lived with hope and strong spirits. But now that her child was lost, all that was left to her was estrangement from Tekkan, and the hardships of poverty.

This poverty was likewise suffered by the two wives who came after her, Akiko and Takino. All three wives, what's more, came from affluent backgrounds. They began from the same place in life, but only Akiko stayed the course. That is to say, it seems to me that of these three from similar backgrounds, it was the woman who most understood Tekkan, in other words whose own life was most analogous to his, who remained his companion to the end. Personality type rather than depth of love is at issue here, I believe. There was nothing undignified about the women who parted from him.

It was after losing her baby that Sadako was at last able to think objectively about her own and her husband's respective personalities and modes of living. She felt within her the stirrings of a desire to begin life afresh. When the thread that bound them together snapped, for the first time in their relationship Sadako regained her real self. She left Tekkan, and returned home.

In his Tokuyama days, Tekkan had had a trusted friend, a young monk by the name of Iwashiro Tatsujo. Tekkan now pursued Sadako to Tokuyama and tried to persuade her to return to him, but she refused. He was about to leave Tokuyama, bitter and hurt, when he called around to Tatsujo's Pure Land temple, and requested that rites be performed for the dead Fukiko.

> You do not know your way
> along the dark mountain road into death.
> Who will you call on
> you who knows no parent's name,
> who knows not my name?

Tekkan no doubt felt upset and frustrated by Sadako, believing that the early death of their child should have drawn them together. He felt, too, an unbridgeable gulf between himself and his wife, who had grown ever more silently withdrawn and depressed. Her leaving had wounded and pained him. He hated this way of parting. It hurt his pride. Moreover, he was tormented by the Asada family's violent loathing for him. He was still young and he took the world's goodwill for granted. It was this that had led him unwittingly to presume on the family's benevolence in relation to their daughter's marriage. While tasting to the full the brutality of the unfeeling world, he could not yet quite rid himself of his naive faith in it.

> With what chaotic feelings
> I watch this autumn pass –
> a poem to mourn the poet
> whose wife
> leaves him behind.

"With respect, we would like not to pursue the question of the monies lent to you in the past via Sadako, in return for which we request that you consider your relations with her at an end."

This was the pronouncement made to him; he was not even permitted to talk to her. The Asadas believed that "Sadako's life has been ruined by that good-for-nothing scoundrel." Their response to the need to protect their own and their daughter's name was simply to cling to silence, bar the gate, close their lips, and ensure that this "shameful misconduct" should not reach the ears of the world. This was at the same time a wordless revenge on Tekkan.

But of course there was no suppressing the rumours – a young girl, heiress to a well-known family, had run off with a man and borne an illegitimate child. One can well imagine what enmity the Asadas felt towards Tekkan. And thus did Tekkan part from his first lover and wife Sadako, never to see her again.

As for Sadako, the year after she left Tekkan, in April 1900, she went back to Tokyo and entered the Tokyo National Literature and Language Training Center, with the aim of becoming a teacher. Her life in tatters, no doubt she felt the only option open to her was to make her own living. She did not, of course, have to provide her own school fees – nevertheless this move suggests that she was a woman of willpower and strength of character. She later graduated from the Tokyo Girls' Secondary School Language and Literature Teacher's course, and thereafter spent her days as an unmarried teacher. No one knew what a passionate youth was hidden beneath the mild exterior of this ordinary-seeming teacher. It is said that she serenely taught Tekkan's famous love poems with apparent indifference. She is remembered as a woman who, though not beautiful, had a fine pale complexion and a beautiful voice. No doubt the times she lived in played their part in this, but she never once spoke of her past love. She did not even mention it to the niece with whom she lived in old age. Her silence on the subject meant that even those close to her had no idea that she had been Tekkan's first wife. She died at the age of eighty-four, in November 1953. Perhaps at the end of her life images of her old love and of the youthful Tekkan came back to haunt her. It is said that, nearing death, she one day heard a flute nearby and composed the following:

Hearing the flute
I wondered at the heart
of he who played upon it
and of a sudden
my eyes filled with tears.

Very few people knew of Tekkan's relationship with Sadako, with the result that few knew that he had had a daughter named Fukiko.

The Pure Land temple where Tekkan went to request the rites for his daughter lay some way outside Tokuyama, in the Saba district. It is still there, in a wood on the left as one follows the Saba River.

The priest, Iwashiro Tatsujo, had known about the affair between Tekkan and Sadako seven years earlier, in Tekkan's Tokuyama days, and he was sympathetic to Tekkan. He did not believe that Tekkan was the scoundrel and rake that the world made him out to be. He was well acquainted with Tekkan's true nature. Tatsujo was a reader of books and poetry, and had a way of understanding things. He did not, however, have the resources to put this to good effect by rescuing Tekkan or mediating to try and help him.

Tatsujo was well aware of the good and bad aspects of rural life, and could understand the feelings of the Asadas. He was in no position to step in of his own accord and protect Tekkan against them. All he could do was hear Tekkan out, and show him sympathy.

Tekkan may have stayed at the temple for one or two days.

Where did he go thereafter? Tekkan's behavior often aroused people's suspicions, and this occasion was no exception.

There are certain things which suggest that, whenever a relationship with a woman failed, Tekkan already had – somewhere, in a corner of his mind – the next woman he would turn to. This is what leads some people to loathe him like a viper. He did indeed have aspects that can be called unfaithful and immoral, but there was on the other hand a feminine weakness to him as well.

"Tekkan the Tiger," the poet of macho swagger, may have been unaware of it, but within him was a tremulous and shrinking self who could not bear to live alone. Ever since he had realized that his relationship with Sadako was doomed to end in failure, the image of another girl had been tucked away in a corner of his heart. He believed that it was love that lay behind it, but in reality it was closer to self-protective instinct. He was intent on shielding his vulnerable heart from further wounds.

The autumn mists lay thick along the Saba River, and the woods and thatched farmhouses, drenched with the chilly rain, depressed Tekkan's lonely heart.

He was twenty-seven, and possessed nothing. All he could call his own was his poet's pride, a modicum of fame, and two volumes of poetry. Now he was about to struggle back onto his feet for a fresh start – and for this, he needed love, and he needed financial support. He was at heart a weak, tender and vulnerable man.

3

Tekkan made his way along the Saba River to the village of Izumo, and casually dropped by the Hayashi household, the home of Takino, once his pupil at the Tokuyama Girls' School.

Like Sadako, Takino came from a wealthy and influential family. The mansion where they lived lay behind a large gatehouse with elaborate ironwork; earthen walls stretched away past vegetable plots, and the grounds, buried in dense copses, consisted of a scattering of outbuildings, storehouses and so on, besides the main house.

"Good morning. I'm Yosano. We haven't met for some time."

"Well, well, Mr. Yosano the teacher, is it?" Kotaro, the present head of the Hayashi household, greeted him with surprise. He had called in from time to time to visit his daughter Takino when she was at the school dormitory, so he had met Tekkan while he was teaching there.

Tekkan was clad in a shabby kimono and dirty *hakama* trousers, the clothes on his back all that he owned. He carried neither book nor bag, and if truth be known, he had not a single yen in his pocket. He was aware of the poor figure he cut, but it was when he was most down on his luck that he was at his haughtiest.

"I'm glad to see you looking so well, Mr. Yosano. To what do I, er, owe the pleasure…?" Kotaro was cordial, generous and good-natured. Revered by the locals in his position as head of an important household, Kotaro had lived a calm and untroubled life, and his was an earnest and unsuspicious temperament. He had no inkling of Tekkan's life of wandering in Korea, nor of the discord with the nearby Asadas, nor the scandal over Sadako. All he had heard were rumours that Tekkan was pleased Kotaro should know, such as the fact that he had made something of a name for himself as a poet.

"I don't know much about poetry, but I gather you have quite a following among the young folks in Tokyo as a poet of the new school. Congratulations."

"Oh, hardly." Tekkan always grew drunk on the wine of hospitality and hymns of praise. This kind of soft-hearted, tender feeling was what he yearned for. He wanted applause – it was the sustenance without which he could not survive.

His host showed Tekkan through to the large guest room that looked out on a perfectly tended garden replete with flowing spring. A tasteful tea house was visible beyond it. The place seemed to offer all that the heart could desire.

"Actually, the reason I've come here today," Tekkan began, politely turning his sake cup face down before him and arranging himself in formal posture, "is simply – well, this is very sudden, but I wish to ask for your daughter's, for Takino's hand in marriage."

"What was that again, Mr. Yosano?" Kotaro was flabbergasted. "You mean Takino? Er, to you yourself?"

Kotaro looked hard at Tekkan. He was gaunt, but he was a fine-looking and youthful man, and he emanated determination.

"I am, of course, most flattered, but I must say…"

"I do understand how rude this abrupt request is. But I have put a lot of thought into this. The reason I've been sending books and magazines and newspapers to Takino is solely so that she can come to learn who I am. I firmly believe that she is the only wife for me."

"But she's my eldest daughter, and I only have four children, all daughters, so I'm afraid she can't marry." The Family Registration Law in those days stipulated that the eldest daughter of the household could not leave it, and that if she married, her husband must be formally adopted into her family. "And then there's the fact that I understand you will be taking over as head of the Yosano household. Your elder brothers have all married into other households, I gather."

"Yes, I'm aware of that of course. But I have a younger brother, and he can inherit. So my hope is that perhaps you might find me worthy to be adopted into your household as son-in-law."

"Adopted, eh? So you're saying that you would be willing to become a member of the Hayashi family?"

"That's right."

"You're prepared to consider going that far, then? But it's not to be taken lightly, you know, to become adopted into a family like that."

"Most certainly. My earnest desire is simply to make Takino my wife. If this were to be possible, I would have no further requirements."

Tekkan had a firm and impressive voice, the result of the sutra-chanting drummed into him during his early training for the priesthood. This, in addition to the rhetorical powers Tekkan could summon at will to present his feelings in such earnest entreaty, swayed Kotaro's good-natured heart.

Kotaro had always felt an unguarded trust in Tekkan, who had been a member of the respected profession of schoolteacher. Indeed, he still held the benevolent opinion he had had of him from that time. He was such an amiable man that he was unaware of how his good opinion of Tekkan was in fact intertwined with the deep admiration he had for Tekkan's brother, Akamatsu Shodo.

Kotaro began to wonder whether this might not be such a bad match after all. Tekkan was from a reputable family and, most importantly, it would be a far from shameful thing for the Hayashis to create a family relationship with the Akamatsu family. In fact they were a good match in social standing. And Tekkan's tenacity struck Kotaro at the time as youthfully impressive.

Takino was called in to join them. Tekkan swallowed when he saw her. She was now a girl of twenty, with shiny jet-black hair and pale skin. She greeted him shyly. Her features still held the look of the young beauty he had known, but they now brimmed with the purity of the white lotus. Takino had grown into a woman far lovelier than Tekkan had anticipated.

She had been constantly approached for her hand, and negotiations were now under way as a result of one of these offers. But Takino particularly disliked the man in question, and her mother and father were distressed by the situation.

Common thinking at the time held that the position of eldest daughter was a very important one. It was a requirement that the family name be passed on via the eldest daughter by adopting her husband into the family register. But this meant, of course, that the other party had to be in a position not only to marry Takino, but also to leave his own family and become a member of hers. Marriage negotiations were constantly foundering. It was only natural that Kotaro should be inclined to listen when Tekkan made his proposal.

Kotaro made up his mind to let Tekkan marry Takino. He was later blamed for his rashness, but from his point of view, the match appeared a good one at the time.

During the flurried private ceremony, the Hayashis' servants peeped in, whispering amongst themselves.

"Good heavens, he's to be Miss Taki's bridegroom?"

"Fancy that. A real bolt from the blue, and there he was in front of our eyes back then."

Tekkan had announced that he wished to take Takino straight back to Tokyo, so his father had hastily sent around to gather the relatives and lay in supplies of food and drink for the ceremony.

Prior to the ceremony, Tekkan had stayed there for several days. It was indeed a casual age, when one pauses to think. Not only had a hasty assent been given to a hasty request, but Tekkan was immediately welcomed in as the husband. Of course Kotaro's easygoing nature played a part in this, but Meiji society seems to have been generous and liberal like this in all manner of spheres.

And so, unlike Ho Akiko, who left home against her family's wishes and fled to Tokyo to join Tekkan, Takino took him as her husband with her family's consent. Yet she surely did not do so simply out of ready obedience to her parents' wishes.

Takino had received the highest education offered to young women in rural Japan in the mid-Meiji period; she had graduated from the girls' school, and she would aim to enter the Japan Women's University that was soon to be established. She was not a girl to blindly do as her parents told her.

Takino had completely forgotten Tekkan, but no doubt when he appeared before her now as the young poet whose name so often appeared in newspapers and magazines, she indulged in girlish dreams. She must have imagined herself in Tokyo as the wife of Yosano Tekkan, this man who would lead a brilliant life and consort with the known and unknown of the literary world. If she had disliked the thought, her doting parents would surely not have pressed the marriage upon her. No, Takino would not have been led weeping to the stake of this marriage.

Tekkan had neither the formal clothes appropriate for the wedding ceremony, nor anything suitable to change into later. Takino's mother, feeling obliged to help, stepped in and borrowed the necessary items from a relative.

"Poets are vagabonds, footloose and free-spirited," Tekkan was wont to joke casually. "We don't give a damn for dress and appearance. I've nothing but the rags I'm standing in!" And he would laugh uproariously. But in his heart, he was always nervously defensive about his vulnerable self-esteem. The Hayashi family, however, admired him as a poet, welcomed him into the family with warm sensitivity, and sent him on his way with a considerable amount of money.

The new couple set off for Tokyo. These days Tekkan was a manly fellow, of solid build, with piercing eyes and lips drawn almost cruelly thin, no longer the young teacher who had been so tender and kind to Takino when she was a girl. She quickly understood the change in him. It seemed to her, however, that this was how men matured. She was a candid and straightforward person. She took on this fate that had fallen into her lap, and cheerfully set about looking after Tekkan as a young wife should. Tekkan was simply entranced by her graceful, slender figure and the limpid beauty of her face. It satisfied him deeply to have won her as his wife.

People have since accused Tekkan of acting from utilitarian motives in snatching Takino away from her parents' loving arms like this, but there is of course much more to the story. As I said above, if one is inclined to see Tekkan's behavior in a negative light, it is certainly more than open to this interpretation, but nevertheless the fact is that he loved Takino all his life with an unwavering affection. This was still the case even once Akiko was his wife.

For Takino, the move to Tokyo was a happy one. Her twenty-seven-year-old husband seemed to her far and away more adult than she. He led her to a land she had never seen before. He was rich with knowledge that she lacked, he knew the ins and outs of the world, and had a wide circle of acquaintances. She found him rather intimidating, but also by the same token trustworthy and attractive.

The only thing that she found somewhat repugnant was the fiery denunciations with which he would demolish others in the literary world, when he and his friends got together and the talk turned to literary matters. She had been brought up in a seemly fashion, never to criticize others, and it shocked her to hear him speak this way.

"The fact is, those fogeys in the old guard don't have the strength for a revolution in *waka* or *haiku*. That's where Ochiai has his advocates. But even Ochiai can't really shed the skin of the old poetry schools. He's useless. There's not an ounce of real power there."

"Gracious!" Takino murmured. "But surely, Mr. Ochiai has helped you enormously to find your feet?"

"That's a different thing altogether. Obligations are obligations, yes, but I'm talking here about achievement. That's the way things are in a man's world. Masaoka Shiki's useless too, for that matter. When you read "Letter to a *Tanka* Poet," it's full of arguments and justifications, but the stuff he writes is just the same old thing. No, there's no hope of anything new in *tanka* coming from the poets writing today and that's a fact!

"Er, *tanka*... You mean...?"

"I mean small-form free verse, that's what I mean. I'm giving a new slant to the old word – I made this up myself. The old *waka* has too many stupid rules about language and form. In order to breathe new life into this boring old 5-7-5-7-7 form, we have to tie in Japanese poetry and the new free-verse style together."

"Yes, I think I understand. I see what you mean now by 'a revolution in *waka*.' I mean, by this idea of a new form of poem you call '*tanka*'..."

Takino herself liked to read and write *waka*, so she was interested in the subject. She threw herself into trying to make sense of her husband's beliefs and ideas.

"But it's all rather difficult," she added, looking charmingly puzzled. "Will there ever be somebody who really writes poems of that sort?"

"Will there be? There already is!" laughed Tekkan, pointing to himself. "Omachi Keigetsu, Kaneko Kun'en, Masaoka Shiki, Sasaki Nobutsuna – they're all just a bunch of worthless good-for-nothings. None of them can hold a candle to me. Right now, if you're talking real genius, I'm the only one around. The rest of them are just talentless riffraff."

Takino was at a loss how to take this braggadocio her husband indulged in. She had never before come across a man who would make such strident assertions and speak so wildly. There was no one, at least in her acquaintance to date, who spouted such hyperbole as this. But she used her woman's intuition to draw her own conclusions.

It seemed to her that Tekkan's arrogant bluster was a kind of act for the benefit of his new wife. A smart woman, rather than despise him for it, instinct led her to respect this husband of hers.

"But Masaoka Shiki and lots of others besides added words of support and praise in your book, *The Four Directions*. Even Mori Ogai…" she said with a smile. "So surely you shouldn't be saying such things about them."

"Ah yes, but that's different. Mori Ogai recognizes my worth. He can see I'm better than him, it seems. One genius can recognize another, you see. But Ogai aside, look at all these abysmal writers who've gotten into the newspapers and magazines and made themselves a name and a following."

Takino was lost for words.

"Those guys have power, they have influence. You've got to play their game." Tekkan chuckled.

Back when they were still on the train to Tokyo, Tekkan had suddenly turned to his wife and suggested they get off when it pulled up at Hiroshima Station.

A man in ragged clothing came over and greeted him.

"This is Wakabayashi. A friend of mine."

Takino was introduced, and Tekkan revealed the fact that she was his new wife. As Takino gracefully greeted the first friend of her husband's she had met, the man took in her silk coat, the round glistening twist of hair with not a strand out of place, and her pearl-like face. While he spoke to Tekkan, he kept stealing covert glances at her, evidently struck by her beauty.

He was shifty-eyed, shabby and undependable-looking. Could Tekkan really have intended to meet him here beforehand? But he had told neither her nor her parents that they planned to stop off in Hiroshima.

When they were settled in at an inn by the station, Tekkan handed the man part of the money he had received from the Hayashis, and the two of them went off together for a drink.

Left shivering in the room by herself and waiting for their return, Takino felt so forlorn she wanted to weep.

Late that night, Tekkan came back alone, quite drunk.

"How much money's left, Takino?"

Takino guilelessly spread out before him all the funds that her generous parents had given her to start her new life.

"This won't be enough." Breathing sake fumes, Tekkan went on casually, "You'll have to go back home and bring some more. I'll wait here."

Takino couldn't believe her ears.

"More money? But we've got enough here to be able to rent a house in Tokyo and live for a while…"

"Wrong. What use is chicken feed like this? It's real money I want."

"But surely we should get settled in Tokyo first, and then maybe write a letter…"

"No way! This is urgent. I'm telling you, go back right now and fetch some money. You're the apple of your parents' eyes, their wonderful eldest daughter. They'll hand over whatever you ask for." Tekkan laughed.

Takino was astonished. "But darling…"

"Shut up! Stop all this 'But but but'!"

Within a few days of marriage, Takino was learning what a short fuse Tekkan had.

"Certainly, I'll do as you say. But what will you use all that money for?"

"I'm going to put out a magazine. I'm going to found a magazine that will spark a whole movement to reform the *waka*, that will be the darling of the new age. I'm the one destined to set the flame alight – but first I need money. I can't move without it. Your parents are bound to come on board if you explain the money's in order to launch a genius on the world. All that money just rotting away in the lonely countryside there – if I set it to work, I'll do it real justice. It'll make the money happy!" He gave a laugh.

"Is your friend a literary man too?"

"No, not him. He's…" Tekkan suddenly shut his mouth. Then he went on, "He's a fellow I borrowed money from in Korea, so I've repaid him. We used to hang out together. Sake, songs, women… Ah, good old Korea. Those were the days. I had this girl by the name of Jade."

Tekkan pulled Takino roughly to him. The innocent bride shrank from her husband's rough caresses. Her body stiffened, as if to fend off a blow.

4

No sooner had the Hayashis settled down again with a sigh of relief after seeing the newly-wed couple on its way than they were astonished to find their daughter had returned. And when they heard what she had to tell them, their hearts bled for her.

"I just had this feeling something wasn't quite right," her mother declared. "There was always something I couldn't quite understand about Mr. Yosano, but your father would insist on having his way in the matter…" She longed to keep Takino there rather than have her return to Hiroshima.

Her father, however, was a thoroughly good and upright man, and he maintained his kindness towards Tekkan.

"This is the sort of emergency that does happen from time to time in a man's career. He must have some compelling reason for this request – and he's putting a lot of faith in our Takino, it seems. He did beg me virtually in tears to adopt him as son-in-law, after all. Well, there you are, I'll lend him what he wants and help him out… But listen, Takino."

"Yes?"

"If you don't want to go back to him, I don't mind. I'll leave it up to you."

Takino hung her head in thought. She recalled the gaiety and high spirits with which she had left this house of her birth with her new husband. She had set off on her new life, had she not, with the blessings and good wishes of her parents and sisters.

It was not her intention to admit defeat and return so quickly.

Her heart swelled, too, with a determined urge to watch over Tekkan as his wife. Whether this was what could be called love, Takino did not yet know.

She sensed that the path ahead would hold pain and suffering far worse than any she had so far tasted – but she was young, and there was a desire to pit herself with all her might against the fate that she had been dealt.

"Mother, Father... I'll go back. I'm sorry to have caused you this trouble... but if I left him now it would all feel so pointless somehow, and I'm sure he wouldn't accept it either..."

"So there we are," sighed her mother.

"Well, at any rate, Takino, you can come back any time it gets to be too much for you. Don't torment yourself. But I can see that Tekkan fellow is quite deeply attached to you, and it would surely be hard on him to have to give you up now," her father said.

Takino's little sisters gathered innocently around, oblivious to the anxiety and hesitancy that clouded her face, and pleaded with her.

"When you get settled in Tokyo you must invite us there, Taki. Promise?"

Brought up in ease and wealth as they were, these girls could only imagine a brilliant life would await them in Tokyo.

And so Takino went back to her husband, bearing a large sum of her parents' money for him.

This was not merely money left to rot away in the countryside, "money that would serve better to launch a genius on the world," as Tekkan had sneeringly declared it. More than simply money, it was an expression of the wonderful generosity and boundless compassion that Takino's parents felt for her. She was still innocent in the ways of the world, a girl brought up without knowledge of the significance of money, but she sensed the scorn behind Tekkan's words, his arrogance and sense of superiority. Her intuition saw through him, and understood that although his boundless self-regard would shrink to timid cowering in the face of adversity, if anyone showed him goodwill it would immediately inflate to a haughty arrogance and scorn for his well-wishers.

In Takino's heart stirred the first faint lack of faith in her husband.

One can find aspects of Tekkan's character that allow sympathy for him – at least he could be perceived as possessing the integrity of his honesty – but for this innocent girl of twenty-one, such cool clarity and generosity of spirit was impossible.

Takino's family would continue to be Tekkan's financial sponsor, even once Akiko had become his legal wife.

To return to the story, the new couple arrived in Tokyo, and to begin with settled themselves at an inn in Karasumori in Shiba. After seeing to the problem of Tekkan's dress and appearance (for he really had been penniless and incredibly shabby), they moved at last to a new home, number forty-five, six Kaji-cho.

The house had one eight-mat room, one six-mat room and one four-and-a-half mat room, plus a small entrance hall and kitchen, and the rent was six *yen* a month.

This was the place that would later become the Tokyo New Poetry Society headquarters, and where the magazine *Myojo* would be produced.

As soon as Takino had settled down she began to set up house, buying household goods and kitchen implements, organizing clothing and other smaller goods to be sent from home and setting them in place – in general creating the kind of home expected of a good wife. She also employed as servant a woman of around fifty, Kawamoto Moyo. Moyo was a formidable woman, clever and worldly wise, who had been the wife of a sumo wrestler named Inasegawa and had once run her own brothel. She proved a hard worker, and she looked after "the young mistress" well; she had a soft spot for Takino, with her refined and well-brought-up ways.

It seemed to Moyo that this young couple were a most unusual pairing.

When she compared the kind and generous Takino, honest and above board in all things, to Tekkan, so temperamental, petulant and short-tempered, so quick to despise others and change his tune depending on whom he was with, Moyo could not but take the wife's side. She had heard that Tekkan taught poetry, but privately she couldn't make out what he did at all. Having been madam of a brothel herself, it was obvious to her that Tekkan was quite a playboy, and shameless in his relations with women. These were the only terms in which she viewed men, so any talents or other qualities of character Tekkan had were irrelevant to her.

What was more, Tekkan was quite unable to earn any money, and was making ends meet by letting his wife's family support them. This alone lowered Moyo's opinion of such a husband.

For Tekkan and Takino, there was no real honeymoon. The money Takino had brought back from her parents was gone in the blink of an eye. The acquaintance Tekkan had met up with in Hiroshima came asking for money again, unknown young dinner guests were always dropping by (Tekkan introduced them as poet friends), advances were paid against the magazine's publication, and each time poor Takino swallowed her pride and wrote home for money yet again.

In November 1899, Tekkan founded the Tokyo New Poetry Society. The members were people he had worked with at Asakasha, and poets he knew on an individual basis. The moment had arrived to hoist the flag of *tanka* reform at last. Among those who joined were Kurishima Sagaromo, Hiraki Hakusei, Kubota Utsubo and Kawada Hosui. In gratitude for Tekkan's earlier praise and support for his own poetry, Susukida Kyukin provided a congratulatory poem.

> Great scholars have chosen you, I hear
> and held a poetry gathering in the capital.
> May you gain a famous name
> and long be wreathed
> in laurel leaves.

The first issue of *Myojo*, the instrument of the New Poetry Society, appeared in April the following year, 1900. It was in tabloid format, with sixteen pages of four columns each, and on its cover was printed in bold lettering, "Editor in Chief: Yosano Tekkan."

The publisher's name was given as Hayashi Takino. This first issue contained poems by Tekkan himself, including "Drinking Long," as well as works submitted by Kawai, but the jewel in its crown was

"Traveller's Lament," sent in by Shimazaki Toson, who was then a schoolteacher in Komoro in the mountainous Shinshu area. I have already described how this poem, with its opening line, "By the old castle of Komoro," so excited Akiko and other young people who read this issue of *Myojo*.

Myojo expanded. As the headquarters of the New Poetry Society, the house was constantly full to bursting and bustling with activity. There were dinner guests dropping by and an endless stream of visitors – whenever someone arrived, out came the sake, and talk of literature and manuscripts went on till all hours of the night.

Poetry competitions were sometimes held at the house, and sometimes Ochiai Naobumi would come along and treat everyone to tea cakes.

Myojo's reputation was high, and as supporters and members flocked to join, the flow of visitors increased yet further, so that Takino was forced to write home each month with a fresh request for funds. This was not only for the two of them – money was also poured into the publication of *Myojo*.

Tekkan had no time to spare worrying over Takino's private hardships. His own inner energies were entirely absorbed by *Myojo*. From his point of view, his ambitions were being fulfilled on several fronts – he had gotten himself a beautiful and adorable wife, had thereby also secured the money to bring out the magazine that had been his cherished dream, and was now its founding editor. He was exultant, dazzled by his own triumphs and, naturally enough, he was too preoccupied to give any thought to how his wife might be feeling.

Gradually Takino grew more isolated from him. She had never dreamed that such a married life awaited her as a new bride. Could it be that Tekkan had been more interested in the money he could gain through her than in herself when he married her? Naïve and virtuous though she was, Takino had begun to be tormented by this doubt.

The young men and women who gathered around *Myojo* held Tekkan in the greatest esteem, as the founding leader of a new movement. His words had an almost magical power to draw others to him. Large numbers of young readers loved his poetry. As he had intended, it had indeed become a reigning star in the heavens, its effects reaching beyond the literary circles to stir the wider world.

"So what do you think? What's your opinion of my poems in this issue?" He was sensitive to what was said of his work, and he went to endless pains to promote *Myojo* and with it his own name.

Tekkan had not a thing to call his own – not relatives nor money. All he had in the world to rely on were his own talents, and the young people who gathered around in support of him. He believed, therefore, that he must sell his own name in order to make the next move. But his driving urgency and ambition were incomprehensible to Takino. She would never understand, or even try to understand, the male world and its masculine imperatives. "He and I simply think differently." This is how she put it to herself when she finally put her finger on the discomfort she felt. It was a belief she held to with stubborn certainty.

Myojo sold well – in fact, it was nothing short of a hit.

The print run soon hit the several thousand mark, and it took three or four days just to write out the names and addresses of subscribers. In the rented house in Kaji-cho that held the New Poetry Society, the air was thick with youthful energy.

The fresh new poetic style of *Myojo* struck a chord with a new generation, but another factor in its success was undoubtedly Tekkan's determined publicity for it.

In those days there was a brand of cigarettes with the English name of "Hero." One pack cost six *sen*. It was Tekkan who came up with the slogan, "You can buy *Myojo* for the price of a Hero."

(It is interesting to recall the intriguing coincidence that a few decades later, in the Taisho period, the author Kikuchi Kan promoted his new literary magazine *Bungei Shunju* with the slogan, "A magazine for the price of Shikishima" – Shikishima was another cigarette brand. These two men even shared the same given name. And while Kikuchi's management skills are well known, there can be no doubt that Yosano in his time also displayed excellent business savvy.)

To give an example, Tekkan devoted a column of *Myojo* to younger people, under the title "School Years," encouraging submissions of poetry and even calligraphy and thereby expanding the magazine's readership range.

Another example: in January of that year he became selecting editor for the poetry column in the magazine *Bunko*, and diverted the submissions through to *Myojo*, thereby managing to poach for his own magazine.

Tekkan had always calculated that the best way of increasing circulation was to swell the female readership of the magazine. This showed remarkable insight for the time.

At this stage, Tekkan was teaching literature at Atomi Women's College as a side job, and he created a new market for the magazine by publishing the poems he encouraged the girls to write. This is one of the reasons for the frequent appearance of female writers in its pages from early on. In fact, both Ho Akiko and Yamakawa Tomiko felt the urge to join the society and submit their poems because of the impressive list of women's names among contributors. Tekkan's idea had hit the mark, and became a powerful priming agent to draw fresh readers.

But such resourceful journalistic skills did not impress Takino – she found them merely petty and frivolous, and hardly what was appropriate for an artist and literary man. Honest and upright as she was, Takino remained unconvinced by Tekkan's tendency to talk big and throw his weight around. It made her cold and uncomfortable to hear her husband loudly proclaiming things she could see very well must be lies, and this sensation hardened in her heart into a stiff resistance.

For Tekkan, these words of his created a lovely aura that straddled reality and fantasy, much like his talk of the tiger-hunting and womanizing days in Korea. They constituted a romantic reality that far transcended mere facts. But he was reaching for rainbows without watching his feet. He was a dupe to his own fantasies, firm in the belief that everyone around him, his wife included, would willingly follow him in his flights to this fictional reality.

"I'm the only true genius!"

"The '*Myojo*' Age' is upon us! The history of Japanese poetry is about to be rewritten by me and my magazine."

Whenever he sat around drinking with his young followers, this was the sort of braggadocio he spouted. He acted the Meiji *littérateur* by behaving with a disciple's reverence and courtesy towards his superiors, such as Ochiai Naobumi, while treating the young followers and fellow-poets around him with relaxed familiarity.

"There are no superiors and inferiors in the realm of literature. We all ride forward together, companions in the battle."

In this, Tekkan was far freer in his thinking than his contemporaries. He liked young people (being the emotional man he was, he had strong likes and dislikes), and they, in turn, adored him. Look at this poem of Tekkan's that they would chant at New Poetry Society events:

> A man am I
> a man of will
> a man of fame and of the sword
> a man of poems and of love
> and ah, a man of anguish.

The New Poetry Society's manifesto read as follows:

1. We believe that we are born with the talent to delight in poetic beauty. Hence, our poems are our pleasure. We would be ashamed to write poetry in pursuit of mere empty fame.
2. We take pleasure in the poetry of the ancients. But we can never bear to till the same ground that the poets of old once broke.
3. We will place our poems before each other. These poems of ours will not imitate the poetry of old but will be our own, nay, will be each his own invention.
4. Our poetry is Japanese, but it belongs to the new Japanese nation, to the nation of Meiji. It is a Japanese poetry that has shaken off the style of the ancient anthologies.
5. We delight in individual creative expression, both in choice of poetic content and in melodic style.
6. We hereby declare that the name for this union of self-willed compatriots, who gather to impose their wills upon the world, is the New Poetry Society.

Myojo was flush with the youthful ambition of spirited new poets.

5

Myojo continued to grow and develop. Within a mere five issues, it had moved beyond the early newspaper-format booklet to something that bore little resemblance to its beginnings. It was now a magazine of 68 pages printed in broadsheet style, with a price of 14 *sen*. The paper was of high quality, and the success of the magazine owed not a little to its bold and original illustrations. These were not the typical colour prints of old, but innovative pictures with a Western feel to them, balancing and echoing the contents they were paired with, and full of stylish youthfulness. They were from the hand of a young artist by the name of Ichijo Narumi, who had chanced by Tekkan's house one day. Tekkan was quite fond of Ichijo, but in discovering his particular talents, once again Tekkan's true genius can be seen.

In considering why *Myojo* should have gained such explosive popularity, one must take into account the intellectual culture prevalent at the time. The intellectual leader of the time, a critic by the name of Takayama Chogyu, had recently begun to propound Nietzsche's ideas. He had devised a set of guiding principles to break up the old ethics-based school of literary theory, by explaining Nietzsche's philosophy in layman's terms.

"The purpose of humanity does not lie in promoting the interests and happiness of the average man. On the contrary, it lies in the production of a minority of ideal humans, to wit, geniuses, or *Ubermensch*… Alas, the present reform pays no thought to the arts and religion. The words and deeds of the vulgar, who hold to no other ideal than that of profit and loss and whose concern is merely with the national polity, cannot but earn our distrust. – Where is Education, where is Ethics, if the essential needs of man are held of no account?"

These words were published in *Taiyo*, one of the leading magazines in its day, put out by Hakubunkan. Public thinkers such as Takayama Chogyu and Omachi Keigetsu were the darling opinion-makers of their day, men who dazzlingly propounded their arguments and ideas in this eminent journal, which swept all before it in the journalistic world of the first two decades of the twentieth century.

Chogyu argued the importance of the dignity of self and individuality. Somewhat after the period discussed here, he published a piece in *Taiyo* titled "On the Beautiful Life."

"Many of us know naught of what it is to lay our lives on the line in the pursuit of knowledge, or to dedicate ourselves absolutely to charity, but is humanity's value not slighter yet when it comes to romantic love?"

Chogyu put forward a concept that deeply appealed to youth, that of "liberation of the instincts." His philosophy provided an outlet for the seething but formless, pent-up frustrations of the new age. The hearts of the young could no longer be ensnared by the literature of feudal ethics and the time-honoured conflict of moral obligations versus human feeling. The floodgates had been smashed open, and the young were now pouring forth in a deluge towards this brave new world of freedom.

(It should be said, however, that although Chogyu had the talent as public intellectual to anticipate the trends of the age, it is questionable whether he had the ability to judge literary works themselves. He was unable to appreciate Akiko's seminal publication, *Tangled Hair*. There is irony in the fact that he damned *Tangled Hair*, which in fact was an expression of his own philosophy, as "lewd in spirit and shallow in conception, unbearably common and clichéd." Compare this with Ogai, who was then beginning to dominate the literary world with his penetrating commentary and profound scholarship while at the same time engaging in his own creative writing and who, when *Tangled Hair* appeared, would heap unstinting praise on it.)

Myojo attained an assured position in the literary world as a new and unique *tanka* society. One can imagine Tekkan's sense of triumph.

But although the magazine sold, it was not such a straightforward matter to actually make money. The household finances were under constant strain from the permanent table guests and the unending stream of visitors, and what is more, the magazine itself was not the kind of thing to turn a profit. So Takino had to go on appealing to her parents for money as before, and found herself having to pawn all but a couple of her kimonos.

Let me live like others
though my prayers
are severed –
ah, so pitiful
the cracks on my lover's hands.

Tekkan was deeply concerned. He was forcing his Takino, who could have enjoyed a life of absolute ease and comfort if she had stayed back in Yamaguchi, to suffer the cruel winds of the harsh world.

"I feel badly for you. Takino. But you married me in the knowledge that you'd be a poet's wife, so please bear with the hardships of our poverty. I have faith that your happiness can make up for it all."

"Is that so?" replied Takino, her voice hard. "So you really believe that a wife can be happy when her husband is involved with other women?"

"Hey, cut the funny talk. You're telling me you think I have some other woman?"

"I don't know. But…" Takino halted, as if words failed her.

Timid, honest and gullible, she was wounded to see Tekkan finding obvious pleasure in what were little short of love letters sent him by the ardently worshipful young literary girls who flocked around *Myojo*. It was true, in fact, that Tekkan was having numerous love affairs.

"Don't be crazy! And even if I did fall for someone, you're different. You can remain calm and sure in the knowledge that you're Yosano Tekkan's wife."

"You're saying that I should remain silent, however many lovers you take?"

"Poets are born to love, to anguish. They mustn't be confused with the average hoi polloi. Look at Byron, look at Heine. How can we poets be measured with the finicky logic of stuffy old Confucianists and would-be moralists, eh? Byron and Heine had more lovers than you can count!"

Takino was at heart a cool person, and the more her husband ranted the more she despised his infantilism and his ludicrous contradictions. She had grown up without brothers, and to her, men were essentially incomprehensible creatures.

Since early in her marriage, she had seen girls come to his home and throw themselves weeping at his feet. Fearing his wife's eyes, Tekkan would sometimes hurry them out with him. According to the maid Moyo, these were "not your usual girls or ladies." Such events, small in themselves, slowly accumulated in Takino's heart and grew into something hard and bitter.

Takino was far from uneducated, and she had some idea of who Byron and Heine were. However, she could not see why her husband should be allowed to claim the same rights and authority as these romantic poets from a distant land. It was different, however, for Tekkan. He felt a kind of emotional self-intoxication that made his blood dance at the very thought of these poets.

"No doubt Byron did have lots of lovers, but I've read other things about him too, such as that he threw himself into the revolution in Greece. Surely you have to consider that aspect of him as well. It seems to me that that's why he's such a fine person, not because of his many lovers."

"Byron could be a hero like that precisely because he loved. A poet's love isn't like the average person's. It moves the world."

"So as long as you're a poet you should be forgiven for making your wife suffer by taking lots of lovers and being censured by the world?"

"You have a very crass way of seeing things. You're just resorting to cold logic. You can't understand a poet by sermonizing, you know. Poetry is a matter of heart, not head."

"Poets are no different from other ordinary human beings, we all have to live in the same world. It seems to me that selfish and wilful behaviour mustn't be tolerated, whoever you may be."

"To hell with that crass and ridiculous 'world' of yours! How can the uncultivated know anything of poetry?"

"For heaven's sake, stop shouting. Moyo can hear you."

They were forever at cross-purposes.

It would seem that a man who is deserted by a woman is more deeply shocked than a woman deserted by a man, perhaps because a woman's self-respect can find a way around it, but a man's will feel the betrayal as a direct hit. Tekkan could feel that Takino's coldness towards him was growing, and he suffered. Bold and brave though he looked, Tekkan was a weakling who could not bear to see the woman he loved becoming distant from him.

Tekkan never considered that the blame lay with himself. Instead, he bewailed the fact that Takino was such a boring, ordinary sort of person, who hadn't the ability to comprehend either art or himself. Why, he wondered, could she not share with him the exultant fulfilment and delight to be had from giving oneself over to the world of poetry and beauty?

"There you are, you see, you always start shouting the moment we disagree. Nothing's solved by a man in your position, with all these people who look up to you, going into such childish sulks, you know."

It disturbed Takino that Tekkan was so prone to argument. He would fly into a temper as soon as anyone differed from him, and start shouting them down with increasing vehemence. She was astonished at this infantile wilfulness in him.

"With all these people's eyes on you, you really must learn to be a little less stubborn…"

"It's who I am."

"You can't just go on getting out of it that way. You have to discipline yourself and develop a little more amicability."

"Amicability! You must be out of your mind! Do you think a poet can be *amicable*, for god's sake?"

"So you're telling me poets are special creatures?"

"Of course we are! We poets can't live in the same world as ordinary folk. *We* soar to the heavens."

"So poets are allowed to lie, and deceive, and hurt others?"

"Are you still harping on about Asada Sadako?"

Tekkan sighed. Takino fell into a stubborn silence.

It seems to me that Asada Sadako was the cause of the initial rift between the couple. One day a letter had arrived from Takino's mother, a letter so full of maternal bewailing that she could not show it to Tekkan.

For the fact was that, after they had seen their daughter off to Tokyo with her new husband, the Hayashis heard some shocking news.

The eldest daughter of a nearby prosperous family like their own had been seduced by Tekkan, made pregnant, and abandoned, and in their despair and shame the Asadas had declared Tekkan a loathsome scoundrel.

Needless to say, there was a good deal of truth missing from this completely one-sided account, which paid no heed to Tekkan's side of the story. Irresponsible rumour though it was, it was more than enough to wound the Hayashis to the quick. Her mother's letter was redolent with her appalled reaction.

"Tekkan gave not the slightest hint of any of this when he came to call on us that day. We had absolutely no idea that he could be such a heartless man. *It's not possible* that the story of the Asadas isn't true, and your father and I are simply horrified by it all."

The letter went on at length to harp about how she'd heard that Takino had been prone to beriberi on account of the water, that she'd had to pawn her kimonos, that she had trouble making ends meet in running the household, and ended by lamenting this man to whom they had married her. But what wounded Takino most deeply was that Tekkan had never so much as breathed a word about Sadako when he came seeking her hand. She could not forgive him for hiding his past.

I'm not just being jealous because I love this man, she thought. What I hate is the way he's chosen to deceive me.

This was how she interpreted her feelings, but the truth was perhaps that they were the flipside of her jealousy. Her understanding of men and women was still quite girlish, and she was overwhelmed by her own tumultuous feelings.

"You apparently even had a child with her. And then you abandoned her…"

"That's not true. She was the one who left. I only–"

"And then you came straight round to our house, didn't you. I was the only one you loved, you said, when in fact you'd left Sadako only a month earlier."

"But–"

"Why didn't you tell any of this to Father? I'm not angry about Sadako, you know, what I can't get over is that you deceived us."

"I wasn't deceiving you, I was going to tell you later. I'm sorry. I never meant the story to reach your father's ears in this way. No, truly. But actually, Sadako—"

"I don't care about Sadako. What I care about is why you kept it a secret. That's what I hate."

On and on, round and round she went, like a madwoman. It angered Tekkan. He was frustrated with this stiff, inflexible nature of hers. Yet at the same time he understood it, and loved it. It was just that she was honest and upright. This is what made her so petty and intolerant.

What's more, Takino was pregnant. Man of feeling that he was, Tekkan could not but pour his whole love into this mother-to-be and her unborn child.

In August that year, 1900, it was arranged that Tekkan would visit Osaka.

Myojo had a rival literary journal, *Shinsei*, run by the young twenty-three-year-old Sato Kikko. His assistant, Takasu Hojiro, had been one of the members of *Yoshiashigusa*, and had come to Tokyo with Sato's help.

Sato had both talent and good fortune as a publisher. He was a rising star in the publishing world who had rapidly made his name in recent times by putting out a number of books of critical essays and novels, and each of them had been a hit. *Myojo* tended to have the lead over *Shinsei* in popularity, but still Tekkan was occasionally invited to submit poems to the other magazine.

When he called round to *Shinsei*'s Tokyo office in Nishiki-cho in Kanda, he was introduced to Takasu, who of course was aware that Tekkan was poetry editor for Osaka's *Yoshiashigusa*.

"Why not go down to Osaka?" he urged. "You should meet the *Yoshiashigusa* group."

"That's an idea. I also have a good friend in Sakai, Kono Tetsunan."

The suggestion interested Tekkan. It would also be useful for *Myojo* if he went to Osaka and met some of its readers. His name had been very familiar to the young people of Osaka since the *Yoshiashigusa* connection was established, and this would be a chance to collect more members and associates for his own group.

The idea was discussed, and it was decided that Tekkan would give a lecture in Osaka on August 5th. On the 2nd, he set off from Tokyo.

Now heavily pregnant, Takino sweated over the sewing of a new cotton kimono and summer coat for her departing husband. She was a wonderfully attentive wife, well-trained in such everyday domestic consideration.

Weighed down by her pregnancy in a summer hot enough to be oppressive in itself, she yet took meticulous care of her appearance. Her hair was done up in an elegant curve, with not a strand out of place. Takino's utter beauty gave Tekkan pleasure, but he also felt uncomfortable at her perfectionism and fastidious way with things, that struck him as somehow common. She was much admired by everyone who came to visit the New Poetry Society, and for her part she did her very best to be hospitable to all within the constraints of their poverty. If Tekkan felt ill at ease with this impressively dedicated wife, to the world at large she was a cause for wonder.

Yet Tekkan loved Takino, there is no doubt.

> What I love –
> a maiden with her hair up,
> whale soup,
> the Fudo mantra,
> white plum blossoms.

In this poem of his, the expression "maiden" is the old word meaning "wife." His later wife was of course Akiko, but this poem appeared in the first issue of *Myojo*, and is therefore from the time before he had met Akiko. Clearly, it refers to Takino.

Akiko is symbolized by the tangled hair which is the title of her famous collection of poetry, but it seems to me that Takino's symbol is the elegantly knotted hairstyle she chose. Of course she also put her hair up in other styles from time to time, but I believe that this *marumage* style, which symbolized a married woman in those days, was her preference. She still went by the family name of Hayashi, but it seems in her heart Takino felt herself truly Tekkan's wife.

Tekkan, for his part, praised her unstintingly.

Like a maiden
who from shame
will not leave the bathtub –
a white iris
reflected in the water
• • •
How lovely the sight
of my wife coming home
drenched
from the pouring rain
in the month of mauve wisteria

"You've remembered your medicine, dear?"

"Mm. You should worry about yourself, not me. It won't be long now."

"Yes. And do be careful what you eat in this hot weather. We don't want that old stomach trouble to cause problems again. When will you be home?"

"I'll be about a week, ten days at the longest. I'll be right back."

"Take good care."

Tekkan set off in high spirits. As he sat in the train carriage he called up before his eyes the beautiful white lotus face of his wife. He was later to give the names of other white flowers to lovers – white bush clover for Akiko, white lily for Tomiko – but now it was the face of his beloved wife Takino that filled his heart as, minute by minute, the train carried him closer to Osaka, where a new fate awaited him.

PART V. THE TASTE OF LOVE

1

Nakayama Kyoan and Kobayashi Masaharu (who used the pen name Tenmin) set about organizing Tekkan's visit to western Japan.

According to one story, Tekkan was meant to arrive in Osaka well in advance of the scheduled lecture time, but as Kobayashi was in the process of making arrangements, a telegram arrived announcing that he couldn't come. The young Kobayashi and Nakayama were indignant at this, and apparently sent a reproachful note asking if it was typical of literary men to break promises in this wanton fashion.

In reply, Tekkan wrote frankly to exculpate himself by explaining that he had had his personal belongings repossessed by a loan shark from whom he had borrowed to support *Myojo*. Since money worries were a permanent feature of life for him at the time, this may actually have been true. The story melted Kobayashi's heart, and from then on his friendship and support for Tekkan never wavered.

Tekkan arrived in Osaka on 3rd August 1900, and put up at Hirai Inn in Kitahama. From there, he sent a note to Kono Tetsunan, saying "I shall wait to hear from you whether I should go there, or you come here. Please pass on the message to Gangetsu and Miss Ho."

It was at the height of the heat of the following day when Akiko, Tetsunan and Gangetsu responded to this message and went to meet Tekkan at Hirai Inn. Gangetsu had met Tekkan once before, with Kawai Suimei and others, when Tekkan had come to Sakai two years earlier, but this was the first time for Akiko to be introduced.

With racing heart, she climbed the stairs behind Tetsunan as he made his way into the room on the second floor. As was her habit, her maid Outa kept herself humbly in the background out in the corridor, in deference to the important personage within.

"Come on in, Akiko."

Encouraged by Tetsunan, she tremulously came through the door, and knelt politely, hands on the floor before her knees.

A cool breeze wafted through the room, and Akiko's eyes immediately took in the sight of Tekkan at the far end, seated comfortably and leaning against the pillar of the alcove. Her first impression was of "someone rather monk-ish."

He was wearing a splash-pattern white summer kimono with a black silk gauze *haori* coat; she thought him a beautiful, tall man, with keen eyes, a fine pale complexion and a long torso. Flushed with nervous excitement, she recalled no more than this.

"Miss Ho?"

Tekkan greeted her with a crisp, clear voice.

"I've been hearing a lot about you, and I'm happy to meet you at last."

Akiko felt sweat break out, and it was all she could do to place her fingertips neatly together on the *tatami* matting and bow deeply in response.

Besides the five or six *Yoshiashigusa* members in the room – Takasu Hojiro, who had come back from Tokyo; Kaneo Shisai, the head of Osaka's new publishing house, Bun'endo; Kobayashi Tenmin and others – there was a beautiful, intelligent-looking young woman who smilingly beckoned Akiko over to her.

"Do come over here…"

She wore a thin white summer kimono tied with a silk gauze obi on which was embroidered a design of morning glories and bamboo fence, and she exuded the glowing vitality of a beautiful lily. She briskly drew up a cushion and broke into delightful laughter as she went on, "Here, please, do sit down… no, closer to Sensei. That's all right, isn't it, Sensei? We two will sit here just like acolytes around the Buddha, and the others will be just like…" She turned teasingly to Tekkan as she spoke. An ingenuously cheerful person, Akiko thought her.

"Just like what?" Tekkan enquired.

"Oh, I get it," Hojiro broke in, "we'll all be just like the Buddha's useless mob of five hundred disciples," and everyone laughed.

They all cooled themselves with cups of cold tea, and the conversation was moving on to a discussion of Tekkan's lecture the next day, when he suddenly broke in.

"Oh yes, I've just realized this is the first time for Miss Yamakawa and Miss Ho to meet." He turned and introduced them to each other, adding, "A meeting of two accomplished women of poetry."

Akiko had realized straight away who this young woman must be. And she had taken a liking to her.

What she responded to so warmly was that Tomiko Yamakawa was just as she had imagined her, a beautiful girl with a gentle face. Akiko liked beautiful people. But it disturbed her a little that Tekkan should be so much more relaxed and intimate with Tomiko than with herself, despite the fact that this was the first time he too had met her. This small flicker of jealousy only served to add impetus to her friendly response to Tomiko.

"But come to that, I think I've met you before Akiko. I used to come into Sakai for study when I lived in the area, and I went past your shop Surugaya, you see."

That day, Tekkan cheerfully wrote a poem on a strip of paper and gave it to Akiko.

> Ten years now
> since I saw you,
> girlish hair hung down.
> Do not hold it cheap
> this fate that brings us face to face.

Akiko read this with blushing face, and mumbled her thanks, but privately she felt this couldn't be her. The lovely girl with her hair down must surely have been one of her older sisters, she thought. But she was not the carefree sort to mention this lightly. She simply smiled reticently. The fact is, she had become interested in and attracted to this man.

Akiko was twenty-three at the time, Tomiko twenty-two, and Tekkan twenty-eight. Sensei and followers, all still young.

The next day, August 5th, Tekkan gave his talk in the conference room of the Osaka Publishers Guild.

It was a small room, seating an audience of about fifty at most, but Tekkan's passionate lecture on the new wave of *waka* writing galvanized its young listeners.

"All standards, all rules of *tanka* writing are meaningless. The poems that each of you writes as an individual are good in themselves. Poems must be poems in your own personal style, the poems of the individual, of the self. You must write directly from your own inner flame, the poem must be that person's cry, that person's life. What worth is there in a poem that does not sing from the heart? What worth can be found in the work of those who do not write from the heart? The new age of poetry, the poetry of men, of youth, is about laying your life bare and letting the heart speak forth. We must smash all those niggling conventions and trade secrets. Not a jot of such things is necessary. All you need do is to transcribe a cry from the heart, each in your own way…"

Tekkan was known as the "Young Warrior of the New Wave." The invigorating effect of his impressive bearing reinforced people's sense of the gallant young soldier, while his powerful theory of poetry struck his youthful listeners deeply.

Among the audience was a smattering of women, but Akiko was unable to attend. Her father would not allow it.

The following day, through the good offices of Gangetsu and Tetsunan, Tekkan was brought to the Jumyokan restaurant in Hamadera, where a poetry-writing competition was held. Thanks as usual to the intercession of her mother, Akiko was able to go to this event. Another factor was that Tomiko agreed to come to the house and take her.

"We were waiting for you yesterday, Akiko. I'm sorry you couldn't make it. It was a great talk."

Tomiko spoke almost resentfully. She was dressed that day in a light summer robe of Akashi crepe, with an obi of wisteria purple silk gauze and black crepe-lined satin, and her hair was up in the style known as the Margaret coil, revealing her white nape. She looked quite the neat young lady, and Akiko's mother was reassured that such a decent-looking girl had arrived to escort her daughter. Tomiko was as relaxed and friendly as if she had known Akiko for ages, referring to her as "elder sis," though Akiko was a mere year older.

"You're so lucky, Tomiko, being able to go out whenever you like…" Akiko mumbled the words, shyly aware of her Osaka accent. She was both quick-eared and clever, and could easily imitate Tomiko's Tokyo style of speech, but she was still too inexperienced to make the attempt. "My dad just won't let me out anywhere. But he said yes today. I don't need to hurry back, he said…"

Akiko's hair was up in the *gingko-gaeshi* style, and she wore a blue splash-pattern kimono, matched with a purple crepe-lined satin and *yuzen*-dyed obi. The fashionable pair of young town ladies chatted happily to Tsune as she hailed a rickshaw, and off they went, to catch the Nankai train to Hamadera Park. Watching them go off together, Akiko's mother was struck by the tender picture of animated affection they presented.

All they talked about on the way there was "Tekkan-sensei." They had both begun to feel an adoring admiration perilously close to passionate love for him, and it intensified the friendly intimacy they felt for each other to share what was in their hearts.

"Hey, sis, tell me, what did you think when you first set eyes on Sensei?" Tomiko was the talker, the one who stoked the flames.

"I thought he looked a bit like a monk. What about you, Tomiko?"

"Me too. But softer, kinder somehow…"

"Exactly. And when you hear him talk, there's this really stern, sharp manliness to him–"

"Yes, yes, exactly!" Tomiko gripped Akiko's hand ecstatically.

"Oh, he's just so much more wonderful than Outa and I imagined he would be!"

Akiko felt how lucky she was, to be able to sing the praises of Tekkan like this with Yamakawa Tomiko, this accomplished and beautiful girl. (Being a lover of beauty in others, Akiko would quite possibly not have befriended Tomiko if she had been ugly, no matter what her talents.) Their love and yearning for Tekkan bolstered their budding friendship, and each one's adoration of him only grew keener as each sought to confirm her own feelings in the other.

The windows of the second floor room in the Jumyokan restaurant looked straight out onto the glittering sea. They were thrown open to the sea breeze, and the room was filled with talk and laughter as men came and went. The two girls were given a warm welcome. Apart from Gangetsu and Tetsunan, those present included Hojiro, Kyoan, and Otsuki Gettei, as well as Tekkan of course, who sat in their midst.

"I do apologise for not attending your lecture yesterday, Sensei," Akiko began, but Tekkan waved away the apology.

"In our New Poetry Society, Miss Ho, we shouldn't go using terms like 'sensei' and 'disciple'. Our society rule is, 'In our dealings with each other, there shall be no teacher and student'. We are all friends who together worship the same god of beauty. Please think of me as your friend."

Akiko felt a happy surge of excitement at his words, and at the atmosphere of the gathering in general.

The flame was lit. The wildfire spread. There was no dousing it now. This was the moment. Almost stolidly plump, Akiko's cheeks creased in a smile, and an obdurate light flashed in her eyes. A poem came to her on the spur of the moment, and she spoke it aloud.

> Pray let me
> call you "teacher."
> For how could
> these reddened lips
> speak the word "friend"?

This was the first time for Akiko to reveal the armour beneath her skirts. She had found someone who could meet her steel on steel.

For his part, Tekkan delighted in the revelation that this burly-looking town girl could in fact strike back with such firm adroitness. He also felt a slight thrill of poetic stimulation from her lively parry.

The poetry competition began with compositions on the theme of "the fan." Akiko wrote:

> That horrid fan
> kept wafting incense smoke
> at me
> until I seized it
> from his hand.

"There you are, a woman's poetry is a fine-scented thing, isn't it?" someone remarked.

Akiko was the first to recite her poem, and other excellent *tanka* followed. Sake and food were brought in, and the atmosphere grew increasingly heady.

From Akiko:

> Gazing out as the sun
> sets on the waves,
> long hair twined
> about the balcony railing
> by the wind from the piney beach.

Tekkan's response:

> The evening tide
> has flooded the pine's roots
> and all are gone.
> Where is it we stand,
> you and I together?

Tomiko was standing by the balcony railing, holding down the kimono sleeve that flapped in the sea breeze. In a composed voice, she recited:

> By the sandy ways
> along Takashi beach
> that grows so thick with pines
> I'll bury my poems
> and go.

Here was a fine and delicate poet too, Tekkan thought, and looking back he likewise felt that Akiko was a talented and brilliant woman, whose eyes flashed a strong gaze in his direction. One outshone the other in sweetness and delicacy, the other in passion and ardour. And when he saw these two, both showering the sparks of an equally powerful genius, holding hands and together adoring him with cries of "Sensei," Tekkan felt a glow of satisfaction. He could only feel that his ideal woman – "If I choose a bride" – really existed, after all. The thought swelled his heart with a new sense of freedom, and sent it fluttering high into the sky's expanse.

Tekkan's lively response to his conversation with the two young women added further life and spirit to the gathering.

"Well well, it looks like the ladies will soon be the mainstay of *Myojo*. Guys, we'd better give Tekkan's favourites our support," said Hojiro with a teasing grin. The sea was filled with the glitter of the setting sun, and the party grew ever livelier.

From Tekkan:

> I take the poem
> tucked in my breast
> and compare it with this sea,
> and cannot think
> the ocean is the wider.

He also picked up a poem card and wrote:

> Suimei alone
> is absent
> and I curse it as
> the lack of one
> of the seven herbs of poetry.

Tekkan loved Suimei's crystal clear poetic honesty. He had gone up to Tokyo that spring, and was studying at Tokyo Senmon Gakko (now Waseda University) while preparing to publish his first book of poems. On the back of the poem card, Tekkan added: "Lamenting how I miss the jewel of your presence at the party at Takashi with the poets Kyoan, Baikei, Gettei, Tetsunan, Gangetsu, Akiko and Tomiko in the summer of 1900."

In the evening, they all strolled on the beach. The day's heat had wafted away, the sand was pleasant to walk on, and pleasant too the evening breeze murmuring in the pines.

"If one were to die, it would be nice to die on this beach on a night like this, wouldn't it Nakayama-san?" Akiko said softly. Nakayama Kyoan was a simple and honest young man, a medical student who boarded and practiced as a locum in the house of a doctor in Doshima.

"Die? You mean you want to die, Akiko?"

"Yes, it's a funny thing, but I have a yearning for death sometimes… I sometimes wonder about committing suicide with one's lover…"

Kyoan let this pass, with the thought that this was a young girl's sentimental fancy. Tekkan was a few paces ahead. He stopped in his tracks, and exclaimed, "Ah, this feels good!" Then he squatted down and touched the wet sand with a finger. Everyone else came to a natural halt as well, some lingering on the knotted roots of the pines, others letting their *geta* clogs be washed by the waves.

Hojiro said something to Tomiko, and she laughed. Gangetsu protectively took her part in response. As if to escape the others, Tekkan turned to Akiko and said, "It's a lovely night, isn't it. A night that only comes once in a lifetime. And I have a feeling that premonition will turn out to be true."

"Yes, Sensei, I think so too." Akiko was kneeling beside him, her sleeves folded neatly over her knees. Tekkan idly wrote something in the sand and let a wave erase it. Akiko watched his thin, beautiful finger as it wrote. There was no way to resist the tilt of her heart towards him. It sought love as a hunter seeks his prey. It tracked love intently, foreseeing nothing. A fierce creature had woken within her, unwitting yet urging her ever forward. Tetsunan stood on the beach alone, arms folded, gazing out at the dark shape of Awaji Island in the night. Akiko's affection for him had not altered, but the attraction and impulse she felt towards Tekkan was a deeper thing. That evening, Tetsunan was largely silent.

When the party returned to the Jumyokan and was about to disband, the restaurateur gave each a fan to commemorate the occasion.

There was talk of each writing a poem on everyone's fan, but it was late, and they contented themselves with signing their names on them for each other. Akiko asked for a rickshaw to be called, and set off alone ahead of the others, tenderly cradling her fan.

As soon as she left, the men began to talk.

"Did you see those flashing eyes looking out from beneath the tangled hair? Quite amazing." This was Baikei, always sardonic and quick to discuss others. He was, of course, speaking of Akiko. The description "tangled hair" made them all nod in agreement, and suddenly all were laughing.

The next day, August 7th, Tekkan gave a lecture in Kobe, and on the 8th Akiko paid another visit to him at his Osaka inn. Her reason this time was to receive practical advice and correction for her *tanka*. Tomiko came with her. Both were by now loath to see him go.

On the evening of the 9th, everyone gathered again for a party at Suminoe. Kyoan was with them, but he found the excited chatter of the two girls who crowded around Tekkan tedious. Kyoan was a sincere and upright young man. Unlike Baikei with his ridiculing and sarcasm, Kyoan tended to grow increasingly mute in such situations.

The conversation of the three of them moved to the subject of Goethe, who had recently been written about in *Myojo*. The two girls could not, of course, follow the original German, but they had rushed to devour translations of Goethe, and Kyoan listened in admiration at their voracious greed for knowledge.

"Goethe gained great success in Weimar," said Tekkan, "but he also gained great success in love. He was an outstanding politician and councillor, not to mention artist and lover... That's the kind of greatness a man must aspire to."

"But Sensei, aren't you that sort of man yourself?" Tomiko said playfully, nodding in assent. "You had a time when you threw yourself into politics, didn't you?"

"You're a kind of modern-day Narihira, Sensei – the romantic lover-poet all over again. Byron, Narihira – you're in the same league..." Akiko broke in. Anyone could see straight away how she adored the way he looked. She was convinced no one could be as handsome as Tekkan.

"Byron, Narihira, East and West, men can sing the praises of love, but what do we have in modern Japan, eh? Fake moralists making a fuss over the least little thing, reducing pure and true love to mere salacious filth. In Japan, one cannot yet truly love. Our long, dark night is still continuing. They speak of the flowering of civilization and enlightenment, but we've seen no true flowering as yet. Trains, electricity – is that true enlightenment? No, it is the human heart. Our hearts are still locked in blind ignorance, I tell you. And self and love, both are still locked in confinement and treated with contempt." Tekkan was by now quite passionate.

"Our duty as poets is precisely to fling open the windows and let the breeze and light in on this world of ours. Let us love, let us establish a modern self, individuality! Take a thousand lovers! I want to yell it at the whole world…"

"Women too, Sensei?"

"Yes, indeed. There is no Man or Woman in our New Poetry Society – we youth must reveal our own love, sing out, open up all the windows of our Meiji era. Polygamy and polyandry is a fine thing. 'It is as foolish/to condemn your love/as to question/the scarlet/of scarlet.' We're the chosen children of the stars, you see."

Even men such as Kyoan felt themselves stirred into passion by Tekkan's eloquence. It was impossible to resist the image of the rebel who battles against the common world. Kyoan could see it was inevitable that girls like Tomiko and Akiko would be inflamed by his rhetoric. And as long as they took on the philosophy of the New Poetry Society, in fact, Kyoan felt nothing despicable in the behaviour of these two girls who gathered on either side of Tekkan.

He was deeply respectful of the genius of both Akiko and Tomiko. He could not, like Baikei, jokingly denigrate them with such remarks as, "Not a bad poem, eh?"

Kyoan had at first assumed that a woman's talents couldn't amount to much, but lately he had begun to find rather terrifying the ability of these two girls in the prime of youth to produce excellent poems on the spur of the moment. Now he felt compelled to interpret everything about them favourably.

It was a bright moonlit night, and figures could be seen taking the evening air on the grounds of Sumiyoshi Shrine. The shrine is the oldest in the Osaka-Kobe area, with ancient links to the imperial family. Beyond its majestic stone gateway, which instils a reverent sense of antiquity in the worshipper, the black shape of the curved bridge floats like a rainbow in the night.

"Ah, what a fine shrine this is!" Tekkan found himself exclaiming. The unique architecture of the shrine hall rose cleanly in the moonlight against the night sky, expansive and elegant, yet with an austere solemnity. One side was bathed in moonlight almost to whiteness, while its heavy, clear-cut shadow lay across the ground, powerful and beautiful.

"I must say, I see it all the time, but seeing it now with you, Sensei, it strikes me with a whole new beauty."

Akiko was finding that everything was bathed in a fresh new vividness. Being with Tekkan, it all seemed to take on special meaning. She could not suppress the excited emotion in her voice.

The curved bridge spanned a lotus pond. Tekkan playfully drew out his little traveller's writing case and wrote a *tanka* on the back of one of the lotus leaves.

> Upon this lotus leaf
> I write of feelings
> I am sure
> even the gods themselves
> know nothing of.

"Now it's your turn," he said with a smile to them.

"Oh dear, do you really think we should break off leaves like this? Surely the gods are watching." Tomiko stretched out her delicate white hand, put her fingers into the water, and drew a leaf towards her. Then, humming to herself, she wrote:

> Thinking to write a poem
> I plucked a lotus leaf –
> what small voice
> whispered there
> on the plucked string of its stem?

A sweet and girlish poem indeed.

How lovable and beautiful, thought Akiko, seeing the smile on Tomiko's pale face. But at the same time her heart was troubled to see that Tekkan was also gazing at Tomiko. There was a stirring of jealousy beneath the friendship she felt for her.

Tekkan spoke. "The response to that is:

> Is it right, you asked,
> to cut the lotus leaf?
> Again I hum
> the poem you wrote
> that moonlit night.

And now Miss Ho, you must have a poem surely," he added, turning merrily to Akiko.

Akiko did not write anything on a leaf. Instead, she lifted the sleeve of the brightly coloured *yuzen*-dyed kimono she was wearing, and said:

> Moonlit night and lotuses
> and the railing
> where you stood so beautiful –
> I will not forget your poem
> writ on the lotus leaf.

"Your poem has a wonderful musicality, sis – your poetry always does," Tomiko said winningly, tilting her head with its dangling white ribbon. It was hard indeed to choose between the talent of these two; not only that, but both had the depth of heart to be able to savour each other's feelings, which brought them yet closer together.

Kyoan drew the leaf towards him and gazed at the inked characters that stood out clearly in the moonlight. "This is a rare and precious thing," he said appreciatively. Then suddenly he became aware that rain had begun to fall on it. "Oh, wait here. I'll borrow an umbrella," he cried, and ran off to the nearby souvenir stall. The three remaining took shelter in a summerhouse. The lotus leaves soon began to dance on the tiny waves that filled the pond.

Kyoan came back bearing two umbrellas. Akiko took one, opened it and held it out towards Tekkan, then stepped over to join him beneath it. She sometimes surprised even herself with her own boldness.

2

Tekkan went down to Okayama, then returned via Kyoto, where he visited the family graves, and on August 19th he returned by train to Tokyo. He was ten days later than promised. Takino had been coping with the mountain of *Myojo* work, and she was weary with waiting for him.

"You're back late, dear. How was Kansai?"

"Fine. I met the poets, and got some new members."

Tokyo was in the grip of an excruciating heat wave. Tekkan was worn out with the rigors of the trip, but he felt keyed up and elated. He was flushed with an enthusiasm for life that was almost like a premonition of love, and the reason was his encounter with Akiko and Tomiko.

Each time Tekkan found love, he felt the blood in his veins refreshed and purified, pulsing strongly.

It was not that he did not love Takino, but simply that his blood seethed with the urge to find new love, a new woman. He was a man who quickly wilted and faded without the transfusion of new love in his veins. He believed this to be a separate thing from his love for Takino. After his return from Kansai, he found himself compelled to read with even more heartfelt attention the poems that Akiko and Tomiko sent for his judgment.

Heavily pregnant, Takino still helped with the editing of *Myojo*. Tekkan had been suffering from his old stomach problems since his return, and had also caught cold, but unwell though he was, as usual he was kept busy running around organizing funds, and had no chance to take it easy and recover properly.

A letter from Kyoan included the words, "Both Akiko and Tomiko are always asking after your health…" One hundred and thirty miles away, the two girls were evidently hanging on Tekkan's every move with gasps of joy and sighs of sorrow.

The flow of letters and poems from them grew still more frequent.

It had been agreed that Takino could open the submissions and manuscripts sent to Tekkan. When one day she happened to slit open the envelope of one of them and run her eye over the enclosed letter, her expression subtly altered.

Turning the envelope over hastily, she read the name "Ho Akiko." The poem inside read:

> Let me wrap
> my arms about your neck
> drawing your poor ill body close
> and drink upon those lips
> so dry with fever.

Takino had felt that there was something behind Tekkan's drawn-out stay in Kansai, and now she felt she had seen vivid proof of it. She was familiar with her husband's propensities, indeed was so used to them that her attitude was tinged with resignation, but she was well aware that this Ho Akiko was a powerful member of the *Myojo* group and an extraordinarily talented woman, and Takino felt she was impossible to simply ignore.

I don't believe Takino loved Tekkan, or was particularly infatuated with him. She seems to me rather to have watched him with a cool gaze of detachment. But when it came to Akiko, her heart grew turbulent. She wasn't like that weird girl who had once turned up crying in the early days of their marriage. Akiko could not be compared with the likes of such girls. She and Takino's husband dwelled together in a world to which Takino had no access – they flew hand in hand to a realm beyond the rainbow. Together they inhabited a magical domain where love and art came together. Whatever she thought, the exasperation Takino felt was most certainly a form of jealousy. And then there was this sort of thing from Yamakawa Tomiko as well:

> I long to die
> calling your name
> upon the path
> of poetry that you
> have newly shown me.

Takino's lovely almond eyes sank in their sockets and she lowered her white chin into the mauve collar of her kimono as she proceeded to take out Akiko's letters and poems and read them one by one. Akiko had even enclosed a photograph of herself. Takino gazed at it with complicated feelings, taking in the tangled hair and Akiko's somewhat eccentric look. Takino was a proud woman of great self-control, and she did not want to believe that she could be feeling jealousy or anger against Akiko. But she found it quite infuriating that this girl could have the gall to assume she could make public such bold and self-indulgent love poetry. Even if it was the mere product of fantasy rather than reality, it was certainly not a poem to be dismissed lightly.

"When I saw you again as if in a dream at the piney beach of Takashi on the 15th:

> Do not rail against
> the god who drew us here
> to meet again
> you and I
> beneath the pines."

Apparently Akiko and Tekkan had had a secret meeting at Takashi Beach, then. Tekkan had told Takino only of the poetry competition at Hamadera on the 6th, and the walk at Sumiyoshi Shrine on the 9th. There may well have been other meetings that were kept from her, thought Takino, and her eyes darkened. Now she also recalled Tekkan's recent fervent poems:

> What is there
> to hate,
> that the hidden genius
> of us two can meet
> here beneath the heavens?
> • • •
> You and I are two
> who must, smiling
> tread the very flames.
> Do not then pray to the gods
> as normal mortals do.

Could these two be Tekkan and Tomiko, or were they perhaps Tekkan and Akiko? In fact, Tekkan was sending frequent letters to both at this time.

> Unarmoured,
> undefended,
> the maiden sends
> winging like arrows
> a rain of letters.

One can scarcely imagine how inflamed the two were. At about the same time, Akiko sent to Tetsunan an announcement of her love.

> Who is to blame, think you,
> that the pure white
> of this robe
> from the realm of stars
> has been dyed so deep?

"I am a child of sin," she added. "It is you who introduced my name to Mr. Yosano. My name today derives from that. And the fact that I have become today's child of sin likewise derives from it. I believe you can say nothing."

One can imagine that the feverish ardour of Akiko and Tomiko was the talk of poetic circles of Osaka and Sakai. Tetsunan was well aware of it before the letter came from Akiko. But this provocative talk of "a child of sin" in her letter seemed to him Akiko's peculiar rhetoric. He had not yet realized that something had happened between the two. Be that as it may, however, he didn't feel this was a matter he should be drawn into. Retiring as he was, Tetsunan withdrew beyond the sphere of friendship, and became a spectator.

There is no question that Akiko sent her letter to Tetsunan on the clear assumption that he was a friend. My own feeling is that the best friend (or one of the best friends) a woman can have is a man. But that man, while being a friend, of course will also have the elements of a male and be the sort of person who, if worst comes to worst, could take the role of lover – there's a particular pleasure in preserving the relationship at the friendship level in such a case. What's more, he must have the discernment, erudition, character, taste and lifestyle to be worthy of the friendship. The best friendship maintains that difficult balance with a friend who is also a man, that dangerous stasis that makes the heart tremble. It seems to me that for Akiko there would have been no greater luxury than to be able to boast of her relationship with the lover and teacher Tekkan to her dear, dependable, familiar male friend Tetsunan.

Yamakawa Tomiko was also transported by love. Akiko would visit her at home, and the two would together practice making the linked verse that was the craze in the *Myojo* circle at the time. Both thought only of Tekkan.

> How nonchalantly she
> writes those love poems,
> those flowery poems
> > (Akiko)
> rumours of you also
> written into poems.
> > (Tomiko)

> Well, then
> the man must be
> blamed as a weakling
> > (Akiko)
> plucking hair from my eyebrows
> to make a fine writing brush.
> > (Tomiko)

The two wrote these lines together on a page, and sent it to Tekkan. They never imagined that Takino would read it.

> Will the gods
> blame me if I call
> him "brother"
> that darling of the stars
> who serves them?
> > (Tomiko)
> Your mouth
> is of that world
> of new stars,
> yet why is my hair
> so faded now?
> > (Akiko)

"Sensei is a child of the stars, sis. He's been born into our world by some mistake."

"It's true. That's why the worldly can't comprehend him."

At the end of the letter, Akiko added: "In the home of Miss Yamakawa in Osaka," and Tomiko finished with: "In a reality that feels a dream. Tomiko."

"Speaking of not comprehending, sis, things are hopeless for me. My father's said he absolutely won't allow any more selfish behaviour." Tomiko spoke in a hushed voice.

"What? You mean all that talk of an arranged marriage is actually moving ahead?"

"Yes, my father's pushing on with it without consulting me."

"But Tomiko... surely you could refuse."

Akiko spoke unintentionally strongly. She was aware of the marriage negotiations for Tomiko. He was someone from the family, a young man called Yamakawa Chushichiro, who had been a secretary in the consulate in Melbourne and was now manager of the Kofuku Company in Ginza. Tomiko's father would not listen to talk of her foolish dreams of wanting to remain single and to go on studying poetry. Precisely because he was so fond of his daughter, he wanted to marry her to a man he trusted.

"Well, as for refusing..." Tomiko hesitated, apparently undecided, a white finger to her cheek. "My father's a stubborn man, and once he's said something he won't hear a word against it. I'm already half-resigned to it myself."

"But Tomiko..."

"It's true. But poetry's the one thing I can't give up, I just can't bear to abandon it."

Akiko longed to say something about herself that would help strengthen Tomiko. She herself was in fact being pressured to marry by her parents. The man in question was Sadashichi from the shop. She couldn't imagine such a prosaic marriage to an employee she had grown up knowing since childhood. She was determined to reject the plan. But she hesitated to speak of this to Tomiko now. She had too much girlish vanity to reveal how poor and mean her own so-called suitor was compared to Tomiko's. She comforted herself whenever they met by singing the praises of Tekkan and bewailing their circumstances.

Takino was struck by the extraordinary hyperbole of them both referring to Tekkan as a "child of the stars."

Takino's discord with Tekkan, if it existed, may have been influenced by the very atmosphere of the *Myojo* group. If this was so, it was a sad thing for her. If Takino felt ill at ease with the air of those poets who published in *Myojo* and gathered under its banner, it was only natural that she couldn't follow where Tekkan went. The poetry she liked was generally restrained, quiet, straightforward verse, and she felt that *Myojo* was full of poetry that blustered and strove for superficial beauty of language. "Child of the stars" was a supreme example of this. She showed it to him, and said,

"I wonder about this. Is this an expression you came up with?"

"No – but everyone uses it a lot. It's girlish sentimentality. They take pleasure in vying to use phrases like this, you know. It's a kind of fashion."

Tekkan did his best to soften his explanation, well aware of his wife's scrupulous, unbending personality.

"'Child of the stars' sets my teeth on edge. It makes you sound ridiculous, as if your group is so much more wonderful than normal people."

On September 23rd, Takino gave birth to a boy.

Akiko learned of it in a letter. Suddenly, the constant flow of letters from Tekkan had ceased, and then came "I have a son." Tekkan had become a father.

The child was named Atsumu. Tekkan was pleased by the birth. He truly seems to have been delighted with the boy.

"Atsumu is a handsomer fellow than his father. I will send a photograph before long."

Tekkan was a man who thought nothing of boasting of his new child to a young female disciple who sent him letters of love. You could hardly say he wasn't honest, but he was certainly excessively self-centred as well. Akiko immediately wrote to Tetsunan:

"I find it just so funny that Yosano-sensei has become a father, the man who advocated polygamy that day by the sea…"

But when Tomiko heard the happy news, she sent this to Tekkan:

Aloft in the heavens
the rock cave of the gods
rent its clouds asunder
and an infant cry burst forth –
a star child!

Akiko also sent a romantic congratulatory poem:

The newborn child
whom you
this morning brought to life
may he soon find
a love truly beautiful.

"Yes, Atsumu. You will have a thousand lovers. Find love, and spread your wings wide in the world, my lad. Live free, big-hearted and manly," cried Tekkan, holding in his arms the baby still too young to see.

3

In October, Tekkan passed once more through the entrance gate of Takino's family home in Izumo village in Yamaguchi prefecture. The money that purchased both his clothes and the numerous gifts he bore had not been personally gained. The Hayashis themselves had sent money (no doubt for the nth time) as a gift on Atsumu's birth, and this had provided him with the funds.

The birth of his son had prompted Tekkan to take this opportunity to finally put a stop to the plan of being officially adopted by the Hayashis.

"I'm grateful to say that I've become well known as a poet." Hayashi Shotaro listened with a grim expression as Tekkan boasted. "Therefore, I've thought things through carefully, and come to the conclusion that I would like to keep the name of 'Yosano', and thus, I ask for your permission to enter Takino in my own family register."

"But Mr. Tekkan, this is not right. I must refuse," said Shotaro bluntly. His expression gave no room for doubt that he would not compromise. "What was it you said back on that day? I believe it was that you wished for Takino's hand on the grounds that you agreed to take on her family name."

"Well, actually–"

"And now you come and tell me that you've made a bit of a name for yourself so you don't want to be adopted into the family after all, you want to take Takino into your own register. Surely this is utter selfishness on your part."

"But since we talked, you see, various things have happened and my ideas have changed. It's only natural that different circumstances change one's way of thinking. I did say that at the time, yes. But now I've become a famous person in the world of poetry. I don't want to bring shame on your name, so I'd like to keep my own. It's only natural, surely."

"It may seem natural to you, but that sort of selfish behaviour doesn't work in the real world, you know. What you say is ridiculous, it's completely disloyal."

Shotaro wielded all the dignity of a wealthy landowner, and this along with his impressive bearing overwhelmed Tekkan.

"If you insist on pressing your case," continued Shotaro, "I intend to consider relations between us as null and void, to request that you separate from your wife, and to take back mother and son to this household."

Tekkan could not believe his ears.

"Separate… you said?"

"This is where my thoughts have arrived. Having carefully considered the life you have lived since taking my daughter to Tokyo, I'm sorry to say this, but as an old-fashioned man I find a great many things to deplore. To begin with, I cannot feel satisfied that publishing a magazine with such an uncertain future is acceptable as a man's work. I am happy to provide a little money to see to your needs, of course, but I cannot happily leave my daughter in the hands of a man who cannot properly support what is now a family complete with child."

"But we poets have nothing to do with normal ideas of prosperity. Takino understands this too. It doesn't matter if there's no money…"

"I know little of poetry and novels. You may claim that it doesn't matter if there's no money as long as you're famous, but I say there has to be substance there. Pardon my saying so, but for all this talk of poetry and genius, I don't believe there's any worth in genius if you leave the straight and narrow path. Say what you will of love, but the first obligation for members of society is to follow ethics and social principles, surely. Do you feel this notion of mine is somehow mistaken?"

"No indeed, sir, you are thinking in terms of the old poetic world. But please consider the new poetry. There, the poet lives in flights of heavenly imagination."

"I don't know about old and new, what I'm talking about is the way a man should comport himself. Any man who has a wife and child in his care has the responsibility to keep them warm and well fed, and since we're on the subject, isn't it true that you're behind in rent, you've pawned Takino's kimonos, and she's undernourished from the beriberi? No, it wasn't her who told me all this. There are people from this backwater who go up to Tokyo to study, you know, and naturally rumours get back. If anything were to happen to Takino or the child, that would be the end of it, and the important thing is, she's the Hayashi family heir. It only stands to reason, surely, that we must find a good husband for her to bring into the family, and have her separate from you."

"But there's Atsumu now…"

"I intend to register him in the Hayashi family, and provide sufficient funds to see that he gets an excellent university education. Pardon me, but I don't believe it's in the boy's future interests to be in the charge of a fellow who comes from a school of poetry where they sing of love and sex and so forth. Well, there you are, I haven't minced my words. We're talking man to man, after all, so I believe it's in both our interests to come to the point and speak our minds."

Tekkan could only conclude that Shotaro had caught wind of some unfavourable information about himself from the Asadas.

Compared to the previous year, Shotaro seemed a different man in his attitude to Tekkan. He was rigid and unapproachable. As Shotaro had said, from the Hayashis' point of view no doubt there were grave concerns over Tekkan's financial situation as well as his profligate ways with women, but the real problem lay in the fact that Shotaro had no standards of judgment by which he might understand Tekkan. Indeed Tekkan would give any father pause. Yet he himself could not see this.

Tekkan was the sort of person who believed his own position was always right, and the blame always lay with the other. He was a man who couldn't be objective about how he must appear when viewed in light of normal social standards. Indeed, he despised this commonsense mentality, and made not the slightest effort to comprehend or empathize with such views. He was the type to never lose his youthful ardor, a permanent late teenager who never matured with the passing years but clung to his fierce self-esteem.

Tekkan left the Hayashi home with a sense of hopelessness, and a wounded heart. Yet he still retained faith that Shotaro would change his mind. Wise in the ways of the world though he was, in some respects he was utterly naïve and lacking in discernment. He had no clue that anything might be wrong with what he himself said.

"The world can never really understand you, cannot grasp your own unique worth and essence," he said to himself, quoting an old Chinese saying.

Exactly as, a year earlier when Tekkan, reduced to utter poverty, had gone to call on the Hayashi home, the poignant autumn mists now too lay thick along the Saba River, shrouding mountains already white with snow. The river wound among fields and ran cold through sodden woods. Unwitnessed, Saba Mountain stood in its coloured leaves, dying toward winter.

Tekkan strode along morosely. He was enraged at his father-in-law, who he felt had proven no more than a common fool. He had no regard for the fact that the honest and good-natured Shotaro had patiently continued to send him money all this time, that Takino had stayed with him despite the poverty and the unease she felt in his milieu, that it had essentially been Shotaro's money that founded *Myojo* and that supported him.

Tekkan could fall into a poetic intoxication about his own circumstances even in a situation like this one. A fragment of poetry floated into his mind.

The poet dwells in imagination's flights –
always the land of his fathers misconstrues
his actions as immoral, fickle, destructive of the public morals.
Ah, would you bind me in humanity's shackles?
It is futile to defy this oppressive age.
I must away!

Tekkan decided he would give this poem the title "Leaving Japan."
He wanted to heal his grief by chanting aloud his own poem. Naïve
and optimistic as he was, and without a way of understanding the
world by its own standards, Tekkan was frequently wounded. His
ego and his bravado sustained his fragile heart.

In the train headed back to Tokyo, he continued to ponder poems
as he gazed out the window at the passing scenery. In free verse,
Tekkan was inclined to strike grandiloquent poses, but in his *tanka*
he was somewhat more thoughtful and objective in his approach.

It should be enough
to grow old in grace
among country fields
and yet my name
and love would be gone forever.
• • •
I cannot stoop
to follow country folks'
diligent warnings to me –
the blood in my veins
flows yet too warm for that.
• • •
Say what he will
yet I will write
inside that purple collar
hidden poems
my wife's father cannot know.

Those hidden poems rang pure in his ears. Two faces flickered before
his eyes. They were the faces of those he had christened "White

150

Bush Clover" and "White Lily" – Tomiko and Akiko. Tekkan needed urgent balm for the wound in his pulsing heart. He was a weak, fragile "child of the stars."

4

Tekkan left the train midway, at Osaka. The ostensible reason was that the Kansai Young Men's Literary Society was holding its autumn meeting at Mino, but the real reason was that he wanted to see Akiko and Tomiko again.

On November 3rd, Tekkan put up at the Hirai Inn. That evening, he called Nakayama Kyoan and told him everything that had happened in Tokuyama. On his lips, the Hayashis' treatment of him sounded cruel and outrageous, and ferociously hard-line. Tekkan didn't consciously plan to present it in that light, he simply couldn't help himself. Kyoan had been hearing rumors that Tekkan and his wife were not getting on very well, but he was astonished to hear that Takino's parents were now threatening to separate them. Not knowing Takino, he naturally took Tekkan's part, yet he couldn't say anything irresponsible, all he could do was try his best to soothe Tekkan's wounded heart. The story of the discord between Tekkan and the Hayashis seems to have spread to others in the group. In a letter to Suimei reporting Tekkan's problem, Kyoan wrote, "These are matters that should not be spoken of, so I will not tell you, but I believe that you yourself know of them."

The following day, Usuda Kyukin paid him a visit, and the three men took a walk around the town together. Tekkan must have been feeling rather forlorn, for he kept Kyoan with him another night, though Kyukin made his excuses and left.

Either that day or night, Tekkan seems to have contacted Akiko and Tomiko, for on the 5th Kyoan was surprised to see the two of them arrive unexpectedly in rickshaws at Matsushita Clinic, where he worked.

"We're to go to Kyoto with Sensei to view autumn leaves," they explained. "Do come along too, Kyoan."

"Well, that's extremely kind of you," replied Kyoan with a wry grin. He was a serious student, and he felt in absolutely no position to take them up on the suggestion. He also remembered the experience of walking about with the three of them at the shrine, bored and annoyed.

"I'm afraid I've got some tiresome things I have to get on with here so I'll have to beg off. Please tell Sensei I apologise that I can't see him off."

The two girls didn't really seem to have expected that he would come along, and they went happily on their way. Kyoan was frankly surprised that Akiko and Tomiko could be out like this, when their parents were normally so strict.

In fact, Akiko had been allowed out thanks to Tomiko's invitation.

"May I borrow your daughter for the day?" she had said winningly. "I'll soon have to go back to Wakasa, and I'd love to have a day wandering around Kyoto with Akiko before I say farewell. Please let her spend the night at my place."

Akiko's mother gazed at Tomiko in her cherry-blossom and grey kimono with crepe coat patterned with chrysanthemums. Her lustrous black hair was up, and decorated with a pale peach-colored ribbon; she looked in the bloom of youth.

"When you say you'll be going back, would this be something I should congratulate you on perhaps…?" she asked, in a roundabout reference to marriage.

"Ah, well…" Tomiko smiled vaguely.

Akiko felt, on receiving Tekkan's message, she would most likely have gone alone instead of waiting for Tomiko.

When she saw Tekkan again, it seemed to Akiko that her own fate and future life were bound up with him. She was happy simply to have been able to meet him.

Tekkan had strong ties with Kyoto from his past, so he knew his way around. He led the two girls through the streets, turning north at Nanzenji Temple to go to Eikando Temple for the autumn leaves. Soon, the temple with its famous forest of Iwagaki maples came into view at the foot of the mountains to their right, and the three were surrounded by the flaming red leaves. Crimson leaves carpeted Benten Pond and the little bridge that spanned it.

"Sensei, this is probably the last time I'll be able to see you like this with Akiko." Tomiko's tone was despondent, and she clung to Akiko's fingers as she spoke.

"There've been marriage offers for a while now, but this time my parents seem determined to marry me off... The ceremony's been fixed for December."

"Good heavens, a ceremony..." Akiko was astonished, and gripped Tomiko's fingers. "Is that really decided?"

"Yes, and here I am with you both..."

"But surely you can go on writing poetry when you're married?" said Tekkan in a reproving voice.

"I do plan to, but once I'm living in another household I don't expect I'll be able to do what I like... I've even found myself thinking I should know my place better than to hope to be a real poet..."

"That sort of weakness is futile. Surely you can't just throw away your precious talents like that?"

"It's true," chimed in Akiko. "It's just as Sensei says, Tomiko. Why can't you pull yourself together and live more strongly? Sensei calls you a star child aspiring to the new *tanka*:

> Child of the stars
> how weak you are –
> raise your sleeve, declare
> that neither devils nor demons
> will defeat you."

Tekkan was astonished at the power of Akiko's ready improvisational skills. Not to be outdone, he said,

> "Such love, such poetry
> will still exist
> at the world's end –
> we three strong ones
> were born in the east

This is my conviction, Tomiko. We three alone are strong. Who apart from us can share this understanding of love and poetry? Ours is the heaven-ordained meeting of three marvellous talents."

Probably all three were secretly and equally convinced of their own genius. Tekkan's words fuelled the flames; the conceit of self-praise fired their volatile spirits.

Tomiko would not be left behind.

> "In our starry world
> where we raise our voices
> unwavering
> the white lily and bush clover
> have one god."

All three felt the pain of parting at this moment. Tekkan wanted to spend the night in Kyoto. He took the two girls to an inn called Tsujino that his late father had known, nestled into Mount Awata on the edge of the city. The spa was called Kacho hot spring, though in fact it was a cold spring whose waters were heated; in the evening light the smoke from the furnace rose into the air.

The three of them approached up the steep hill in separate rickshaws. It was only a small inn, but the view from the garden was magnificent. To the northeast of the city, Mount Hiei was shrouded in evening mist, while below them lay the quiet city. Through the trees and houses they could make out landmarks here and there – the great gate of Nanzenji Temple, or the pagoda at Kurodani.

Autumn's evening breeze had a chill to it that drew them close together.

"The three of us here like this somehow feels as comfortable and familiar as if we were sisters and brother fallen on hard times together," said Akiko when the three had taken their baths and were gathered around a table for the evening meal.

"Oh no, not brother and sisters surely – Sensei is a star child, after all. He's a sort of divine messenger. We couldn't call him brother. For me, he's more like a god."

Tomiko was the most excited of the three. Now that she was to be married, she seemed unable to suppress her overwhelming emotions.

"To *Myojo*, and to Sensei!"

"To *Myojo*, and to Sensei!" Akiko repeated after her, and the three raised their sake cups.

Akiko tossed back the alcohol. It snaked crazily through her body like poison. Had Tomiko and Tekkan become physically intimate? The intuition came to her in a flash.

Tomiko had laid her head weeping on his knee, drunkenly sobbing, "Sensei, Sensei," while Tekkan patted her back.

"I'm unhappy too. I may have to separate from Takino…"

Both girls raised their faces to look at him in astonishment.

"It's true. Takino's father is a stubborn old ignoramus, who hasn't got a clue about poetry. He has no understanding of art, and Takino is a woman with a heart as cold as stone. You'll remember my 'Poem of Yearning' – 'If I choose a bride/she will be gifted/lovely of feature/tender of heart…' Ah yes, the wife who will take my hand and walk with me through life must be a passionate-hearted woman, one who understands poetry. That's what I believed. A woman of genius, whose hot blood rushes through her veins… someone like you both."

Tekkan's gaze was fixed beyond Tomiko, on Akiko.

Just as Tekkan and Tomiko had some secret between them, there was something hidden from Tomiko that he and Akiko shared. Back in summer, after the poetry competition at Takashi Beach on August 6th, the two had met again by the sea, on the 15th. Akiko knew the taste of Tekkan's embrace and kiss.

Now, however, all that seemed neither dream nor reality, but sheer fantasy, while yet it had the raw vividness of real memory. Now that she was face to face with the real Tekkan once more, her blood sang, and she could no longer be sure whether indeed that memory was fantasy or reality.

> "It was yesterday
> I sent a poisoned dart
> into your breast,"

murmured Tekkan, and Tomiko immediately responded with the last two lines, like an echo's instant answer.

> "And it is tonight
> we meet and embrace."

It was yesterday I sent a poisoned dart into your breast – Akiko had tasted how deadly poisoned love was. She was afraid of her own love, which grew fiercer and fiercer within her.

"How swiftly comes
the punishment for sin."

Akiko trembled as she continued the poem.

"Sensei, I don't want to leave you," sobbed Tomiko on Tekkan's lap. "I want to stay with you and never be apart from poetry. But I'm simply too weak to stand up to my father…" She seemed no longer to care that Akiko was watching.

"You must fight, Tomiko. You mustn't give your ideals, our ideals, over to the devil. You mustn't let marriage make you give up poetry. Not even the devil himself can overcome the human heart."

"It's not just poetry, Sensei, it's you my heart belongs to."

Tomiko wound a white handkerchief around her little finger, took out the little make-up box she always carried, and jabbed the pointed end of the manicure scissors lightly into her fingertip.

As she sucked at the blood, Tomiko threw a meaning glance at Tekkan.

"Sensei, I will write a vow with this blood. Even though I may go, my heart will never leave your side."

"You're going to write in blood? Tomiko, me too. I too belong to you and Sensei."

"I'll write too," declared Tekkan, putting down his sake cup.

My heart and my poems belong to you.
May I never betray this oath.

Each wrote these words on a piece of writing paper with their blood, and exchanged them as keepsakes.

Akiko gave her oath to both Tomiko and Tekkan, and received theirs in return. Later, Tomiko wrote the following:

Forever I weep
and writhe in agony
and cut my finger
and yet deeper
do I go on loving you.

5

There are those who dig about in search of the bizarre in this story of the night they spent at the inn on Mount Awata, but this kind of ridiculous curiosity and vulgar speculation has nothing to do with the real nature of these three.

All were young, and flush with intelligence and talent, and Akiko and Tomiko were in love with Tekkan to the point of adulation. Tomiko was in turmoil, poised on the brink of marriage, and Akiko's own love may well have been spurred to new heights by her knowledge that Tomiko would no longer be there to share Tekkan with her. As for Tekkan, no doubt he was drawn to these two above all others, and found it hard to rein in his rush of emotion for both Tomiko and Akiko.

Tekkan was a wounded man. The hurt he had received at Tokuyama was unchanged from that first love of ten years ago. And when his heart ached, he always turned to love to help him bear the pain. He was reborn like the phoenix through new love, a new lover. Through loving he revitalized himself, restored his self-respect, and brought fresh youthful energy to his art. Now he sought love instinctively. And both Tomiko and Akiko were wellsprings overflowing with feeling, more than able to accept what he brought to them. Toward dawn, the long tale came to its end, and the two women retired to their room to sleep together under the one coverlet. They talked on softly together, from time to time hearing the sound of Tekkan's sleeping breath through the paper doors that separated their rooms.

"Sister, I'll give Sensei to you. My time for parting has come, like it or not. I mustn't love Sensei any more… you don't write love poems once you're married."

Tomiko was still gently sobbing as she spoke. Her white, sweet-scented arms were wound frantically around Akiko's neck.

"Of course you can write love poems…that would be an interesting thing to do, it seems to me. You could bring stormy seas to this marriage of yours, and make your husband suffer…" Akiko responded, her face buried in Tomiko's hot, tear-soaked hair.

157

"Good heavens, you say some scary things. You'd be prepared to hold onto your love for Sensei despite his wife and child, wouldn't you? I wouldn't want anyone else to have him, but you, sis, I'm happy to give him to."

"Tell me honestly, Tomiko, have you and Sensei…?"

"Don't, don't! All I'm saying is I'm prepared to leave loving him to you. That's the real meaning of the oath I swore tonight." Tomiko beat her heels on the mattress in agony.

The mist lay thick as the autumn morning dawned.

Akiko softly slipped away from the sleeping Tomiko who lay beside her, her face half buried in the bedclothes. She went out into the corridor and gently slid back one of the heavy wooden panels over the window. At this point, Tekkan emerged.

"They say autumn nights are long, but ours was short, wasn't it?"

Akiko's hair was tangled, and her eyes shone. She looked at him, and said casually, "Sensei, Tomiko's feet were cold last night."

Tekkan was jolted. Akiko had a way of doing this to people. Sometimes something smoldering suddenly flared up in her and surprised others.

Before breakfast, as Akiko sat painting her lips with the red brush they had used to write their vows the night before, she saw Tomiko walking mutely in the garden. The garden too flamed red with the leaves of large maple trees.

"Oh look, sis, there's an old well here…"

Tomiko seemed to be peering into it.

Akiko laid down her brush, and hastily slipped on sandals to join her in the garden, saying, "What are you doing, Tomiko?" On the impulse of the moment, she spoke with a broad Osaka accent. She pulled on Tomiko's sleeve. "That's dangerous."

Tomiko folded her sleeves and pressed them against her face.

"I want to die. We have to part come the morning… I'll never be able to be with you and Sensei like this again…"

Tekkan held her thin, trembling shoulders firmly in his arms. He too felt a gaping hole in his heart at the thought that Tomiko must leave and get married.

In fact, he did not see either Tomiko or Akiko as a possible wife. His ideal was for the two to remain forever by him, loving him and not seeking another man, while Takino continued to remain his wife. Such a selfish desire did not seem irrational to him. He could not bear to lose Takino.

Akiko dipped a comb into the water that flowed from the bamboo pipe, and tenderly combed Tomiko's tangled hair.

It was a little chilly, but when the paper screens on the windows were opened, Mount Yoshida rose through the autumn mists beyond.

A strange mushroom appeared on their plates at breakfast.

"It's better not to eat that, Sensei. You mustn't get poisoned," said Akiko.

"If it's poisonous we'll all be poisoned," Tekkan replied. "What about it, Lily? You wouldn't mind dying if we all died together, would you?" He turned to Tomiko with a little smile.

"Truly…that would satisfy me."

Akiko was the first to take the mushroom in her chopsticks.

"Well, this girl is good enough to speak of love," said Tekkan admiringly.

"I believe I am too," declared Tomiko, and popped a morsel into her mouth.

"Oh, it's so bitter!"

"Hey, I mustn't be left behind here…" said Tekkan, taking a bite. "There, now the three of us have tasted poison."

"If it really were, perhaps that's a good thing," said Tomiko dispiritedly.

They decided to go for a walk along the nearby mountain path. The forest dripped with mist, and the path was rocky. The three walked happily, Tekkan teasingly asking, "Whose hand will I take?"

"Do you know what this is?" he said, pointing to a red flower on a red stem at his feet.

"That's a mountain knotweed."

The three looked down through the mist onto the sunken city. They could not say when they would meet again.

> We spread our fragile wings
> to shelter each other
> but this too was in vain
> my beautiful friend
> that autumn in the capital's west.

Akiko was deeply saddened by the departure of her talented friend, who was leaving behind love and poetry. They had tried without success to shelter each other with their fragile wings, but Tomiko had been forced to admit defeat against the irresistible powers of the wider world. Akiko could not believe that she would ever again be blessed with such a friend, one whose talents matched her own.

Yet she also felt a kind of demonic joy and relief that there would be no more anguish over Tomiko's relationship with Tekkan. For Akiko, marriage was synonymous with the extinction of youth. She could not but feel that Tomiko was letting herself be defeated without a fight. Some of the poems she wrote for her thus had the quality of a tolling funeral bell or elegy.

> We will meet again
> as stars
> until that time, remember
> the voice of autumn that we heard
> together in our room.
> • • •
> My friend, your genius
> has made its name known wide
> and now how sad
> that fame must meet its end
> this dying autumn evening.

In the middle of November the two met again at Akiko's house, and that night once more they shared a room to sleep. Tomiko was about to return to her country home to prepare for the marriage.

"I've given you a wonderful thing by giving you Sensei, sis…"

Tomiko's warm sweet breath was on Akiko's neck. Tomiko had borrowed Akiko's under-robe to sleep in for the night.

Akiko turned to Tomiko. "But Sensei has a wife and child, you know…"

"Good heavens, that's not like you, sis… And besides, they may well be parting. You don't want anyone else to get him, do you, sis, promise? He's yours. I can give him up if you're the one who gets him."

"Tomiko!"

"It's because it's you… If you're the one he loves, it's the same as if I'm loved myself, see."

Through their crepe night robes they clasped each other in warm arms, soft breast to breast.

> Casually I turn
> my back and leave
> to my friend all the crimson flowers
> and weeping, pluck
> the grasses of forgetting.

This poem of Tomiko's reveals the subtleties of a relationship that was part friendship and part romantic rivalry. It was in December, just before Tomiko's wedding, that they next met. Akiko wrote to Tekkan about it.

"I called today on White Lily. She will return to her home tomorrow. There is nothing more hateful than a railway station platform, I told her. There we were the three of us last autumn! Today she had her hair up in a high coif, and looked extraordinarily mature for her years. She was beautiful. She gave me a photograph of herself dressed up similarly and holding a lily. As I left the platform, that place of reunions and endless absences, and headed south, the wind was cold upon me."

How did Tomiko feel as she sat in the train bound for Wakasa?

> Oh distant sky
> that we once saw together
> over the western hills,
> have you no cloud to carry me
> northward to her in Wakasa?

This poem of parting by Akiko, and Tomiko's "crimson flowers" poem, are famous, but not many people know another poem Tomiko composed at the same time.

Say what you will
congratulate me as you will
yet I a maiden
this morning have ripped open
my scarlet sleeve.

Even after his return to Tokyo, Tekkan did not have the courage to tell Takino of the separation that the Hayashis had asked for. What's more, there was a mountain of business to attend to from his absence, and he was also busy with the editing of *Myojo*.

That month, *Myojo* was slapped with a ban on sales owing to some nude illustrations it ran. Tekkan was deeply indignant at the highhandedness of the authorities, and he sent an open letter of protest to the Home Minister, Suematsu Kencho, titled "Letter Addressed to All Readers, Expressing My Position on the Oppression of the Arts and Requesting the Minister's Clarification." In the special edition of the magazine that appeared minus a cover, looking something like a pamphlet, Tekkan called for contributions to the New Poetry Society. Naturally enough, he knew he couldn't rely on support from the Hayashis now. He was desperately searching for any contingent to stave off his dire financial straits.

Busy and harrassed, Tekkan fell ill from his old stomach complaint. To make matters worse, baby Atsumu had digestive troubles and diarrhea, and his young mother was upset. Swollen with beriberi, Takino had been ordered by the doctor to cease breast-feeding, so they had to buy milk for the baby. Both parents were flustered and unsettled. Takino even had difficulty paying the wages of her servant Moyo, yet she couldn't dismiss her because she herself was so taken up with housework, helping to run *Myojo*, and looking after Atsumu. She had pawned all she could, and was living from hand to mouth. She had no way of knowing that her parents had told Tekkan that they must part and were awaiting her return.

Akiko greedily devoured *Myojo*'s letter of protest. She absolutely no doubt that Tekkan was perfectly right to be enraged.

"It's only natural if they're going to publish a nude picture of a woman," said her mother in astonishment. "How can they do something so obscene?"

To which Akiko replied, "But Mother, all the pictures in the West are like that, they're really lovely. There's absolutely nothing obscene about them. That's art, that's the art of the new age."

"West is West and Japan is Japan. It's wrong to publish such things."

> How hard to explain
> about you
> to my mother
> who has caught
> the faintest rumors of you.

Behind her mother's back, Akiko continued to send two- or three-*yen* donations with a card. She was unbearably moved at the figure of Sensei, living on such a pure plane and doing endless battle with the world. She suddenly felt her love for Tekkan moving into the dimension of reality.

Every time a letter from Akiko arrived, Tekkan opened it with beating heart. He did not cease to think lovingly of his wife, and therefore he was loath to send her home as her parents had requested. Here he was, temporising by hiding the talk of separation from his wife on the one hand, while on the other enjoying thoughts of how things would develop with Akiko. A typical man's irresponsible hedonism in the ways of love.

> Ah, how hot
> that night
> your breast when I
> left tangled
> my fringing hair.

This poem of Akiko's struck Tekkan like a gust of wind head-on. What an extraordinary woman – she spoke little when one met her, but her fierce gaze could pin you to the spot and make the heart leap. Such a bold, willful, wanton look. And yet both her heart and her talents still lay not fully roused from their deep sleep.

But little by little, the time of awakening was approaching. The thought only increased Tekkan's affection and interest in her.

He could not resist composing poetry for her, poetry full of love and praise.

> She would commit
> her very life
> to my poetry, she said
> and tears stood in her eyes
> her hair tangled.

In *Myojo* he published two free-verse poems, one titled "Long Drunkenness" with the dedication "For you with your tangled hair," and the other titled "Mountain Knotweed" inscribed "For that person with cold feet."

"Mountain Knotweed" began with the following verse:

> Like powerless parents all ideals failed
> and the young friends turned from the world in loathing.
> At evening, trembling hand in hand
> they laid their heads in the western hills.

and ended as follows:

> Well, my dear,
> little one
> beautiful one,
> still unfulfilled
> in the morning we part.
> Do not leave forever
> upon the palm of your brother and sister
> only your white lotus heart
> do not ever forget it.
>
> Treading in light mist the mountain path
> how should you regret
> the breath upon the red stem
> of that mountain knotweed drawing us to part?
> Remember how, cold-sleeved in our ideals,
> we swallowed poison that evening
> and how our living blood flowed with that color.

Tomiko responded with this:

> How ill I was
> for your sake
> whom we both loved,
> jealous of my sister
> lamenting the transience.
>
> You did not tell me
> so how could
> this ignorant child have known
> how bitter the taste of love
> in that mountain knotweed.

Myojo was publishing for the public eye what amounted to love letters.

PART VI. MEDUSA'S HEAD

1

In January the following year, 1901 – the start of a new century – Akiko received an express delivery letter from Tekkan. He wanted to meet her in Kyoto after attending the January literary competition in Kobe later that month.

Now that Tomiko had married and left, Akiko would meet Tekkan alone, and place her feet firmly on the path of her fate. She trembled as she awaited the approaching day.

There was still time to say no. She could avoid the approaching comet, the thunder and flames of the fierce shock of impact that would shatter the life she had lived until this moment and open up new worlds for her. *I can still choose to live my life unbroken in tranquillity and security*, she told herself. She could do as Tomiko had said, marrying according to her parents' wishes, bearing children, and quietly ageing and decaying in her hometown, an old woman who would laughingly mention to others that she used to write poetry in her youth.

In an agony of indecision, Akiko lowered her face to the desk and wept. It was no doubt quite literally as her poem expressed:

> My thoughts,
> my thousand thoughts
> tangled, twisted
> like my thousand
> tangled strands of hair.

But in the end she knew. Her will to go and meet him had never really wavered.

Standing now
and turning to look back
I see my love was then
like one blind
who does not fear the dark.

That day, Akiko gained permission from her mother to go away for two days, on the grounds that Tomiko had come back to Osaka. It was January 25th.

She did up her hair in the swept-back *gingko-gaeshi* style, and put on a dark red coat bearing the family crest, the collar tucked under a woollen shawl. It was a suitable outfit for a New Year excursion, but her mother couldn't help grumbling when she saw it. "Here you are at your age, still dressing as an unmarried girl…" Akiko was twenty-four this year, an age considered late for marrying.

Akiko was aware that her parents had more than half made up their minds to marry her to Sadashichi. If her mother so much as hinted at this, Akiko always diverted the conversation. Even when she was sitting at work in the shop's little office, her heart inhabited a different world. Thanks to this other world, there was now no turning back for her. But no matter how she loved and yearned for Tekkan, she knew her parents would never allow her to be with a married man.

"And when will you be back, Sho dearie?" asked Outa as she set out Akiko's shoes for her.

"I'm not sure – tomorrow, maybe the day after…"

Outa offered to see her to the station, but Akiko said she would go on her own, and off she went alone. She left the house without a word, looking exactly as usual. *I choose my fate in silence*, she thought, *telling no one*. She was one who could maintain her silence to the end when she chose.

When she arrived at Tsujino Inn in Kyoto's Mount Awata, the short winter day was already coming to an end. Tekkan had not yet arrived.

"Please take a bath if you'd like…your companion won't be long now I'm sure," said the maid. "At least do change out of your outdoor clothes, ma'am."

But Akiko was unable to settle. She restlessly opened the doors of the side room and went out into the garden, then came back in and sat in the room, warming her chilled hands over the brazier. Dusk came early to this mountain inn, and the surroundings were already growing dim. At last she thought she heard the distant rumble of a rickshaw's wheels.

Hurriedly, Akiko slipped from the outer veranda into the garden. The scent of plum blossom came drifting in with the smell of the bath's steam. Yes – the man who was suddenly striding towards her through the dark was Tekkan himself.

"Sensei! You're so late…" Akiko fell into his embracing arms.

Tekkan was gaunt and haggard. Yet he seemed elated, and his eyes shone.

How lovely a lean man is, thought Akiko. Until now, she had revered him as her senior and Sensei, but now this reverence gave way to a different emotion. The man who stood here holding her was a touchingly powerless being. A sudden rush of poignant love overwhelmed her.

The bath water and the hot sake warmed them. Like sinners huddled together out of sight, who begrudged an instant's separation, they crouched there willing time to stop, clinging to this passing night and its fleeting moments. In the bath, Akiko drank in the fragrant breath of a man, and at the table a man's hand held her sake cup to her lips.

"Thank you for coming, Miss Akiko… On my way here I feared that perhaps you wouldn't come to me, that you too would have abandoned me…"

"But Sensei, how could I? My mind was made up. Still, there must be many others you love more than me – your wife, Tomiko…"

"No, no one as much as you."

"Sensei, please call me Akiko! I won't mind." Akiko's provincial lilt delighted Tekkan's ears. She snuggled in against him. Fresh from the hot bath, her body burned like fire. Or was it the effects of the sake she had just drunk, that coursed through her veins like a poison? Tekkan put his lips to her wild black hair. How thick and hot it was! It gave off a strong scent of oils.

"You don't regret this, Akiko?"

"No, neither regret nor bitterness…"

She remembered how, when the three had stayed here together months ago, she had spoken the lines "How swiftly comes/ the punishment for sin." How could she not wager all for this moment, no matter how cruel the punishment for the sin of loving? Let her name be sullied, her fate be altered – how could she not choose to flame for this one moment with the man who had come to set the light in her, despite that he had a wife and child?

"I've been waiting for a woman like you, Akiko… You don't mind? Truly?" She felt a man's hands, a man's fingers, lips.

"No, if it's Sensei…" For her, his hands and lips swept the present moment away and in its place she felt the longings of past and future, all her desires, life itself, her very soul leap beyond the heavens, in an ecstasy full of the harmonies of death.

"How rich…you spill from my hands…such rich strength brimming! Ah Akiko, what a wonderful woman you are!" cried Tekkan, holding her hot breasts. He felt a free, bold passion break the fetters of reason, rise and take wing in him. Here was a woman strong enough to lure him to such a pitch. Were it not so, these hot, firm breasts would not be in his hands.

> Oh, only let
> this fire rage
> and burn on –
> thus do I feel
> as spring flames to its end.
>   (Akiko)

Akiko awoke early. The cold was sharp, but it was a bright, clear, late January day, and sky and earth were crystalline. Bells tolled near and far, perhaps from the great temples of Chion-in and Shogo-in.

Akiko called someone in to dress her tangled hair in the adjoining room. She gazed at herself in the mirror in the morning light, and felt she had never looked so beautiful.

The temple bells had not woken Tekkan, but when she went to his side he opened his eyes. "That was a bush warbler singing just now," he said.

"Really? You heard it?"

"I thought I did, yes… Ah, you've done your hair up so prettily." Tekkan sat up, and looked at Akiko's hair with a smile. "I was woken by the scent of your hair oil."

"You don't like it?"

"I love it."

Seen from Tekkan's arms, the city below, shrouded in morning's pink mists, seemed lovely as if a dream.

Familiar with Kyoto as he was, Tekkan pointed out to her Mount Nyakuoji and Mount Daimonji. The great gate of Nanzenji Temple, Kurodani Temple's pagoda, and the houses at the foot of the eastern mountains floated hazily in the mists, like a world below viewed from heaven.

The white powder she applied to her face was cold to the touch in the pre-spring air, and did not go on smoothly. Tekkan put his hand on the hand that held her rouge brush, drew it over to a piece of paper, and guided it to write two words there: "Yosano Akiko."

"There may be a day when you will write this," he said. The words struck Akiko with the force of a marriage proposal.

The two walked the mountain path together. A bush warbler sang on a distant mountainside, and the path was strewn thick with the crimson of fallen camellia blossoms.

"Tomiko was with us last autumn, wasn't she," Tekkan remarked. Instantly, jealousy sprang up in Akiko's heart.

"You're always thinking of Tomiko, Sensei. It's true, isn't it?"

"No."

"Just for today, think only of me, will you? Please?"

"But of course, Akiko!"

Yet later that day as they lazed at the inn, Tekkan asked the maid to lend him an inkstone and brush, and wrote a letter. What an unfathomable heart the man had! The letter was to Takino back in Tokyo. Aware of this, Akiko sat with shoulders hunched, enduring what she felt was almost a rebuke aimed at herself. She could not let herself feel jealousy towards this woman who was after all his wife, and so her suffering was turned inward against herself, and ate at her frail heart. The hatred she felt was turned against Tekkan. How could he, at this precious time, before her very eyes!

Tekkan seemed to be excusing himself when he remarked, "I've been away from home longer than expected, so I just thought of a few things that need attending to…"

"I guess you love your wife, don't you, Sensei? I understand."

"Well, as for her…" He laid down his brush and put his head in his hands miserably. "Even if my father-in-law in Tokuyama insists we separate, I would keep her as my lover. But she's a cold-hearted woman, that one. She doesn't understand my love."

For Akiko, this felt like a fatal declaration. This man knew nothing of how terrifying it was to tell one woman that he loved another. He was as devious as a child when it came to women's hearts. She trembled. She should now have grown angry and despised him, but it was all too late. Even so demeaned, so trampled, still she wanted to be with him. Though she knew that his heart did not belong solely to her, she needed him to embrace her. Cruelly treated though she may be, she could only cling to his feet.

How far will people debase themselves for the sake of love? Crushed with grief, Akiko carried Tekkan's letter to the maid to be posted. That evening once more she soared, flaming from the hellish depths of sorrow to the heights of bliss. They spent two nights together.

2

After Tekkan had returned to Tokyo, Akiko wrote a letter. She wrote and wrote until she could write no more and found it had become poetry; the words, the verses, poured from her as if some other stood behind her guiding the pen. Each moment's memory from her time on Mount Awata tortured her, driving her to a madness greater even than before they had met.

In the land of spring
the sacred land of love
first light, the clarity
is it hair?
Oil of plum blossom.
I have turned my back
on the gods to whom I pledged
to meet you no more.
Farewell to all farewelling!
Sin will not trouble my heart again.
No talk of moral paths
of what's to come, of reputations –
here in love,
loving we meet.
You and I.
Your five fingers
so frail to clutch
the sword you turn
against the demons –
I take them in my mouth.
The morning I
rose early and bound up
my tangled hair into the *Shimada*,
though I would let you lie
I shook you awake to see.
The morning holds no chill
for the bush warbler's voice
here in Kyoto's mountains where we tread
together, intimate,
the fallen camellias.

The poems were sighs, groans of despair, chortles of victory, sobs of anguish, whispers of a devil foretelling destruction. Sunk in gloom, her heart distrait, as each new feeling and thought issued from her lips, it flowered resplendent and transformed into a distilled jewel of poetry.

In the same issue of *Myojo*, Tekkan's poem titled "Spring Thoughts" appeared, a poem that raised its voice in praise of the blissful realms of love. It was as if they were breathing in unison.

> Abandoned flaming arms twisting
> we two drown in each other

> And how should we look back?
> At the end of the world lies the sacred…

Tekkan's wife Takino was stunned by Akiko's poems, and hurt by her husband's. She had long been aware of how matters stood, but when she saw what Akiko had sent her husband, the truth of it came home to her. Tekkan neither hid nor threw away the letters; he was indifferent that his wife would see them.

"I was worried that you may have trouble meeting your commitments on the 31st of last month – child of a merchant household as I am, I know something of such worries," Akiko wrote, concerned at how Tekkan would have been able to make ends meet.

"My thoughts are constantly dwelling on death, but always after all I think 'And yet, how I love'…

> You have gone, and
> now you must forget
> your wife of one spring night,
> that dream maiden of myth,
> until our next world's meeting.
> • • •
> Feelings that seem
> not those of the common world
> I feel, and now,
> ah here is
> you…"

And in another letter:

"Every night before sleep I read your "Spring Thoughts," and after that I look at your photograph, and then I sleep warm… Today, the 15th, all the shop's employees have a holiday, and I am writing this in the room next door, planning how to open the door so no one will hear me and run to the post office with it... At least, my love, may I be your marriage cup in the world to come – although for this lifetime I will not hold you to this promise."

What was coming has arrived, thought Takino. Yet even so, she could not throw herself trembling and weeping upon her husband. Perhaps if she were married to a different man, but with Tekkan she could never give herself over so completely. She had automatically steeled herself with an instinct of self-preservation, closed herself against him for protection in order to withstand the pain of his actions. This was a man who could write:

> It is as foolish
> to condemn your love
> as to question
> the scarlet
> of scarlet.

"Darling, I read that poem of Akiko's about the fallen camellias. Tekkan the Tiger seems to have turned into Tekkan the Lover. So you've let Akiko draw the tiger's fangs, eh?" Takino smiled mockingly. "How did that poem of yours go again?

> Seven feet of red scabbard
> dew drips from the drawn sword
> Who is the sword-maker? Bizen Kanemitsu.
> Gaily I stride the six lands, sword in hand
> not yet placed on the grave of my friend.

That was it, I think. That's the sort of bold, manly poem you once wrote, remember? But seems there's no new moves left in the repertoire of the old Tiger School, eh?"

This was the only way Takino could express her jealousy. There was in Tekkan something cruel and brutal that drove women to react like this, something that he did not recognize as his own fault. He only felt peevishly that Takino was a cold woman.

"That's not so. The love of an artist is simply the action of the heroic man. The battle for such love is the same as a sword battle, it's a fight against the old ways, against custom, to bring ideals to realization. Goethe had twenty mistresses, you know. Byron had uncountable lovers."

"Here we go. Goethe and Byron again, is it?" Takino's lips closed tight in an icy, bitter smile. She regretted having begun this pointless conversation. There was no way she could have a real dialogue with her husband, she thought grimly.

One day, when Tekkan was absent for the day, someone suddenly appeared at the door.

"Anyone home?" came the voice. It was a man in priest's clothing. Takino went to the door with Atsumu in her arms, and was astonished to find there Iwashiro Tatsujo, the priest from the Pure Land temple near her old family home.

Business had brought him here, he told her. But his business was apparently with her rather than with Tekkan. He had been asked by the Hayashis to report on how Takino was doing. They were worrying about whether she was well, whether she had recovered from the beriberi, whether perhaps Atsumu was still too young for the journey. They were waiting for her to come home. This was his message.

Takino's mother had been badgering her in letters to return, but she'd assumed this was more of the usual pleas. Atsumu was still too small, she'd decided, and besides, it was hard to decide to leave Tekkan. And so the days had passed. But now, Tatsujo gave her the story more directly than her mother had.

"When your father met Tekkan back in October, he apparently demanded that the relationship be severed."

Takino had heard nothing of this from Tekkan. What it amounted to was that her father had refused to allow her to be formally entered in the Yosano family register. But she did not want to let Tatsujo know that she'd been unaware of all this, and thereby reveal how little her husband communicated with her.

"I'm just here to deliver the message. Anyway, you seem well, and the baby's growing nicely, so I'll simply tell them nothing's wrong. It's just that your father's been worrying." It was almost time for him to catch the train, so he left, asking her to convey his apologies to Tekkan that he had not been able to see him.

Takino, of course, could hardly wait till her husband returned so that she could cross-examine him.

Cornered, Tekkan had to admit that it was true. "But I didn't keep it from you on purpose, you know. I asked your mother to intercede for me. Besides, it was never my own intention, so I didn't really know how things would turn out, and what good would it have done to worry you by telling you about it before it was all clear…"

"I hate this sort of hypocrisy, hiding things like that!" Takino was sobbing with anger. The house was so small that the maid Moyo, who was looking after Atsumu, would have overheard, but at this point she wasn't able to pause and worry about that. "This is just typical of the sort of thing you always do. I find your behavior quite unreasonable and incomprehensible… Why do you never tell the truth? You're perfectly happy to show the world at large everything about Akiko and Tomiko, and here you are keeping hidden something that's really important. It's disgusting, that attitude…"

Takino was sobbing hysterically. She herself did not realize that all this was in fact an expression of her jealousy.

"You're wrong! It's all because I love you! I don't want to lose you, that's why I kept quiet. I couldn't tell you because you'd leave the moment I did…"

"You're just selfish, that's all! You're an emotional cripple who only thinks about himself. To say such things!"

Their voices had risen. The next day Takino attacked Tekkan again.

"Hold on! Hold on a minute, that's not how it is at all…" he protested. He was caught in a predicament. The fact was, in order to publish the financially troubled *Myojo*, he had asked his friend Utsumi Getsujo to borrow money at high interest. Two of Getsujo's colleagues from work had agreed to stand as guarantors for the loan. If Tekkan couldn't repay the loan, there'd be more than trouble for Getsujo and his colleagues – their employer was the Ministry of Education, a notoriously inflexible institution, and they could well lose their jobs.

The only thing that sustained Tekkan in all this was that *Myojo* was just now entering its full flowering. Women in particular had flocked to join the group, and there was something of a *Myojo* craze going around among female readers. The magazine was full of poems submitted by these contributors: Akiko alone was sending 70 or 80 fine poems each month, and although Tomiko was now married and therefore rather distant from the activity, there were poems by women such as Masuda Masako (later Chino Masako), Tamano Hanako, Nakahama Itoko, and Hayashi Nobuko – poems of maidenly purity, of gorgeous excess, and of fierce emotion, dotting the pages like flowers.

Just at the moment when, with the help of the young men, *Myojo's* members were blossoming and the future looked glowing, now came the worst possible crisis.

"Because of me, because of the mistake Getsujo and I have made, three men of literature have lost their position as public officials," Tekkan wrote to Akiko. "I have done a sorry thing." The three had indeed been dismissed, simply for being guarantors for Tekkan's bad debt.

To add to Tekkan's troubles, in March he was incensed by the circulation of an anonymous work attacking him. The booklet, which slandered and maligned his personal character, was called *Yosano Tekkan, Portrait of a Demon of the Literary World*, and its appearance became known as the Literary Demon Incident.

The pamphlet that appeared in bookshops and was sent out to people in the literary world was dated 10th March 1901. The publisher was listed as the Dainippon Purification Society in Yokohama, but both this and the few names that were listed were fabrications. The malicious intention of the work was to ostracize Tekkan. The anonymous author was evidently thoroughly familiar with Tekkan's behavior, and attacked Tekkan in minute detail under a series of shocking headings.

The sixteen "Criminal Acts" of which Tekkan was accused: "Tekkan Sold Wife," "Tekkan Drove Virgin to Madness," "Tekkan Raped," "Tekkan Tried to Shoot Girl," "Tekkan Committed Robbery and Arson," "Tekkan Adept at Not Paying for Food," etc. – and detailed the evidence under each one. Readers were stunned by these headings, as well as by the fierce rage and personal animosity of the writing.

177

The accusations were either groundless or much exaggerated and distorted. The fact that he had used money from his wife's family to publish *Myojo*, that he lorded over his young male and female followers like the founder of some sect, details about his two followers Ho Akiko and Yamakawa Tomiko, and his arrogant belief that he alone was a new-style poet – all these were true, and all could be seen as scandalous depending on how they were presented.

Tekkan was furious. Judging from what was written, he decided it must be the work of someone who had free access to the New Poetry Society, either Takasu Hojiro or Ichijo Narumi. Both were close friends of his. However, Takasu wrote for the rival magazine *Shinsei*, and the popular Ichijo, who had done illustrations for *Myojo*, had also recently been poached by *Shinsei*. Ichijo had lived for a time in Tekkan's household, so he knew various intimate facts, while Takasu was a member of *Yoshiashigusa* in Osaka, so he knew a great deal about Tekkan's affairs with Akiko and Tomiko, and had a source of further news. Even if they themselves had not written *Portrait of a Demon of the Literary World*, there was a strong possibility that they had fed information to the author.

Tekkan suspected that Takasu himself could well have written the damning criticism of him as a poet: "Tekkan came to be lionized by the world for producing tiger and sword, and flashing around his grandiose gestures; for his flamboyant heroics at a time when the world was tired of the old poetic school's shilly-shallying ways... He has exploited his present fame to establish his power, and is feverishly seeking to extend it yet further... He is held to be the most peaceable (nay, lethargic) poet in the literary world, but he wears a mask, and deceives all his followers with his wheedling and cajoling. I hereby publicly denounce him as follows: 'You are a traitor of conscience, and a scoundrel who corrodes society.'"

If this incident had amounted to no more than the publication of the pamphlet, it would have been merely an instance of the kind of harassment that occurs from time to time, and the rumours would have died.

But when Takasu aired the contents of the pamphlet in the fourth issue of *Shinsei*, the scandal spread. *Portrait of a Demon* took on fresh meaning. Why did Takasu feel he must take up this underhand personal attack and parade it before his readers so ostentatiously, rather than ignoring it as it deserved? Surely this was something that no gentleman or person associated with the artistic world should do? Even if he hadn't written the work, surely to make a point of laying it out for all to see like this amounted to the same thing?

Tekkan sued Takasu, whom he saw as the author of the work, and Nakane Komajuro, who was registered as the publisher of *Shinsei*. It was clear to anyone of any conscience who read the piece that those at *Myojo's* rival *Shinsei* had slanderously fabricated tales out of jealousy of Tekkan's fame and *Myojo's* popularity, but public opinion had been fanned against both the journal and its leader, and abuse rained down on them.

Portrait of a Demon had branded him as "Demon Tekkan." It had spread the image of him as a man who had taken a wife for the sake of gaining money; who had compromised the chastity of his female followers; who was talentless, arrogant and rude; and who was a vicious and evil schemer.

"Takino, do you believe I'm like that?"

To his chagrin, he was deeply hurt by this base plot. And his wife should have been the one to support him with love and encouragement at such a time, but Takino was preoccupied with a different matter.

"No, I don't think you're such a dreadful person — but it does seem clear it wasn't just an innocent relationship with Akiko and Tomiko. Tell me the truth. It's true, isn't it?"

"What would you do if I said yes?"

"So it's as I thought. You really did!" Takino was jubilant. She was engrossed in her own female anguish, rather than in Tekkan's predicament. For her, nothing was more important than her husband's relations with other women. Tekkan had always been an incomprehensible, incompatible person, but to betray one's wife with other women was unforgivable to Takino, who had been educated in the new era.

The result of the suit was that the defendants were declared not guilty. Tekkan gained nothing but defeat and further notoriety from the case. Taguchi Kikutei, a reporter for *Shinsei*, struck a fine pose when he wrote, "Our party does not deign to pass comment on the likes of a small-fry like Tekkan," Research now suggests that Taguchi was in fact the author of the original work.

Readership of *Myojo* fell sharply, and many female members dropped out. One can see just how badly Tekkan had been hit by the fact that he ceased to use the pseudonym he had always so loved. In a poem, he compared himself to a wounded and bloody dove.

> That dove returning
> in the spring sunset
> wings deep dyed
> in its own blood –
> can it be myself?

Mindless of her suffering husband, Takino wrote to Akiko. She was planning to leave Tekkan and return to her parents, she said, so Akiko should feel free to marry him. Her mind was made up. She was not doing it for Akiko's sake, she had planned to leave for some time. Please don't misunderstand me, she wrote, I am not saying this out of jealousy of you.

Back came a letter from Akiko.

"I am happy, happy for your sympathetic understanding. Please imagine how my heart is in turmoil. You will surely have guessed, gentle sister, that I had no idea such a sorry event would occur, or that you and I would come to exchange such letters as these. Those vain poems I wrote have led to unfounded aspersions being cast upon your husband. Can you ever forgive me? This child of sin is so sad. So ashamed. Your letter, so kind and gentle, drew tears to my eyes. Please forgive these wild words I write today, please forgive all, all."

3

In her letter, Akiko used the expression "child of sin" to the woman who was her lover's wife. These were the words of a woman who still held to the old ethical system of feminine virtue in her heart, much as her head understood the need to challenge this feudal morality. That competitive spirit that burned so fiercely in her in relation to other women friends in the group, such as Tomiko and Masuda Masako (also a beauty), for some reason turned to a timorous, shrinking creature before Takino.

Takino seems to have been the exact opposite type of woman from Akiko. On the surface she had all the bearing of a fine old-fashioned wife, but in fact she seems to have been a rational person whose way of thinking was determinedly realistic and modern.

She was giving up all hope for her life with Tekkan. She had put up with poverty and her husband's affairs, but face to face with Akiko's fevered passion, she could not muster the desire to battle it out and defend her place as wife. She was a resolute and decisive woman, not the sort to temporize with half-hearted jealousies and nagging and sulks. I imagine her to have been the kind of woman who, for all her apparent obedience, had none of the old-fashioned belief that one must stand by one's man in his time of adversity. She intrigues me, this woman with such an unstained, unclouded nature, a nature reminiscent of a perfect white sphere. She strikes me as a modern Meiji woman in the real sense, the sort who could break through and discard the old morality of "The chaste wife does not take a second husband." She was certainly not one to be blindly subservient to her husband's demands.

Here are two poems Takino wrote:

> Abuse me as you may
> and call me cold
> yet surely
> you are at heart
> one drawn to coldness.
> • • •
> As a water drop
> holds all the many
> shapes of its surroundings
> so my body holds
> all women.

One has a vivid image of a chilly, intelligent woman.

Tekkan was a defeated man. He had suffered for months with the fear that his wife may leave him, and now he faced the unavoidable

181

moment itself. A letter arrived from Takino's family urging her to come home. As Takino's poems relate:

> I tell him I will go
> and yet today too
> my husband
> does not say yes,
> does not say no.
>
> • • •
>
> I turn you away
> with the excuse
> of beri-beri
> and yet I am sure
> that you love me.

Since Atsumu's birth, Takino had used various pretexts not to sleep with Tekkan (apparently because she feared that she might fall pregnant again and thereby lose her chance to part from him). Even this no doubt only spurred Tekkan's desperate attachment to her.

Besides, Tekkan absolutely adored his son. He would often walk about holding him in his arms. The seven-month-old Atsumu was Tekkan's dearest comfort, and he could not bear to lose the child if his wife went.

"Come on, Takino, change your mind, I beg you."

"It doesn't matter how long we talk, nothing will change, will it? You have plenty of lovers, plenty of friends…I want to make a new start myself. You should remarry the girl in Sakai."

"No, it's not like that. If you leave, that's half my life, gone in a flash."

> Your mouth speaks
> of a long separation –
> so strong you seem
> and yet
> in truth how weak.
>
> • • •

Parting from you,
this hand
can place no flower
to adorn your hair,
that hair so groomed and neat.

Those "plenty of friends" that Takino referred to, people who had shown their friendship by refusing to desert *Myojo* during the Literary Demon Incident, were silently sympathetic with Takino. They would not say so aloud, but to them it seemed inevitable that the marriage must end.

As for the maid Moyo, though she was on Takino's side, she had devoted herself to helping raise Atsumu for the last half a year, and she was loath to part from the two of them.

"You should hold out, ma'am, and keep a careful eye on your husband. What if he takes up with some wicked woman?" Moyo was afraid Takino was feebly resigning from her position as wife rather than putting up a fight.

Takino continued exchanging letters with her parents, and it was finally decided that she would take her baby and go back home on April 9th.

"Send a telegram as soon as you arrive, won't you... I'm worried about you. Look after Atsumu." Tekkan, who had accompanied them to the station at Shinbashi like a faithful and loving husband, had tears in his eyes.

"And you... take care of yourself."

Takino was tearful too. The fact is, she and Tekkan were temperamentally incompatible; he was simply too different, someone beyond her understanding and outside her imaginative scope. *If only you were a more modest and conscientious person, I could have loved you!* she cried in her heart. She could not forgive him for his lying, secretive ways, first over Asada Sadako, and then over his discussion with her father about the separation. *You're a vain, arrogant, deceitful man, with a cowardly spirit!* her heart accused.

No! cried Tekkan's heart to her, *No, it was all because I love you. Why can't you understand that? You're truly the only one I love...* The wife who had just left him filled his heart.

Once home, he threw himself into writing to her. "I do hope you have arrived safely," he wrote. Then he proceeded to harp on and on about the fact that she had not sent a telegram on her arrival as he'd asked. "I think of you with love and longing. Stay there until the autumn, for our son's sake, then come back. You must absolutely set about enrolling in the women's university. No one should be left to rot like plants or trees do."

The university he referred to was the Japan Women's University that had been founded in 1901 by Naruse Jinzo. It was a focus of aspiration for modern girls and according to Aoki Takako, author of the biography of Chino Masako, it was "well known as a mecca for progressive women." Partly due to his own lack of academic qualifications, Tekkan had a deep respect for universities, and he encouraged his lovers, Tomiko and Masuda Masako to enroll.

"I have been declared bankrupt, and intend to move with Moyo to a place where I can commute by train, to somewhere really really small. I haven't yet been able to pay last month's rent... I am overwhelmed with gratitude, with appreciation that you should have been so kind as to undergo the sufferings and heartache you did on account of one such as myself. What manly tears I weep in my heart, unworthy that I am! She (Akiko) lives at home, and cannot share a life with me. She is resigned to loving me from afar, I who must live my life alone...

"I hope to publish the next issue of *Myojo* on May 5th. I am today a poor poet, without even loose change to my name. I pity you – you must be worrying. If all goes well for me, I hope to go to Mitajiri to meet you, so that together we can go to Miyajima and comfort one another. I also plan to meet Akiko and Masako in Osaka en route. Don't catch cold, and don't let the boy catch cold. I love you and long for you, and tonight I have written some poems to send you. Please make sure you give the boy good cow's milk."

> This spring
> at twenty-nine
> cherishing you, Takino,
> in letters
> I yet love Akiko

he wrote. It was a letter full of schoolgirlish, clinging sentiments. He was thrashing about, unable to accept things and resign himself.

The only thing that could sustain him at this moment was to write. Tekkan's bad reputation had caused the public's image of *Myojo* to change drastically. The high-flying "child of the stars" had plummeted to earth, and lay there muddied. Tekkan was defeated.

It was all very well to be deserted by friends in the group and readers – good riddance to them, thought Tekkan – but what pained him irrecoverably was that his own name had been so besmirched. He wrote a rebuttal to the *Portrait of a Demon*, but he felt helplessly lonely and bereft.

What was more, the woman who should have been there in his hour of need, to praise and encourage him and breathe fresh strength into him to battle on, had left him. Tekkan was someone who needed constant love to reassure him. His foundation stood upon the respect and admiration of others, and his abandonment by the one who was closest to him had rocked that foundation deeply. All he could do was to go on writing desperate letters.

Even in these letters, however, he couldn't resist mentioning meeting Akiko and Masako. Furthermore, while he was writing like this to Takino he was also shooting off a string of letters to Akiko. One can only conclude that he was a truly complex and fascinating man. Any woman who became involved with someone like this would be worn to a frazzle, yet on the other hand it seems to me that this type is wildly attractive to certain women.

The Literary Demon Incident, which had provided the impetus to Takino's departure, brought Tekkan and Akiko closer.

News of Tekkan's reputation had of course spread to Sakai. Akiko, who had begun the task of revealing to her family that she and Tekkan were in love, was now miserably caught between her worried parents and her brothers who were against the relationship.

"Just look at the sort of man Tekkan is!"

Akiko found it unbearable to hear her parents insult him like this, believing what they heard.

But Sensei's honest! she thought. *He's honest to himself, and tries to live according to the dictates of his own heart. That's what common folk find provoking, and that's why they resent and loathe him. He's actually an honest man, incapable of lying.*

Akiko's idea of Tekkan was as different from Takino's as light from dark – that's the sort of man he was. Perhaps he swung too widely between the extremes. When Akiko learned that Takino had left him, it aroused her feelings to a still higher pitch. She grew thin with anxiety and fretfulness over why he didn't call her to be with him immediately. Yet she had still not brought herself to decide finally to leave her family. She was being increasingly criticized and reprimanded at home.

Tekkan wrote tirelessly to Akiko.

"Yesterday I received a visit from Kimura Takataro (translator of Byron). 'Come on,' he said, 'confess this relationship with the fine lady from Izumi. It's dreadful to cram the pages of your rag with it like this. Everyone knows now, so no excuses. Byron wouldn't have paled in this situation, after all. At it, boy!' I must say I had to smile. You cannot rail now against the gods. We must love with pride. Our love is greater than poetry can ever express. For this I must be proud. I am remembering our time together in Awata. I long to see you. The end of April is so very very distant."

This was Tekkan, a man who could pen love letters to two women simultaneously (or perhaps even three, if he was also writing to the poet Masuda Masako, whose talent he admired) – on the one hand wracked with love for his wife, on the other hand dallying with seductive words that would pour oil on the already inflamed fires of his lover's passion – and who could happily live with these contradictions within him. What's more, he was in earnest with both women. To Takino he wrote, as if in defense of Akiko, "Miss Ho says that she will always consider you a sister. She is a dear person. You must never never think badly of her."

Meanwhile, he wrote to Akiko twisting the facts in apparent self-protection: "Takino is a pure-minded and determined person, who obeys her parents' injunctions. She is a brave woman with a lonely fate, and I cannot bear to hurt her. It makes me tearful to think how dear she is, how determined and silently long-suffering."

Essentially, he desperately wanted both his wife and his lover to be friends, and to join hands in loving him. He was lacking an adult's rational mind. This chosen "child of the stars" wanted to believe that all women were drawn to him, and wished to love him and to be loved by him.

Takino's parents, who caught glimpses of the flood of letters he sent her, were astonished at how utterly lacking in common sense he seemed. She had determined to leave him and taken the child with her, and from their point of view the ties with Tekkan were thereby broken.

"You must not take another husband. I love you deeply, and you have been always deep in my heart even when I was with Akiko and others – you and Akiko."

"We are lovers for all eternity. I want to seal your name in history as such. Yet it is not conducive to your happiness to be by my side. I am more full of error than the average person. I cannot now become a calm and gentle poet. I believe I will continue to have troubles, commit errors, and be in debt, until I have gone to the West and returned."

"Please look on Miss Ho as your true sister. You must please permit us our love together. I will also have other loves besides this one. And yet, I still have not decided to make her my wife. I want to keep her forever as a lover, because I must somehow avoid making any wife as unhappy as I have made you, and Miss Asada. This is not something that should be condemned too harshly in a poet. Official accounts alone put the number of Goethe's lovers at twelve, while Byron had countless numbers. I have heard that Byron ended his life unwed."

"You must be broad-minded, you must put away your narrow, earthbound heart."

Don't remarry, be my lover, and what's more overlook the fact that I have affairs with other women – what an utterly astonishing, brazenly selfish request!

"I wonder if this Tekkan is a bit soft in the head," remarked her mother. Takino tore up and disposed of the letter with a thin smile.

"That's the way they all are there, such oddballs…"

But Takino was deeply intrigued by her husband's suggestion about the Japan Women's University. In those days even middle-aged women could freely enter the university, and it was the sole opportunity

available for women who wanted to gain their independence as
school teachers. And Takino longed to be independent.

Tekkan urged her in every letter to go to the university, and always
added endearments: "I long for you and love you." "Everything is my
fault. I loved you from youth, and I have driven you away although
I still adore you."

Takino, who had registered her child as fatherless, and who hated
being back in her family home, found her heart gradually swayed by
these entreaties.

In May she returned to Tokyo, with Atsumu in her arms.

4

Tekkan had moved from Kojimachi to 272 Nakashibuya. He had
been served a warrant of repossession, and been deserted by his wife,
so he needed to make a new start in life.

"Oh madam, welcome back," exclaimed Moyo when she saw
Takino. "Stay here this time and hang on to your husband." Moyo
believed that Takino had withdrawn because she was too meek. "It'd
be terrible if that grasping girl from Sakai seduced Mr. Tekkan, and
snuck into your place."

"Moyo, that's enough…I intend to part from him. I've decided I'm
going to go back to studying and make my living as a girls' school
teacher. My parents have both told me I should do as I want."

"But madam, this is terrible. You'll gain nothing by being so
fainthearted. All the neighbours are on your side, you know. They're
impressed at how well you put up with such a terrible husband…"

"Moyo, please don't criticise my husband."

Takino's feelings were complex. She had made up her mind to part
from him, but now that she was back and saw how madly delighted
he was to have the child in his arms again, and ran her eyes over
the familiar things that filled the house, she felt her good sense
being assailed. This man was the father of her son, she felt, and her
own husband.

Though it seemed on the outside a restoration of the former
peace of the family, hearts once broken cannot be brought together
again as they were before. Takino continued subtly to elude her

husband's seeking hands. She followed her parents' advice and set about preparing a way to eventually rent a house from which she would be able to commute to the women's university. Her plan was to spend a little time sheltering in this house while she looked for somewhere to rent.

Akiko was writing to Tekkan saying she wanted to come to Tokyo, to which he replied: "It really is not the time right now. I ask that you put off the plan until the beginning of June. I hate to do this, but for the moment we cannot go against the gods…"

He swung between agonizing and soothing her. At the same time, he was writing: "As for me, I would love your hands to be removing my summer clothing, and to bury my head in the scent of your hair. Never believe that we will not meet again. I long to see you. The wisteria blossoms are already tumbling, yet still we are apart. I would rush to your arms."

These were cruel words, aimed on the one hand at throwing her naive girl's heart into a turmoil of love, while on the other restraining her. He made no attempt to consider how painfully her passion must have burned, and how his letters must have inflamed her further, in the days since they had last met in January and over the distance of three hundred miles that separated them. Later, Akiko describes the love she was feeling:

> Ridiculous
> those topsy-turvy claims
> by all around me
> that it is I
> who call you to me.

Tekkan was the one who called – or at the least, it was he who had driven her to her present state. Akiko was sending devoted love letters, and letters are things that intensify the force of fiction rather than reality. It seems to me that perhaps if that distance had not separated them, their love would not have developed as it did.

Distance sent their letters to and fro, and those letters mixed dream and desire inextricably with reality, dyeing the relationship with the single colour of passion. To go to Tekkan, to live with him, to pin one's life and one's poetry on this man…this was all she longed to do. The letters that came from him and those she sent in return gradually drew them both into a fierce intoxication.

Moyo had referred to Akiko as "that grasping girl from Sakai" because the progress of their love was palpable from the letters that poured in.

Tekkan was on tenterhooks at the thought that the impetuous Akiko could at any moment leave home and appear. He didn't want to let her know that Takino had come back to Tokyo; he didn't want Takino to see Akiko. He was afraid his wife and his lover would clash, but there was also the fact that Takino was again suffering from beriberi, Atsumu too was in poor health with diarrhea, and the doctor had advised them to leave Tokyo's heat and retreat to the cool of the countryside. Takino was inclined to leave Tokyo once more. Tokyo's water just doesn't suit me, she thought, miserably turning the problem over in her mind. Meanwhile days passed, and June arrived.

Akiko was impatient. Her heart had already flown to Tokyo and to Tekkan. She recalled her first experience of love – a feeling so innocent and ingenuous it could scarcely be termed love at all – for the artless young man Kono Tetsunan. What tender palpitations of infatuation that long-ago heart had felt! she said to herself. How different from her present suffering, this hellish madness of carnal desire.

Her letter dated June 1st is full of a fantastical delirium: "I will fall into yet more agonized turmoil when tomorrow comes. I am amazed at how I have survived February, March, April, May… In two days' time it will indeed be the 3rd, and from there in due course the 5th will arrive. Darling, but darling, how I suffer, oh how I suffer. Even one day sooner! Such pain, such pain… I know nothing of weakness or strength or suchlike things. If only I could meet you! If I must wait another week, I feel my soul itself cannot bear it. I pray and pray. I cannot simply bow and call it fate."

Thus she wrote as if possessed, from the tangled tresses of her passion-tossed emotions.

"Come and have dinner, Sho dearie," came a call, and with a start she returned to her senses, and hastened to conceal the letter paper. She was about to leave behind this dear familiar home of twenty-four years, turn her back on it without a backward glance, and choose for herself a life full of suffering. When she was feeling strong, she longed to rush to Tokyo then and there; then she would reconsider, and decide that for the moment she would stay and mollify her parents.

Her spirits drooped. A listless inability to feel pleasure gripped her. Did Tekkan's hesitancy mean that he had returned to Takino? With the heightened awareness of one who loves, Akiko intuited that Tekkan was still very much in love with his wife. At the thought, she longed to leap on the earliest train to Tokyo. She would fly the whole distance like one with wings, and rush to his side. She did not want him ever in anyone else's possession again. She was in an agony of jealousy.

At other times, when she was serving her father his dinner, for instance, or sewing with her mother, or while her fingers raced over the abacus in the office, she even now found herself wondering if she could ever leave this place. When she saw the familiar local stream, or gazed at the mountain ranges of Ikoma and Katsuragi, she could not bring herself to believe that she could ever live anywhere else. She couldn't conceive of herself as someone who could do such a thing.

Lately, her mother had begun to talk quite openly about her plans to have Akiko engaged to Sadashichi. Akiko did not reply directly, she simply repeated some vague, half-hearted words in automatic response. It was as if her eyes were fixed somewhere in the distance beyond Sadashichi's small pale face, the ears that stuck out on either side of it like a pair of shelf fungi on a tree, and his permanently sad eyes.

That year, Akiko registered keenly the passing seasons of the first six months – the snow that whitened the peaks of Mount Katsuragi on the day after New Year's; the road to Tonobaba Girls' School, yellow mustard blooming all along it; the white clouds of summer reverberating with the roar of the distant waves; the evening primroses flowering on the banks of the Yamato River. She could still choose to spend her life in peace here in her home town, beside her parents…

And so Akiko spent her days, her heart skittering about, wracked with doubt, now suddenly determined, now full of doubts once more.

A letter from Tekkan arrived, with a woman's name given as the sender. Wait for me on the 5th, it said, at Mount Awata, at the same inn as last time, Tsujino. The situation was urgent.

Akiko gathered up all the money she had at her disposal.

"Tomiko's here, Mum," said Akiko, wheedling. "There's a message saying she wants to meet me. Can I go please?"

Her mother looked displeased. "Your father's worried about you at the moment, dearie… He's in a bad mood, and if he learns later that you've been out and about like this…"

But Akiko ignored her, and went ahead with her preparations.

Don't you dare stop me, Mother, she said in her heart. *Patience, please, patience.* She peered out from wisps of hair that hung about her face, her eyes glittering like an animal's. Yet the eyes saw nothing.

> Family, the gods themselves,
> what do they all amount to?
> I tell myself.
> Ah, my heart,
> be bold!

A fine poem. Elsewhere she calls this her "feeble heart," and another poem refers to it as the "wound from a Naniwa upbringing," as well as its charm and elegance.

> My heart
> loving you
> swells high –
> how small now my parents
> how small that "moral path."

she wrote, and indeed she could not bring herself to act unless she scolded her heart to "be bold."

Tekkan had said that he would come to meet her in Kyoto. He also openly confessed that Takino had returned to Tokyo, and although she said that she was going back home she still hadn't left.

It being Tekkan, no doubt he was wishing and fantasizing that the two women would make friends and behave like intimate sisters, and go through life, one on either side of him. For Akiko, this kind of childish selfishness and ignorance of women was attractive in a man.

While Akiko was resting after her arrival at Tsujino, it was not Tekkan but a telegram from him that arrived for her. He couldn't come, it said, so she should leave on her own.

"Oh, you're going out, ma'am? Dinner's all ready… When will you get back?" asked the astonished maid as Akiko hastened out the door.

"I won't be returning. I'm leaving. The bill please…"

I can't go back, she cried inside, *I can't go back to my parents' house, where I grew to girlhood counting the distant sound of the waves.* She could not return to all her memories, to her infant self, the warm protection of her family, the world of morality, all those old-fashioned precepts about women's behaviour…

Akiko went straight to the station and boarded the train for Tokyo. All she had with her was the bundle containing her make-up bag and a change of clothes – a serge striped kimono and Hakata obi – along with the sun umbrella she held modestly at her side. She had left the house looking casual, so as to avoid any challenge from her mother.

Akiko did not need the usual accoutrements of a dowry, the furniture and kimonos that a bride traditionally took to her new home. She loved the feel of beautiful brocade gauze or crepe cloth, but she was prepared to forego all that now. The only things she clung to for encouragement were the recent throwaway words of her brother Chusaburo: "You like writing poetry and you're planning to keep on writing it, aren't you, sis? In that case, you should go somewhere where they write poetry. I believe a girl should be more free to live as she pleases than a boy. Why? Because if she just gets married straight off, it's really hard to go back and do things differently later. You do what you want, don't worry about what the family says."

Thanks, Chu! she said to herself. *Please forgive your bad sister. But I just couldn't do what Tomiko had to do…* Akiko recalled that autumn night when Tomiko had sobbed. *I won't make the same mistake,* she vowed. *I hate the thought of crying over things later.*

Finally, the train pulled into Tokyo's Shinbashi Station. Tekkan was there to meet her. It was early the morning after she had so impulsively set out, on the 6th.

He was beautiful. His strained face, haggard with emotional suffering and poverty, gaunt with love, eagerly sought her out.

What beauty of heaven's beauteous realm
to see you now
you whom I have sought
in the god of beauty,
knowing naught of love.

Akiko felt she had never seen him look so handsome. Aware of the eyes of those around them, they met in mute silence, their looks speaking to each other of the thousand feelings within them.

"You got away from home? It's wonderful you've made it!" Tekkan felt himself buoyed and supported by the fact that this fine strong woman had left home to run to him.

Your delicate hand I take
frail moonlit flower
on Musashino's field –
and yet what strength in you
to flee the capital and come to me.

He felt his eyes grow hot with emotion at the thought. *Restore me, Akiko. Help me.*

"You brought nothing?"

"Nothing. I've come bringing nothing but myself."

Akiko's face was full of emotion that threatened to spill over into an outpouring of tears at any moment. Tekkan hastily took her back to the house in Nakashibuya.

Moyo came out and greeted her suspiciously. She was quite justified in showing her antipathy and hostility to the strange woman who was elbowing in like this. Tekkan had only that morning seen Takino to the station; he had left with Takino and Atsumu, and brought back with him this odd woman.

194

5

Tekkan himself must have felt guilty about bringing Akiko back as replacement for Takino. In his letter to Takino, he reports that Akiko arrived on the 14th. (Takino, however, had learned from a letter from Moyo that she actually came on the 6th.)

"And she was just like some spooky ghost," Moyo told the local storekeeper, gleefully expounding her tale. "And shameless! Well, I may not look it but I've been in the profession myself and it takes more than a bit to surprise me, but let me tell you, when the girl arrived she was simply all over Sensei, making a dreadful fuss. I just couldn't stand to see it, so out I ran."

Tekkan brought the two women together and said, "Moyo, this young lady has come up from Kansai to study. She'll be living here for a while. Please call her Miss Ho."

He might refer to her as a young lady, thought Moyo, but to her this girl with her hair all awry and nothing but a little bundle in her hand was a hard nut to crack. She could only conclude that no sooner did her master get rid of his wife than he was bringing in a mistress. And she wasn't exactly attractive, either, she thought, with that hair and those eyes. She looked like a mad woman or a ghost. Moyo threw together a meal, while the two were hidden away together in another room. It was only natural that she found herself keeping an eye on the situation, and bravely deciding she must tell madam what was going on.

Akiko was aware of Moyo's vigilance, and felt unable to talk at ease with Tekkan while Moyo was hovering.

"I've come at last, Sensei!"

Akiko gazed in disbelief at the ceiling and the sliding doors. About now, perhaps back home her mother would be discovering the letter she had left on the little desk, and being berated by her father. Or perhaps her parents were rushing around gathering people together, enraged and grief-stricken.

"It will be hard being with me, you know."

"Sensei, is your wife ever going to come back to Tokyo?"

"She said she'd be back come September when the weather's a little cooler… she plans to go to university."

195

"She must be distressed about me."

"No, she's not the type. Even while she was here recently, she was urging me to marry you."

"Was she... was she living here for long?"

"No, it was Kojimachi where we lived in together. She's only spent twenty days with me since I moved here."

Tekkan spoke of Takino with a warm familiarity that infuriated Akiko, but her anger was turned not towards him but against her own self, for finding herself in a situation in which she was forced to hear all this.

"You still love your wife, don't you, Sensei?" she said in a small, sad voice.

She was expecting Tekkan to deny it immediately, but he was silent for a moment, then said, "But she's gone, isn't she?"

That's no answer, thought Akiko. *It's no way to answer me.* Had Takino and Tekkan slept together in this bed with Atsumu between them? But Akiko could not speak of her sadness. It was not simply her genteel Naniwa upbringing that stopped her. Tender and pliant, Akiko was afraid of Tekkan.

He was adorable, yet he also had an intimidating manliness that kept her from speaking.

I don't mind what humiliations I suffer, as long as I can be with this man... "You're here with me now, so I'm happy."

Tekkan drew her face under his arm. This is Tokyo, she thought, Tokyo! It's not a dream, I really am here with Tekkan in Tokyo.

> How it rings out
> with manly firmness
> the temple bell that sounds
> through the night as I lie
> to sleep in Tokyo.

The rumour spread that this poverty-stricken poetry master had chased his wife out and installed a mistress. Moyo was adding her own lurid elaborations to the tale.

The cheerless days of the rainy season dragged on in Tokyo, while back home in Sakai, her shocked parents had sent Sadashichi to pursue the runaway Akiko in Tokyo. When he arrived, Akiko left via the back door in her socks, and hid in the closet of an empty house two doors away. She had no wish to see anyone from home just yet.

We don't know what was uttered between Tekkan and Sadashichi, but it seems highly unlikely that Sadashichi could have had much to say. Surely he must not have believed he'd be able to take Akiko back with him then and there.

Her brother Hidetaro proved more painful for Akiko. He was absolutely furious, and declared that he was severing relations with her forever. Her father also stated that he disowned her. He was apparently very angry that he had suffered such a loss of dignity.

The news that Akiko had gone to Tokyo rapidly spread around the New Poetry Society and the literary world as well. The *Portrait of a Demon* incident was still recent in people's minds, and Takino had only just left again with their son, so disapprobation and censure were heaped on their heads.

Her mother seems to have given in to pity before long though, for most of her kimonos and everyday things eventually arrived for her. This too upset Akiko, but what distressed her more was the difficulty of their life, and Tekkan's requests to Takino for money. In a letter to her, he wrote: "What with that *Demon* incident, and the economic recession, and the fact that *Myojo*'s sales have dropped to two and a half thousand, and the fact that our publisher costs one hundred *yen* a month, I have no income, and furthermore I am determined not to borrow any more, so I am finding it impossible to meet monthly expenses… I deeply apologise that I haven't sent a single summer robe to the little boy, and in fact you are the one who is helping me out…" Later: "Could you possibly manage to send the rent money to me by the end of this month? I have not been able to pay last month's rent either, and the situation is desperate."

Tekkan and Akiko's honeymoon was a cramped and miserable affair.

"Sensei, please don't ask her for any more money. And another thing, could you please send Moyo away? I hate all the things in this house, the kitchen things, the cushions, all of it. They're all the things your wife used. Please get rid of them."

Akiko was sobbing hysterically. While her love was strong, her hatred and jealousy were equally above the ordinary, and once a certain point had been reached she could stand no more.

"What can be the matter?" Moyo spoke casually, but her words struck home. Moyo was out to bully her.

"Madam was tall and elegant, and she was beautiful too, you know. It's no wonder he can't forget her. And what a dear little thing the son is… I've been helping out ever since he was born, you see, and he's like my own flesh and blood. The two of them got on so well together…" Moyo's expression was fierce. Her eyes were cunning, and her wrinkled mouth was turned down with ill temper. She'd disliked Akiko from the moment she laid eyes on her, and Akiko had no fondness for Moyo either. Whenever Akiko was silent, Moyo made a point of plaguing her with tales of Takino.

A hatred that was more than mere jealousy grew in Akiko's heart. She had never met Takino, but she could imagine what a wonderful woman she must be, to be so adored even by Moyo, and to be sent such endless love letters by her husband, and even asked for loans. If she was so marvellous, surely she wouldn't have left him?

"Please don't ask her for money. It hurts me, Sensei."

"But how are we going to make ends meet? I've gone everywhere I can asking for loans, and I've run out of places. I've even unforgivably gone to Ochiai-sensei and Kobayashi in Osaka. Where else can I go? We've hardly been able to eat gruel these last few days. This isn't what's really important, it's the determination to devote ourselves to art that matters. I'm not ashamed to bow my head to Takino and ask her to send money. A poet cannot be hurt by such things. The shameful thing is not to be able to do the work I'm meant to."

Tekkan held her gaze. "Let's think about the first collection of your poems we have to get out, Akiko… Let's not trouble our heads over these boring things. We mustn't let ourselves become obsessed with questions of shame and obligation like ordinary people. You have unquestionable talent…your poems will never die, they'll be loved by people down the ages. There's never been such a beautiful poet as you… Your poems are like bombshells. Let's hurl them at those impudent folk out there. The world will reel with astonished praise. *Myojo* will rise again… You wait and see. We'll blow away whoever wrote the *Demon* booklet."

Tekkan drew her to him.

"*Tangled Hair*. How's that for a title, eh?"

"Yes…" In his arms, Akiko finally broke into a little smile. "It was November, wasn't it, when you wrote that poem for me:

> Let me give
> to you a name
> befitting to the autumn wind –
> 'Maiden with the distracted heart
> and tangled hair.'"

"That's true. There couldn't be a more appropriate title, for you or for the book."

"I'm happy too, to think there'll be a book of poems. But still, somehow I'm scared…"

"You're amazingly timid considering how powerful and bold your poems are, aren't you, Akiko? Just leave things to me. I'm sure it'll succeed."

Akiko forgot her jealousy towards Takino, and her worry at the lack of any home to run back to. In Tekkan's arms the rest of the world grew misty, and only the two of them seemed vivid and real.

But her sense of happiness was based on a powerful uneasiness. There were just too many women who fell for Tekkan.

A strength gained from passion that rivaled his own was what had brought Akiko to his side. Had either Tomiko or Masuda Masako had this strength that poured through Akiko, would he have chosen one of them instead?

Although Tekkan was all Akiko had, it seemed things were different for him. Within a month of their living together, she was already in an agony of worry over when his love would fade. She was constantly watching his reactions and anxious to do as he wanted, tremulous lest the depths of her love be discovered and he should turn away from her.

Ceaselessly
I burn
with fires of love
yet some day you
will have grown tired of me.

This fear haunted her. Yet in fact, a man who betrays was just what Akiko wanted. She was drawn to someone who made her scared.

As for Tekkan, his energy was restored by winning Akiko. The fact that she loved him, or rather was head over heels in love with him, gave him stability. Only genius or a woman's love could replenish his spirit and inject him with fresh vitality. And now that Akiko was his, he had them both.

He was no longer a "child of love." He had thrown himself into being a "child of work." This energy had come boiling up in him once more. He had dedicated himself to the revival of *Myojo* and the success of Akiko's volume of poetry to the point where he seemed to be putting his very life on the line, nay even his fate. Akiko was his trump card. She was the means by which the *Myojo* School would challenge the world and test its true worth. This lay behind the choice of the name *Tangled Hair*, with its daring poetic innuendo of nights of passionate love.

Tangled Hair appeared on August 15th. It was published by Bunyukan, but since the publishers were as poor as Tekkan, they had a hard time meeting the four hundred *yen* costs involved.

The binding and artwork were strikingly fresh, and suited the contents well. It was a long notebook-style shape, printed on nonstandard three-by-six size paper, with three poems to a page and a total of 139 pages. Some claimed that the thirty-five *sen* price was expensive, but the book quickly elicited a strong response from the public, helped by advertisement in *Myojo*, and by the gossipy interest in personal scandal that attended it.

It seems to me that what makes readers love *Tangled Hair* is the way it takes the thousand-year-old traditional *tanka* form and manages to turn it upside down and pour fresh wine into it. Akiko based her poems firmly in the honed and perfected ancient five-seven-five-seven-seven syllable poetic form that had been thoroughly polished and withstood the test of time, and infused it with radically opposite content.

You draw me in to love
then brush my hand away
in curt farewell –
the scent of your robe lingers
soft in the darkness still.

• • •

Spring is short.
What has eternal life?
I said, letting your hands
seek out
my powerful breasts.

• • •

Pressing my breasts
I softly kicked
open the portals of mystery –
rich crimson
of this flower.

• • •

So that men of much sin
should suffer I was made
skin so glowing pure
black hair
so long.

• • •

Child of comeliness
child of spring, of flame
of pulsing blood – now
surely you have the wings
to soar free.

• • •

Don't catch cold!
I drape my robe
about your new-bathed body
crimson purple
you so beautiful.

Although the translations cannot convey this, the rhythms she uses are the stable traditional ones, but they are undermined and subverted by the material and the highly individual grammar and vocabulary, destabilizing, shocking and bewildering readers. Lulled toward passivity by the familiar rhythms, readers find themselves shaken awake, kidnapped and swept off to an utterly new world. They read of love, of flesh, breasts, kisses, black hair, embraces, and closeted virgins; images that make the cheeks blush run free through its pages.

What's more, these old-fashioned rhythms are flooded with references to Western art and mythology and the Bible, all popular subjects for the young of the day. The fiercer the disparity between old and new, the more bewildered the reader would inevitably have felt.

> Purple my dawning
> realm of love
> both hands
> scented, a following wind
> stretched far behind.

Surely this is a close echo of the color reproductions of Western paintings that readers would have seen in magazines. For young people of the day, who only knew such paintings from photographs and reproductions, one can well imagine how moving this was. This poem was most certainly created by seeing a color reproduction of a painting.

Akiko's position on love as equal to the male standpoint was yet another radical aspect of this poetry. The poems of *Tangled Hair* were not like those written by women of old, poems of secret longing or waiting for love.

> In Kyoto's Shimogyo
> a man ducks into
> a cosmetics shop
> delightful
> in the moonlit spring night.

The daring ability to state that a man is "delightful" shocked people's sleeping hearts awake. Now men and women loved and hated on equal footing. The freshness of this love poetry that could trample on thousand-year-old poetic custom to make such unflinching declarations stunned the reader's eye to new vision.

There is color, light, and wind in this new world. The poetry is like a hot breath, the voice unabashed and beautiful, like a god's or a demon's. With each poem, the reader is lured into a sense of lascivious beauty. Reading it, one grows elated by the demonic whisper seducing to immorality and dizzily drunk on the sweet poison of its fierce wine, until the mind grows numb. Who until then had commandeered love so arrogantly, incited others to live through instinct and impulse, and brandished their way of life before the eyes of the world so brazenly?

The world already knew that Tekkan had sent his wife and child away and was living with Akiko. A whisper ran through the reading public that the demonic portrayal of Tekkan in *Portrait of a Demon* was not necessarily completely false. Tekkan and Akiko were spoken of together as a pair, he a libertine and she a sex maniac, and there were many who were inclined to stone them.

The two of them stood exposed to this rain of abuse. Their philosophy was that poetry and life must be unified, that you can only sing true to your self if you are prepared to wager your life on the self's freedom. *Myojo*'s pride and challenge to the world was to expose the heart through poetry. It was a declaration of the supreme value of love.

"The world's moralists may claim the superiority of reason and justice, the excellence of language, but were they to have the courage to confess the naked truth of their innermost hearts, they would surely acknowledge that the highest happiness for mankind lies in fact in the pleasures of sex."

So wrote Takayama Chogyu in "Concerning the Aesthetic Life," published in *Taiyo*, volume eight. Although this lends philosophical support for *Tangled Hair*, when the volume appeared Chogyu failed to understand it. "This work is so affected as rather to be almost pretentious," he wrote. What part of *Tangled Hair* can he possibly have been reading?

Chogyu also condemned the volume in the following terms: "For a time *Tangled Hair* seems to reveal an uncanny gift, but one cannot long bear the lascivious feelings and shallow thinking contained therein." Tekkan immediately responded in the pages of *Myojo* by saying that for all his youth, Chogyu was already evidently senile.

In the Chikuhakuen School's magazine, *Kokoro no Hana*, Sasaki Nobutsuna criticized the volume by writing "I have no hesitation in judging it detrimental to the human heart and poisoned in its public teaching... She spews forth vicious language such as common harlots and whores would voice, and promotes licentiousness."

Susukida Kyukin and Kawai Suimei both praised it in their respective magazines *Shotenchi* and *Bunko*, but they could be considered as predisposed to be sympathetic through personal association.

The well-known critic and poet Ueda Bin sent out a volley of defensive support in *Myojo*: "Any who denounces the work out of astonishment at the fierceness of its tone and the extravagance of its thought is no friend of literature." Aside from Kyukin and Suimei, Ueda Bin and Mori Ogai alone showed praise for *Tangled Hair* when it appeared. Indeed, these two remained understanding and appreciative of Tekkan and Akiko all their lives.

"There you are, it's as I thought," declared Tekkan exultantly. "The established old fuddy-duddy poets and hypocrites have no comprehension of Akiko's fineness. Have you seen the latest *Imperial Literature*? Those pig-headed idiots haven't the strength to savor Akiko's poems. All this scathing criticism just shows what a powerful punch we've landed. The whole pack's rushing about in a panic from the shock. Just wait and see, the youthful supporters will emerge any moment now. *Myojo* will draw new breath."

As he had foretold, *Tangled Hair* was ecstatically welcomed by the young. If anyone stepped forth to abuse it, this only served to bring a fresh flood of members to the New Poetry Society, and *Myojo* became still more of a focus for the *tanka* revolution. Romantic literature, symbolised by Akiko, had at last attained the literary success to be able to assert itself.

Akiko, however, was more caught up in the obsessions of petty female emotions than with her splendid literary debut and the praises being heaped on her talents.

"Sensei, what's happened to the flower? Someone's pulled it off," she cried in surprise one morning when she saw the early-flowering cotton rose she'd been so carefully cultivating. It was a much-loved plant they had bought together two months earlier and planted in the garden. Every morning Akiko had gone to look at the bud, happily anticipating its flowering.

"Oh, I picked it and enclosed it in a letter to Takino," Tekkan replied casually. He was still tapping Takino for money. No matter how well *Tangled Hair* sold, it wouldn't be enough to cover their loans, and he was having trouble paying the interest to the pawn shop.

"September 1st. Dear White Cotton Rose, I am at present in deep financial trouble... If you can, I would ask you to help me as a matter of urgency by sending 30 *yen* by the 15th. Do look after our son with all the care you can... A white cotton rose has flowered today, so I enclose it for you. Please I beg you send the money (just ten *yen* will do) straight away. It is the absolute truth that I am in dire straits. Take all care of Atsumu please. Yours faithfully. Tekkan."

Akiko felt as if she had been hit. Tekkan's head was full of Takino and their child. This family had irrevocably permeated his life, and their influence would never fade. Akiko's heart swelled with hatred. She loathed Takino so much she could kill her, this woman who could monopolize a man's heart and then attract him still more strongly by leaving him.

"Sensei, if you love Takino so much why did you ask me to come here and join you? If she's so wonderful, you should still be living with her instead of letting her go back home like this."

"Shut your mouth!"

"All you do is think about her day in day out. Why should you still be so tender with someone who went and left you like that?" Akiko was standing rigid in the garden, sobbing. "Have you ever considered my feelings? To have left my home and my parents for you, and come up here all alone... I'm sick of your constant 'Takino, Takino.' What's so good about her anyway? A woman who could leave you and go off like that..."

"Takino's not like you. She never criticizes others. She's a generous-hearted woman. She's always telling me I should get properly married to you. Stop putting her down, you don't even know her... You know perfectly well it's only because of the ten *yen* here and twenty *yen* there she's been sending me that I've made it through till now, though she knows there's no chance it'll get repaid."

"That's what I hate! I don't want to be beholden to Takino for money like this. And I'm not going to marry you because she tells us we should... If that's the way it is I'll leave!"

"What rubbish! Go then, go if you want to – go!"

"What? You...you..." Akiko blurted out, and with that she impulsively gripped the little cotton rose and hauled it out by the roots. It was almost as if she was dragging Takino herself by the hair.

Tekkan, always short-tempered, flew into a fury. Akiko's anger took him by surprise, and he had no idea what was enraging her. What to a woman's heart was perfectly reasonable and straightforward seemed from his male point of view the sheerest irrational capriciousness. He leapt barefoot into the garden and seized Akiko as she stood snapping the branches of the uprooted plant, then punched her full in the mouth. "White Cotton Rose" was his pet name for Takino. This was well known in the *Myojo* circle. For Tekkan, the flower's nobility and bewitching elegance were the perfect embodiment of Takino's form and face. He could not stand to see the leaves of this beloved plant being scattered about and its branches broken. He loathed Akiko's appalling presumption.

Shocked by Akiko's cries, Moyo intervened and tried to hold Tekkan back, but he went on beating her. He beat her relentlessly and mercilessly. He was a man who lashed out physically when he lost his temper, and he didn't pull his punches.

Tekkan was used to Takino's obedient ways. While Takino hid an ungovernable strength beneath her meekness, Akiko could show flashes of boldness but her love for Tekkan made her at heart weak and fragile. Tekkan was not even aware of this difference between them.

"What are you doing? How dare you? You have no idea about my relationship with Takino! Stop your meddling!" Tekkan was dragging Akiko about by the hair, infuriated, hitting her until he gasped for breath.

These words hurt Akiko even more. Howling, she bit his hand, flung Moyo away from her, and rushed off.

"Hey, Miss Ho, Miss Ho! Sir, you mustn't let her go like this, let me go after her." Moyo was pale and beside herself.

"Leave her be! Stupid jealous bitch!" Tekkan exclaimed bitterly, and he too left the house.

When he returned late that evening, Akiko was sitting there dejectedly. Moyo seemed to have gone off to bed, for there was no sign of her.

"Sensei...I'm sorry. I was wrong." Akiko hung her head, her tangled hair hanging about her face. "I lost my temper, and I'm sorry."

Tekkan grunted a response, and sat down at the desk in front of its piles of books and manuscripts. "Let me just say this."

"Yes?"

"You must understand that I want to keep Takino as a lover even though she's left me. I've told you that before."

"Yes."

"Takino doesn't have any objections to you, you know. She's never been at all jealous. She's let me do what I wished. I wish you'd learn to be even half as good as her."

Akiko remained silent. She was twisted up inside with unhappiness. She simply nodded, desperately holding back her tears, fearing that if she cried she would upset Tekkan again.

"If you'll agree to put up with it, I'll forgive you." Tekkan drew over a lamp, and opened one of the manuscripts.

There's nowhere I can go, whether I put up with it or not, Akiko thought. *He knows that perfectly well.* But she still could not bring herself to rebuke him. Thanks to the love that pervaded her, her self-respect was in tatters.

The house had come to distress her. Everything in it had been touched by Takino; her writing was still in evidence, and a toy of Atsumu's lay forgotten on the shelf. When she found an item of child's clothing left in the corner of a drawer full of Tekkan's things, Akiko forgot herself and flew into a rage again.

Moyo kept up a flow of honeyed praise for Takino. Akiko never deigned to respond, she only listened till she felt the poison flow from her ears: "This house was kept together by the money from her home, you know. She was so nice and polite that she never said anything about it... Oh yes, she was such a good person, she did everything for him, sending money all the time like that... But she would never lord it over him. She was a gentle person, who always put her husband first. Everyone who visited the house loved her..."

All this had the effect of provoking violent emotions no doubt undreamed of by Moyo. Akiko longed to beat Takino's ghostly presence from all the corners of the house that it still inhabited. She didn't want to hear what Moyo said, yet at the same time she slunk about like a dog on the scent, sniffing out any whiff of Takino and Tekkan's life together, while if she did chance to hear some new piece of evidence it made her pale with pain and she fervently wished she had blocked her ears.

"My, how delighted he was when the little boy was born!" Moyo was at it again, spilling out an endless stream of remarks as she and Akiko worked together in the kitchen, Moyo tossing wood into the cooking stove while Akiko wielded a knife. "He walked around holding the little fellow all day long, and everyone who came along to congratulate them, he'd ask them, Does he look like me? D'you think he looks like me?" and she chuckled.

Akiko could just imagine Tekkan then. Atsumu had been born in September, and it was August that she'd met Tekkan and fallen head over heels for him. She'd spent her days writing love poems and love letters. To him. "Would that we could meet..." All she could think of was how she loved him and longed to see him again. And meanwhile, he'd been holding Atsumu and delightedly showing him off to everyone.

"And that darling child of his..." Akiko shot back, "The apple of his eye, was ripped from his arms and carried off. To think of it!" she spat out, as if to stop the old woman's mouth. "Hardly a tender-hearted wife, surely?"

"Well, her daddy just wouldn't hear of it, you see."

"I'd follow my husband through thick and thin no matter what my mother and father said. I'd go to hell if I had to. I don't know if she's a good person or not, but she strikes me as a very cold-hearted lady."

When things had gone this far, Akiko could come on very strong. If her opponent grew spiteful, she grew more spiteful still. This was the aspect of her that people later focused on, and that gave her the reputation of being headstrong. But when the other was weak and virtuous, she was capable of taking on the same qualities. Arimoto Hosui, a poet who was a frequent caller at the Yosano house in his youth, said of her, "She gave the impression of being an amiable, attentive, gentle girl." With these two opposing sides, Akiko must have been easily misunderstood by many.

Astonished at Akiko's unusually forceful tone, Moyo closed her mouth and said no more. She had underestimated this apparently dull-witted country lass. Now at last she'd caught a glimpse of Akiko's strong, resilient, fierce will to win, and she flinched. Akiko was bristling like a hedgehog, convinced that if she showed any weakness Moyo would lord it over her. But essentially this was not antagonism directed at Moyo so much as a form of hatred of Takino.

She abhorred Takino with a deep, seething hostility. And yet, oddly, she felt not the least hatred for Tekkan, the prime cause of her situation.

"Sensei, do please send Moyo away somewhere, I've asked you this before," Akiko pleaded.

She had said this so many times that Tekkan grew tired of hearing it. He now remembered that the pregnant wife of Kurishima Sagoromo, a member of the *Myojo* group who had recently moved in next door, was in need of household help, so he decided to send Moyo there.

"Thank you for the long service you've given, Moyo."

"The thanks are all mine, sir. I just adore little Atsumu. If they ever come back to Tokyo, do please let me know. I keep wondering how much he must have grown…"

"Me too."

Akiko could tell that Tekkan found it hard to let Moyo go, and felt her request was selfish and unreasonable. He couldn't even manage to give her the full parting salary of twelve *yen*. "All I have is ten yen," he said. "Could you wait till next month for the other two?"

When Moyo left, Akiko felt relief that the memories of Takino had left with her. She immediately tore up and sliced into ribbons the things of Atsumu's left lying about and Takino's obi that lay in the bottom of a drawer, wrapping them in paper and throwing them away. Then, pained by her own cruelty, she wept. It would be impossible to live with a man like Tekkan if she felt such powerful jealousy. Yet even so, she could not leave him.

I burn with jealousy.
And today too
my heart flutters
with its flames
the curse of love.

6

Around the middle of September, a token wedding ceremony was held with the critic and translator Kimura Takataro as formal go-between, and the marriage was announced in *Myojo*.

Tekkan and Akiko moved to another house higher on the hill, about half a mile away, this time a freestanding house. They were living alone together for the first time. They put up a sign saying "Tokyo New Poetry Society." It was a peaceful, almost bucolic scene, the house surrounded by flowers with paddy fields stretching away beyond the hedge, and Shibuya Station a little over a mile away. It seemed precisely the scene celebrated in the old poem, "The crimson mists/fall on the plain of Musashino."

Once again, it was thanks to thirty *yen* sent by Takino that they were able to move there.

Takino was resigned to never seeing this money again, but she begged for her parents' help, saying she couldn't abandon her son's father to his own devices. At least this was the reason she gave. But perhaps she felt that by doing Tekkan and Akiko this favor she was creating some sort of alibi for herself. This too was no doubt behind her advice to Tekkan in a letter that the two of them should marry, otherwise poor Akiko would forever be referred to as his mistress.

It also seems likely that Takino, who had lived with Tekkan for more than three years and knew very well what the reality entailed, would have heartfelt sympathy for Akiko. Could this nicely brought-up girl manage to put up with that poverty-stricken life and that extraordinarily fickle man?

It seems to me that even though Takino had left him of her own free will, she would still have had some vestiges of feminine pride as well as curiosity. Perhaps she didn't feel too bad about maintaining a connection by sending money.

The move to the house on the hill meant that Akiko and Tekkan really were living as a couple. Visitors came and went from the house all day, and poetry competitions were held, while at night there was drinking. Unlike Takino, Akiko was a talented member of the group, so she became a kind of queenly presence, sitting amongst the visitors. Otherwise, however, they were alone together. For the first time, at last, Akiko was happy that she had come to Tokyo. Tekkan relaxed and enjoyed their life together. There was no hint of Takino in the place, and Tekkan had finally ceased to write begging letters to her and to others. Akiko no longer felt diffident. Morning and night, the two could freely express their love for each other. When she awoke, Tekkan was beside her, and she could greet each morning with her face buried in his chest, as she had longed to do. That first morning together in Kyoto, a terrifying anxiety and despair had lain behind her love, but now their mornings together stretched ahead to infinity.

The morning mists in the oak wood that they saw together, the view of Mount Fuji on fine days, the dew-wet autumn flowers in the hedge – for the first time, Akiko knew happiness.

> For twenty years
> my happiness
> was a shallow thing –
> such a simple dream
> all that seems now!
>
> How bitter
> my parents made me
> those twenty years
> and now it is all nothing
> since I have gained you.

Poetry welled up in her like a victory song. The brilliantly ornate diction that was a hallmark of the *Myojo* School was being polished to perfection and made her own. With her at its center, the atmosphere of the New Poetry Society gained fresh delightfulness, burgeoning like a circle of sunflowers about her.

Tekkan wrote:

> How shallow I was
> to think that I alone
> was earth's genius
> in the days
> before I met you.

> Our love is no mere love
> for she and I together
> have made anew
> the poetry
> of this land of the rising sun.

Suddenly, however, the dream was broken.

On the 21st of September, Moyo arrived at the door. She appeared to Akiko like one who bears evil tidings of things to come. She was elated.

"Sir, your wife has come, as you know, and I'm just going to show her the house to rent…"

"You mean Takino has come?" Akiko felt she was in a nightmare.

Averting his eyes from Akiko, Tekkan said to Moyo, "Is it the Kanda one?"

"Yes, that's right."

"Now hang on, it's not a good idea to rent a place in Kanda. The air's bad, the location's inconvenient. Better to wait a few more days at least and try to find somewhere nicer. If you put them there, Atsumu's bound to get ill."

"I see. Well then, where should madam stay while we're looking…?"

"She's at Kurishima's now?"

"Yes, that's right."

"Right, I'll just slip over there." Tekkan hurriedly turned to Akiko. "I'm off to Kurishima's…" and he and Moyo left together.

She had heard that Takino was planning to come back to Tokyo once the hot weather was over. But this was the first she had heard of precisely when that would be, or of the rented house in Kanda. It was clear that Tekkan had been in secret communication with Takino in Tokuyama as well as with Moyo. He hadn't been writing letters recently because he knew that Takino would soon return.

It was afternoon when Tekkan left the house, and completely dark by the time he returned. Akiko had prepared dinner and laid it out on the table, but he strode abruptly past it.

"I've eaten," he informed her.

"You had dinner with Takino?" Akiko hung her head, her shoulders hunched in misery. She had spent the hours weeping, so her eyes were swollen, her head ached, and her voice was thick and heavy.

"Kurishima pressed it on us." Tekkan turned his back, took up a book and pretended to be reading.

"You and your wife and child had a happy meal together, did you? Didn't you realise that I was back here feeling lonely? All alone here..."

"But think of Takino, staying in someone's house like that. If I hadn't gone over she'd have felt awkward and out of place." Short-tempered as always, Tekkan's voice was now rising. When he was angry, he looked and sounded as though he would bite. "Why are you always so self-centered? She's come all this way to Tokyo with a little child, and has to camp in someone else's house. Don't you feel sorry for her?"

"What on earth has she come back for?"

"She's going to university."

"You asked her to come. Why didn't you tell me?"

"Why should I have to tell you everything I do? Takino feels bashful."

Akiko was infuriated all over again by Tekkan's gentle tone. Why did this man always sound so tender when he spoke of Takino?

"Bashful? Is she going to have another child?" Akiko's lips were pursed sharp as a needle. Tekkan looked at her in astonishment.

"What are you saying? How could she be?"

"Really? Nothing I heard would surprise me..."

213

"Fool!"

The two slept that night turned away from each other. Tears streamed down Akiko's cheeks. In the night she woke to blow her nose.

"Cut the noise!" Tekkan was up, the lamp burning. He had changed his clothes.

"Where are you going?"

He didn't respond.

"Are you going to see Takino?"

"Do you think I'd go round to Kurishima's house at this hour?"

"You really can't forget Takino, can you? Why did you bring me to Tokyo, if that's the case?"

"There you go again. Are you going to keep at it all night? There's no use trying to explain to someone as jealous as you, you just wouldn't understand."

"I just want to die…"

"If things are so bad you want to die, we should part…" He spat the words out. Akiko shrank as if she'd been hit. This man could say such cruel things, and so glibly! He could just toss off remarks that made the heart clench with terror. "I'll see you on your way tomorrow, then."

"No! I'd rather die than leave you! If I go, you'll get back together with Takino, won't you?"

"How can I do that, when her parents are against it, eh? If we were going to get back together again, I would have refused to listen to them earlier. Whatever they said, I could have stayed with her, after all. But I let her go, for the sake of my pride and sense of moral obligation as a man. I was a fool."

Akiko couldn't believe her ears. Tekkan was in earnest, and there was pain in his voice. Akiko felt dazed with the extremity of her suffering, unable even to cry.

"I see…so that's the way it was. That's how you felt, is it?" She staggered to her feet.

"Where are you off to?"

"It doesn't matter, surely. Don't worry about me."

"Wait. I'll take you to the station tomorrow."

"No! It's better to die."

"I've told you already, it's better to part."

214

Tekkan's voice was raised. Akiko too was in a fever of emotion.

"I don't want to part! I'll die, but I won't part from you!" she sobbed.

Tekkan rose and slammed the wooden shutters together with all his strength.

"Shut up! How many times do I have to hear this? If you don't want to leave, then put up with it! Can't you do anything but sulk and pout?"

Akiko desperately gulped back her tears. Tekkan had slipped on his wooden clogs and gone into the garden. He was someone who, once he grew excited, couldn't sleep for several nights.

She wept until sleep overcame her. When she woke the next morning, Tekkan wasn't there. He must have gone to Kurishima's place, she decided. Then Moyo arrived. She was beaming cheerfully.

"I've come to get the little fellow some milk. Could I have Sensei's?"

"Certainly. Is he over there?"

"No, he hasn't come yet this morning."

"I see." She got herself dressed and went down to the shop by the station, where she bought a box of sweets and carried them home. She had decided that it wouldn't do to pretend she didn't know what was going on, so she would call in and meet Takino. There was a timid, upright side to Akiko that tended to temporize in typical feminine style.

She went around to the house after lunch. Neither Tekkan nor Kurishima were there, nor was Moyo. Kurishima's pleasant wife was sitting dandling a little boy and talking to a woman with her hair done up in the style of a married woman. She was a fair-skinned, elegant-looking lady.

This must be Takino, thought Akiko.

Takino also seemed to have immediately recognized Akiko, for she bowed. Her smile was neat and refined; there was no hint of vulgarity in either her manner or her expression. She was lightly made up, and the hair coiled on her head shone black and beautiful. This was a woman whom people would consider a beauty. The little boy had Tekkan's mouth.

Strangely, once Akiko saw her in the flesh, she felt none of her previous hatred for her. All resentment melted away, like mist in sunlight. She even registered an indescribable liking for this woman.

All jealousy aside, she struck Akiko as someone with whom she might be friends. She was astonished at this feeling, almost a nostalgic warmth, that held the promise of mutual confessions and complaints about Tekkan. Until this meeting, Akiko had been wracked with hatred and unhappiness as she imagined Takino now this way, now that, while a crushing sense of humiliation pervaded her. Now, however, face to face, she saw that there was nothing hateful in the beautiful Takino. She was a perfectly normal person with, moreover, a gentle face and a sweet, lyric mouth.

Takino too was startled by Akiko, observing how she blushed like a child whenever she spoke. She had imagined her as much more impetuous and demanding, pushier, more brazen. The woman she now saw was not what you would call beautiful, but she was a pale-skinned girl in the flower of her youth, a handsome young lass with lovely hair. She spoke with a shy, mumbling Kansai accent, and looked terrified that Takino might do something dreadful to her at any moment. It seemed a miracle that this sluggish, countrified, timid girl could produce those dazzling poems.

Akiko thanked her for sending the recent money, and asked what plans she had.

"My father has said I can't make my living by being a scholar so I should give up the idea of university… he's finally agreed to let me go to sewing school."

Both Takino's manner of speaking and her mouth as she spoke gave an immaculate impression.

"That's really hard… with the little boy."

Akiko reached over and took the child onto her knee, but he immediately began to whimper, so she passed him back to his mother. When she held that soft body in her arms, she was struck with a sudden realization: How could she ever understand the depth of relationship that Takino and Tekkan had together, this profound bond of having a child? She realised how strong were the ties that bound two parents together.

It seems to me that Tekkan had every reason to feel drawn to this mother and child. The adorable child and the intense bonds had etched themselves deep into his soul. These things had dwelt in his heart since before Akiko's arrival there.

Once Akiko saw how beautiful and decorous Takino was, her jealous feelings sank far out of sight, and did not raise their foolish head again. Yet by the same token, her suffering drove her all the harder.

> Wild-haired
> Medusa-headed
> this mask of furious jealousy
> raving at you –
> would that it were not I.

The next day was Atsumu's birthday, and Akiko followed the Kansai custom for the occasion by making sushi, and asked the two of them round. Tekkan went over to fetch them, and the three set off to walk back the long way round, Tekkan holding the child, like a typical family of three.

"Are you well? How's your stomach?" asked Takino.

"My stomach's fine, but Akiko's kicking up a fuss." Tekkan seemed overjoyed to be alone together with Takino again after the long absence. "She's an incredibly jealous type. I really copped it for that white cotton rose I sent you."

"Moyo told me." Takino gave a little laugh.

"She gets mad, she sulks, she cries… Life's never dull with Akiko. When I was with you, I was a free man."

"I should say this degree of constraint is actually just what you need." Takino smiled as she spoke, but suddenly she added, "Akiko came to Tokyo on the 6th, didn't she? She came the same day I left. Why did you lie to me and say she came on the 14th?" The question was a rebuke, from one so upright and honest that the smallest discrepancies demanded correction.

Ah, she never changes, thought Tekkan, but far from feeling alienated, he even registered a certain nostalgia. "Well, I was kind of constrained in various ways at the time, but yes, it really was on the 6th she came," he confessed. "She's been disowned by her whole family, you know. She's burned her bridges. That may have something to do with it, but let me tell you, she makes things rough for me, jumping on every little thing I do and say, madly jealous…"

"You'll just have to put up with it."

From her short conversation with Akiko, Takino had gauged her character well enough to feel she could understand the jealousy. For all Akiko's meekness and diffidence, Takino could feel a fierce heat smouldering deep inside her. She guessed that when this came pouring furiously forth, Tekkan would find himself flinching and staggering. It amused her to imagine his bewilderment and defeat as he struggled against this uncontrollable force.

And with this, Takino suddenly realized that she was no longer jealous. She had the sensation of gazing down from some slightly elevated place at the human attachments she observed. She had left the arena of tormented relationships, the jealousies and fights, and the knowledge made her as happy as if she had graduated.

It induced in her a generous goodwill towards Akiko. Smiling, she said to him, "I think she's a fine person. *Tangled Hair* has had a good reception," she went on. "But of course it's not just her talent that's earned it, it's thanks to you, you know. Everything you've undertaken has been praised for being a step ahead of its time. Half the success of *Tangled Hair* is your own. You really do have that power and ability. You're a great man."

Intuition had revealed Tekkan's essential nature to Takino. She had perceived exactly how this man longed for these words just now. They were words she could not have spoken if she were living with him, truths she would be too blind to see. But for this woman, who had stepped back outside the circle of attachment, only now was it possible. She could say the things she had been unable to utter while she lived with Tekkan.

Tekkan, however, had no such self-awareness. He attributed it to her temperament.

From listening to him, Takino understood that he still loved her. But this no longer upset her. She was surprised, too, at how it calmed and pleased her to be walking along like this, the three of them together. She now felt a much warmer understanding of Tekkan than she had during their marriage. Of course this was thanks to the peace that had come with severing relations with him, but it did not seem so to Tekkan. He seemed to believe that this connection between them could continue for ever.

This may be the last time we three walk together in this way, Takino told Tekkan in her heart. Now that Tekkan was living with Akiko, Takino had no intention of meeting and walking about with him like this again.

"Atsumu's grown heavy." Tekkan happily shifted him onto his other arm.

"Shall I take him?"

"No, it's fine."

"He's your father, Atsumu. Okay? This is your father."

When his mother spoke, the boy beamed and put his arms around Tekkan's neck. They were indeed just like a typical couple with a young child.

Tekkan went on to fuss about whether the child was a little thin, again just like a normal father.

Akiko was waiting for them, with everything prepared. Tekkan arrived first, alone.

"What? Where's Takino?"

"She'll be here shortly. I left a bit before them," Tekkan said. Just a little earlier, he had hastily left Takino behind, saying they mustn't make Akiko jealous by turning up together. Takino had taken Atsumu and wandered idly about for four or five minutes, half-amused at how nervous and fearful of Akiko Tekkan was. He would blithely hurt others as a rule, but he had this other, cowardly side to him, that was wary of causing pain.

Akiko bustled about, a kitchen apron over her kimono. "I'm embarrassed that this is all I have to offer, after inviting you over like this," she said to Takino politely. "It's poorly made, I'm afraid, but I hope you'll accept it as a gesture of congratulation on Atsumu's birthday. I hoped I might be able to find some special celebratory sea bream, but I couldn't lay hands on any. This is a Kansai-style sushi mix, I hope you'll enjoy it though."

"But doesn't it look delicious! You'd have grown up eating lovely fish in the area where you lived, I'm sure, so it must be quite disappointing moving up here. There's nothing in Tokyo."

"Well, actually…" Akiko smiled as she laid chopsticks out for her guests. "Food's been the most difficult, coming here. But when it comes down to it, I wouldn't be able to buy things even if they were available here, so it doesn't make much difference."

"'Poverty is the curse of the poet,'" said Takino, imitating Tekkan's voice, and the two women laughed together.

"Hey, don't go ganging up on me like that," protested Tekkan. He was delighted. What he saw before him was the scene he had been picturing in his dreams. He loved Takino, his darling son was on her lap, and here she was with Akiko, exchanging jokes. Akiko was his powerful partner in life, and now she was chatting intimately with Takino. He must have felt an exceptional pleasure to have these two fine women by his side like this.

"What would the little boy like to eat?"

"He can eat what we do."

"I've bought some milk for him… Aren't you a bright boy! Can he talk yet?"

"No, he's a bit slow at talking, he can't say much yet."

"They do say boys are slower, don't they. Girls learn quite fast."

"It must be because we girls are such chatterers."

"That's how God ordained it, it seems."

And the two of them laughed again.

The meal continued amid genial chat. The talk turned to a discussion of *Myojo* members, and Takino asked after various people she remembered fondly. Among them were some who were unknown to Akiko. Takino had no fear of Tekkan in front of Akiko, and felt free to open up and say whatever she wanted. She showed no hint of choosing her words with an eye to his reactions.

Ah, thought Akiko, *she doesn't love him. Yet this insouciance may well make her all the more attractive and alluring to Tekkan. I'm different,* she thought. *I love him from my whole heart. I have more right to him than she does.* A sense of self-assurance swelled in her breast as she thought of Takino, yet when her gaze fell on Atsumu her confidence shrank again. The boy was perched on Tekkan's lap, and he was popping something into the child's mouth with his chopsticks.

She knew that when Takino's father had insisted on their separation, Tekkan had hoped at least to be able to keep custody of the child. It was at this time that he had written the poem:

Strongly, how strongly
I would hold the infant child.
These man's hands would sew
winter robes, would bring
the milk to feed him.

This is Tekkan's first child, Akiko told herself. *If I were to bear him a child, he would probably not love it as much as he does this boy.* She gazed enviously at the father and his son.

Even though the talk and laughter flowed amiably enough, beneath the surface there swirled a sense of rivalry and envy. For Takino too there was a feeling of something between envy and sorrow as she watched Akiko coming in and out of the kitchen, or gazed about the house, taking in the new items of furniture and utensils. She had no urge to try living with Tekkan again. Yet a woman's heart is strange indeed, and she felt a sudden jab of jealousy and pain at the sight of Akiko seated beside Tekkan. Though merry laughter arose from time to time from the two women, in the privacy of their hearts they were both preoccupied with melancholy feelings. To see them there, each appeared quite without any dislike for the other woman. If Tekkan had not been the pivot that drew them together, they may well have met as good friends. Both Takino and Akiko had a great respect for each other's character and talents.

"Masuda Masako has also said she wants to be a student at Japan Women's University," Tekkan remarked, after they'd discussed the doings of various other acquaintances.

"She comes from an old family too, I gather, so she'd probably have difficulty breaking away to come to Tokyo." Takino was evidently conversant with the family backgrounds of the *Myojo* members as well.

"Still, she's determined to come, no matter what."

"You've seen her recently?"

"Yes, when I went to Osaka in January."

"I see. Well, if she comes to Tokyo, the New Poetry Society will be an even jollier group, won't it." Takino's remark was offhand, but it dealt a shock to Akiko. January was when Tekkan and Akiko had spent their two nights together in Kyoto, surely? Before or after their time together, Tekkan had met with another woman.

PART VII. THE NAIL IN THE ASHES

1

About a year later, Takino married the poet Masatomi Oyo, who had become her teacher of the Japanese classics *The Tale of Genji* and *Man'yoshu*.

Oyo was his pen name, his real name was Yoshitaro. He was born in Honjo village in the countryside of Okayama prefecture, and his early schooling was in the local old-fashioned clan school of Shizutaniko – its ruins are still proudly preserved, tucked away in the mountain village, harking back to the scholarly local feudal clan that founded it. He left before graduation, and arrived in Tokyo the same year as Takino's return, to begin studies at Tetsugakkan (later Toyo University). Oyo had been an avid follower of the arts since his early youth, and while a student at Tetsugakkan he studied *tanka* under Onoe Saishu. Onoe had been a disciple of Ochiai Naobumi at *Asakasha* in the days when Tekkan was also in his fold, but had since formed the Ikazuchi Society with Kubo Inokichi and Hattori Motoharu, and undertaken a *tanka* reform movement. The Ikazuchi poets had a different approach from the *Myojo* group, choosing to emphasize a quieter style of clarity, simplicity, and harmony.

Oyo met Takino while he was still a university student. He was three years her junior, and when the relationship developed to the point of marriage neither family was pleased. Oyo was the eldest son, so his parents had had dreams of him marrying well." To think of you marrying a woman older than yourself, with a child in tow…!" his father stormed. In response, Oyo only hung his head in silence without attempting to defend himself. But his will never wavered.

Takino's father was also against the match, but he was favorably impressed by Oyo when he met him. The fact that almost no one had a bad word to say about him suggests that Oyo had always been an earnest and sincere young man, quite the opposite of Tekkan. By chance, he and Takino found themselves sharing lodgings. No doubt Takino first began to study the classics with him because the sewing school failed to fulfill her academic longings, and we may imagine that before long she found herself pleased and impressed by his character.

Angered at the marriage, Oyo's father disinherited him and cut off his school funds, so Takino went to work in the post office. After the marriage, Atsumu was taken back to the country by the Hayashi family and brought up by his grandparents.

Both their parents were finally reconciled to the marriage in January 1903, and Takino was formally entered in the Masatomi family register as Oyo's wife. She said later that her life with Oyo at last allowed her to taste the happiness of married life where respect and love were balanced. Oyo was an honorable and peaceable man, and she found nothing incomprehensible in him, none of the irritating elements that her former husband had. Through this new marriage she realized just how very different she and Tekkan were, and was delighted and grateful at her luck in having met Oyo.

Takino's marriage angered Tekkan. When he learned of her intended marriage to Oyo, he did his best to hurt him by making disparaging remarks about him to others.

Until her marriage, Tekkan had visited her frequently at her lodging and often taken her out. Takino was sharing rooms with a friend (a woman called Irie Shin), so she found Tekkan's visits unwelcome and did her best to avoid them. Tekkan would attempt to keep her from leaving him by feeding her distorted gossip about Oyo. These desperate efforts to turn her against him only served to reinforce Takino's attraction to Oyo, but even this was something Tekkan could not grasp.

Last year, I had a chance to visit Oyo's home village in Okayama. It's close to where another poet, Takehisa Yumeji, also grew up, and across the way from each other on the road stand two monuments inscribed with their poems. Takehisa's free verse poem reads:

> Living here
> waiting
> for one who does not come
> like the drear grasses
> that await the evening –
> tonight, once more,
> it seems the moon
> will not shine.

Oyo's monument stands in a somewhat more elevated position, on a hill in a wood. His family traditionally produced the village headmen, so the house that stood here would have been substantial, but there is no trace of it now. The wood is hushed and quiet, the only sound birdsong. Oyo's monument is a large, long stone laid lengthwise, and the paper I'd brought to make a rubbing of the poem inscription was too short. The poem, in free verse, reads:

> The persimmon tastes as persimmon will
> the apple tastes of apple –
> cut it, hack it as you may
> the savor will remain.
> Slandered, wounded you may be
> yet still remains
> the taste of staying whole, unhurt –
> the savor of a good man.
> Oyo

It was peculiarly moving to stand there amid the endless flow of the wood's tiny sounds and trace with my fingers the carved words of this open-hearted poem. I can't help thinking it conveys something of the feel of Oyo himself, and I can somehow understand how Takino would have felt in rejecting Tekkan and choosing him. It seems to me that the poetry of the *Myojo* School was fundamentally incompatible with Takino's poetry and given this, we can imagine how difficult it was for her to have faith in its founder and proponent, Tekkan. The problem is one of inherently different natures, and it would be hard to claim any right or wrong in the matter. When it came to Oyo, Takino was prepared even to relinquish her own child in this marriage to a younger man, and her steely will overcame each obstacle in turn. Her attitude to life impresses me deeply. This pair remained a mutually loving couple through to their golden wedding anniversary, and never parted until death separated them.

A month before Takino's marriage, Tomiko lost her husband, and overnight was transformed from wife to beautiful young widow.

> And so a rainbow
> too must disappear?
> For whose sake now
> am I left here alone
> upon this earth?

She had been married a mere two years. Chushichiro, her husband, had contracted tuberculosis, and very shortly after their marriage he took to his bed. He died in December 1902.

Tomiko was stunned. All that was left to her now, one may imagine, was poetry. She had nowhere secure to stay even if she went back to her family home – she couldn't have stayed there long, with her brother and sister-in-law now installed, forever dependent on her parents. And so Tomiko made the same decision as Takino, to stand on her own two feet. She would go to Tokyo. She was a widow and a beautiful young woman of twenty-six, and she was about to set up life as a single woman in the world. One can guess that, as she gazed into the future, somewhere in her line of sight was her old friend Akiko.

Akiko, of course, was now Yosano Akiko, the queen of *Myojo*; she had both love and work, and her poems sang of this golden age in her life. In November 1902, what's more, she was blessed with the birth of her first son, Hikaru (a name given by the poet and critic Ueda Bin). They were still poor, but Akiko's poetic fame hung over the New Poetry Society like a glittering halo; if anything she was held in higher esteem than Tekkan now.

There were those in the *Myojo* group who were not pleased by Akiko's lifestyle. Kubota Utsubo was a long-standing *Myojo* member, and he didn't look kindly on the progress of Tekkan and Akiko's developing relationship, from love through living together to marriage. He decided that his own style of poetry was different, and he left the group. Mizuno Choro, a handsome youth who was very friendly with Akiko, was said to have been driven out of the group by the jealous Tekkan. Akiko was no doubt all too well acquainted by now with the fact that the egotistical Tekkan, for all his demands that women suppress any jealousy, had a deeply possessive nature himself.

At around this time, the group welcomed two new members who would become famous poets in their own right, Ishikawa Hajime (who later took the pen name Takuboku) and Hagiwara Misao (later Sakutaro). Shortly after came dramatist and poet Yoshii Isamu, the poet Kitahara Hakushu, novelist and poet Kinoshita Mokutaro, and novelist Nagata Mikihiko. *Myojo* was more than ever a hub of literary activity that satisfied the aspirations of young writers. Later, as these young men began to develop in their own literary directions, *Myojo* evolved from its emphasis on fiercely subjective poetry towards a Western-style symbolism.

Akiko's own poetry, meanwhile, grew and transformed with ceaseless energy. Tekkan was full of praise for her work, adding his own commentary to each poem, and even sometimes using a poem of hers as a model for instruction in poetic technique.

Someone described Akiko at this time as "a meek and docile lady, who spoke little and always modestly supported her husband." Like Atsumu, little Hikaru was small, weak, and premature, perhaps because like Takino, Akiko was malnourished. He was settled in a little muslin bed beside the group when they met to compose poetry together. Akiko made her newborn son his first kimono from a large wrapping cloth. There is a story of one young member of the New Poetry Society, who often visited the house, one day finding Tekkan asleep on the tattered matting of his little home, wrapped up in an old futon flattened with use, his bent, spindly legs sticking out of the narrow cylinder like a prawn's. This man had brought along a gift for the baby boy which happened to have the name "Candied

Gold." Faced with this scene of abject poverty, he said, he was struck by the awful irony of the name, and could hardly bring himself to hand the gift over. For all the privation, however, beautiful poetry nevertheless continued to pour like a gushing fountain from Akiko's pen. She might sleep huddled under a battered old futon, but she never lost her mettle.

> When I look back
> over the path I've travelled
> I bow low in awe.
> How huge, how superhuman
> my love looks now!

This is not in fact a late poem. It stands at the beginning of the volume *Little Fan*, which appeared in 1904. Akiko was still only twenty-seven, but already she was full of "self-praise" for her own loving.

How must Tomiko have felt about Akiko's love, a love that she herself could proudly proclaim as "like a giant"? The following tells of Tomiko's feelings when she relinquished her own love for Tekkan in favor of her friend that day back in Kyoto:

> In my next life
> I will seize from his right hand
> the demon's whip
> and strike down
> all beautiful love.

Why should Tomiko's poetry be so horrifyingly bitter? Everything she wrote is fraught with pent-up, resentful rage, a powerful crystallization of anger that hovers in the realm of the inexpressible. They are like the poems of some vengeful spirit. Tomiko's poems strike the reader as even more imbued with the dark energy of ferocious attachments than those of Akiko, and for this reason, at times they are better than Akiko's; they have more depth, more strength. It could be claimed that Tomiko rivalled Akiko in establishing and refining her own unique poetic realm. I find her poetry irresistible, and in my opinion she is a poet worthy of being ranked with Akiko, indeed above her.

Tekkan was delighted that Tomiko was coming to Tokyo to become a student at the women's university. We can imagine that he would have felt elated that the gods had recompensed him in this way for the blow from the loss of Takino. Akiko wasn't particularly concerned about the fact that Tomiko's arrival would bring her into close proximity with Tekkan. No doubt she would be in and out of the house as a member of the New Poetry Society, and she and Tekkan would grow closer, but after all, the relationship among the three of them was no longer what it had once been. Besides, Akiko was in the throes of jealousy over Takino.

Akiko's heart was thoroughly bruised by her suffering over Takino and Atsumu, and their mutual relation with Tekkan. Her pain was caused by the knowledge that it was impossible to return Tekkan's heart to its pristine state before he had known Takino or, for that matter, Asada Sadako.

In *Akiko Mandala*, the poet Sato Haruo treats Tekkan's former wife Takino unfairly, in a way that can only be put down to his lack of understanding of women. Akiko herself, in her autobiographical novel *To the Light*, writes of Takino with an unflinching jealousy that still had not faded ten years after the event. Indeed, right through until Tekkan was on his deathbed, she couldn't prevent herself from endlessly mulling over the same old story.

Why would Akiko have been so full of loathing and jealousy for this woman, so sure that Takino still secretly dwelt in Tekkan's heart? Which of the two, Tomiko or Takino, made her more jealous? I believe it was Takino. Tekkan certainly did love Tomiko, and there are poems of Akiko's that express jealousy towards her, but his feelings for Tomiko were probably not much stronger than those for Masuda Masako.

In her autobiographical novel, Akiko writes of the secret Tekkan kept from her for ten years.

> You hid
> your heart from me
> these ten long years –
> and how diminished
> I became.

I would guess that what caused Akiko's jealousy was the sheer weightiness of Takino's life with Tekkan. After all, the two had shared poverty, humiliation, and joy, and finally produced a child together. In the face of this whole shared life, I think Akiko would have despaired. It would have driven her repeatedly into a state of mad, tortured, accusing jealousy.

She must have been perpetually aware of young Atsumu, now being brought up by his grandparents. It would have been to Atsumu rather than to Hikaru that Tekkan's thoughts constantly returned, though no doubt he never admitted as much. Feminine envy and resentment, suppositions and distrust must have oppressed Akiko's heart, driving her to a consuming suffering – the profuse suffering implicit in human life and its sexual relations.

Compared to this, one may imagine, a lover from the past would seem no more than a distant and hazy figure. In the more than four years since that time, Akiko had lived with Tekkan, born his child, and formally married him, something even Takino had not done. Who could appear between them at this stage to threaten such an accretion of life?

But Tomiko no doubt did not have the same view.

2

On 11th February 1904, the twenty-five-year-old Masuda Masako, "wearing a delicate-patterned crepe coat over a finely striped kimono, hair up in the *gingko-gaeshi* style and sporting a handmade silver ornamental hairpin… stepped out of Shinbashi Station in the dusk and took her first step into a Tokyo that seemed sunk in a somehow tragic silence" (as described in Aoki Takako's biography *Chino Masako*).

The times were tense. "Vague, troubling rumors were rife. When her Tokyo-bound train reached Shizuoka Station, she had learned that diplomatic relations with Russia had been severed."

Liaotung Peninsula, which Japan had briefly been awarded after the successful war with China a few years earlier, was forcibly restored to China, and Japan had gritted its teeth and prepared for future war. Both Japan and Russia were plotting to advance their territories into

Manchuria and Korea; they were two wolves seeking the same piece of meat, and a battle was inevitable.

The public debate that raged at this time between the pro- and anti-war advocates, however, would become a source of later pride for the Meiji period. It sprang from the spirit of the times, the same zeitgeist that had also produced the *Myojo* School and *Tangled Hair*. The pro-war school of thought, backed by the military and the government, emanated from right-wing militarists who sought to agitate public opinion towards the conviction that Russia must be attacked. The anti-war school, according to *Yorozu Choho* (a newspaper of the time), preached "against opening hostilities with Russia." To a man, these Christians and Socialists did all they could to prevent the approaching war.

The Christian commentator Uchimura Kanzo concluded: "I am not only against the opening of hostilities with Russia, I am a believer in absolute pacifism. War kills. And killing is a great sin. An individual or a nation that commits such a sin can never profit from it…"

Not long after this, however, *Yorozu Choho* went back on its principles and shifted to a pro-war position. Uchimura left, along with two other staff-members, Kotoku Shusui and Sakai Toshihiko. These latter two immediately began to publish the *People's Paper*, where they continued their anti-war campaign. Among those they attracted were novelist Kinoshita Naoe, and commentators Katayama Sen, Ishikawa Sanshiro, Abe Iso, and Nishikawa Kojiro. After war was declared, Kotoku continued to inveigh against it in the *People's Paper*, writing: "War has now arrived, yet we will continue as long as our voices, pens, and paper allow us to raise our voices against the fighting."

Meanwhile, an endless stream of soldiers was setting out for the Manchurian front. "Soldiers, go forth! We now have no way to bring a halt to your actions… All we can now do is devote our energy to abolishing the present evil system, so that your descendants may never again meet with such tragedy as we see today… Neither citizens nor soldiers have ever once been consulted on this war."

The movement for democratic rights continued unabated – at least for the moment. "Oh soldiers, your fields are in ruins, your work destroyed, your aged parents will lean solitary at the gates of their houses, your wives and children weep from hunger. What hope that you will return alive? And although in truth you do not wish to go, yet you must, for as soldiers, you move as a single machine..."

Meanwhile, in Russia, Leo Tolstoy brought out a Christian rebuttal to the war, entitled *The Case Against the Russo-Japanese War*. The *People's Paper* in Japan quickly published this. It is surely fair to say that Meiji society, where such a healthy ongoing anti-war debate could flourish, was a finer age, and one more robust and made of sterner stuff, when compared not only to the subsequent period of the Second World War but to the seventy years that have since elapsed. This was a time when the blood of modern humanism still ran hot in our veins – so different from the chill that later descended on us.

It was at this troubled moment in Japanese history that Masuda Masako arrived in Tokyo to become a student at the women's university. The fact that this was precisely when Yamakawa Tomiko also became a student there can only be called an extraordinary coincidence. Tomiko came to study English literature, while Masako majored in Japanese literature.

Masako was the daughter of a merchant in Osaka's Doshomachi who sold wholesale ingredients for Chinese medicine. Her photographs show her as the epitome of the typical Japanese woman, gentle and beautiful. She was a warm and charming girl, liked by both men and women, a fact that Akiko refers to in *To the Light*. Her placid face was precisely that of a typical downtown Osaka beauty of old; she had elegantly sloping shoulders and a graceful figure, and her poetry too was like a direct expression of her appearance, redolent of a tender femininity. Tekkan gave it the name *Seien-ha* (literally "The Pure Anger School").

> Seventeen –
> in old Osaka
> deep in Nakasenba
> beyond the reed blinds
> she plucked her *koto*.

This was the kind of traditional upbringing Masako had had. Her parents forbade her to follow her academic urge, and she did not manage to come to Tokyo to study until the age of twenty-five.

It seems that all these Meiji women, be it Masako or Tomiko or Takino, had a strong desire to learn. In this era of *Sturm und Drang*, it seemed, some powerful force flowed through society, one that uprooted these girls from their sheltered lives. One cannot help but be aware of how in our present age of equality, when women are educated on a par with men, their drive has lessened rather than grown stronger.

It was at the women's university that Masako and Tomiko first met. They had both long been contributors to *Myojo*, so their names were known to each other but, oddly, it took coming to Tokyo to effect a meeting between them. The two became close friends. Both had been freed of the shackles of their families and were now able to go where they wished. On Sundays, they generally left their university dormitory and made their way to the meetings of the New Poetry Society in Shibuya.

Another woman who arrived in Tokyo at this time was Tamano Hanako (whom the poet Hirano Banri later fell in love with and married), a delicate beauty. There was much delight that the "four flowers" of *Myojo* were all assembled in Tokyo; the group's monthly poetry competitions and special gatherings to compose a hundred poems on a set theme were more popular than ever, and the New Poetry Society seemed to have reached its apogee.

Tomiko and Akiko met again. Akiko by now was already pregnant with her second child. In January 1904, she brought out two volumes of poetry: first, her collection *The Little Fan*, then a joint collection with Tekkan, *Poisoned Herbs*. She was by now an established poet with an unassailable position in the literary world and her own unique style. Tomiko, on the other hand, had not only met with huge setbacks in her personal life but had aborted her poetic career, and was now embarking on it afresh, with nothing to her name.

The two women could no longer return to those foolish days of their maidenhood, when they had called each other affectionate girlish names. Tomiko had lost her cheerful, unshadowed smile of old and become a woman of new depth, etched deep with a mature melancholy. Akiko, however, greeted her as a long-lost friend despite her new air. She had so much she wanted to tell her! And so much to ask.

"How utterly unthinkable that your husband should have passed away so soon, Tomiko!"

In response to Akiko's heartfelt emotion, a faint smile hovered on Tomiko's thin and beautiful face, which had only grown more refined and charming with the years. "And your father has passed away too… It must haunt you, not to have been there."

"Yes, it was hard," Akiko replied. "Still, he forgave me before he died, and that's something. My brother is apparently still declaring he's severed all relations with me for the next seven lifetimes."

"There's nothing you can do about it, I suppose."

"Yes, I guess you're right. Still, I get sad sometimes when I see how this little one looks more like my brother than like his own father." Akiko stood little Hikari on her lap as she spoke. "And I have to say, Tomiko, he also looks like the previous wife's son Atsumu."

"No, really?" Tomiko stared intently at the child. "Where is the boy now?"

"He's back in the country, I understand, being brought up by his grandparents. Tekkan sometimes goes off on the excuse of some trip or other and sees him, it seems. He'd be four or five by now. At his cutest. And Tekkan's brother lives in Tokuyama too, so he has a good place to come and go from… Tomiko, does it seem to you that people always love their first-born best? I can't help feeling it's true."

Tomiko hadn't been anticipating that their conversation would broach such private matters. On the face of it, it seemed Akiko would be the proud wife of an adored husband, flowering splendidly in the sun like the proverbial sunflower in the hedge. Yet the woman Tomiko saw before her seemed simply an utterly normal woman. This impression of a typical, gossipy housewife was reinforced by her appearance – the hair was tangled as of old, and she wore a silk and cotton weave kimono with a soft, rather tired satin obi. She was five or six months pregnant, and next to the still smooth-cheeked and fair-skinned Tomiko, she looked aged and haggard, and ten years older.

"Yes, I guess that may be true… I don't really know. I've never had children," Tomiko faltered. "But surely it's the people you live with every day that you love most. I'm sure it is."

"And it's not just children. It's the same with Takino. Tekkan's never forgotten her, you know."

"But I heard that Takino's married the poet Masatomi Oyo."

Where once they had indulged in talk of dreams and longings, these two women in their mid-twenties now embarked on secretive, catty whisperings together.

"Yes but Tomiko, he still can't give her up you know. He always just adored her. It was like cutting off a limb for him to give her up when her parents put their foot down and made her leave. He didn't part from her because he didn't love her, that's for sure."

"And what about her? What did she feel, I wonder?"

"She didn't really love him. That's the impression I get. I guess he just wasn't her type. So she was happy to leave him, but he went chasing her, and wrote asking her to come back to Tokyo… I know for a fact that he sent someone to spy on her and check out whether she had another man… He's not a bad man, Tekkan, but he's impatient as a child, he can't put up with things. Well, after all manner of carrying-on and fuss Takino decided to marry Oyo, and when Tekkan got wind of it he went limp and miserable about the fact she was marrying."

"Good heavens."

"When he told me I didn't say a word, and then he turned around and accused me of having a heart of stone for not comforting him! The very words he used about Takino to us both long ago, remember?"

Akiko laughed bitterly. Tomiko had been nodding silently as she listened, and now she said, "But you're the only woman in his life now, Akiko. You've got to forgive what's passed and done with."

"It's there in the past, that's what hurts… I've forgiven, as far as that goes." Akiko sighed, and lowered Hikari to the floor. "You know, Tomiko, it always seems to me that a woman can forgive but she can't forget. Women can use the word 'forgive,' but the word 'forget' just isn't in their vocabulary."

Some petty, fleeting, childish complaint had only to pass Akiko's lips for it to turn into a poem that emanated like a sigh from her. She could turn any old bad-tempered grumble or trivial remark into poetry, like a silkworm spinning a silken cocoon.

> Though men
> are fickle and forgetful creatures
> this one alone
> cannot forget
> past love.

From their first reunion, Tomiko could not help registering a strong sense of discomfort. It disturbed her to find Akiko so taken up and obsessed with worldly trivialities. From Akiko's point of view, on the other hand, she felt she could tell all this to Tomiko because of their friendship. The fact was, their differing fates had led them both in different directions, and they were no longer their former selves.

Tekkan took great heart from Tomiko's reappearance, and began to plan a group collection of the poems of the three women – Tomiko, Akiko, and Masako. Tomiko was delighted by his goodwill. He was still an attractive man in her eyes, a fearlessly honest poet, upright and single-minded in his approach to things, hasty and impulsive, and for that reason easily misunderstood.

Tekkan looked a little tired that day. The proofs of *Myojo* had finally been completed the day before. Akiko had gone out on an errand, taking Hikaru.

"You haven't changed a bit, Tomiko." He gazed at her fondly.

"Neither have you, Sensei," she replied, aware as she spoke of a slightly lost, forlorn air about him. These days the set of his shoulders exuded a certain world-weariness that she hadn't detected back in the days when she and Akiko were his adoring disciples. Now, indeed, Akiko was her *sensei*, on a par with Tekkan. In fact, in terms of poetic achievement, Akiko was more suited than her husband these days to be the real head of *Myojo*.

It was surely true to say, she thought, that these days Tekkan had relinquished his former role as *Myojo*'s leader both in name and, in fact, in favor of Akiko, and had retreated to the role of supporting promoter. He must have had complex feelings when he considered his present status as "Akiko's husband." Now that her light had grown so bright, he was overshadowed, for all that it had been his own plan for her to develop and become famous. Tomiko felt an affectionate tenderness for him. Akiko struck her as selfish, with her trivial obsessions and lack of thought for how he must be feeling. Tomiko could only see Tekkan from the outside, and from this perspective she found Akiko almost incomprehensible. She was particularly put off by Akiko's fierce jealousy. Yet if Tomiko had been in Akiko's position, she too would surely have tasted this most feminine of emotions.

I'm the only one who can understand Sensei, she thought to herself. *Neither Akiko nor Takino can any longer.* The thought made her feel even closer to Tekkan. He for his part was also moved by her. Tomiko's talent was on a par with Akiko's. If it had not been left by fate to stagnate, it could well have been honed to something finer yet than Akiko's.

> I who watched
> the flowering
> of your fresh youth
> you who saw
> my own youth at its end.

This was Tekkan's later elegy to her. He was, I feel, a natural poet, who from time to time wrote perfect pieces that went to the heart of the human condition. All his elegies for Tomiko are masterpieces. He and Tomiko together saw "youth at its end" – surely they would each have felt something in themselves that resonated with the other. Who could condemn them for that? One lonely heart was responding to another.

"You made a sad marriage, didn't you, Tomiko."

"The past is the past. I've managed to come and be here like this with you now, Sensei, that's what matters. From now on, poetry is my life. Please let me stay here by you forever, Sensei."

As she spoke she fixed her great eyes on Tekkan. Gaunt and large-eyed, she was bewitchingly beautiful. Seeing her thus brought back for him those days of their youth. She had been dear to him. Now, however, all he could do was publish a collection of her poetry for her, and thereby help her revive her career.

"I'm wondering whether we could bring out a collection by the three of you."

When she heard Tekkan's plans, Akiko liked the idea. "It would encourage Tomiko, and also be good for Masako. Let's do it."

"Tomiko hasn't published a single volume yet."

"It's true. And I guess your plan would be to publicize *Myojo* by bringing out the work of its three finest women poets. It would attract attention, wouldn't it, and make the advertisements more effective. Trust you to come up with this. You have a fine talent for devising ways to get people really talking about us."

Akiko was laughing as though she found the whole thing rather funny, but Tekkan was suddenly aware how much she sounded like Takino. He was evidently a man who drew comments, critical and otherwise, from women.

The war dragged on. In July Akiko bore her second son, Shigeru. At the end of the month, Japanese forces attacked Lushun.

Akiko's younger brother Chusaburo had joined the Fourth Division Eighth Regiment and gone to the front, and his regiment was now involved in the Lushun attack. The place was an impregnable stronghold, and as the Japanese troops flung themselves into the mortal combat, the mountain of corpses only continued to rise. For days the deadly battle raged. Again and again the white-sashed suicide troops were hurled into the fray, none to emerge alive.

This was the base for Russia's Navy in the Pacific, so Japan had been doing its best to storm the fortress ever since the war began. "Corpses piled till the mountain's shape was altered," as General Nogi's poem described it, and still with the passing months the numbers of the Japanese dead only rose.

The September issue of *Myojo* included Akiko's poem "You must not die," a poem constructed, as it were, out of the commentary of Kotoku and others in the *People's Paper*. Even more than *Myojo's* judgment in publishing this poem in the midst of the war, what impresses me is the atmosphere of those times that would allow such a thing to appear and not ban it. This decade still retained the romantic elation of the dream of freedom. For this reason, I would like to include the whole poem, despite its considerable length.

> Oh brother, I weep for you.
> You must not die.
> You the last-born,
> so loved by your parents –
> can they have taught you
> to take sword in hand and kill,
> raised you to twenty-four
> to slaughter others, and to die?
>
> You, inheritor to the name
> of the proud family
> of a Sakai merchant shop of old.
> You must not die.
> What is it to you whether Lushun's fortress
> be ruined or prosper?
> Do you not know, there is no rule
> in a merchant's house for this?
>
> You must not die.
> Could our great emperor
> who has not gone to war himself
> order you to die upon some animal path
> leaving behind the spilled blood of another?
> Could he declare that death is fine,
> out of the wisdom of his heavenly heart?
>
> Oh my brother, do not
> in battle die.
> Your mother, mourning already
> her husband's death last autumn,
> now has the added sorrow
> of her son's going. In this reign
> of our "gentle" emperor, "protector of homes,"
> her hair is whiter still from suffering.

Do you forget your sweet, new, youthful wife
who weeps behind the curtain of your shop?
Do you not think of her?
Think of her girlish heart
torn from your side these ten months past.
Who but you on this earth
has she to lean upon?
You must not die.

Akiko loved Chusaburo. It was he who had warmly welcomed her when she went home on her father's death. She was terrified that he would be killed in battle.

The poem was no sooner published than it was bombarded with criticism. Poet and commentator Omachi Keigetsu, who was in charge of the arts column of *Taiyo* in place of the late Takayama Chogyu, criticized the poem as anti-war and wrote of it, "This is the expression of dangerous ideas." He pointed to the third verse in particular as open to accusations of slander of the imperial family.

Akiko was not a woman to sit silently by at such times. For all her apparent docility and gentleness, she had a steel within her that was capable of protean transformation depending on her opponent. In the November issue of *Myojo* she published an open letter, written as if to Tekkan, which contained her comments and rebuttal.

"What could be wrong in the poem I attached to the end of my letter to my brother? It is a poem. I was born in this country, and my love of it is inferior to none... There was no master of a merchant house who loved our emperor more than my late father, or who could forget his own needs to serve his emperor.

When I hear of those people's comments in the pages of the *People's Paper* and elsewhere, I tremble.

Yet all young girls are against war.

I am a poet, and thus I wish to leave behind poetry true to my heart, that will not be the butt of jokes of later generations...I do not know whether or not Mr. Keigetsu has a younger brother, but even if he does not, if he stands an hour at Shinbashi and Shibuya Stations when the trains bearing fresh troops for the front are about to leave, he will most certainly be witness to those scenes of parents, siblings, friends, and relatives clutching the hands of the departing sons, each repeating the words, 'Come back safely! Take care!' and raising their voices in cheers of '*banzai*' for the emperor…It seems to me that those words – 'Come back safely! Take care!' – are what my own humble poem expresses. Theirs is a cry from the heart, and so is mine. I know of no other way of writing poetry than to express the truth of the heart in true words."

Keigetsu responded with a counter-attack, but Akiko found herself protected by supporting fire from an unexpected quarter. The very same journal in which he was writing published a poem by the woman poet Otsuka Kusuoko, titled "The Hundred Day Pilgrimage," a reference to the prayer ritual that consists of walking the circuit of a shrine a hundred times.

> With the first step I think of my husband,
> With the second, of my country,
> And with the third, of my husband once more.
> What is there to blame in a woman's heart?…

Kusuoko was the wife of a professor from Tokyo University, a beautiful woman of thirty-one. She had been moved by Akiko's poem and her "open letter" to make her own declaration of a "woman's heart."

These two women's poems were talked about and savored by many. It was not as a barometer of anti-war feeling that they were appreciated, but as the impetuous expression of the "woman's heart," as moving expressions of true feeling. Akiko, a woman who "trembled" at the discussion of "those people" in the *People's Paper*, was not one to support her own spontaneous words and feelings with argumentation. The only support she ever relied on was the single truth of the human heart.

3

The three-person collection of poems by Akiko, Masako, and Tomiko was titled *Robe of Love*. Masako was delighted with the name – "It's perfect for a women's poetry collection!"

Akiko was aware that her husband felt a special love for Masako, but this didn't bother her. Face-to-face, there was nothing hateful about

Masako. She was quite simply a beauty, with a hint of forlornness about her but in no way gloomy, and she said entertaining things. Akiko may have had reservations before she saw her, but when they met she instantly liked her. This could be partly put down to her own good nature. Akiko was skilful at uncovering the virtues of others, and she generally felt goodwill toward those she met. Takino had been the same, in fact.

"I've been wondering whether we should dedicate our collection to Kyukin-sensei," Akiko said. "What do you think?"

Masako and Tomiko both unhesitatingly agreed. It was true, after all, that all three had first spread their wings and learned to fly under the influence of Susukida Kyukin. It would be a meaningful gesture to dedicate their first joint collection to this man who had stayed so long with *Myojo*, and who understood it so thoroughly.

Respectfully dedicated to the poet Susukida Kyukin, said the dedication at the beginning of the book.

Robe of Love was widely advertised. The Japan Women's University reacted fiercely by expelling Masako and Tomiko. They had chosen to take no action over the fact that these two were known to frequent the New Poetry Society and have dealings with the notorious womanizer Tekkan, not to mention his wife, who had been attacked as a traitor for her recent poem – but they claimed that this bold publication of a collection with the word "love" in its title, whose poems spoke openly of such matters, sullied the name of their institution. Tomiko's father came up to Tokyo from distant Obama to support his daughter, and Tekkan engaged the *Myojo* member and lawyer Hiraide Shu to help him negotiate with the university authorities. Together they finally managed to persuade the university authorities to drop the proceedings against the women, and *Robe of Love* was published without incident.

Tomiko, outraged at the university's philistine attitude, wrote:

> Cast in the same mold
> surely what emerges
> when the kiln is opened
> is figures of one shape alone
> a single, boring color.

Look back on us
you of the distant future
to this fine world of ours
where writing poetry
can be deemed a sin.

Her poetry was growing more and more inward and fierce, taking on a strength that spoke of inner truth.

January 1905, the month that *Robe of Love* came out with much fanfare, also saw Tokyo seething with the news of the defeat at Lushun. While the streets at New Year were thronged with celebratory lantern processions, on the other hand the *People's Paper* had closed down. With the run of prohibition orders, bans on public meetings, and court cases, it had found it almost impossible to keep publishing. The final edition, which came out on January 29th, was printed entirely in red ink. Kotoku wrote his farewell editorial as the news of the "Bloody Sunday" upheaval in the Russian capital Petersburg resounded all about him.

Robe of Love received critical acclaim, and both Tomiko and Masako were acknowledged by the literary world as promising young women writers. The opening poems by each of the three poets are interesting in the way they establish the individual voices.

As a low makeshift pillow
she laid precariously
one upon the other
copies of two old classics –
alas, it toppled over.
                    (Akiko)

We are shown, as it were, a brightly colored ukiyo-e picture of a beauty napping on a spring evening.

Born a maiden
with long hair
I hide my face
in a white lily
thinking of you.
                    (Tomiko)

There is a sense here of proud isolation, with a chill passion hidden within the beauty. The poem burns with the fierceness of white silver.

> She only gazed
> on the sweet-scented
> white plum of his robe,
> she did not speak his name
> that dream on a spring night.
>
> (Masako)

The sweetness and elegance of this gently flowing poem in the style of the great *Shinkokinshu* poetry of old suggests how Masako would have been more loved by others than Akiko.

Personally, I am fonder of Tomiko's chilly ferocity than of Akiko's poetry in the early poems. Tomiko's poetry attained still greater heights before her death four years later. Her poems emerged like blood that flowed from her own torn throat. Akiko, who had already reached a position of pride in her own work and had established her place in the sun (true of her work, if not of her inner state), would need more years and more suffering before she could write poetry of violent pathos.

We have no way of knowing how far the relationship between the newly re-encountered Tekkan and Tomiko progressed. I myself cannot imagine that Akiko and Tekkan would have exchanged heated words over it. I don't believe Akiko was that sort of woman. She was by now almost thirty, with two children and a third on the way.

No, in fact I think Akiko was afraid of Tekkan. He was everything to her. She later said that he was still a rather cold person at this time. He was apparently quite open about being attracted to other women, and tended to sink into moody silences. We can judge how intimidating he was from her later poems:

> Moving to see
> my husband
> approaching forty
> now a man
> without anger.

How sad I find it –
that man who once so grimly
pressed in on me
white sword in hand
has vanished.

Tekkan still flourished his "white sword" in these early days, it seems,
and I can't imagine that Akiko would have raised her voice and
called him to task. The days when she had occasionally stood up to
him were past. She had been at the height of her youth back then,
and still too innocent to know him well.

The longer Akiko was with Tekkan, the more like Takino she
became, and she could not but be aware of the fact. It seemed
that a woman could only survive life with this difficult man
by armouring herself against him, hardening like ice or stone.
Akiko's jealousy must only have intensified with the deepening
of her empathy for Takino.

So remote
so intimidating
you always were –
off to see the mountains
of Tokuyama, you said as you left.

This poem suggests that Tekkan's visits to Tokuyama threatened
and intimidated Akiko. Her mind must have leapt from one
assumption to the next as she envisaged him going to see his son
there.

Forgive me
I love two women
you weep before me –
but I am no all-forgiving
Mother of God.

Who would these two women have been?

I would have been
more easily consoled
was there not another name
besides my own
that you could not forget.

This suggests that Tekkan had only one person besides Akiko whom
he "could not forget." This was the woman who had long been his
love. Who but Takino?

Of course this may have been Akiko's imagination. Perhaps her
discovery, that day she arrived in Tokyo, of how unexpectedly
vivid Takino remained in his heart had thrown her into a despair
whose shock waves continued to haunt her, later inducing paranoid
conviction. It may be that Akiko, already all too easily thrown into
jealous fits over Takino, now suffered an added torture from Tomiko's
recent arrival on the scene. But who knows how much truth there
was in all this, and how much was merely her own delusion.

Make of this long night
in the home where you
do not return, a temple –
gouge out those crimson plums
by the roots and hurl them!
• • •
That autumn day
I cursed
his cold, silent indifference –
"May the woodpecker
hammer at your ears!"

Who knows how much Akiko suffered in her relationship with her
husband when she was with her fellow members of *Myojo* or in
society generally? If either *Myojo* or Akiko's poetry was adversely
criticized, Tekkan was quick to fly into a rage. And no sooner did he
lose his temper with someone than he intentionally caused trouble
or severed all relations with them. He was so volatile and honest to

a fault that he readily lost his temper over the least trifle, and was quite without the breadth of vision to take things in stride. There's no way of guessing just how much Akiko bustled about covering for him here and there, unbeknownst to others. (Tekkan crossed swords with both Keigetsu and Shiki, for instance.)

Akiko was certainly aware that Tekkan loved Tomiko, and it was surely out of consideration for him that she refrained from unseemly blame. To her, he was not only an intimidating man but also had elements of an overgrown child. As she became increasingly renowned, his own name slipped further into the shadow of obscurity cast by hers.

Tekkan was slowly vanishing into history, his main claim to fame merely that he had been a pioneer in his time. Akiko, on the other hand, had gone on from *Tangled Hair* to evolve into a poet of yet more depth and beauty. As a woman's heart matures with the years, so her poetry grew rich with the weight of experience.

I will here give a few examples of poems I particularly like from this period of her life. The choice is arbitrary and personal, and some may complain that I could have chosen better poems, but I believe these give some idea of the beauty of her poetry.

> The earth seemed a single
> vast white lotus
> that moment when the sun
> rose up
> out of the snow.
> • • •
> Spring rain. Can this be
> the day the little acolyte
> enters the priesthood
> of Mount Koya's temple?
> So many bells ringing.
> • • •
> Chaos of cuckoo calls
> at dawn's first light –
> they seem to toss
> white waves
> about the lake.

Akiko's later poetry ceased to be so fantastical and lyrically descriptive, and became more and more realistic in focus.

When I was young and busy creating small, short-lived journals brought out by the various literary groups I belonged to, one of the members happened to be a young man who was deeply involved in political movements. In those days, I was devoting my energies to writing evanescent little romantic novelettes, under the impression that this was the only sort of thing that women could write. Endless novels about love are possible for women, and I found I could write any number of them. I believed that this was all the world consisted of.

But when I showed them to this young man activist with the hope that he'd praise them, he denounced my novels as utterly worthless, and read me a sermon on the existence of things more important than love, and on the need to write about them. And what might they be? I asked eagerly, desperate to gain his approval and literary admiration because I liked him so much. To which he arrogantly responded, "The question of where the next meal will come from." It would have been one thing if this were just after the war ended, when food was in short supply, but by then the problem no longer existed, and I was sadly at a loss how to please him by writing the kind of novel he described. Even now, I still cannot feel that the need for tomorrow's food is greater than the love of man and woman. I'll never be able to win that young man's approval.

> As for me, I swear
> by the gods that love
> is a great
> a shattering event
> in the annals of the world.

I was delighted when I came across this poem of Akiko's. For a woman, love is not merely a personal matter, it is no less than "an earth-shattering event in the annals of the world."

But I digress. To return to my theme, as the beauty and depth of Akiko's poetry grew, she was glorified with the title of "the greatest woman poet of the age," while Tekkan increasingly gave the impression of being remembered simply as "Akiko's husband."

In fact, Tekkan wrote some fine poems. There are poems from his middle and later years as well as from his youth that I love. True, some of the early images (for instance in *The Four Directions*, *Heaven and Earth*, and *Poems of Loving*) are rather too strong. But this is clearly related to the deep emotion that his particular genius provoked in others, and I wonder too whether it is not also connected to the ease with which his words and actions tended to invite misunderstanding. He was a passionate and loving man, but he seems to have had an equally strong ability to hate those who criticized and parted from him. His childish selfishness and exactingness no doubt made him appear more intolerant than he actually was. I believe his poems should be regarded more highly.

Akiko certainly thought so. She believed in her husband's talents, and was convinced that the cool reception of his work was unjust. She took care to gently enfold and protect his heart from hurt. Jealous though she was, she would not have expressed it openly but rather turned the feeling in against herself, where it ate at her own heart. She wrote an excessive number of poems of jealousy. One who sought to give vent to her indignation in poetry in this way would be unlikely to release it through real-life arguments. The resentments that she could not express to her husband's face instead crystallized and took form in poems.

> Most painful
> is when my breast
> is wildly plucked, strummed hard
> by some plectrum
> that suddenly invades.

> Still more severely
> punished
> than long ago
> when molten lead
> was poured upon my back.

Working shoulder to shoulder with a man as she was, Akiko came to understand the sorrows of a man's life. She knew what it was for a man to have to make his way in the world, and this surely gave her the skill to see the world through the dual perspective of male and female experience.

Life is hard for men, while women too have much that is painful in their lives. Akiko, who straddled both experiences, had ways to understand when Tekkan was drawn to other women. But when her masculine discernment was disturbed by her feminine emotionalism, she suffered. She then became simply a middle-aged woman, a wild-haired hag, two children at heel and pregnant with a third.

Among the young men who frequented the New Poetry Society at the Yosano house were two lads in high school, Chino Shosho and Hirano Banri. They remained close friends from their schooldays onward, together joined the society, and were both ambitious up-and-coming young poets. Both found lovers in the New Poetry Society – Hirano fell in love with Tamano Hanako, and Chino with Masuda Masako, two of the flowers of *Myojo*.

Hirano tirelessly pursued and soon won over Hanako, but Chino found Masako elusive, and he suffered. Every time he came face to face with her at the society's regular meetings or all-night poetry sessions, he loved her more, but she remained cold, so he finally left in despair and went travelling. Masako, it seemed, could not consider this young student (by now he had entered the German Literature Department at Tokyo University) who was three years her junior as a serious marriage partner.

Fearing that his friend might commit suicide, Hirano sent him a telegram: "There is hope. Return." Wildly happy, Chino came back to Tokyo. He was a small, insignificant-looking young man with glasses, but purehearted, and he had been recognized from an early age for his poetic talent. His poetry was quiet, yet with impressive depth.

> Here and there I roam
> hand pressed
> to wounded heart
> that spills the blood
> of agonizing love.

Masako's heart was moved. Chino pressed his case, seeking to sway her further.

> Winds, blow wild.
> City, turn to flames.
> So I may snatch you up
> and float with you
> among the waves.

At last he succeeded. Filled with respectful affection for his character, Masako agreed to marry him.

No sooner had he heard than Chino flew around like a whirlwind, setting things in motion for the wedding. He needed a go-between to help gain the consent of the two sets of parents, and planned to ask Tekkan. To this end, he first wrote a letter to Akiko telling her of his plans. Akiko, however, was dismayed. She knew that Tekkan loved Masako and had the foolish dream of keeping her forever single, and she felt that if she approached him on this matter he would be very likely to misinterpret her motives. She crumpled up Chino's letter. Undeterred, Chino proceeded to bombard her with letters.

Tekkan did indeed misinterpret the matter, and become angry at Akiko. However, the parents had by now already agreed to the match, and he found himself in the role of official go-between at their request.

A large number of men had courted Masako, but few of them would have had the selfless dedication of pursuit that Chino did. The two held their wedding in the summer of 1907, when Masako had graduated from the women's university, and lived together in Tokyo for a year while Chino completed his degree.

The year that Masako graduated, Tomiko formally withdrew from her studies. A diary entry from Chino's early time at the New Poetry Society as a high school student, when he first fell in love with Masako, reads: "Went to meeting of New Poetry Society in Shibuya... Miss Yamakawa Tomiko has a mature, forlorn-looking face, and must have had much cause to weep in her life. Miss Masuda Masako is otherwise, an angelic girl with a delightful smile."

"Forlorn-looking" Tomiko had been hospitalized the autumn of the year that *Robe of Love* was published. She had contracted her husband's tuberculosis. She left the hospital the following spring, but that summer it was decided that she would return to convalesce at her sister's home in Kyoto. She had a temporary remission, during which she came to the New Poetry Society meetings, and both she and those around her hoped that a summer spent recuperating might restore her health. Her new start on her poetry career had been all too short. How could she have known, as she set off for Kyoto, that she was looking her last on the Tokyo where she had so recently arrived?

"I'll be back at the end of summer," she reassured them. Akiko gazed at her old friend, and her heart was pierced. On that beautiful countenance she could see a pitiless decay. Struggling with her tears, she responded, "Yes, yes, you'll be better soon. Come back quickly and let's see you at our meetings again. I'll be so lonely without you…"

The thought flashed through her mind that the woman before her may well be long bed-ridden, and she grieved over the parting. Tomiko's pale cheeks, thin and etched deep with illness, nevertheless managed a cheerful smile.

"I'll bring you a present from Kyoto, Hikaru," she said brightly to the four-year-old boy.

Tekkan went with her to see her off at the station.

"Sensei, I really do want to get better again, you know," she said to him on the platform. Standing there with her silk parasol, dressed in a summer kimono, her body so thin it seemed it might snap, she looked light enough to be carried off on a passing breeze.

"Get well and come back soon. Without you here I'll feel empty and lonely, Tomiko. Promise me you'll be back." Tekkan, fresh in a white cotton robe, stood before her as if shielding her. Pale and straight-backed, at thirty-four Tekkan was at his most bewitching. To Tomiko, he was as handsome as long ago. He was that teacher whom she had desired. Alone with him, Tomiko immediately reverted to the innocent maiden of that early time. It was only five or six years earlier, but what a long time seemed to have passed.

"I want to live again, Sensei. It's leaving too much unfinished to die now…" The train pulled in. Tomiko's pent-up tears overflowed. She reached out from the train window, her slender fingers twined about his, sobbing, oblivious to the eyes of others. "I'm only twenty-eight… I just want to live. To live, and to write…"

"Don't just live to write, Tomiko. Live for my sake too."

"Sensei…"

"Come back. For my sake, come back."

Tekkan stayed standing on the hot platform, watching Tomiko's pale face receding into the distance. They had only once spent time alone together since she had arrived in Tokyo. Their feeling for each other was not so much romantic love or simple affection, but rather the sentiments of two mature people who have traversed difficult landscapes in their lives, and who tenderly protect and soothe each other's wounds.

Masako, and now Tomiko, had both left him.

> More fleeting than meteors
> all the women
> have fled through the sky
> before the eyes
> of this Don Juan.
> • • •
> I cut
> this love I cut this love –
> cut as if hacking
> thick sheets of metal
> with great hacking shears.

Tomiko spent the year convalescing at her sister's home.

> May I be born once more
> a lovely maiden
> into this world
> to love again the flowers
> the dear moon.
> • • •

Ice
against my forehead
I can scarcely bear to see
the setting sun's bright gold
streaming through the window.

Her illness would improve a little, only to worsen again, and slowly
the sense of death thickened in the air about her.

Did the lord of death
also mourn
my unhappy youth?
No book of judgement
lies before him.
• • •
May it snow too like this
the day I die
Kyoto's mountains
towering white
and Kurodani's dark pagoda.

In a constant fever, Tomiko lay between sleep and waking, looking
out at the tall dark shape of the pagoda of Kurodani Temple against
the eastern mountains. Into her vision also floated the white frost
and the crimson stalks of the wild knotweed. She had believed that
Kyoto would be a better place than her hometown both climatically
and in terms of medical access, but it seemed she would never recover
her health even here.

As she lay ill, news reached Tomiko of the death of her old friend
Tamano Hanako, wife of the poet Hirano Banri, who had died within
about a year of their marriage. Hirano was deeply grief-stricken.
Lying there, she wrote to Masako of her memories of Hanako and
of her own condition.

It was no longer Akiko to whom she felt inclined to open herself
up in letters, but this woman who had become her friend at the
women's university. She had grown distant from Akiko. She thought
with longing affection of the sweet-natured, easygoing, gentle

Masako. Together they had had the experience of being temporarily expelled from the university after the publication of *Robe of Love*. It was also Masako who had been a frequent visitor to her bedside when she was hospitalized in Tokyo. After her marriage, Masako had written worried letters to Tomiko. It eased Tomiko's heart to think of her. She longed to be soothed by the gentle spirit of this friend. To Tomiko, Akiko now felt far in the distance.

I think it is the flicker of dark, pent-up will-o'-the-wisp emotions in Tomiko's poetry that moves me so. It feels as if an inexhaustible flame of oppressive resentment burns behind the words. At first glance it seems she is resigned to her fate, yet as we read we are struck by the smouldering bitterness that can never quite accept what life has given her.

Both Tekkan and Akiko felt this as they read the poetry she sent them back in Tokyo.

> The leaden bird
> the dark great-beaked raven
> comes torturing me
> beating at my breast and crying, Die!
> His wings cover the sky.

The poem is a scream. In a vision she sees the implacable fate she cannot accept turn to a leaden bird and press in to attack her. It sings of the endless bitterness that is like her own hand clawing at her breast, with the pain of this cruel fate that has wrenched from her hand both poetry and love.

There was much she longed to do were she to live. She could not bear the thought of dying. If she died now, what would have been the point of living? Yet the shadow of death drew closer. She could feel it. Her strength was rapidly failing her. Now what emerged were poems of mad self-mockery to freeze the heart.

> What fun
> to taste now
> the happiness
> of sleeping
> on ice.

It made Tekkan weep bitterly. His tears flowed at the poems that Tomiko was pouring her remaining strength into for *Myojo*. He had never felt so strongly for her as now. She was the symbol of his youth. And now she was fading and wasting away. He wept not only for her but for his own youth.

Akiko watched him. It was painful for her to witness Tekkan's heart withdrawing from her and going out to Tomiko. Yet she could only feel that there was nothing she could do about it. She had loved her husband more than had any other woman, loved him and thrown herself into her poetry under his direction. *What sin could I have committed that would remove me from his heart?* she asked herself. If there was any sin, it could only be that of loving him too much.

"I'm envious of Tomiko for being able to possess your heart to such an extent, you know... I can see you've loved her more than you ever did me." So she found herself saying accusingly, her voice trembling and halting. She knew perfectly well how things really stood, yet could not prevent herself from speaking resentfully.

"That's not true. It's just that I feel an unbearable empathy with how she must be feeling..." Tekkan lifted his head from his hands and muttered. "What she's going through is something a woman like you couldn't understand. Do you know how it feels to be pushed to the brink? You live only for the day. All you care about is to fulfil the moment's requirements. How could someone with that life comprehend Tomiko's despair?"

Akiko was silent. She was afraid that if she spoke, her breast would heave and her tears overflow. If she didn't work, if her work didn't support the family – if she didn't think of "the moment's requirement" – the whole family would starve. Tekkan had pinned his hopes on *Myojo* and was inextricably involved with the work for it; he could not carry the burden of looking after the household.

Akiko would write anything to order. Fairy tales, novels, essays, occasional pieces, anything would flow from her pen. After her son Shigeru, she bore twin daughters, Yatsuo and Nanase. She was in no position to pick and choose what she did for a living.

What's more, she was on the verge of making a brilliant entrée into journalism.

She was now recognized as having established her own style in the poetry world, with three more collections of her poetry in the two years since *Robe of Love*: *The Dancing Girl*, *Dream Flowers*, and *Black Hair*. Since 1907, she had held the position of poetry editor for the *Yorozu Choho* newspaper – the pay was poor, but it was a symbol of her recognition as a fine and first-rate poet. She was still only thirty.

Akiko could understand why Tekkan should be particularly moved by Tomiko's poetry. But she was by now well-embarked on her own life. Tekkan was only reacting against superficial manifestations, he didn't pause to consider her heart.

> Not many days yet
> since you began to hate me
> yet already
> I am lonely
> as a nun.

There was something that served to increase Tekkan's isolation. Youthful and talented young members of *Myojo* were leaving the group. It was now nine years since *Myojo*'s establishment; an era was drawing soundlessly to an end.

4

The decline of *Myojo* was caused by the sudden rise of the Naturalist movement – but Japanese poetry itself was undergoing changes. Kanbara Ariake from *Myojo* had begun his own experimental style of poetry using a 4-7-6 syllable rhythm, an intriguing and disturbing form completely at odds with the traditional 7-5 rhythms espoused by Shimazaki Toson, Yosano Tekkan, and Tsuchii Bansui. Young poets saw in Ariake's poetry a new direction.

The French Symbolist poet Paul Verlaine was only beginning to be known in Japan, and it was through Ariake that young literary people came under his influence.

"The time for a new poetry has arrived. It was a splendid new dawn," wrote Toson in the preface to his poetry collection. Toson himself had already begun to make the shift from poetry to prose.

Among the young writers who joined him in exploring the way towards a new form of novel were Kunikida Doppo and Tayama Katai. The earlier Ken'yusha Society literature no longer reached readers' hearts. The death in 1903 of one of its key members, Ozaki Koyo, affected many in different ways.

Koyo was not so much the leader of the Ken'yusha group as its powerful central figure, and his funeral was a grand affair, "fit for a *daimyo*." His death was deeply significant. In everyone's eyes it was clear that the Ken'yusha era was over, and a new literary age had come.

In the same year, Ochiai Naobumi died. Naobumi had been Tekkan's teacher; he had first made his name under Naobumi's patronage. Naobumi had loved Tekkan above his numerous other followers, and when many had deserted Tekkan over the *Literary Demon* scandal, he had remained to protect him and lend his support.

With Naobumi's death, Tekkan felt that the age of old-style *tanka* poetry had finally died. Naobumi had written free verse poems, and preached the virtues of the new *tanka*, but his own poetic talents were limited, and his poetry smacked of the old sensibility. The *tanka* revolution that he'd planned had been effected instead by his more daring followers, among whom were Onoe Saishu, Kaneko Kun'en and of course Yosano Tekkan.

Tekkan took control of Naobumi's funeral. He had lost a benefactor who had given him such affectionate patronage in every way, and he was as lonely and bereft as a child at the death of a parent.

Just before Naobumi's death, poet Masaoka Shiki and the great critic Takayama Chogyu had also died. A great wave of reform was washing over the literary world. Toson's ground-breaking free-verse poetry collection *Seedlings* had been published only a few years earlier, in 1897. The vibrant, youthful period of the Meiji era was all too soon at an end. The flowers of Romanticism were falling. Meiji literature was awakening from its dream, and the time had come to face reality. Historically too, the time for a new maturity was ripe, now that the nation had undergone the transforming experience of victory in the Russo-Japanese War. Within the short space of a decade or less, young people had ceased to be fulfilled simply by poetry that sang of love and longing. Now they were giving themselves over to poems whose lifeblood was everyday reality. To the day's youth, *Myojo* seemed redolent of an old-fashioned romanticism.

In 1908, the following piece appeared in *Myojo*'s "News from the Publishers" section: "Yoshii Isamu, Kitahara Hakushu, Ota Masao, Fukagawa Amanokawa, Nagata Hideo, Nagata Mikihiko and Akiba Toshihiko have left the group, citing the desire to pursue their independent literary careers." Ishikawa Takuboku also left. Hakushu, Isamu and Ota Masao had been bright stars in the later *Myojo* years. After they had gone, Chino Shosho and Hirano Banri were the only good young writers left in the group. *Myojo* had effectively disintegrated.

When Hakushu and the others left, they had poured criticism and slander on Tekkan, claiming he'd plagiarized the poetry of Hakushu and other younger poets. "He's no poet, he's merely able. He's a man of policy," it was also claimed. It's unclear how far the charge of plagiarism was correct. We do know that the early work of both Hakushu and Isamu was in the style of Akiko's poetry. Their writing evolved into its own style in time, but it seems natural to assume a mutual influence.

That year, the September issue of *Myojo* did not appear, and in November the journal closed with its hundredth issue. The final issue was full of the work of all the old members and contributors.

Myojo, the literary journal that had led Meiji's poetry, was defunct. Tekkan wrote a farewell message in the final issue.

Our journal has now reached its hundredth edition, and to commemorate this we bring you a special expanded issue.

Our first issue's appearance feels far in the past. There have been various ups and downs in operating the journal over that time, and I myself have likewise tasted some bitter experiences. I wish to express my deepest gratitude to all my teachers, respected friends, readers, and the members of *Myojo*, without whose ardent support this journal could not have succeeded in maintaining its original purpose, or managed to the end to cultivate the ground of the New Poetry, transplant to our shores the poetry of the Occident, and promote woodblock art... There are two reasons why we have determined that this issue will be our last. One: I have been unable to recover losses incurred in running the journal. Two: I have decided to devote the mental energy required for this task to self-cultivation instead… However, although *Myojo* will no longer exist, my determination to pursue my career as a poet is and will remain as steely as it is today, and it is my earnest desire that in another ten years this determination may bear fruit in my poetry. I humbly beg, therefore, that I may have the good fortune be blessed with your patronage to this end.

November 1908, Tokyo.

"Thank you for all you've done, darling," Akiko found herself saying with heartfelt feeling to her dejected husband. "It's a sad thing, but there's also some relief in it somehow. I must admit it feels a bit like losing a child, though…"

Myojo had been Tekkan's life and lifeblood. Its demise left him stunned, and with a gaping hole in his life. "I just wonder what I've been doing all this time," he said miserably.

"But you've been doing something hugely important. If the New Poetry Society hadn't existed, poetry wouldn't be anything like the popular thing it is today. It's fledged so many people into the world. Surely this was a fine thing to have done."

But Tekkan could not be comforted. Akiko felt unbearably tender towards him. She decided she would leave him be and not badger him with talk until he began to feel better.

The new year brought sad news, however. Tomiko had suffered a relapse. In January she had made her way through the winter snows to her hometown of Obama on the Japan Sea, at news that her father was on his deathbed, but once arrived she had taken to her own bed, unable even to visit her father in his room. He died without her being able to be by his side.

> Drive the nail
> into the white wood
> of my heart, this dead of night
> as I hear his coffin
> pounded shut.

Faithfully
my fevered illness calls up
visions of my father
flickering before my eyes
day after day.

The only people there to nurse her through her illness were her
mother and twenty-year-old brother Akira.

She died on the 15th of April, on an overcast day, just when
the cherry blossoms were poised to scatter. Her mother and brother
were beside her.

Even in my next life
let alone in this
I could not hope for such a thing –
a scattering petal come
to rest next to my heart.

I saw
my coffin go
into the lonely plain
with none to watch over it,
trailed about with mists.

Her premonition of loneliness was right. When her beautiful young
life was snuffed out at thirty-one, her older brother Kinjiro, fearing
infection, immediately stripped her still-warm bed and burnt it in
the garden, along with all her dearest possessions. It was all Akira
could do to hastily hide a few of her things. Among them was her
poetry notebook.

The funeral was a lonely affair.

Tekkan heard the news in Tokyo. First he had witnessed *Myojo's*
demise. Now came word of Tomiko's death. He could not but feel
that all his youthful dreams had quietly faded and now were slipping
away before his eyes. Tomiko took with her the life of his own youth,
his best years, the extravagance of his springtime flourishing.

When he had first seen her long ago, Tomiko had been the

White Lily maiden, lively and bright. Tekkan's heart returned to that moment nine years earlier.

"My heart and my poems belong to you. May I never betray this oath." He still had the piece of paper they had exchanged at the inn in Kyoto, written with her blood, and his heart was still etched deep with the unforgotten poetry of his While Lily maiden. But her body had passed on, and with it, a part of Tekkan's heart also died.

> So you
> are gone?
> Tomiko of Wakasa
> precious jewel
> darling girl
> broken and undone?
>
> What rumor
> has it that you are gone?
> Rather it seems
> that I myself
> have died today.
>
> Two maidens who
> cleansed the way
> for me –
> one is with me still
> the other flies the heavens.
>
> Crying for you
> thinking of you
> the frost at dawn
> on Mount Awata
> looks so white.
>
> No, do not speak it –
> those parting
> words of long ago
> like a secret held
> by the vast empty sky.

Tekkan published these poems under the heading "Mourning Yamakawa Tomiko," in the New Poetry Society's monthly newsletter *Tokiwagi*.

Akiko's heart was pierced when she read them. What wonderful poems of fierce and bitter sorrow! Every one of them was brimming with love and anguish, and the hot tears of grief. These poems must surely have poured forth from a heart broken by sadness, she thought.

While sympathizing deeply with Tekkan's bitter blow, Akiko could not help feeling "envy for my dear dead friend." She was plagued with the suspicion that Tekkan and Tomiko had once secretly confided their bruised hearts and comforted each other. Could they have sought together to share their memories of the past in exclusion of her? She could see that in Tekkan's heart Tomiko alone possessed the most beautiful parts of the memories of that night on Awata Mountain that the three had shared together what felt so very long ago, and the lotus poems of Sumiyoshi Shrine, memories that he held as uniquely precious. Akiko had no means to reclaim them for her own.

"Those who die first are lucky, aren't they," she couldn't help remarking with feeling. "Those left behind have to go on simply working and suffering day after day."

Akiko had been busy simultaneously bringing babies and poetry collections into the world. Her third son, Rin, had only just been born early that spring. Now she had five children. The house was a dreadful place, crowded with people. Meanwhile, two new collections of her work had appeared, *White Light* and *Eternal Summer*. What with work and family, Akiko had not a moment's pause in her day.

Akiko was hurt by Tekkan's "Rather it seems/that I myself/have died today." He was happy to let her carry all the hardships and pains of day-to-day living, while he sank himself in pure grieving.

"I do think there's a kind of karma that follows each of us, but I must say, I envy Tomiko for dying early... She gets these beautiful poems by you, after all. I don't imagine you'll write such poems for me when I die, will you?"

Tekkan didn't reply.

"But when I think about it, I do feel sorry for Tomiko. She probably wouldn't have been able to achieve release and salvation if it weren't for these poems of yours, it seems to me. She died still unable to accept what life had done to her."

Akiko too wrote and published poems as elegies for Tomiko. Among them are:

> Ten years ago
> you and I
> learned poetry together
> and called "teacher"
> the man now my husband.

> Wicked as I am
> in the one breath
> I mourn and envy her
> she who in life
> called me her friend.

Yet Akiko's poems lack the fierce sorrow that resounds like a wail in Tekkan's poems. This is strange, when we consider how close they had once been, sharing their innermost feelings, more intimate than sisters. But as people's lives change so do their hearts, and what was uppermost for Akiko now was the sense that Tekkan was monopolising the grief of the occasion, leaving no room for her to feel any herself. It was as if he had seized the initiative from her.

"You may well be right about her dying with bitter feelings over her fate. She didn't have much to laugh about during that brief year or so she was in Tokyo – that was the way things were for her, poor thing. I find it hard to contemplate that, it just makes me so sorry for her. I guess now she's dead I can say this... I was fonder of her while she was in Tokyo, you know, than in those early days. She understood me better than anyone. And she's taken that person she understood with her when she died. She cried when she said to me she just wanted to get better again; she felt she could neither live nor die the way she was..."

"She said that?"

"She said she was just twenty-eight, she wanted to get well, and to write." The message of Tekkan's tone was that he couldn't bear the weight of this sorrow himself, and Akiko must bear some of it with him.

Akiko listened in silence, while he spoke contritely of how he and Tomiko had met just once together alone, and what they had said. He wasn't seeking her forgiveness. He was confessing so that he could lighten his own sorrow a little by sharing the burden of it with her.

"It feels so strange to think that she's not in this world any more. I just can't accept it's really true. I was sad when Masako got married, but not as sad as this. I guess if I were to point to another moment when I felt this degree of sorrow, it's when I heard the rumor that Takino had gotten married."

> Such a child he is
> who can believe
> that simply to confess
> will make the sin
> vanish from the heart.

> Hard to forgive
> when I think how he
> has all this while held her
> tighter in his heart
> than me.

Akiko tried to sympathize with this husband who kept endlessly harping on Tomiko.

> Did he not know
> that for a woman
> to hear a man confess
> brings only
> fresh suffering?

Weeping, she wondered how much longer she had to go on living with this eternally childish man. Whether he spoke of Tomiko or of Masako, it always ended with Takino. She was the counterweight against which all else was measured. Knowing this for the ten years she'd lived with him, it was only natural that she should have aged quicker than many, she thought. And Tomiko's death had served to stir up the thought of Takino in his heart again. Akiko had been drawn to Tekkan's honesty when she married him, but it was clear that his honesty was sustained by a strength derived from a blithe disregard of others' feelings.

Late that night, having made Akiko suffer with his confessions, Tekkan slept an easy sleep. As he was drifting off, he remarked, as if in praise of Akiko for listening to his tale, "But it's you who've stayed with me to the end. You're the only lover I have left."

Akiko could not sleep. Whatever she thought about drew fresh tears. There was the question of Tomiko, and of Masako, but it was Takino that she really hated now. And she hated the man who could not forget her.

"Wake up!" Finally the dam of her emotions burst, and she pounded on Tekkan's pillow until he woke. She was still crying. "Why do you keep harping back to Takino all the time? You're forever comparing me with her."

"That's not true."

"I've been with you longer than she was. We've had five children together, yet you still love Atsumu best."

"Who said I did?"

"You wrote letters to him, didn't you. You asked someone on the sly to give them to him, didn't you."

"But I…"

"Oh yes, I know. I just don't talk about it, that's all. You don't love our children as much as him. You think of him as your precious firstborn, don't you."

This was the fact that caused Akiko endless pain. She was overcome with pity for her children whenever she told herself that her father's love was focussed more on Atsumu, now ten years old, than on his own sons. It hurt her that there was someone who had tasted with her husband the awe and hope that parents feel with the birth of their first child.

"But even though poor Atsumu's not an orphan, his parents are both scattered to the four winds," Tekkan responded. "You ought to pity him. Neither Takino nor I can do anything about it."

His words only drove Akiko to wilder suffering.

"The boy's frail, you understand. Takino conceived him when life was at its hardest for her, so he was born sickly. He's often in bed with this or that. It's hard for the poor kid, lying there ill without a mother or father to care for him."

"It's harder for our own children. It's just as if they don't have a father. All you think about is Atsumu."

"Don't be ridiculous. Stop this talk! You go on and on about it."

"Didn't Takino go on and on about things too?"

"She wasn't the sort of nag who'd wake her husband in order to quarrel with him."

"You say that because you don't understand how I feel."

"Enough!" Tekkan said crossly, as if trumping her argument with ill humour. But now that Akiko was thinking of her own children, she grew emotional, and she spoke with fresh vehemence.

"You don't need any other children as long as you have Atsumu, do you. That's what you feel, isn't it. I'll bet you think you might be able to use him to get to see Takino."

Jealousy ate ceaselessly at Akiko's heart like acid, eroded it inch by inch. Long ago, she had heard Tekkan grieve that he could have stayed with Takino if he'd chosen to, no matter what anyone did or said, and he'd been a fool. They were words she could not forget. She felt very alone. There was no home she could return to if she and Tekkan parted. Chusaburo had returned safely from the war and taken over the family home in Sakai, but her mother had died at the age of forty, and Akiko and her elder brother were permanently estranged.

Tekkan's voice was rising now too. How long was she going to harp on like this? When would this jealousy end? But it's your fault I feel like this… You're wrong. You're the one who's going out of your way to pick quarrels… And so they went on.

> These lonely
> quarrels we have –
> you beat
> against yourself
> and I beat myself.

Akiko was weary. To breathe fresh life into the stalemate that their relationship had become, and to bolster her husband's state of mind, she decided that he must have an overseas trip. More and more people from the literary and art worlds were travelling abroad at that time, although they were all going there to live and study for months or even years, rather than taking a week or even a month's short trip.

> Whenever he hears
> the world's ridicule
> my husband
> lays down his brush
> and slumps in despondent thought.

Why did people flog poor Tekkan like this? Day after day, month after month, the newspapers and journals carried the jeering voices, claiming that he was a thing of the past, already over the hill at forty. His own youth had coincided with the youthful moment of the age, and thus as that time passed and the age changed, he was left behind. How could he be blamed for that?

Tekkan had virtually no work during this period. After the demise of *Myojo*, both he and Akiko became no more than guest members in the *Subaru* group formed by the original New Poetry Society members, with the novelist Mori Ogai as its central figure.

Encouraged by Akiko, Tekkan began to study French in preparation for the European trip. Once the teacher arrived and Tekkan settled down to his lesson, Akiko found the time to move ahead with her own writing. She got a certain amount of work out of the way before he rose in the morning, but once he was awake she had to lay this aside and prepare his breakfast. She left the children in the care of their maid, but she had to keep an eye on the twin girls who were not yet at school, and the baby Rin, while she put an egg in the pan or made miso soup and seaweed rice for him.

After breakfast, Tekkan spent time going through journals or reading the paper, and Akiko could only pray painfully that he wouldn't see the occasional pieces that appeared there praising her and scorning him. He suffered from constant mood swings.

When she grew excited, Akiko could really say what she felt to him, but for the most part she kept an eye on what mood he might be in, and spent her time worrying over what might have upset him. She felt she shouldn't do her own work while he was just reading listlessly, at loose ends. So she sat on with him, holding herself back from rising to go and get on with her writing, this woman in her striped muslin kimono and crepe obi, her tangled hair held up with a lacquered comb.

"Well then, I suppose I'd better get on with some work," she'd remark in a carefully casual tone, although inside she was dying to get going. She wrote whatever she was asked – novels, children's stories. This year, too, a book of essays was due to come out. It was a busy life she led. There were times when every minute was accounted for. Yet she could never bear to let Tekkan witness this frantic activity. She was also concerned that the constant flow of guests were there to see her rather than Tekkan, and was continually monitoring the effect on him.

Tekkan was squatting in the garden, squashing ants with a rusty knife.

Akiko retired to the study to work; three hours later, she emerged to find him still in the same position, engrossed.

"Darling... are you still killing ants?"

Tekkan made no response. Often, he would reply by saying, "Well, I don't have anything else to do." When he had come back inside and was napping, Akiko settled herself beside him.

"It looks like it's going to happen, dear," she said. "Kaneo has said he'll lend us some money, and Kobayashi's said he thinks he can fix things with that gold screen I asked him about... You'll get to Europe after all."

"What's this about a gold screen?"

"I showed you yesterday, remember? I'm going to write a hundred of my poems on a gold folding screen and he'll buy it. Along with some poetry calligraphy pieces."

"How much will we need?"

"I'm not really sure, but I'm guessing around two thousand *yen.*"

"Why don't you go too while we're at it? Come with me."

"I..." Akiko smiled sadly. It was all her womanly strength was capable of to muster the funds to send him alone. But the words "there isn't the money" must never pass her lips in front of him.

Folding one of his kimonos as she spoke, she went on, "I don't really want to go. The children are such a worry, and there's no one I could leave in charge here..."

"If it's the money, I can see to that, you know."

"See to it?"

"I plan to go to Tokuyama before long."

How typical! Akiko thought at these unexpected words. Rather than blame him, something like resignation flooded her heart.

> And so, in our different ways,
> you have a world
> known only to yourself
> while I
> gaze at days that are mine alone.

This was how she chose to think about it, indeed the only approach that allowed her to forgive him.

5

A letter came from Tekkan in Tokuyama.

"To my surprise, it turns out that most of the money for the trip can be supplied from here, so I can assure you that there's no longer any need for you to worry over the question." His brother in Tokuyama had solicited five hundred *yen* from various interested parties and handed it to Tekkan.

Akiko had never been so upset by him. She had borrowed against future royalties, she had pushed herself day after day to write the hundred poems for the screen, nursing an arm numbed by her tight shoulders, while her two oldest boys had been kept busy grinding the ink, but she hadn't resented the fact that this was all for his sake. No doubt Tekkan was only trying to save her the burden, but to her it seemed he was snubbing her. When he returned, however, she couldn't say so.

"Isn't that good news, dear?"

To her relief, Tekkan was looking cheerful. Yet she found herself wondering whether his good mood had anything to do with the fact that he'd seen Atsumu. And so she was happy to hear Tekkan say to Hikaru, who had caught cold while he'd been away, "You all right? How many days' school did you miss?"

She was delighted or downcast by little things. In this she was simply a typical woman, quite unlike the person one imagines from the firm, forceful, heavy-handed opinions she voiced in her criticism, or the calm and meditative verse of those middle years she had now reached.

For the first time in a long while, the children were gathered around their father, laughing happily. Akiko longed to finish her work as quickly as possible and join them. But someone was coming the next day to collect the manuscript. Once it was handed over, she would get the payment within the month. Akiko's thoughts were set on the future.

"Come on Mum, how about joining us from time to time?" Recently, Tekkan had begun borrowing the children's name for his wife. The children were used to having a mother who wasn't constantly with them, and when she laid down her pen and came over, they scattered awkwardly.

On 11th November 1911, Tekkan set sail on the *Atsutamaru* from Kobe. Akiko accompanied him to Kobe to see him off. Many other old friends were also there to fare him well, including the Chinos and Kobayashi Tenmin.

When the gong sounded for guests to leave the ship, Tekkan quickly went round gripping the hands of the people gathered around him.

He came to his wife. "Akiko. Till we meet again, eh?"

"Take good care."

"Look after things while I'm gone. And make sure you follow me over there. To France, right? We could manage it."

"Yes, I'm sure someone could help. I'll get there."

"Of course you will. Oh, and…" He gazed into her eyes. "I heard while I was back in Tokuyama. Apparently Takino now has four children."

Akiko was silent.

"I've made you suffer over me, I know, but I truly do not think the way you believe I do. I just wanted to say that. It made me sad

to think that if I'd met you first…" The second gong rang, and the
visitors were gathering at the side of the ship, ready to step into the
launch that would take them back to shore. "I wouldn't have put you
through all that anguish." Tears spilled from Akiko's eyes. "Though
really, you're the only one in my life."

When she heard this, Akiko wept. She felt wretchedly as if they
were saying goodbye forever. Waves of people pressed around her,
while Tekkan went on around the group, gripping hands in farewell.

Looking up from the launch, the *Atsutamaru* looked even more
massive. For months and years, they would not meet again.

The launch carrying well-wishers set off around the ship, away
from the passengers leaning over the railings in farewell, and headed
off towards the port. The ship's horn sounded, and the *Atsutamaru*
left the harbor.

> The man departs
> leaves me and departs
> sets off to Paris
> sad, yet
> not sad.

> You will cross
> the seas
> and wander lonely on your travels
> as if pursued
> as if in flight.

Tekkan had gone. Akiko already yearned after him madly. It was as if
he were carrying her own life away with him on the *Atsutamaru*. She
couldn't even bear to turn and face her children just then. She felt as
if she couldn't live a day without Tekkan beside her.

"I'm going to get to Paris, no matter what it takes." With Chino
and Masako on either side lending a supporting hand, at last she
managed to stand. The *Atsutamaru* was already small on the horizon
of the blue autumn sea.

It was May of the following year that Akiko crossed the ocean
and joined her husband. Together they travelled around Europe, and

renewed their love for each other. Yet there must have been further turbulence between them after their return.

This man
seems to me
something like a nail
I have plucked
from the ashes.

Both were strong characters, yet Akiko remained forever womanly. No doubt it was the friction this created that led this extraordinary couple to go through so much of their life together attracted and repelled by each other. Yet if it hadn't been for Tekkan's genius, Akiko's own genius may well not have been elicited. His life was thanks to her, hers was thanks to him – his poetic endeavors, and her art, were woven together to create something that belonged to both.

Akiko raised eleven children, and saw her husband to his grave when he was sixty-three.

His hand in mine
he died,
this man part of myself
unforgotten
all these long years.

Akiko died of angina seven years later, while recuperating from a brain hemorrhage. She was sixty-five. She was buried next to her husband, in the Tama graveyard. Her posthumous Buddist name: Hakuo-in Hosho Shoki Daishi.

Their souls are now in heaven, their flesh returned to the earth. All the passionate attachment, the jealousies, joys, and sorrows of Akiko and Tekkan, and of Hayashi Takino, Asada Sadako, and Yamakawa Tomiko, have blown away like mist. The hot ashes of those passions are now cooled, and all that still resounds of them in the world is in the poems they left behind.

The many joys
I have known from you
have passed. Today
I die.
God is good.

(Akiko)

Akiko sleeps quietly now in a corner of Musashino, close beside the man she never ceased loving, in whom she entrusted all her dreams. These are the poems on their gravestones.

Along the road
by Naniwa Bay
the flowers bloom.
Yet until you came
the path was choked with weed.

(Akiko)

I know
almost all
that is so hard to know.
Where do my eyes turn now?
They turn to the heavens.

(Tekkan)

In *Murasakigusa*, their daughter Uchiko described her mother's death as follows:

"She was dressed in the purple-skirted kimono she loved, in her handbag the fountain pen she always used, her glasses, and a notebook. She was a large woman, but her bulk had suddenly fallen away. She looked as if modestly setting forth to meet my father, slender and beautiful once more."